CAROLINE
...THE CAPTAIN'S DAUGHTER
A Novel

JOANNE EAGLES HONEYCUTT
BOOK 2 OF THE EDGECOMBE TRILOGY

simply francis publishing company
North Carolina

Copyright © 2024 Joanne Eagles Honeycutt. All Rights Reserved.

No part of this publication may be reproduced, stored in a retrieval system or transmitted, in any form or by any means-electronic, mechanical, photocopying, recording, or otherwise without the prior written permission from the publisher, except for the inclusions of brief quotations in a review.

All brand, product, and place names used in this book that are trademarks or service marks, registered trademarks, or trade names are the exclusive intellectual property of their respective holders and are mentioned here as a matter of fair and nominative use. To avoid confusion, *simply francis publishing company* publishes books solely and is not affiliated with the holder of any mark mentioned in this book.

This is a work of fiction. Any references to historical events, real people, or real places are used fictitiously. Other names, characters, places, and events are products of the author's imagination, and any resemblance to actual events or places or persons, living or dead, is entirely coincidental.

NO AI TRAINING: Without in any way limiting the author's [and publisher's] exclusive rights under copyright, any use of this publication to "train" generative artificial intelligence (AI) technologies to generate text is expressly prohibited. The author reserves all rights to license uses of this work for generative AI training and development of machine learning language models.

Library of Congress Control Number: 2024905598
ISBN: 978-1-63062-058-5 (paperback)
ISBN: 978-1-63062-059-2 (e-book)
Printed in the United States of America
Cover and Interior Design: Christy King Meares

For information about this title or to order books and/or electronic media, contact the publisher:

simply francis publishing company
P.O. Box 329, Wrightsville Beach, NC 28480
www.simplyfrancispublishing.com
simplyfrancispublishing@gmail.com

Dedication

For my husband Rhett
and my wonderful family

In memory of my maternal grandmother
Mary Caroline Robinson Holland

Cast of Characters

Primary Characters
Hap - Thomas Rolland Tyson
Caroline Cromwell Bagley - daughter of Elijah and Sarah Cromwell
Willie - Willa Abigail Pridgen
Elijah Cromwell - Caroline's father
Sarah King Cromwell - Caroline's mother
Coeffield King (Coffie) - Caroline's grandfather, Sarah's father
Litchfield Jacob Bagley - Caroline's husband

Secondary Characters
George Edmundson - retired overseer of Shiloh Plantation, Maggie's husband
Maggie Edmundson – housekeeper of Cromwell Hall
Fate Edmundson - George and Maggie's son
Shug Maples Edmundson - Fate's wife
Doctor MacKinley – "Mac" Foster
Pamela Martin - Hap's friend at UNC
Craven Peacock "Banks" McCloud - Pamela's grandfather
Michael Collins - Caroline's former tutor
Doc Sims - professor friend of Hap's at UNC

PART ONE

Prologue

Life as she knew it was over. No longer was she the young mistress of Cromwell Hall, or the darling of Tarboro, or the granddaughter of Coeffield King…or even the Captain's daughter. Her vows had made her Litch Bagley's wife. She had said them, and she would honor her troth to this man as long as they both breathed. She had vowed, "I will," when asked, "Caroline King Cromwell, wilt thou have this man, Litchfield Jacob Bagley, to thy wedded husband."

Yet, no one, not even God, could ever erase the memory tucked in her heart of Hap Tyson. As a child, she had loved him as a waif. In her youth, she had loved him as the meanest scoundrel in all of Edgecombe County. As a blossoming woman, she had loved him as the young man from the other side. However, the tragic death of her brother had ripped them apart, but not before they had loved once, as a good-bye, not a new beginning. It was over…

Chapter 1

1882

THE HONEYMOON

*T*he honeymoon suite at the Claiborne in Rocky Mount was magnificent. Litch had filled each room with roses and gardenias. The perfumed atmosphere intoxicated the wedded couple. Caroline sat on the loveseat by the fireplace and waited for her glass of champagne. She figured she would need several to blur the memory of Hap Tyson; she had made a choice and she would die with her words, "...until death do us part." She could not believe that she thought of Hap as she looked over at her new husband. Her last meeting with Hap had been closure, had it not?

Litch Bagley's graduation from the University of North Carolina in Chapel Hill had arrived last May with such fanfare, with the families staying at the Patterson Hotel on Columbia Street just one block away from Hap's rooming house. Hap was starting a new life now, getting himself educated to be a doctor of the same ilk as his old friend Rufus Knight from down east, but Caroline could not resist one final contact before she became Mrs. Bagley. *Such foolishness,* she thought, as she slipped down the steps of the Patterson, hastening toward his rooming house, but it was goodbye, wasn't it?

Her knock was ever so slight, the second a little hesitant, but as Hap's door swung open, a shaft of light from the porch lantern lit her golden hair. Her face appeared in a halo. Sheepishly she slipped by Hap, as he stood, shocked, curious, and yet a little amused. His crooked smile flickered across his face.

Closing the door, he watched her slow steps around his room,

Chapter 1

apparently acquainting herself with his new life without her. She stopped at his bureau and studied the photos of his family. Picking one up, she smiled, glancing at him, acknowledging who they were. Eventually, she came to his bed and stood staring at it, her fingers brushing the counterpane.

In seconds, she flew against him, burying her golden head in his chest, her arms locking around his waist quickly and hard in desperation. He inhaled her fragrances, as his own arms draped across her shoulders as he sensed loss of control.

For minutes their bodies fused, until she lifted her head to his and invited a kiss, one for which he had yearned since youth. It was passionate.

They parted, their eyes smoldering.

"Love me, Hap. Love me as your wife," she'd whispered.

He'd reached for her, swinging her slowly around and gently laid her small frame in the center of his bed. He stood back looking down at his bride with the loving eyes of the bridegroom. *I, Thomas Rolland Tyson, take thee, Caroline King Cromwell...*

For this one night, she would be his bride and he, her groom. A tear formed in his eye, as he slowly unbuttoned his shirt and laid it neatly on the back of his chair, his chest rising and falling with desire for the young mistress of Cromwell Hall.

She'd held outstretched arms to him, an invitation he had longed for. He could hardly believe that she was real and the moment was real, but in his heart, as he looked into her eyes, he recognized closure, not a fresh beginning. Another tear trailed down his face. This time, she caught it with her fingertips before it got too far.

"I know, my love, I know..."

Litch stood before her with champagne. Reaching upward with an alluring smile, she accepted his toast to their future. Breathing deeply, she downed the sparkling liquid and raised her glass for more. Surprised, he poured the next one even fuller.

Mrs. Bagley stood and excused herself to dress in the wedding night attire that Sarah Cromwell had chosen for her daughter.

Thanks, Mother. You made another very good choice. There is no way Litch Bagley will not be enthralled. Throwing her clothes aside, she slipped into her robe. *I've never seen such frills.*

Looking in the mirror, she wrapped her arms around her body and closed her eyes. She could no longer delay. Pushing the door, she stood in the opening.

Her husband lounged in a silk robe with his legs crossed and his arm resting on the back of the couch. He sipped more champagne. As she approached, he remembered sitting in her room at Cromwell Hall, watching over her the night her brother Will died. He remembered her passing his chair to the window. Never once did she suspect her gown had glided over his hand. He had hurt with such desire then, and presently felt that same tightness, that same hurt, but now he would release these long imprisoned desires. He was about to make Caroline Bagley truly his wife. His wife, in his bed.

Slowly, he placed his glass on the table and met her in the middle of the room. His hand caressed her face as he bent to kiss her lightly. Then, as if she were weightless, he swept her up into his arms and carried her into their future.

Oh, God, she's mine.

Chapter 2
NEWS IN OAKWOOD

Oakwood became home for Litch and Caroline, an area not far from humming downtown Raleigh. Jacob Bagley had set up his son in real estate as promised, but the political itch lurked in Litch. He had always enjoyed sparring with the politicos, and with the granddaughter of Coeffield King at his side, he would embrace that arena in a heartbeat.

As the weeks flew, Caroline busied herself with their new home, a wonderful Georgian archetype that reminded her of her grandparents' house. She had always loved how theirs sat on the Town Common in Tarboro. This yard was not Jackie Thrash's with the huge boxwoods across the front or the lush backyard with clusters of flowers, and soon Caroline would put her touch to the blank spots.

Both families had given them furnishings, but Raleigh offered antique dealers to fill the gaps. It was fun for her to explore and learn this city, a favorite pastime being to sit under the trees on the capitol's lawn, feeding pigeons and watching mothers stroll their babies.

Settling in to their married life, Caroline looked at Litch with new eyes and new hopes that the past was fading. She and Litch were ardent lovers now.

One morning after breakfast, she excused herself from the table. Nausea hit with a vengeance. Litch left the house, never once suspecting his wife was ill. She sat with a cup of tea, trying to figure it out. Was it a virus, food poisoning, a cold? She was never sick. Another bout struck her the next morning. *Oh my*

God! A baby? So soon? Denial failed the newlywed, when another morning of sickness proved this conjecture. She had news for her new husband.

"Darling, you know I hate eating alone," Litch announced, frowning at the one place setting on the table. Puzzled, he looked at her.

"Whhhatt?" he dragged out the word, as her grin would not quit. "What's going on? Why have you got this silly grin on your face?" He looked around. "I am missing something, lady. What is it? I demand to know and no joking!"

"No," she finally got out.

"Okay, it is a joke. What is it?" he quizzed, throwing his hands up in the air.

"I'm sorry, Litch, but I just wanted to wait for the right moment to tell you something important for both of us."

"Tell me what, Caroline. What? You're driving me crazy," he replied impatiently.

"I'm going to have a child." She wrung her hands, as she looked for his reaction.

Litch froze. Initially, his face appeared as granite, yet in seconds he came to life. He could not have been more stupefied. He stuttered. He stammered. Finally, coming to his senses, he jumped up from the table and grabbed her.

"A child. You're having my child?"

Surely, this sign would seal the past for him and for her. *My child. Oh, joy. Our child. Tyson, you're out, man, out of our lives forever.*

Litch Bagley was fully aware of the shadow that Hap Tyson cast on Caroline's earlier life. He knew about the accident with her brother Will, for he had even testified at the murder trial against Hap. The birth of this child would be huge in slamming the door on that part of their lives. Litch held her gently, as he whispered endearments of this wondrous thing happening between them.

Chapter 2

"Think of Coffie, sweetheart. He'll be a great-grandfather."

"Mother's last letter really worries me," she murmured, her head against his shoulder.

"Moving him to Shiloh permanently was the right thing."

"I know, but, Litch, I just can't imagine that old house on the green standing deserted." She sighed. "I've got to see him soon. Mother says he's so feeble. I think it would be better for me to go now before traveling gets too difficult. Please, understand, Husband Mine. This news might give him a boost, a new lease on life. I have to go."

Caroline only called him Litch or Husband Mine. No other endearing names. He embellished their conversations with enough for both of them that she never thought he'd ever notice. Her response to his declaration of love only prodded from her, "I do, too." She could not say the word *love* to him; yet, maybe after the baby, she could and would without hesitation.

Enthralled with the miracle growing inside his wife, Litch would have granted any wish. Leading her across the room to the settee in their bay window, he sat her down, kissed her sweetly, and pulled her to him, as he laid her head on his chest. Even food seemed unimportant now. He was going to be a father. He had hardly been able to grasp being married, but to be a father so soon just added to his joy of making this golden-headed woman his wife.

Burying his face in those curls, he pledged, "Oh, darling, I will love and care for you and our child until I take my last breath."

His mind framed the same old stanza again. *She's mine. Finally, she is truly mine.*

Chapter 3
THE NEW LIFE

Hap Tyson could no longer live at the boarding house where he had lived his first year in Chapel Hill. Everywhere he turned, he saw Caroline. Each move she had made around his room that night in May was imprinted in his brain. After countless hours of unrest, he conceded he must get away, holding out the best he could until the first summer session was over. His childhood sweetheart was Mrs. Litch Bagley, now. He had no claim. Frankly, he needed distance from Chapel Hill, from school, even from Tarboro, to help heal this wound, and he knew where the answer lay. He was going home to Pitt County.

Wendell Tyson was surprised to find his son on his front stoop.

"Hap?" he asked quizzically. "Why aren't you at school?"

"I've decided to take some time off, Pap. Would you hire your son for the rest of the summer?" he spoke with a sheepish grin.

"A job? Well, first come in and sit a spell, so we can talk."

He pulled Hap through the door and awkwardly hugged his strapping son, before directing him to a chair, all the while dragging one close for himself.

"So, you want a job?" An amused look covered his face.

"I do. You know, to have a little change in my pocket for up at school."

"Won't you get behind missing a session?"

"I've looked over my schedule, and I promise that I won't fall behind."

Chapter 3

"Good, son. Well, how about this! You want to work with me! Listen you know I'll give you what you need."

"I know you would, but I want to do this. My life calls for a change right now. Working here with you seems the perfect answer."

And he did. By spending the latter part of the summer with Wendell Tyson in Pitt County, helping him in his tar pitch business, became the salve for his wounded heart, while his father relished watching his offspring work. By summer's end, Hap knew his father had done well in his business.

Returning to Chapel Hill for the fall session felt strange, but sitting on South Building's steps facing Polk Place, Hap sensed he had returned home. This university was his new mother, and she was there to care for him, guide him, and teach him a new life. He had a great opportunity in front of him and he would not, could not, fail. He owed thanks to so many who had helped him along this way, and he would do anything not to disappoint one of them.

His most important declaration on those steps that afternoon concerned Caroline and his survival without her. Now, he would see her as a life-long friend, an important ingredient in his youth, his first love, never to be forgotten, and one who had taught him so much about the affairs of the heart. He'd been so naive, so ignorant. She'd given him a look at a gentler side of life, one that he had never known. He had learned much and he would never forget her. Perspective was the key.

"Well, Lordy me, if it ain't my new roomie. And your name, buddy?" a voice boomed from the doorway of Hap's new dorm room.

He jerked around, startled by the voice, and even more so by the size of his roommate. The young fellow filled the doorframe.

"It's Thomas Rolland Tyson, sir, but my friends call me Hap."

The crooked grin slowly crept across his face.

"I hope we'll be friends?" he asked, looking this sturdily built young man over from head to toe.

"Hey, guys," the giant of a fellow hollered, as he turned toward the room across the hall. Three heads popped up, peering around the young man. "This one's called Hap...by his friends. What do you think we should call him?"

All four stared at Hap and then chorused loudly, "Hap!"

Rushing forward with outstretched hands, Randall Moffitt, Stuart Tyndall, and Nicholas Fornes shook his, welcoming him to the bosom of the pack. Lastly, Ashe Randolph swaggered over and introduced himself as the new roommate.

The big lummox wrapped his arm around Hap's shoulder and declared, "I will be the best roomie you'll ever have, my man. From this day forth, we'll be known as the Fearless Five. What say, gentlemen? Here's to the Fearless Five."

He stretched out his arm and the other four slapped their hands down one at a time upon his.

Organized baseball had just come to Carolina a couple of years before. When Ashe Randolph walked out onto the diamond for try-outs, the coaches watched closely. He could out pitch, out hit, and out run anybody on the playing field. He was the best freshman prospect, and now as a sophomore, he'd be a star. He was tall, lean, and mean on the diamond. He was a natural.

However, he was an enigma to Hap, for one moment Ashe was the fierce, loyal family member or friend, and, in the next instance, he would roughhouse, hoisting any one of them above his head. A lunch wager was an eager bet for him to put their arms down.

Ashe stood four inches taller than any of the others and constantly said, "Nobody's gonna mess with you guys as long as I'm around. I'll hog-tie, horse-whip, and cow-rope any yokes who step out of line. They'll answer to old Ashe."

Hap could not have choreographed a better change to erase Caroline's memory. These four young men became his blood brothers. They were inseparable, their lives knitting quickly.

Chapter 3

One day, an inquisitive Ashe pressed his roommate.

"Hap, if we're gonna be roomies, we can't have secrets, so who is she?" he asked, slapping his chest as they sprawled on their beds.

"For a baseball player, you certainly are a sensitive joker," Hap kidded.

"Well, I'm not kidding. Who is she? I know the symptoms."

"My first love back home. It's getting better, but it's slow. God, it's slow."

He raised his head up from his pillow.

"Thanks, Ashe, you're my best friend and the best roommate I've ever had," he said with sarcasm.

"Get outta here. I'm the only roommate you've ever had," he jawed, throwing his pillow.

"Whoa—" Hap yelled, sailing it back.

"Seriously, any time you want to talk, Buddy, just let me know."

Hap knew he meant it. In fact, the next day, as they sat on Polk Quad, Hap spilled his story.

"I really don't know when I have not loved her," he began, gazing down at his hands. "I think I loved her the first time her mother brought her down Station House Road. The church ladies were delivering shoes to the children. Can you believe this young lady of distinction once loved the meanest scoundrel in all of Edgecombe County?"

His crooked smile etched his face. "The meanest what?" Ashe boomed, ignoring a passerby.

"You've got to be kidding. You, a scoundrel? Nah! Now, I'm a scoundrel and proud of it," he said, puffing up his chest. "You're a pussycat compared to me."

Laughing at his friend, Hap continued, "We used to meet on a grassy knoll in the lower 40 on the Cromwell land, Shiloh Plantation. Her family hunted and fished on this woodland. I could wait all day long some times and never see her or another soul."

"All day? This is serious," Ashe said.

"Or, miraculously we might show up at the same time. We were both misunderstood young people, her by her family and me by the townspeople. When anything went awry in town, the authorities always knocked on Willie Pridgen's front door at the end of Station House Road. 'Where's your son, Miz Pridgen?' they'd ask."

"Pridgen? But your name's Tyson. I don't understand."

"My mother died at childbirth, leaving a bunch of young'uns. Pap just couldn't handle us all. He brought me to Willie. She'd helped us on the home place over in Pitt County before returning to Tarboro. I reckon my howling long and loud enough did the trick. She took me in. Poor Pap... He was at his wit's end trying to raise six of us. Anyway, as we grew up over the years, Caroline—"

"Caroline?"

"Cromwell. Caroline Cromwell. Her parents own Shiloh outside of Tarboro. Anyway, we became close, very close, until one day I realized my world wasn't hers. I tried to let her go, but I lost my nerve every time. Do you know what really galled me?"

"What?"

"I hated anybody who said we couldn't be friends in public, or anything more."

"Well, that's crummy. Go on. I got a feeling somethin' big's about to happen in this saga."

"You're right." He paused. "A real tragedy..."

His voice trailed as he reached down and pulled a piece of grass.

"We were meeting at the lower 40 one day. I swear I was going to stop the madness. Unfortunately, her brother happened to get there before I did and accused her of having seen me on Shiloh land. He thought it was disgraceful. Her reaction surprised him. She lunged at him like a cat, catching him off guard."

"Oh no, and that's when her hero came up."

"Right. He'd caught her by the wrists just as I came through

Chapter 3

the woods. Gallant me rushed to defend the lady in distress."

With a sigh, he looked off in the distance before picking up the story.

"It was just a dumb, stupid mistake," he spoke through gritted teeth as he threw the blade of grass in frustration.

"What do you mean a stupid mistake?"

"He turned into an animal. The man pounded me, but I never laid one cotton-picking fist on him."

Hap paused, trying to contain his growing anger.

"Look, Hap, you can stop right here, if you want to, if it's too painful."

"No! I want you to know. I need you to!"

"Okay, Buddy. I'm here for you. Just take your time."

He lightly punched his shoulder for encouragement. Hap took a deep breath and began again.

"Caroline just stood there screaming. I kept begging her brother to lay off, but he kept coming. The groin and shin kicks got me. I bent double, but when I righted myself the best I could, my head chin-butted him in just the right spot. I knocked the poor fellow out cold with my head."

"Jeez, man."

"Ashe, he didn't crumple like he should've, but fell straight backwards. His neck smacked a fallen tree trunk. I swear to God. The sound was sickening."

A shiver ran through his body, as he hesitated.

"He was dead."

"Good Lord! Her brother died! I can't believe this. What-what happened after that? My gosh, I had no idea you were going to tell me this," he clamored.

"I know, I know, but you have got to hear the rest. I was tried for murder."

"What? No way!"

"We thought we were goners coming up against the DA and Tarboro's favorite son, Coeffield King."

"Wait! Who is this Coeffield King?"

"Her grandfather. He's a well-known and respected lawyer from down east."

"Uh," he grunted. "Well, did the DA question her?"

"Yes, but first he asked her just general ones that weaved the strongest story of love between a brother and sister. The DA finally got around to asking Caroline what happened on the lower 40 between her brother and me."

"What did she say?"

"Just that there was a scuffle between us, and that Will died. The DA excused her after that."

"Uh-oh... What did your lawyer do when it was his turn to cross-examine?"

"I hated it, Ashe, but he had to draw the truth out of her for the jury and the court to hear. She broke down. Just like a china cup crashing to the floor. You would not have believed the echo of her cries in the dome of the courtroom. 'It was all a horrible mistake, an accident.' Time and again, she hollered. The people in the courtroom all seemed to talk at once, with the judge's gavel pounding through the noise. Ashe, I never believed for one moment that she would let me down in the end. Never."

"How do you know that?"

Looking down the grassy bowling green of Polk Quad, he nodded, "I just know. The jury acquitted me, and Judge Barnes dismissed the charges against me, slamming that gavel down on my case forever."

Hap quieted and then continued. "But another strange thing happened that day. Her grandfather suffered a heart attack right there in the courtroom. It was tough on the family. I have to tell you that he forgave me after he knew from Caroline's testimony that it really was an accident, just a horrible, freaky accident."

"What do you mean forgave you? You should have been forgiving him for accusing you unjustly," Ashe said.

"He asked me to come to the hospital to see him. I went, and he told me that he accepted my situation with Will as an accident, just as Caroline had said, a horrible accident. Then he turned

Chapter 3

around and asked me to forgive him. I really did, Ashe, without hesitation. He was so humble and made me feel worthy of being in the same room with such an important man in our county."

Ashe just kept shaking his head in disbelief at all the tragedy his friend had experienced.

"Where is she now? At Shiloh?"

"Oh no. She's married. This past summer. In June..." His voice lowered to a whisper.

"I'm sorry, Buddy, but you just wait. The Fearless Five will have you out of this slump in no time. You gotta come to the fall dance. You've steered clear of the gals so far, but now I know you gotta make a move."

"It's not that easy, Ashe—"

"Aww, don't give me that bunk. I guarantee your life's about to change. Randall will fill you in on the dance. It'll be great. I promise."

"But-but," Hap stuttered.

"Spit it out, man. What gives?"

"My-my social graces with young ladies are lacking, and all I know is the Virginia Reel, and besides, I don't have the clothes to wear to a shindig like that."

"Oh, for Pete sake, Hap. Do you think I knew all that stuff when I got here?" Ashe laughed and jumped up. "Come on, Buddy, we've got to find Randall. He's our society man extraordinaire. I was putty in his hands and you will be, too."

Chapter 4
ROUGH EDGES

Randall Moffitt stood in the middle of Hap and Ashe's room and bowed.

"Put yourself in my hands, Hap, and I'll have you dazzling the ladies for sure. Hmmmm," he said, as he walked around Hap. "Are you willing to be putty in my hands?"

"Do I have a choice? I suppose," Hap said with gritted teeth, shaking his head.

"Good, now Stuart and Nicholas will be my support. Guys, I think my barber needs to tame his locks a bit. Then—turn around, Hap."

He followed instructions.

"Lockhart's has the perfect jacket and pants. You're my size. I've got a hundred shirts in my bureau. I'll make you a gift of three. My mother overdoes everything."

"I do have money from the summer for the coat and pants," Hap said. "I just don't know how to buy these niceties."

"Leave it to Randall," Stuart and Nicholas chimed together.

"Now, Stu, be the young lady, and let's get Hap brought up to snuff on his social graces," Randall said. Laughing, Stuart stood and curtsied for the crew.

"Don't get fresh, Stu," Nicholas joked. "We don't want you and Hap to have black eyes for the big event."

The next week was intense. Hap had much to learn.

The morning of the dance, Hap's eyes popped open. He froze in his dorm bed, reaching quickly to touch his forehead. It was dry. What? No dreams? In the months since Caroline had taken

Chapter 4

her vows, he had awakened in a sweat after seeing her and Litch on the stage of his mind. They would stand in the middle of a bedroom, those azure eyes lovingly staring at her husband. And it was not him. He should be the one gazing back, not Litch. He should be the one tracing her face, shoulders, and arms with the tips of his fingers. He should be the one to taste the passion in her lips, the fullness of her body.

Where are the dreams now?

Slowly, he turned his head and looked over at Ashe, asleep with little puffs slightly moving his lips. The big guy hardly fit on his bed, but somehow, he always awoke refreshed, devoid of any nightly disturbances. Hap continued to stare at his best friend.

"Okay. Okay. I know you're staring at me. Was I snoring?"

Then one eye opened under a raised brow.

"You're incredible. How did you know?"

"Powers, boy. Pure ingenious powers."

He sat up and stretched, looking over at *his* best friend. "Well, did it happen?"

"No."

"What? You're kidding. Not one little peep into the bedroom?"

"Not the first glimpse."

"Oh man, it's happening. Do you feel the shackles falling? Do you feel the scales dropping from your eyes?"

He leaped out of bed and crossed the room.

"Get out of that bed. I want to shake the hand of a healed, refreshed, renewed body and soul."

Whether Hap wanted to or not, he was coming out of that bed. He laughed as he clasped his best friend's hand. God, he loved this lummox.

No one could have pulled him from the mire like Ashe Randolph had done. Well, except maybe Willie. He'd never be able to repay him.

"I'm going to tell the rest of the guys. They are not going to believe it."

"Ashe, it's six-thirty. They may throw you out."

"Are you kidding? This news can't wait."

Hap fell back in his bed, his head sunken into his pillow. Once more he replayed his new perspective of Caroline in his mind. She was his first love, an important ingredient in his youth, and most important a life-long friend, never to be forgotten.

The Fearless Five stood at the door of the gymnasium.

"Good golly! I've never seen so many streamers," Hap said, excitement in his eyes.

"Streamers? Look at the girls, man. The girls," Nicolas instructed.

The young men scattered, leaving Hap to drift farther into the room, the smile still plastered across his face. He felt good, excited, uplifted. He didn't know why. He just did.

"What's your name, fellow?" a throaty voice rang out behind him.

Slowly turning, he stared into the eyes of a tall, willowy girl with a broad smile.

"Thomas Rolland Tyson, miss. Most just call me Hap," he said with his crooked grin.

"Now, where'd you get a name like Hap?" she asked, cocking her head and cutting her eyes at him. "Well?"

"Uh, I have this crooked grin and it seems I laughed a lot as a young'un, according to my brothers and sisters. They just dubbed me."

He shrugged.

"Oh, I see, Hap Tyson."

This night might be interesting, he thought, as he looked into her pretty face, with a turned-up nose and dark, sparkling brown eyes.

"Hey, would you like to dance? I'm not much good, but I'm sure you can teach me what I don't know."

"Oh, I can, Mister Tyson, I can," she answered as she took his hand, following him into the middle of the dance floor.

"By the way, my name's Pamela Martin."

Chapter 4

"'Nice to meet you, Miss Pamela."
They danced the rest of the evening as long as the music filled the air.

"Well, who is she?" quizzed Randall as they all bunched into Hap's and Ashe's room. "C'mon. We're all dying to know."

"Give him room, guys. Give him room," Ashe demanded, tossing clothing aside as the friends muscled in to hear every word.

"I can't believe you all, but if you must know, her name is Pamela, Pamela Martin."

Grinning, he shrugged his shoulders and sighed.

"She's nice. Stuart, get that stupid look off your face. I just met her."

"Maybe I'll ask her to dance at the next social," Randall said.

"And, me, too," added Nicolas.

"All right, all right, enough's enough. And lay off the lady, you characters. If she'd wanted to dance with any of you jokers, she would have talked to you, but she didn't!"

His voice grew louder. Then Hap burst out laughing. For the first time since his trial and his breakup with Caroline, he had really enjoyed himself without thinking of his past. Maybe his heart was starting to heal.

But old, daunting thoughts returned as Hap lay in bed after the dorm settled. For some strange reason, Litch Bagley's searing words in an earlier confrontation at the university filled his head: Caroline will have a passel of Bagleys gathered at her knee.

Flipping over, Hap burrowed his face in his pillow. He would get over her. He would. Maybe he had a reason, now...

Chapter 5
VISIT AND RETURN

The Farmer's Almanac predicted a nasty season for North Carolina in the winter of 1882. These words and her pregnancy prompted Caroline's decision to make her way down east in mid-September. She stayed for three glorious weeks at Shiloh.

"Coffie?" she whispered that first day. "Are you awake?"

He smiled with his eyes closed and mouthed a "hello."

"I've got some news."

His eyes opened; his brow furrowed.

"What?" he mouthed back.

"You're going to be a great-grandfather. Litch and I are going to have a baby," she said, fondly rubbing the furrow in his brow. His face relaxed into another smile. He raised his bony hand to clasp hers.

"I...wish...Jacksie...was here. Your grandmother...would...just love this...news," he whispered. Closing his eyes again, he drifted off to sleep, but the slight smile remained.

During her visit, Caroline spent every waking moment she could with Coffie. She had been right about sharing the news of her impending motherhood; he'd been elated. Rarely did he speak now, with most communication coming through nods, a few grunts, or maybe a scrawled note. The granddaughter seemed to have the sixth sense about what he wanted or needed.

"I wish you'd stay longer, Caroline," Sarah whispered in her ear as they both stood watching the rise and fall of Coffie's bony, sunken chest. Both women loved the old man as much as any daughter and granddaughter could. They would do anything to

Chapter 5

extend his life and happiness, but the old man still had his wits.

Coffie's eyes fluttered. He stuttered and tried to speak. "Sarah...she...must...go...home. Caroline...you...belong...with...your...husband...at home."

Both women looked at each other astonished. He was still the patriarch.

Coffie could not imagine the loneliness Litch must be experiencing. If Jacksie had left him for that long, he knew he would have been crazy. Caroline had to go home.

"Litch, hello. Anybody home?" she called from their doorway. The housekeeper scurried to greet her and took her wrap and bags from the stoop.

"Litch Bagley? Where are you?"

She had missed him, but she could not imagine his not rushing in to see her. Didn't he miss her? She walked through the house to the breakfast room, and then, she saw him through the window.

He was groping in the rose bushes, pricking his fingers, sucking them, and cursing the thorns. He made a clip with the shears, just as she tapped on the pane. He reared up quickly, his hair falling on his face. The frown from the pricked finger quickly fell, replaced with the smile that she had expected at the door. She retreated to the parlor couch, squeezing her eyes shut in excitement as the door slammed. She knew he would not believe the size of her belly.

Her husband raced to stand in front of her with his hands behind his back.

"Choose," he instructed as he always did when he had a surprise.

"The right." He produced an empty hand.
"Again."
"The left."
He produced an empty hand.
"Litch, play fair. You're teasing."

"Alright, my dear. For you, I have a most unique surprise. It's the last rose of summer, paid with a huge price."

He showed her his red finger, pricked by the nasty thorn.

With much fanfare, he presented her his treasure. He had found just one, hidden low and protected by remaining foliage. It was beautiful, sequestered just for this special return. Only then did she reach for his hand. As he pulled her up, he placed the rose behind her ear.

"I've missed you more than I can tell you."

His kiss was hungry, almost desperate. Pulling back, his eyes dropped to her midriff. He'd felt her size against him.

"Caroline...you—"

Her husband stood speechless. He stared at the growing child. Startled from his stupor, he stammered again. Laughing, she let go of his hand and twirled.

"Can you believe this is me, all me?" she gushed as she led him back to the couch and sat him down. He had yet to speak. She took the rose from behind her ear and laid it on the marble top table in front of them, its fragrance permeating the room.

She placed his right hand on her swollen side just as the child moved dramatically. Litch jumped. Her eyes, closed in ecstasy, showed she coveted this moment for both of them.

"Oh, Caroline," he whispered. "Thank you, darling. Thank you."

The Bagley household was quiet the week before Christmas. Caroline and Litch sat in front of the fireplace in their bedroom suite. They had retired early as they had each evening for the last month. Mrs. Rumley had drawn baths for each to soak out the day's kinks.

"Darling, wait. Let me help you."

Quickly drying himself, he tossed on his robe. "Give me both your hands," he instructed, as he leaned down to help her.

"I'm not going anywhere without you, Husband Mine."

"No, you're not," he laughed, grabbing the towel from the

Chapter 5

washstand. Litch loved to dry her swollen body with the pride of an awaiting father.

"Oh, what joy that lies within," he'd say each time. Both would laugh.

Wrapped in their warm, fleecy robes, they sat and talked, a brandy snifter twirling in his hand. Finishing his last sip, he knelt before her and massaged her feet and legs. When he reached her belly, he touched her with such reverence. Placing his head on her stomach, he caressed her and talked to his child.

"Oh, little one? Can you hear your father? Let me tell you a story."

Caroline's hand fell on his head with her fingers rhythmically running through his hair.

"We were on vacation down at the seashore. Do you know what, wee one? I knew I would marry your mother from the first time I saw her. Do you know what else, my precious baby? I love her more each day that passes."

His hand played over her midsection as if he were taking possession of her. He peeked at her face as she lay back on the couch, seeing the immense pleasure he gave her with this ritual of pure adoration and love. Litch could no longer be her lover with her growing size. He had missed their intimacy, but he could wait. He nudged her.

"Bedtime for you, my lady."

"Hmmm," she murmured.

Pulling her to her feet, he led her to her dressing gown. Standing on tiptoe, she kissed him full in the mouth.

"Thank you, Husband Mine," she whispered.

He kissed the curvature of her neck and shoulder.

At daybreak, Caroline padded to the window and absorbed the early sounds of morning. She turned toward the bed and stared at her husband. Would he ever really believe that she was his wife in every sense? It amazed her how insecure he was about her and how important it was for him to caress her and cling to her and endear himself to her as if momentarily she would vanish. She could not ask for a kinder or more loving man. She did love him. She did. She smiled as she saw him stirring.

Raising up on his elbow, he squinted at her outline with the rising sun behind her. Throwing back the covers, he leaped out of bed and raced to embrace her as both greeted the new morning. *Oh, surely, this lovely creature is mine. Oh, yes.* He stood behind her and stretched his arms to encompass her and enclose her swollen body with his own. *Oh, ...*

Chapter 6

EXCUSES, EXCUSES

The sophomores had one more social before the holidays. Hap knew he would see his tall, willowy dancing partner once more. Maybe, just maybe, she could continue to distract him from his aching heart.

"Hello, fellow," Pamela greeted him as before. He turned around on the edge of the dance floor and held out his hand and waltzed her around the floor, twirling until both were dizzy.

"Whoa! My head's spinning," she said. "Sit with me a moment until I get my dancing legs...and head back."

"I like your red gown. It suits the season," he said as he escorted her to the sidelines. "Punch?"

"Oh, yes, the whole bowl, after that last dance," she laughed.

He loved her laugh, deep and throaty. He handed her a cup, as they walked to nearby chairs and sat quietly for several minutes, resting and watching the other dancers.

"Are you all right, Hap? You seem occupied or distracted tonight."

"Me?"

"Yes, you."

He looked away, sighing. "Hey, look at me. You're troubled by something. What is it?"

"School, I suppose," he lied. "Exams are coming up and I have one more paper to finish before the holiday. Just my studies," he tossed her way, shaking his head, and scrunching his shoulders.

"Hap, I've known you a few months now and I've never heard this concern from you before. No, it's something else, and it's fine if you don't want to tell me. It's your business."

She paused, then grabbed his arm. "Okay, handsome, I'm ready to twirl again."

No girl had been that familiar with him before. He liked the sound. At nine o'clock, the dance ended.

"I can't believe the holiday is already here. Can you?" Pamela asked as they left the building holding hands. "Will you go to Pitt County for Christmas?"

"Oh yes, I'm excited. I've had so few holidays with my Pap. I'm sure he's got loads of plans. And you?"

"My grandfather will come to Hillsborough this season. He's a banker on the other side of the state, but we're hoping he'll retire soon and come to Chapel Hill. He loves it here. I bet it won't be long."

They ambled as if they hated the night to end, and being last to reach the long horse drawn carriage seemed to suit them just fine. With enough darkness and swiftness, Pamela brushed his cheek with her lips. No one saw, but he certainly felt the softness of her mouth. She squeezed his hand and climbed aboard. One day, he knew he would kiss those soft lips the way a man should.

The young ladies from the academy always stayed overnight at Mrs. Canright's guest house. He wondered if he should try to see her tomorrow before her departure, but as he waved goodbye with the rest of the guys, he knew he wouldn't. Exams. His imaginary paper. His excuse, but he did want to make the dean's list for Pap, Doc Knight, and-and... He choked on her name, the name he was used to saying every other breath. He had to stop this nonsense and now.

The Christmas holidays had come and gone too quickly for Hap. He could not believe how much he had enjoyed his Greenville family celebration, but he was anxious to get back to Chapel Hill to see the Fearless Five and to test his relationship with Pamela Martin. The urgency pressed hard to know if he was free from the past.

Chapter 6

"You look different, Roomie. What gives?" Ashe asked, then broke out into a big grin. "My God, you're ready, aren't you?"

"What are you talking about?" Hap retorted.

"She's fading, and that, my man, is good." He waggled his finger.

"Maybe," Hap shrugged.

"Look, man, you have ached too long. I'm glad, Hap. I really am. Now, you can concentrate on your new lady friend."

"I am seeing her this weekend," he said with a smile.

"Good deal," he hollered, hurling himself across the room for a brotherly tussle. The laughter brought the others to their door.

"What's going on?" they all chimed.

"You'll know soon enough," Ashe laughed.

In seconds, he lifted his roommate from his bed and stood him upright. Slinging his arm around his shoulders, he announced, "This, my friends, is a new man."

He slapped Hap's back, winking at the rest of the gang.

Pamela Martin became a frequent guest at Mrs. Canright's Boarding House, whether Hap's invitation was for a concert on Polk quad, a play at Smith Hall, a football game, or watching Ashe perform on the baseball diamond. Their favorite pastime was simply a basket lunch sitting under the Davie Poplar Tree down from South Building, then strolling up Franklin Street.

Every time Hap called for Pamela, he was always amused by Mrs. Canright. She stood only five feet two inches tall, but her voice penetrated the air whenever she spoke. No one disputed her authority over "her girls." Her rouged face made Hap wonder if she had a fever, but her funniest facial feature to him was her mouth. He swore it looked like a bow tied in a knot.

"She's waiting for you, Mister Tyson," she would say every time, turning to call up the staircase. "Pammie, dear, Mister Tyson's here."

One night after a mouthwatering meal at Mrs. Canright's, Hap and Pamela sat down on the swing at the end of the porch. They snickered at the loud creaks. Both swore that Mrs. Canright built the swing with squeaky boards, just to know that silence meant the two swingers were "up to no good," her very words to "her girls."

Abruptly, Hap's toe stopped the swing. He stared forward, his face serious. Slowly, he turned toward her.

"Why, Mr. Tyson, are you up to no good? I've got a feeling that you're going to kiss me."

Pamela never minced words, but slowly the humor left her face. Her heart raced. They had only been good friends, so far. Of late, she had sensed earlier wounds, but she wanted no part of picking up pieces and binding a man back together. No, she wanted everything between them to be whole and real and free from past ghosts.

Hap took the back of his hand and touched her cheek. How soft. Her eyes closed for a moment, as his hand dropped to hers. She realized his difficulty, slipped her other hand to his chin, leaned forward, and brushed his cheek with her lips. Before she could pull back, he turned his head, quickly locking their mouths in a long-awaited kiss. Their lips melded perfectly. Breaking away, their eyes posed a thousand questions.

"Mister Tyson, Mrs. Canright might come outside. The swing's not creaking."

Both burst into laughter, easing the tension. They'd taken a step from which neither wanted to retreat.

Chapter 7
REALITY

*I*n Raleigh, the last months of Caroline's pregnancy seemed to drag. The expectant parents could not have been any more eager for the birth of this child.

"I believe this baby will come any day now," Doctor Frawley said, as he looked at her over his wire-framed glasses. She sat on the examining table in the doctor's office.

"Mrs. Steuben says you've begun to show signs," he continued. "I wasn't expecting this so soon, but some ladies deliver early and in a hurry."

Normally, her last appointments would have been in the downstairs guest room in Oakwood. Doctor Frawley and the midwife always visited their patients in the homes near delivery time, but for their first child, Litch was nervous as a cat and insisted they use the new nearby Presbyterian Hospital.

"Doctor? Any day?" Caroline looked at him in wonder, as he nodded.

"Let's call Litch in and tell him he'll be a father soon."

She hesitated. "Dr. Frawley, please. Allow me the pleasure to fix my husband a special dinner with all the trimmings to make that announcement myself. Litch has done so much for me. It's one little thing I can do for him in return," she sweetly charmed him.

The doctor shrugged, "Whatever you say, my dear, but you better get everything ready. You'll be a mother in a few days, mark my word."

The doctor left his puzzled patient.

Caroline sat, absorbing the startling news.

"My God, the man has credentials," she mumbled, looking up at the diploma on the wall from The Jefferson Medical School.

Couldn't he count? She and Litch had been married in June. June, July, August... January, February. January? They would have had to have been married in May. *May?* Her hand flew to her mouth. *May. Oh, God in heaven. Not May.* She grabbed the sides of the examining table before crumpling into a heap on the good doctor's office floor. *It just cannot be true. Please, God, not true...*

She braced herself just as the nurse came in to assist her, but a tear spilled from her eyes too quickly for her to hide it.

"It's all right, my dear, all new mothers have little crying spells. Come now; let me help you. Mr. Bagley and the doctor are talking. They'll want you to join them."

How could she face him? The man adored her. What had he not done to win her affection? She had given herself to him as fully as she knew how and it was all a lie. A lie! She dabbed her eyes as best she could and was grateful her hat had an attached veil to hide her reddened features. She must recover before they arrived home.

Over the months, Litch had insisted on being with her for her appointments. He had chosen Doctor Frawley for his reputation in progressive obstetrics.

"It's the least I can do, darling. I want to be with you."

Sometimes, she had shooed him off to the office, but lately it was nice to have him help her because of her size. Her size! Good grief! No wonder he had marveled at how swollen she'd become so fast. Well, why shouldn't he? She was one month earlier than they had thought. Oh, the misery she had set upon her head, upon all their heads.

Mustering her courage—*God, help me*—Caroline opened the door and walked out. Amazingly, she was able to smile at her husband, as he rushed to her side. The weather had broken finally and given them a clear day. Litch rubbed her gloved hand all the way home and babbled about the nursery that had taken

Chapter 7

shape since the holidays. He was delirious.

His humor temporarily blocked Caroline's misery. Leaning out of the carriage, he shouted for all to hear.

"She's mine, all you people! All mine!"

"Litch Bagley, you're an outrage," she scolded, but only for a second. Her own laughter matched his. Sending him back to his office was difficult, but after numerous attempts, she commanded, "Go!"

Their dinner was carefully laid and quite intimate. She and Mrs. Rumbly had worked diligently. Caroline prayerfully rehearsed her words, words that would not hurt her adoring husband.

When he arrived, it was she who opened the door, not their housekeeper. His brow furrowed only for a second as she gave him a bewitching look and an ingratiating smile. He forgot himself immediately and swept his wife into his arms and kissed her, only to feel her giggle under his lips.

"What?" he asked, looking down at her quizzically.

"You're standing on the hem of my dress. One more tug and it just might fall off. Oh, get that gleam out of your eye. Later, Husband Mine, later."

He returned her laugh, pinched her nose slightly, and walked her into the parlor. Catching his breath, he spotted her preparations through the dining room doorway.

"I'm speechless."

"Isn't it lovely? Mrs. Rumley and I worked hard. Sit down. Sit down," she encouraged. "Doctor Frawley says I am in good health and the baby seems alive and well."

"I know, darling. I'm so glad," he sighed. Picking up the starched napkin, he draped it across his lap.

Breathing deeply, she began to serve him his favorite meal, roast beef, sweet potatoes stuffed with currants, and crowder peas. Her baked apples with cinnamon always made his mouth water. Selecting a special Bordeaux from the wine caddy, she poured him a glass.

"A toast, Husband Mine. To you and to our child." She raised her water goblet to him, his face covered with adoration for his wife, soon to be the mother of his child.

Serving herself from the buffet, Caroline prattled on, her back to him. "The doctor thinks that I might deliver any day. He says that some women have babies early. I might be one of those."

She strategically failed to tell him that her birth canal had shown signs of opening. Thinking she had told him enough, she turned and sat, chatting fast and furiously about the nursery.

"Whoa, slow down," Litch demanded. "Did you say you could have the baby any day?"

She froze. Finishing her mouthful of food, she nodded. "Why didn't you tell me at his office?"

"Well, I thought a special meal for special news."

"Oh," he hesitated, "but do you know what that means? We'll be parents in a matter of days, maybe? Frawley's not sure, or is he? Darling, just think this ordeal for you will be over in a few days. Oh, my God. Just a few days."

He was crazed with emotion. Flying around the table, he knelt at her feet and buried his head in her lap. Lifting his face to her, he placed his hands once more on her swollen belly.

"Are you a bouncing baby boy or an adoring little girl who'll wrap me around your finger like your mother has done?"

"Litch," she laughed.

He raised himself up to kiss her smiling mouth. Her fingers traced through his hair. As she pulled his head back, she looked him in the face and told him what she had not been able to tell him since their marriage.

"I love you, Litchfield Jacob Bagley."

The pain of all the past months of not hearing this pronouncement lifted from this man's soul. She crushed his head against her bosom.

Oh, surely, she's mine now. Oh, yes.

The pain hit mid-afternoon the next day. Doctor Frawley was

Chapter 7

right. This baby was coming. Truly, she had hoped that he would be wrong, for the longer away from her due date, the less suspicion that the baby could be anybody's other than her husband's.

Husband and wife had shared lunch that day. She'd used more spices than usual, but mothers-to-be have cravings. How she regretted it now as she held her side, for the cramps were not just from the food. The little mister or miss was clawing on the walls, wanting out into the world.

"Caroline," Litch hollered as he dashed into the house.

The expectant father fortunately had sat with a client in his office when the next-door neighbor's son delivered the news.

"Oh, my God, Caroline," he murmured, scooping her up in his arms from the parlor sofa and walking quickly to the carriage, hardly noticing her added weight as he strode with determination.

Mrs. Rumley stood and wrung her hands. The neighbor's son drove as fast as he dared.

"Darling, we're hurrying. Don't fret," he said as he held his wife and soothed her. "I love you so. You have made me the happiest man in the world."

Only then did he notice the wetness on her dress. He bit his lip to prevent words of worry.

At Presbyterian Hospital, Litch rushed everybody in sight. No one moved fast enough for him.

"Can't you hear her agony? Please hurry!"

"Sir?" A voice boomed behind him.

"Huh?"

He turned in response to the tapping on his shoulder. A foreboding nurse ordered him from the room, and she meant every word.

"But—"

"No buts, Mr. Bagley! This hospital has rules and you will abide them."

Frantically, he looked at Caroline as a bevy of people worked over her. Couldn't he tell her that he loved her, just once more?

"Out! You're impeding our work."

The nurse's arms were crossed, and they were healthy ones. Litch threw up his hands in defeat and backed toward the door.

Being pushed out was not sitting well with him, as he presumed all husbands acted this way when their wives were in labor. Reluctantly, he trudged down the hall, past the hospital chapel. How he wished for Reverend Barkley's prayers. He turned back and peeped inside. The quiet and the coolness of the chapel startled him, as he slowly drifted to the altar and draped his big frame over the railing. He clasped his hands and raised his face toward the simple cross above his head.

At first, Litch seemed confused, but then in a whisper, he slowly found words.

"Lord—Lord, I don't know what to say." A long moment passed.

He breathed deeply, "I guess I just want you to protect my wife as she delivers. You know the strength she needs. Give it to her."

Another moment passed.

"And—and heal her body, Lord. This trauma can't be good on her. Give her back her health. Please!"

His voice raised to a higher pitch, only to drop once more.

"My—our child. Oh, God, grant perfect health to this child. Let this son, or daughter—I don't care which—bring us happiness. Help me...help me be a better man for having loved her and give me a love for this child that is totally, totally without bounds. Thank you. Thank you..."

His voice trailed into silence as he rested at the rail and stared upward. Pushing back on his heels, he stood up, then sat on one of the meager benches and just thought.

"Litch? Litch?" Doctor Frawley had stepped to the doorway still dressed in his blood-splattered white hospital garb.

"Car-oline," Litch said, his voice breaking.

"Litch, you're the proud father of a handsome young son."

"A son? A son? Jacob. Oh, my God, we have a Jacob," he shouted.

Chapter 7

Even the shushing of the doctor could not keep Litch's voice down. Rushing to the man, he shook him and demanded to see his wife.

"Look, Litch, be thankful it happened fast. I know how anxious you are, but we have to wait a little while for Caroline to be ready to see you. Give us a few minutes. Sit right here and I will personally come get you. By the way, she did great."

Shaking his head, he mused at the many speeches to new fathers he had made in his lifetime. *Too many,* he thought. He walked away from a happy, but frustrated man.

Chapter 8
THE BAUBLE

Old Doc Sims looked over his protégé's shoulder. The man had continued through the year to use Hap in his laboratory on campus.

"Son, have you thought about medical school? We haven't talked about it in a long time."

Hap put down a beaker and turned to his friend.

"I really want to, Doc. You've been such an unbelievable help. Here, look at this paper."

He handed the old gentleman a rumpled-up page from a tablet.

"I've tried to do a little figuring. With all the extra classes, summer sessions, and labs, I should be able to finish undergraduate this coming summer and could start the medical program next fall."

The old man nodded and smiled, slapping his back. "You've got my vote, boy. I've just been waiting for this moment. I'm not your pa, but I think I feel how he would, and Rufus."

He spoke the name *Rufus* with admiration.

"You know he keeps up with your progress," he grinned as he thought of his friend. "Son, I cannot tell you how happy I am."

"Hang on, sir, here comes the shocker. I want to get married."

"Wh—what? Married? Have I been asleep? Who is she?"

"It's Pamela Martin from Hillsborough."

"Banks McCloud's granddaughter?" Doc asked.

Hap nodded.

"That's right. Do you know him?"

"Oh yeah, everybody knows Banks McCloud," he said stroking

Chapter 8

his scruffy goatee. "He's been a tremendous benefactor of the university. Yep, when you're a good alum as he's been, you get known around campus."

"Uh-oh. How good?"

"There'll be a building with his name on it for sure."

"Tell me about him, Doc."

"Son, the man went to New York City after a stellar record at the University in Money and Banking. He sat under the guidance of J.P. Morgan for a time, but wanted to come back to North Carolina. He ended up in Winston-Salem to help set up the national bank there and that is where he has been."

"How'd he get the name Banks?"

"Well, when rumor had it that he was coming South, many a bank clamored for his attention, but he already knew what he intended to do. I don't know, someone just dubbed him Banks and it stuck."

Hap gulped when he thought of his meager budget. Surely, the man was well heeled being a financier and such.

"When did all this happen with your young lady?" Sims marveled.

"This last semester. We got pretty serious after the holidays."

"Want me to stand up for you?"

"Naw, my Pap'll do that, but I want you to be there for sure, along with my family and friends. My buddies can't believe it, but we're very serious. Right now, I just need some more lab time so I can pay for a ring."

"Well, well, well... Now, you *are* in a predicament. You just happen to be the best laboratory assistant I've ever had, *and* you will need a good recommendation for med school, will you not?"

They both nodded.

"Well, to get my *John Hancock*, you'll have to work hard for the old doc. Hey, I like this proposition better and better."

Cocking his head, he asked, "When are you going to pick it out?"

"The ring? Today, probably during lunch. Pamela's grandfather has retired from that bank in Winston Salem and has returned to Chapel Hill. He'll be living in the McCloud family home on Rosemary Street."

"I'd heard that rumor," Doc said.

"There's a family retirement party. The Martins invited me. I thought maybe I could ask Mr. Martin's permission, and if he says yes, I'll have the ring with me to give to her."

"I like this plan. Hap, let's go get that ring. I haven't done this sort of thing in thirty-five years."

Mrs. Sims had left the old professor a widower fifteen years earlier.

The two men, one old and bent, the other towering and tousled-headed, stood in front of the jewelry counter staring at Hap's choice.

"Now, son, I like your pick, but I need to think of a wedding present for the two of you, which, frankly, I would like to do now, since I see an opportunity. Can I throw in a few extra bucks for, let's say, hmmmm, that one?"

He pointed a crooked finger at one perched on a small pedestal under the glass of the display case. Its brilliance dazzled in the sunlight.

"You sure would get me off the hook, struggling with a choice that is. What say, boy? Do it for an old man who wants to do something special for you."

Hap could hardly speak.

"I-I don't know what to say."

"How about yes?"

Slowly, Hap pulled his money from his pocket and handed it to the jeweler.

"Put the difference on my account, Withers. Mister Tyson would like to take it now. I think he has a *rendezvous* tonight," he spoke with a twinkle in his eye.

The jeweler bowed slightly and disappeared.

Hap had experienced few family celebrations in his lifetime;

Chapter 8

Pamela, many. She'd invited him to McCloud's retirement party without a qualm as if it was natural that he should be with her and her family. The night could not come fast enough for him.

When it did, the young man strode quickly toward her grandfather's house on Rosemary Street in the brisk wintry air, his warm breath streaming in long puffs behind him. He patted the small box in his pocket at least one hundred times.

Stopping short, the excited young man studied the imposing house, activity brimming through the windows. The bell by the front door jamb beckoned a pull, which he jangled nervously. Lucas, the old gentleman's butler, opened the door, his smile soothing any anxiety that Hap had.

"Good evening, Mister Tyson," Lucas said. "Miss Pamela's been waiting."

As he followed the soft-spoken Lucas, Hap embraced the family scene, quite different from the quiet ones with Willie, or the few lively ones with Pap. Then, he heard her voice.

"Oh, Hap," she said, peeking around Lucas. "Welcome. Everybody's anxious to meet you." She motioned him to follow her, as they weaved through family. Many he knew; others, he didn't. He nodded to all, then stopped quickly behind her.

"Grandfather, I want you to meet my friend," Pamela spoke softly. "His name is Hap Tyson."

"Well, well, young man. Welcome to the McCloud household," a voice boomed out at him.

The voice and his handshake did not match the size of the man. McCloud wasn't much taller than Mrs. Canright, but his shock of gray hair added at least four inches. Hap smiled. Willie would have called him scrawny.

Lucas jingled a small bell.

"Dinner is served, Mister McCloud."

Everyone rushed into the large dining room, eagerly looking for their names on the place cards. Hap had never seen such a table, nor had he ever seen his name on a place card. Mister Tyson, no less. He smiled and remembered to help Pamela with her chair. The food came, the family ate, the conversation flowed.

When can I tell them my intent? Hap worried. *Are there no quiet moments?*

His hand slipped inside his pocket to find the small present, miniature in size, but large in significance.

Banks McCloud rose, scraping his chair back from the table, tapping his spoon against his crystal goblet for attention. Mouths closed.

"Family, it gives me great delight to welcome our guest tonight, Mister Tyson. This is your first time with this family and may it not be your last..." The old gentleman droned on.

Hap began to wonder if he ever would finish. Finally...finally, he offered the floor to his family, but it was his guest who sprang from his seat.

"Mister McCloud, sir..." he gulped, looking around at the expectant group. Pamela sat with her admiring eyes gazing over at him, since someone strategically seated them across from and not beside each other.

"Everyone, I am very humbled by this grand evening. Pamela's grandfather has been kind to include me in this family celebration, but, sir, frankly, I would like to come back...over and over..." his voice trailed. "You see, sir, I visited the Martins last weekend and asked for Miss Pamela's hand in marriage. I would like to join your family."

A faint smile crossed Pamela's face. *What a perfect time. He could not have picked a better opportunity.*

"What ?" her grandfather sputtered, "Nobody told me."

The Martins clapped their hands.

Banks McCloud's face froze in a frown.

"Father," Bethiah Martin laughed. "Could this be the first time anybody's ever pulled one over on you?"

The entire family roared, and quickly the retiree's deep frown disappeared.

Moving around the table, Hap continued to speak, "I have a

Chapter 8

gift for you, Pamela. Would you honor me by wearing this ring as a sign of our engagement? Hopefully, yes?" he pleaded with his words and eyes.

Blushing, she quietly looked for approval from her parents and her grandfather.

"Pammie, if you don't say *yes* to this young whipper-snapper, then I'll answer for you," the old man ordered.

"Yes, oh yes," she whispered with her hands shaking as she took the little box. A tear hung on a lash, as she opened it. "Hap," she gasped, calculating the size of the stone and the size of Hap's budget.

"May I?"

"Of course," she said, stunned at the ring being placed on her finger. The family applauded and listened once more to a long and flowery toast by her grandfather. It was a good night in the McCloud household.

Yet, Hap soon discovered that their decisions would become family decisions. Everyone agreed, even over Hap's hesitation, that a summer wedding, before the fall session would be perfect. And, before the question was hardly asked, McCloud, as Hap suspected, pressed the school board, and the village gained a new teaching staff member by the month's end, by the name of Pamela Martin, soon to be Pamela Tyson. And, yes, they could certainly have the bedroom suite upstairs in the McCloud house. Fresh paint, new wallpaper, and the works would make the comforts of home for his beloved granddaughter and her groom.

McCloud even donated his desk, upon which he'd written his very first paper. It would be perfect for the little office off of their bedroom, a true private haven for his studies. The old gentleman almost seemed as excited as the mother of the bride.

And, yes, he could call her grandfather by his nickname, Banks, as she had been doing since she was sixteen.

Weddings do strange things to folks, Hap thought. He had a feeling he would have to rein in McCloud's gift-giving. This could get way out of hand.

No words from her son could convince Willie Pridgen to attend his wedding. She refused more than once. In most of her letters, she tried to keep him abreast of Tarboro news, but there was that one item she could not decide whether to tell him about. However, at the end of one of her refusals, she scrawled a line that burned into his brain as he read it over and over.

By the way, Caroline Bagley gave birth to a baby boy back in January.

Chapter 9
MRS. TYSON

"Do you, Thomas Rolland Tyson, take Pamela McCloud Martin, to be your lawful wedded wife…"

It was happening, actually happening. He was getting married and not to Caroline. Surely, this could not be. Too clearly, he could hear Pamela's words ringing in his head.

"Darling, we can make this work. Just listen to me. I have the job. We have a place to live. Banks wants to set up a fund, just in case we need a few dollars in a pinch. Hap Tyson, this ring is driving me crazy. I want that other band, my dear, and in June."

"Whoa! June? You forget that I have obligations to Doc Sims about that ring on your finger. Let me work this out in my own mind and my own time, please."

Hap had never heard such insistence in her voice before. He was not quite sure how to take this new sound. Was it the one of a spoiled granddaughter? A spoiled daughter? Whatever, he felt uncomfortable, as she continued with either a pout or a whine, when the subject came up and that was quite often.

Could he actually live in the McCloud house? And with a bride? His first reaction was, of course not, but, otherwise, they would have to live in any cramped quarters he secured. The more he looked around her grandfather's house, the more appealing it became and the more credible the possibility. He would consider it strongly.

"Do you, Pamela McCloud Martin, take Thomas Rolland Tyson, to be your lawful wedded husband…"

Reverend Simons continued the charge as the two young

people stood before him and a full congregation at the Presbyterian Church in Hillsborough. They had made it this far with no hitches. Vowing to cherish each other seemed the easiest part they'd experienced so far. Between her grandfather and Mrs. Martin, the young couple had been entertained by almost everyone in the village and Orange County.

For the wedding, Pamela's huge family had come from across the state. Being hugged and squeezed by so many females amazed Hap. He pitied the poor politicians who had to shake hands all over the countryside; his knuckles were raw from the last few weeks.

And, of course, Willie had not come. Stubborn as she was, she stuck to her resolve that no one would understand their relationship. Saddened by her decision, Hap was equally thrilled to see his Greenville family disembark at the Carrboro train station. He'd housed them at the only small inn in Hillsborough with thoughts that they would be more comfortable there than in the homes of Pamela's family. He wished privacy with them, as they shared his joy. Wendell Tyson could not have been happier.

"The Lord's honoring your hard work, Hap. You're jes' doin' better all the time. You make your ole man right proud."

In Orange County, the Martins' wedding reception ranked nothing less than phenomenal. As the buggies approached, the wedding guests gaped at the gazebo and orchestra tuning up for dancing on the lawn. Banks McCloud reveled as he watched his granddaughter and the groom dance the first dance as Mr. and Mrs. Thomas Rolland Tyson.

Her grandfather would stay with the Martins for a week to allow "the young'uns a little privacy," he'd said with a guffaw as if he expected a great-grandchild immediately.

Hap kept reminding him, "Sir, I have to finish my education before we start a family."

"Sure boy, I hear you, but don't wait too long. My wobbly knee won't be able to hold the scamps when I tell them stories," he'd

Chapter 9

chortle and punch Hap in the ribs with countless winks.

"Weddings do funny things to folks," Hap would mutter incessantly.

"I'm exhausted," the new bride declared after the reception. Hap had reached over and patted her hand as they rode back to Chapel Hill.

"It's almost over," he assured. "I can't believe your grandfather. He's tireless." Both had turned as they rode away to watch Banks holding court in the Martins' yard, his wild hair flying as he jerked his head and shook his finger.

"Pamela Tyson. That sounds marvelous, doesn't it?" the bride murmured, as she settled back in the carriage, her head on Hap's shoulder. "I cannot think of one thing that I would have changed. Every single solitary part of the celebration was perfect."

"And the honeymoon will be perfect as well," he whispered in her ear.

"Ahhhh, Mr. Tyson. Is that devilment in your eye?"

She snuggled closer.

The house on Rosemary Street stood lit as they rode up, each knowing the housekeeper and the butler waited within to serve the couple a wedding supper, quiet and intimate, with candlelight, in the dining room. As ever, they performed their task efficiently and promptly.

"Sir, madam, we'll excuse ourselves now. In the morning we'll come, but not too early, to prepare your breakfast. What time would you suggest?"

"Lucas, no time. We'll be just fine. Mrs. Tyson and I would like for you two to take a week's vacation. We promise you we will survive."

"But, sir, Mis—"

"Lucas. We can do for ourselves just fine. Thank you."

"Yes sir. We understand. The larder's well stocked, sir. The missus and I wish you all the best in this new life."

"Well, thank you, Lucas. We appreciate that."

The older couple left, shaking their heads and smiling. The backdoor clicked shut.

"Mister Tyson, we're alone," she laughed that throaty laugh. "Where are you going?" she asked, throwing her napkin down on the dining room table.

"I'm just going to lock the front door," he said over his shoulder. "Well, well, well. Pamela, come look what Banks has left in the parlor," Hap called out to her as she came through the door.

"What? Why that romantic old coot. Champagne!" she laughed as they sat down on the sofa.

"This is perfect, for I have a toast." Struggling slightly with the cork, he assured his new wife, "I can do this."

Grinning at her when it popped, he caught the bubbling liquid in one of the crystal flutes.

"For you, my dear."

He filled the other and raised his glass.

"To you, Pamela, and our years together. May my devotion never fail you."

"Thank you," she whispered.

"May happiness, satisfaction, and love beyond your wildest imagination fill our lives."

The fine crystal tingled at each toast. They sipped.

"And," she interrupted him, "here's to the future generations that will come from our marriage."

They sipped.

"Also, to a night of wedded bliss, and if we sip any more, I won't be able to even crawl up the stairs."

Laughing, she jumped up making a mad dash for the staircase, with her bridegroom in pursuit. He caught her before she entered their bedroom door and swung her up in his arms as he walked toward their bed. He had only done that once before, with Caroline. How could he think of another woman on his wedding night?

Gently, laying his wife on their bed, he looked down on her

Chapter 9

just as he'd gazed at Caroline those countless months ago in his boarding house room.

"Darling, let me prepare myself for you," she softly whispered as she rolled off the bed and disappeared into her dressing room to leave him with his troubled thoughts.

God in heaven make me forget. Please... Please, he silently begged, hoping his new wife would squelch these resurgent memories.

"Ahem."

Pamela cleared her throat.

His head popped up from deep thought. He gasped.

"Pamela. Pamela," he whispered.

He'd never seen such lace on a robe and gown. It was stunning, but the woman who wore them was even more so. Scrambling to his feet from the bedside, he held his hand out to her and slowly drew her to him as he soaked in her every essence. Putting his hands on her shoulders, buried in lace, he allowed his eyes to lock with hers as they both leaned toward one another for a kiss, their eyes wide open.

"Hello, Mrs. Tyson, how ravishing you look on our wedding night."

"Thank you, Mr. Tyson. Could it be you think that way, 'cause you love me?"

"Oh, yes, Mrs. Tyson, oh, yes."

With that acclamation, his thumbs hooked the inner neckline of her robe, and with his hands moving ever so slowly, he exposed her creamy shoulders. The robe dropped to the floor in a mountain of ruffles with a slight swishing sound. Once more, she took his breath as his eyes absorbed her, but mainly his eyes saw a face that glowed with a love to sustain him through whatever lay ahead.

Slowly, they walked to the wedding bed, his hand on her silken waist. Turning her to face him, he kissed her once more on the mouth, then on her neck, and lastly on her shoulder. Placing his hand on the small of her back, he pulled her close. They had never really embraced, and he desired to feel the full length of her body against his. Soon, they would meld in another way, but right then he just wanted to hold her and endear her to him.

Once more he picked her up and placed her on their bed. Slowly, he undressed himself as she watched. He reached to lower the light, but she stopped him, wanting to see her husband as he laid claim to the love she waited anxiously to give him. He eased in beside her and reached for her. Never again, that night anyway, did he venture a memory of Caroline Cromwell Bagley.

I, Thomas Rolland Tyson, take thee, Pamela McCloud Martin...

Chapter 10

THE CHRISTENING

The Bagleys proved the perfect doting parents. Even business seemed unimportant to the new father.

"Litch Bagley, we'll be in the poorhouse. Go to work. What am I going to tell our child? 'Oh, your father has just decided he won't work anymore so he can stay home and play with you.' Now, what kind of example will you be for your son? Join us for lunch and we'll all take a nap to restore ourselves. After last night, we both can vow his lungs are probably the healthiest part of his body."

Reluctantly, Litch left, promising to return promptly at noon. Caroline sighed as she watched her husband walk to his carriage, throwing one last kiss. Quickly, she turned and carried Jacob up to the nursery. She sat in the rocking chair that Coffie had sent to her and the baby. Rubbing the smooth finish, she held the child in the crook of her right arm. Surely, she had been wrong yesterday. Jacob had peered at her with a little crooked smile that froze her heart. Surely it was a coincidence.

"All right. All right, little one, don't be so cranky. Just a minute. Goodness. All right," she soothed the child as her buttons popped open exposing her swollen breasts.

Jacob's mouth began to suckle the nourishment, his hands grasping. The new mother rocked and treasured this intimacy as a lullaby broke from her lips. Laying her head back on the rocker, Caroline Bagley felt at peace with herself and this child. For how long, she didn't know.

He did it again. Oh, no! Please, God, do not let him have that smile.

For weeks now, the crooked smile spread frequently, unmistakable to her, but, of course, she had privileged information. His facial features reflected the Cromwells and the Kings for which she was grateful, but little by little, she watched Hap's wavy hair sprout on that precious head. What would he say if Hap knew she'd given birth to his child? Her body shuddered at the idea. Litch was no fool. He would figure out this secret. What had she done in her own selfish need to risk so much, and for what? A memory? *I, Caroline King Cromwell, take thee, Thomas Rolland Tyson...*

"Caroline, darling, what's the matter? You look so strange," Litch inquired as he came through the doorway of the nursery one day. Quickly, her features changed.

"I'm just a little uncomfortable." She wrinkled her nose as her hand brushed her chest. "Your son's a hungry boy." She mustered a smile.

"You go right ahead. We certainly want those lungs to grow," he said, laughing as he turned to leave them to their task. Caroline placed the baby at her breast.

"There, little one. Your papa is right. We want those lungs to grow. Yes, we do."

Their ritual of rocking and nursing and singing seemed such a soothing effort, but her fears nagged continuously. How long would Litch be satisfied with all her explanations?

Days later, Caroline looked up at her husband from the opened letter on the marble top table in the parlor.

"Coffie's dying, Litch. I've got to go to Shiloh." She paused. "Listen, my love. I have been thinking about something." She paused again, as she sipped tea. "I would love to have Jacob christened at Calvary, hopefully with Coffie with us. If we wait much longer, he may not be able."

Her head turned at Jacob's cry.

Chapter 10

"Excuse me, darling. Our son calls."

Litch had come home early to celebrate a business coup, but realized his news paled to the letter's content. The old patriarch was failing. They needed to go.

Baby Jacob looked handsome in his christening gown. His round, startled eyes peered over Litch's shoulder at the congregation of family and friends at Calvary Episcopal. Coffie had survived to watch his great-grandson, christened and blessed in the church. His wizened face showed a glow of yesteryear.

Only Caroline could even begin to tell what the old barrister meant by his garble and his scrawled notes. It was amazing to everyone how she just seemed able to interpret his every thought, his every wish, but she was confused by something he kept saying about his lawyer, Carleton Phillips. She knew that she would figure it out or would be told by Mister Phillips.

Cromwell Hall brimmed with activity. One more time Maggie's cooking tweaked the family's taste buds.

"Litch, just look at these tables in the yard. Don't they remind you of our wedding reception?"

He smiled at her, holding Jacob, kissing his child continuously.

"It seems so long ago, but it's not even a year. I'm amazed," he said. "Life has changed so in such a short time, hasn't it, my sweet child?"

He jostled Jacob, who gurgled in response.

"I miss Will," she said, fingering her handkerchief.

"I know you do, sweetheart."

"He'd be a proud uncle."

She smiled at her men, but her face darkened. She sniffed, then blew her nose.

"You know, it's been forever since I've even said his name. Litch, I want to walk to the cemetery. Would you mind?"

"Are you kidding? My dear, have I let you put your arms around Jakie in the last hour?"

"No," she mouthed and slipped past him, heading toward her brother's grave. *Oh, Will...*

On their last morning, Caroline rose early. A stable hand saddled one of Elijah's horses for her. Compelled to ride the lower 40, she once more remembered her days with her pony Nellie on these familiar roads through the plantation. The air was crisp and clean, as she inhaled deeply. She'd missed her riding and knew she would find a way for Jacob to enjoy that tradition. The freedom of those rides welled in her chest. How simple life had been back then, how complicated now as a mature woman with a husband, a child, and a secret.

Caroline slowed as she neared the grassy mound. How strangely the grasses intertwined a curious webbing around the hidden site. Years back, Old George had religiously used a sling blade on the haven. She supposed the unkempt undergrowth somewhat allayed the pain and sealed away the hurt of the tragedy for her mother and father. And, what about Jacob? What if he were seized from Litch and her, just as Will had been from her parents? She shuddered at the thought.

Breaking the spell, she urged her mount through the thicket into the inner part of the grassy knoll. The willow still stood by the little creek. Even the infamous log lay in decay where she and Hap Tyson had sat countless times and where Will had died. Lichens clung to the undersides, creating a strange, ruffled attire. Never dismounting, Caroline pushed through the wild grasses. The trickling creek lured her where she had last spied Hap disappearing around the bend, as he would slip back through the woods to Willie Pridgen's house. So, so long ago...

Turning her horse, Caroline started.

"Father," she called out, seeing the Captain sitting on his horse just outside the haven.

"I ride every morning, Caroline. You must have come out right before I did."

Sweeping his arm before him, he sighed.

Chapter 10

"As you can tell, we've just let the lower 40 go these last few years. Come, daughter, ride back to the house and talk to your father."

Sidling up beside him, she smiled feebly, only to hear his very pointed question.

"Did you come here because of Will...or Hap?"

"Father," she exclaimed.

"Oh my God, Caroline, forgive an old fool. I cannot believe I asked such a thing. I suppose I associate the lower 40 with Will and Hap. I'm so sorry."

He turned his head in pain.

Her eyes fluttered.

"I-I especially missed my brother this trip. I would have given anything, *anything,* if he could have seen Coffie's face, or yours, or any of us, at Calvary. Surely, you must have thought the same?"

He sighed.

"Of course, I did and do. Every day of my life and even Fate's, we both visit Will's grave, sometimes together and sometimes alone. It's so strange how close we've become and how amazing we both have loved Will as much as anybody on this earth. It's like the Lord's given us each other for comfort. His Shug helps Maggie the best she can since they have a little boy now. When they are older, their son and Jacob can play together, just like Will and Fate did. How about that! It's almost like a reward from the past."

Father and daughter passed the last crop in the field when Caroline turned to Elijah and challenged.

"Race you, Poppa," and took off in a gallop and a puff of dust from the road.

Laughing, he dug his heels in and chased, never wanting to beat her, but he enjoyed watching the golden curls bounce and gleam in the morning sunlight.

"Caroline," Litch called from the back door of the main house. "Where have you been?" he questioned looking from his wife to his father-in-law.

"Little Jacob is squalling for his breakfast. Maggie has him sucking milk from a little rag she keeps dipping. Come on," he urged. "The little fellow's hungry."

The mother took her son from Maggie's arms.

"Thank you, Maggie."

"Jessie will come up and clean him up later," Maggie assured, rubbing the soft skin with her finger.

The young mother smiled and nodded, climbing the stairs to her old bedroom in Cromwell Hall and laughing at the baby's urgency in her arms.

"I hope I have enough milk for my growing boy. What a hungry little fellow you are."

She nuzzled his head, settling down in a rocker.

"I believe you will grow to be as tall as your father. Come here, Jakie."

Finding his nesting place, the child quieted and busied himself, gratifying his hunger. Leaning back in the chair, Caroline closed her eyes and rested from her ride. She was grateful her father had not pursued the other side of his question. She knew she would have lied to him in hopes of not distressing him.

Of course, she had thought of Hap Tyson, a forever ingredient in her life. Gazing down at the child at her breast, she said aloud, "Of course, I thought about the father of my child. Of course, I did."

Chapter 11

OLD FRIENDS

The Captain laughed as he dismounted his horse in front of his oldest friend. Willie Pridgen sat on the front porch of Fate and Shug's house within view of Cromwell Hall. She rocked their baby boy and smiled up at the only man she'd ever loved in her entire life.

"What a sight to behold, Willie."

"Children soften the rough spots in life, don't they?"

He nodded.

"It was good seeing Miss Caroline and little Jacob, wasn't it?"

He nodded again.

Elijah Cromwell and Willa Abigale Pridgen had grown up together on Shiloh, her parents were slaves freed by Elijah's father. They called her Willie for short. Over the years, these two had sat in the small haven in the lower 40 under the weeping willow, talking by the hour. Parental pressure to become a gentleman farmer forced a disgruntled young man to turn to Willie to share his feelings. He was seventeen, and she was a year younger.

"I want to be a soldier, Willie. Father won't hear of it, but the Citadel is just waiting for my letter. A war's getting ready to break and I want to fight to save our homeland."

"But he's your pappy."

"I know, I know. That's what hurts. I'd be defying him."

"Mister Elijah, can you really go against him?"

"But I can do and be the other later. And Sarah..."

His voice dropped.

"Miss Sarah? What about her?"

Willie was afraid she knew.

"I want to marry her after I get out of school and finish my training. Father approves of Coeffield King's daughter, as much as he hates my becoming military."

Willie's breathing almost stopped. What in the devil was she thinking? Of course, he'd be thinking about Miss Sarah. She had no claim on her young master. Miss Sarah did.

Only once in her lifetime did Willie Pridgen have a claim on Elijah Cromwell. He'd won the battle with his father about the Citadel and met her in the lower 40 to tell her the good news.

In their jubilation, she'd said, "Leave me a memory, 'Lijah."

He did. They did. And the evidence of that memory lived right on Shiloh, unbeknownst to the Captain.

How many times had she recalled that memory at the lower 40? And what a precious memory...for her. He'd left her with her only child, a son. Willa Abigale Pridgen was the only living soul privy to Fate Edmundson's real identity. She'd moan every time she'd remember that painful morning of placing the basket with Fate inside on the porch of Maggie and George Edmundson.

Oh, God, my only child... Why, why, did I give up my own flesh?

And how many times had she scolded herself for reliving such pain? She had protected the Captain, her family, herself, but especially her child, their child.

Willie continued rocking her charge. She laughed inwardly, as her heart raced.

It's amazing how you still make my heart pound, she said to herself.

Finally, she let her eyes drop from the man before her to the babe in her arms.

Elijah had given Fate a few acres and built the young couple a house not far from the Cemetery of Angels and the main house. Fate had taken over the responsibility of the plantation by then,

Chapter 11

for his father, old George, had phased out.

"You like taking care of Little Ozzie?" Elijah asked, peering down at the sleeping child. She frowned.

"Of course. Who wouldn't?"

Willie had jumped at the chance to help Fate and Shug when they had other duties on the plantation. She would ride from Tarboro regularly with Maggie and George when they would come to tend to Cromwell Hall. *How unbelievable?* she thought.

Every time she rode with them, she'd listen to their talk about Fate this and Fate that. Sometimes it hurt to hear the details of her son's life, but other times she would laugh with them. She would not have known these things if she had not had this opportunity. Of course, Fate and Shug knew nothing of her secret, and neither did Elijah.

Keeping this secret was becoming harder and harder. She sensed an urgency to tell, especially to Elijah, as their lives became more seasoned.

"Come sit a spell with your old friend, will you? Feast your eyes upon peace, real peace," she said.

He dragged a bench over and sat close, gazing down at Little Ozzie's relaxed face, as he dozed in the sunshine in the crook of her arm. They both smiled at the involuntary twitches of his sleep.

Placing his hand on her shoulder with affection, Elijah told her, as he had a million times.

"Willie, you would have made such a wonderful mother. Look at you, even now."

He paused and rubbed the child sprouting fuzz.

"I'm just sorry you never knocked the right man over the head."

Somehow she would always manage to turn away, so he could not see her pained expression.

"Why don't you hold this growing boy, Mister Elijah, so's I can get us something to drink?" she asked, handing Little Ozzie to the startled man.

She disappeared into the cabin just in time before the tears ran down her face. She just didn't know how much longer she could be silent.

She returned with two glasses.

"Lemonade for my friend." Retrieving Little Ozzie, she sat down. Elijah handed her a glass and sat by her side until they could see the parents coming up the drive. Willie's insides screamed: *He's yours and mine, Elijah! Fate is your son!*

Her real voice never sounded.

I just can't last much longer.

One day Willie sent for the Captain in what she hoped was a casual note, but, when she heard the hoofbeats pounding down Station House Road, she closed her eyes and felt faint.

I can't wait; I just can't... Something could happen to one of us. He has to know, since his only son is dead. Lordy, Lordy...

His heavy boot hit the step, followed by an impatient knock. Opening the door, she stared at a perplexed face.

"You don't ask me to come without trouble brewing. This is no casual conversation you want, woman. What is it? You've worried me these last twenty-four hours."

His hand came to rest on her shoulder as he gazed down at his best and oldest friend.

"For God sakes, Willie, what's going on? You're driving me crazy."

She backed away from him, gesturing for him to sit. He strode to the chair, more questions on his face. How could she begin? Her face bent toward the floor; her voice failed.

Elijah jumped up and shook her slightly. "Tell me, Willie. You're scaring me. Ar-are you sick?"

"Oh, no, Captain, I'm not sick, like you mean, but I have to...tell you...a secret that I've hidden from you for most of our lives. Sit down. Please. I—I just have to take my time."

His eyes never left her face as he backed to the rocker by the

Chapter 11

fireplace.

"Both of us are moving along in years. Maggie might say we're old enough to die. Well, you know that something could happen to either one of us all of a sudden. I—I just don't think that I could leave this earth without your knowing somethin' that's very important between you and me."

"Yes? Yes?"

He remained impatient.

Willie paused, gaining momentum. Clearing her throat, she continued.

"Do you remember that time on the grassy knoll when I asked you—to give me a memory?"

Her voice lowered.

Then, his voice softened.

"Of course, I do, Willie. I'll always treasure that time with you. The first time you love someone, it's a special memory. Willie, what does that have to do with us *now*? That was so long ago."

Not for Willie. She'd relived that lovely moment almost every day of her life.

"Oh, it was a sweet memory, Elijah, but you left me more than a memory. You left me with your—child."

Watching his face blanch, his mouth dropped open, and his eyes widened, Willie cowered, trying to catch the tears with the back of her hand.

Once more springing to his feet, the man whipped her around in a dizzying fashion.

"I what? Let me get this straight. *I* left *you* with a *child,* and you never told me. *My* child? When? How?"

His voice was thick with emotion and fringed with anger.

"Are you telling me when you disappeared that you had my child? All those years, you hid a child from me?"

He shook her with each question.

Willie struggled slightly against his strength and broke free finally to back away from this angered man.

"I just knew something had happened. You would not go away

from me without even saying goodbye. You were my best friend. God, how stupid I am!" he scolded himself, staring down at clinched fists.

His shoulders slumped. He ran his fingers through his hair, pacing the floor in front of her as she collapsed in the chair left empty by him.

"Where is the ch—young man...or woman?" he pried, stopping to tower above her.

Looking up into his contorted face, she gathered her last ounce of courage and said, "It's Fate."

"Fate! Oh, my God, Fate? Will's best friend is my—my son. Will had a brother and never knew it. God in heaven."

He turned and paced again in front of her. Her anguished moans matched her rocking.

"I have to leave. I-I can't stay any longer. I just have to think."

Then, he turned abruptly.

"You be here tomorrow morning," he said, punching the air with his finger.

She nodded through her whimpers, tears streaming profusely.

The next morning, Willie greeted Elijah at her door, a cup of steaming coffee in her hand. They settled down by the fireplace and rocked in quiet.

"Willie."

He broke the silence.

"We have to tell Fate I'm his father and Will was his brother. I just cannot go on without doing that."

"Oh, please, Elijah."

She realized she had slipped into calling him by his first name. Well, why shouldn't she?

She continued, "Think what that would do to Miss Sarah and Mister King. I didn't tell you, so you could go blabbing to everybody. No, I ges' wanted to die knowing I had told you, only you."

"You mean you don't want me to be a father to my own flesh?"

Chapter 11

"But, you have already. Look at the house, his job, your bond...You've been a father to him in every way, but one. Nobody gets hurt this way. You would save me shame, too. Remember that Fate knows nothing about me. We have something very special, now. I don't want to mess it up, Elijah. Listen to me. Listen," the mother pleaded her case.

"If you want to tell him, let's do it by letter after the two of us are gone. He's always felt like a brother of Will's. We'd just make a man happier in his older days. But now? We'd cause more misery than you could shake a stick at. Think of all the folks we'd be hurting. Think of Maggie and George."

Elijah listened and weighed every word. Her thinking made sense. Had they not all suffered enough with Will's dying? Looking at her with a knowing smile, he reached over and took her hand as they sat in her small house.

"You are the dearest friend I have ever had."

He pulled her up from her seat and crushed her to him.

"Thank you for giving me this child."

He held her close against his big frame, took her face in his hands, and let his finger trail her entire face. He kissed her forehead and then faintly brushed her lips, just an old friend kissing an old friend. She accepted him for the first time as just that, the dearest friend she had ever known. They walked arm and arm to the door, where he once more hugged her and took her hand up to his lips. For one moment, he was hers again, just one fleeting moment. Then, it was gone.

Once again, they were just old friends.

"I love you, Willa Abigale Pridgen," he said smiling.

"I love you, too, Elijah Cromwell," she smiled in return, as they basked in the peace between them.

Chapter 12
RANKLED

*H*ap looked at his wife in disbelief. She had entered his little study situated off of their bedroom.

"He's what?" Hap's voice rose a decibel. "Pamela, tell me this again."

"Grandfather has set up another trust fund for children we might have. The boys should attend the University and the girls the Academie where I went. Isn't that wonderful?" she gushed.

Hap shook his head and said, "No," very quietly.

"No? My God in heaven, you said no? Why? I think it's the most generous thing I've ever heard. Banks only wants to help us, Hap. He knows that we're not comfortable... yet."

She looked down at her hands.

"Is there something else you're not telling me?"

She bit her lip and with a little flip of her shoulder said, "All right, I'll tell you the whole thing."

The words poured.

"He also wants to give us a fund to help us while you're still in school."

Hap's mouth dropped open. His eyes widened.

"Oh, please, Hap, he's an old man who wants to help two people he loves. He won't be around too many more years, and he wants to see us taken care of while he's still alive. Don't be difficult on this."

Hap knew affluent gifts could pose problems. Most assuredly, they were strapped with just her meager teaching salary and his work in Doc Sims' lab. Maybe they had jumped too fast into this marriage, but he'd better not think like that. They were married

Chapter 12

and very much in love. It would be a miracle if she did not conceive before he got out of med school. He just had two years left, but if she did... Then McCloud's offering could be an answer.

"Pamela, if—"

"Oh, Hap."

"Pamela, I said if we accept this trust. I promise you and God that I will pay every penny back when I get my practice established."

He could hear his father's words ringing in his ears: *Owe no man. Pay it all back, son. Go to your grave owing no man.* Hap meant it just as much as Wendell Tyson had, as he took his wife by the shoulders.

"Hap, I knew you'd see it our way."

She threw her arms around him in celebration and led him up the stairs to really celebrate. When his wife was insistent, he was doomed.

The next evening Hap sat in his study, plagued with thoughts. It was late. Pamela had retired early. He was grateful for no distraction. If things went well, he would be through with his undergraduate studies and medical school in two years, counting summer terms. The pressure was great, but he was determined to keep his vow to Coeffield King and to himself to accomplish and serve people for the rest of his life.

He remembered how he had stood by the old barrister's bed in the little hospital in Tarboro. King had collapsed at Hap's courtroom trial, the trial of murder charges of Will Cromwell, King's only grandson. He could still hear Caroline's screams, as she told the court the truth. *It was an accident, just a horrible, freak accident,* she had hollered. Hap had never laid a finger on her brother. She had freed him.

His eyes closed.

"Forgive...me...Hap," the old barrister had said, "for not...believing...in...you...or my own...granddaughter."

He intended to keep his vow to serve, as Coeffield King had done. Yes, he would do the same.

Chapter 13

MISTAKES

Litch stood in front of his wife in the nursery and demanded an explanation. "Caroline! I can't believe what you've done to our son's head. Why did you cut his hair so short? He's almost a year old. My gosh, he was just beginning to get a head full. Darling, what's gotten into you? He looks like a skinned rat."

"We just got it a little too short. I'm sorry, dear. Don't be too upset. Hair grows, for goodness sakes."

The shorn look was indeed intentional. Hap Tyson's features were coming out stronger and stronger in his son's face, as well as his brown, wavy hair. A new look was the intent, but now, her fear had drawn attention.

"I just cannot imagine you doing this. The boy's got beautiful hair. I can't even see that little glint of gold from you. Wife of Mine, lay off the shears. Come on, Jacob. Daddy will take you outside to rock on your horsey, okay? I'll hold you, young man, so you won't fall off."

Father and son left the frustrated mother wringing her hands and kicking herself for failing miserably. What could she do?

"Oh, my gosh, Caroline, come here. Come here!" Litch hollered.

"What is it?" she cried, running through the door, fearing the worst.

"Jakie took his first step. I swear he did. Watch...Come on, Jakie, stand up by yourself, now...Ohh...That's it. Now, come to Poppa... Righttt...Right!" he shouted as the little fellow legitimately took one step...then two steps...then, boom, no steps, but the excitement of his parents made him smile the biggest,

Chapter 13

crooked smile. Litch never noticed the Hap smile as he swooped the child up in sheer joy. Caroline froze in horror but quickly joined the celebration, the only way to keep her sanity.

Months slipped by with the household calming after the haircut. One shopping day, Caroline spied a special dress in her favorite shop, a perfect distraction for Litch from scrutinizing their son, as Jakie grew more in the image of Hap every day. The pattern of waves formed more prominently, as well as the crooked smile. She had lavished her affections of late, trying to endear herself even more to this man who seemed to worship her next to God.

Mrs. Rumley greeted her at the door and took her packages.

"Mister Litch is upstairs getting Jacob settled for an early bedtime," she informed the mistress of the house. "I've fixed the two of you a little supper on the breakfast room table. Mister Litch said that the two of you would be just fine and has released me. Does this agree with you, Madame?"

"Of course, Mrs. Rumley, thank you for taking care of things."

"Good night, Madame, I'll be here in the morning after my shopping."

The housekeeper bowed slightly and left immediately, grateful for the extra time with her own family.

Caroline removed her cape and hat, and looked up the staircase, but saw no one. She would freshen up, she thought, and bring up their supper on a tray, along with her new dress.

Climbing the steps, tray in hand and her new dress slung over her shoulder, Caroline still heard nothing from the chambers above, not one sound. As she entered their bedroom, she saw her husband standing by the big window across their room, staring out into the early evening. As he turned, she spied a brandy snifter, which he raised in salute. The low lighting hid his face, but she knew he watched her as she crossed to the settee and placed the tray on the coffee table, throwing the dress on a nearby chair.

Nervously, she prattled on about her new dress and Mrs.

Caroline...The Captain's Daughter

Rumley's fixing such a nice supper for them.

"Come, Litch, and have a bite to eat."

Serving his plate, she smiled and held it up toward him, but noticed he never budged.

"Put it down, Caroline. I'm not hungry at the moment."

Was this her loving husband's voice? She looked startled toward his darkened outline in the window.

"We have something to discuss. Now. Put down the plate and answer one question for me."

Her hand trembled as the china plate clattered on the table. Fear crept up her spine as she waited for her husband to speak.

"Is Jacob Hap Tyson's son?" he asked, his voice a dead monotone, but the second question, he hurled at her with a roar. "Is that precious boy down the hallway Hap Tyson's seed?"

There was no way the woman could lie her way, or her son's way, out of this dilemma. Her head dropped; her eyes closed. Her mouth could not work to refute the question, to scoff at such nonsense, or to shame him for asking such a preposterous thing. The lady sat totally useless. Litch strode over and stuck his contorted, reddened face inches from hers and screamed for an answer.

Shaken, she finally stared into his grief-stricken face and whispered, "Litch, please sit down and talk civilly to me."

"Civilly!" he shouted. "You want me to talk civilly with you. Tell me, woman, is it true?"

His hands clamped down on her shoulders, raising her up off the settee, shaking her like a rag doll. Wincing from pain, she began to nod uncontrollably, saying ,"Yes...yes...yes."

The back of his hand clipped her, snapping her head as she stumbled backward, fortunately catching herself on the arm of the settee. Deeply frightened, she backed around the sofa and fell upon the seat as he loomed over her.

"You Jezebel! I devoted my life to you! I gave you everything you could have ever wanted."

"I know-"

Chapter 13

"Shut up," he interrupted. "When? Where?"

"I went to him during your graduation. Litch, it was before we ever said our vows. It was over, that's all. It was over. Then, I fell deeply in love with my husb-"

"You betrayed me!" he hollered in her face.

She could smell the brandy heavy on his breath, which frightened her, not for her own safety, but for the boy's. If Litch did anything foolish...

"Go put on your new dress."

"What?"

"You heard me. Go put on your new dress," he snarled. "You know, the one that was supposed to distract me, like your cutting Jacob's hair. You know, just one more of your deceptions."

Unsteady, she tripped slightly, making her way over to the dress. Turning her back, she disrobed and slipped the dress on with fumbling fingers. She knew once more that he morosely watched her every move.

"Now, come over here and have a little brandy with your husband to celebrate your confession. You must be terribly relieved to have this burden lifted from your saintly shoulders."

"Litch, you know I don't care for—"

"Come here anyway, woman."

Slowly, she walked to him as he stood by the window, her head dropped in shame.

"Look up, lady, into the eyes of your beloved."

And with that declaration, he hurled his glass into the fireplace and crashed the fine crystal goblet into smithereens. His big hands locked on her shoulders. His disturbing face inched slowly toward hers.

"No, Litch. No."

"Oh, yes, my dear," he sneered, as his mouth covered her last "No" and ground her lips bloody.

Grabbing her thick shock of hair, he jerked her head back, laughing all the while with a drunken, devilish laugh, and buried his cruel mouth into her neck. Suddenly, he pushed her away and looked down at her bodice.

"Nice."

Grinning wickedly, his hands took the front of her dress, and in one swift motion, he ripped the entire front off and the busk's hook and eyes of her corset. She stood half-naked. Stunned, her free hand shot upward to hide herself, but his hands swiftly grasped both wrists and held her arms high. Her head hung in humiliation, but he was not through. Once more, he grabbed her golden hair dragged her to his bed, and slammed her body down.

His hand muffled her cry as he tore off the rest of her clothing. Suddenly, her body grew limp. Frustrated with the lack of resistance, he shook her from her swoon. With just enough fight from her, he took his wife as a madman, violating her in every way he could think. Once more, her body grew limp. Pulling himself off her, he shoved her aside and rolled off the bed. Litch reached for his robe and the decanter of brandy.

Oh, yes, surely she is mine.

He stumbled from the room.

Chapter 14
RETRIBUTION

Answering the light knock, Caroline called out, "Mrs. Rumley, please take Jacob visiting today? I'm not well."

She fell back on her lounge, averting her face.

"He's taking a nap, but the weather's good for a stroll."

"Certainly, Madame. Can I do anything for you?" Mrs. Rumley asked, peeping around the door.

The draperies darkened the bedroom, making her mistress a silhouette.

"Oh, no. Just take care of Jacob."

Caroline could hear the housekeeper busying herself in the nursery. Muffled sounds from the stairs soon faded. Relieved, she was alone with her wounded spirit and body.

A sob caught in her throat.

"Oh, Litch, what have you done?"

His brutality was etched across her. She ached all over. Too much brandy had made him a devil in the flesh. Hiding her torn dress and undergarments would be no easy task under Mrs. Rumley's scrutiny, but somehow she would manage.

Even her eyelids hurt as they had fluttered open earlier that morning. Litch's stirring below had alarmed her. Feigning sleep, she'd heard his step on the stairs, then felt his presence in their room. Her heart pounded. She sensed his eyes on her as she lay, restraining a hiss at his violation of her. Her own guilt checked any response.

He left the room.

Why, oh why do people do the things they do? she moaned. If she had been faithful to their engagement, none of this cruelty would have happened. They would be the idyllic couple, the darling lovers, and the happy parents. Now, they had nothing, nothing. Their marriage was faltering because of her selfish desire for Hap Tyson.

Mid-afternoon, Caroline heard the creak of the downstairs door. She scanned the mantle clock. It was too early for her husband to return from work. She gripped the lounge's arm, as his large frame filled the bedroom doorway.

"Where's the child?" he dully asked.

"Mrs. Rumley put my son down for a nap before she left."

Litch winced at her words, *my son*. He stepped closer, but stopped abruptly when she shrank back. His lip quivered. He saw the swelling on her face. Rouge helped, but he knew that face.

"Litch, we're leaving," she said, her voice unbelievably steady for the emotion she felt.

"Leaving?" He caught his breath. "What do you mean?"

"Jacob and I are going to Cromwell Hall for a visit."

"How long?"

"I-I don't know." This time her voice faltered, but she quickly regained her composure. "It'll be good to see Coffie and the family. I need time to think."

"I understand." His head dropped. "When?"

"In a few days, after..." she hesitated, "the swelling goes down."

He flinched again.

"What about Mrs. Rumley?"

"Send word to her this afternoon that you're going on a business trip with your father and that I'm going to Shiloh. She'll appreciate a few days off. I'll be gone when you return."

"I suppose an apol-" he started to say, but she curtly cut him off.

"Litch, say nothing more. It's all I can do not to scream at you."

He bowed slightly and backed out of their bedroom. How he

Chapter 14

got his valises packed and out of the house the next day puzzled her. The important issue was his absence. She could nurse her wounds, pack her own bags, and head to Shiloh, hopefully, to heal with the love of her family.

For two weeks the Cromwells spoiled their daughter and grandson, not knowing they were the balm in the healing for Caroline.

But, Coffie was not fooled. He sensed an uneasiness in her. One day when they sat alone in his room, he looked directly at his granddaughter and croaked, "What's...wrong?"

Caroline looked up, startled. "What do you mean, Coffie?"

He waggled his finger at her.

"I can't even fool you, can I?" she said.

He shook his scraggly head. She took her handkerchief and caught a quick tear.

"Litch and I have had a misunderstanding. We need a little time apart to think."

Coffie frowned. Talking had always brought solutions for him and Jacksie. He didn't see a solution with her at Cromwell Hall and Litch in Raleigh.

"What?" Coffie strained.

"I-I can't say," she stuttered.

Coffie quieted. He had stepped where he should not have. He reached over and patted her hand.

"Make...it...fine," he said, laboring with each word.

All she could do was smile and nod.

The next weeks slipped by quickly. Caroline could no longer put off her return to Raleigh.

"It's time to go, but I hate to leave my family," she said, standing by her trunks in the entry of Cromwell Hall.

"Darling, you have Litch waiting," Sarah said. "You sound so sad."

"Come, girl, give your poppa one more hug. It has to last until

Christmas," Elijah said. She smiled and wrapped her arms around his neck.

Looking over her father's shoulder, she spied Coffie staring intently at her. She walked over and dropped down on the chair beside him.

"Goodbye, Coffie." She put her arm around his bony frame and kissed him on the cheek.

"Fix..." he whispered.

She squeezed his hand.

Jacob toddled over.

"Goo-bye, Coff."

The old patriarch chortled and tousled his great-grandson's thick, brown curls.

Their coach arrived on time in Raleigh. As Caroline suspected, she saw Litch's carriage standing outside the way station. Her heart beat swiftly as if she had run a foot race. She had no idea how she would feel toward this man who had physically and spiritually crushed her. They had spent six weeks apart and the next few minutes might determine their future.

Litch Bagley stepped through the door of the station and stopped her heart. She had never seen him more handsome. Her hand went to her chest as if to hold her heart in place. She felt faint but knew she had to be strong for herself and her son. As he walked to the coach to help her, she saw brightness in his face, even a peace about him. Once he held out his hand to her, she knew he was a courtier again, determined to win her favor.

"Da-Da," Jacob interrupted both their looks and thoughts.

The tyke had already climbed down the steps and clung to Litch's legs. He turned to his wife, his eyes questioning. She nodded.

"How's my little man?" he asked and swung him up in his arms. "I love you," he said as naturally as he'd ever said it.

Mrs. Rumley greeted the threesome at the house, totally beside herself, as she kept rubbing her hands on her starched apron.

Chapter 14

"I'm just so glad to see you two. Now things can get back to normal. This house has missed you, Madame, and the little mister."

She took her handkerchief from her pocket and blew her nose.

"Hi, Miz Roomblee," Jacob said, as he buried his face in her apron and wrapped his arms around her legs.

"Ooh, hi to you, little sir." She patted his head, then turned to help her mistress get settled in.

Jacob retired early.

Litch and Caroline ate quickly in the breakfast nook, exchanging platitudes while Mrs. Rumley fussed over them. They left her with the dirty dishes and retired to the parlor, wishing that she would finish soon.

"Is there anything else I can do for either of you?" she asked, when she had finally chased the last crumbs off of the counter into her hand.

"No," they chorused as she bowed slightly and wished them a good evening. The front door clicked shut. Soon they heard Mr. Rumley's horse's hooves hit the brick pavement.

They were finally alone.

"You look well, Litch."

"Thank you. So do you. Tell me about Coffie."

"He's a miracle. The man just keeps breathing. I'm not sure how."

Silence grew between them. She looked down at her clasped hands. He gazed at the floor. Each looked up at the same moment.

"Caroline, I have to apologize now. You wouldn't let me before, but I have to. I can never forgive myself unless you do. I'm not saying now, right this moment, but I want to convince you that the devil you saw in me is gone. Our rector at St. Patrick's has been unbelievable."

"Reverend Forsyth?"

"Yes, I hope you don't mind."

"No, I suppose not."

"Caroline, for years I have put you on a pedestal, expecting you to be perfect. No matter how hard you try, or I try, we're not, simply put."

He quieted.

"That is true," she sighed.

"What pressure you must have felt from me. My God..." He shook his head.

"I see."

"It will take time, Caroline. I know that, but I am asking you for another chance. Tyson knows nothing about the boy?"

She shook her head.

"Then I'm the only father Jacob knows and has ever known. I love your son, Caroline, and I'd like to raise him as ours."

He smiled faintly, waiting for the lump in his throat to subside. "That is if you'll have me..."

"I cannot tell you how badly you hurt me, Litch."

His eyes shut tight.

"You're right," she continued. "It will take time, but I have something to tell you."

"What?"

He looked hopeful at his wife.

"I'm carrying your child."

Chapter 15
SURPRISE

Litch sat stunned in disbelief. "Are you sure?" he whispered.

"Yes," Caroline said, watching his chest rise and fall as if momentarily he would be gasping for breath. In seconds, his demeanor cracked. He clasped his head in his hands and sobbed.

She let him cry.

Finally, he collected himself and looked up at her.

"Never would I want a child under these conditions, but this blessing may save my sanity."

He jumped up and strode to the front windows, wiping his tears with his handkerchief.

After a moment, he looked back at her and asked, "What do we do?"

"We go on, Litch. Down deep, we both want this child. If we salvage our marriage along the way, then so be it. You can stay in the other room upstairs. We'll simply tell Mrs. Rumley I'm having trouble sleeping right now. She'll understand."

"Thank you. I think I would have died if you asked me to leave."

The next six months brought a deep friendship into the mix of Litch and Caroline's marriage. Never once did he make advances to her. Their only physical contact was by hand, his helping her into their carriage or through a door. They'd talk by the hour about his business or her revived interest in art.

She had started painting again, a lost love from her youth in Tarboro. She would smile countless times, thinking of her mother's encouragement in the arts. Most of what Sarah

Cromwell wanted for her daughter, she had run from, but not art.

"Mrs. Gillespie thinks I have a knack for portraitures," she said one day, as they sat in the sun porch, her favorite spot to paint.

"Oh, really?" Litch asked, looking up from his newspaper.

"I need a subject."

"Oh really... Certainly not Jacob." He laughed.

"No. I was thinking of a more mature subject." She eyed him closely.

"Me?"

"Why not?"

"But can I be still long enough? You know I'm almost as much of a wiggle tail as our...your son."

"You can say *our*, Litch. I have no problem with that."

"Thank you."

A smile flickered across his face.

"Litch, please do me a favor."

She had been sitting with her easel and canvases for most of the afternoon.

"Can you help me take my lace-ups off. I know my feet are swollen. This big belly makes it harder to do by the day."

"Of course."

He quickly stooped in front of her and unlaced her shoes.

"Oh my gosh." He gaped at her swollen ankles.

"Caroline, do you...I mean, would you—"

"Yesss. Rub them. Please."

Her head fell back on the chair. Her eyes closed in sheer pleasure as he massaged her feet and ankles. Opening an eye, she watched him in curiosity. He was attending her as he always had, as if rubbing her feet was the most important thing in the world. He looked up and caught her spying. His boyish grin caused her to blush.

"Thank you, Litch. That's enough."

"Are you sure?"

"Oh yes. If you don't stop now, I'll never get out of this chair."

Chapter 15

"Here. Let me help you."

He reached for her hand, but somehow it slipped from his grasp.

"Litch," she hollered.

The man dove for her, but in doing so, they both landed on the floor.

"Are you all right?"

"Yes," she laughed. "What a silly predicament."

She kept laughing.

"You better find me a chamber pot or we're both in trouble."

"Mommie? What you doing on the floor?"

Jacob and Mrs. Rumley had returned from a walk in the park.

"Madame, are you hurt?" Mrs. Rumley asked, stepping forward with a look of concern.

"No. Fortunately. My hand slipped from Mr. Bagley's and we both took a tumble. I'm fine. I'm sure we're a funny sight."

"Mommie? No shoes?"

Jacob pointed at her bare feet.

"Your father was rubbing your mother's poor, swollen feet, son."

"Mrs. Rumley, help me get Caroline up. I don't trust just me right now."

"Of course, sir," the housekeeper said.

"Gracious, I'm receiving such special attention," Caroline said, as all three looked down at her spraddle-legged.

"Caroline, give Mrs. Rumley your hands. I'll support you from behind. Ready?"

"Yes, sir," Mrs. Rumley said.

"Can I help, Daddy?" Jacob begged.

"No, son, we'll handle it. You can hug your mother after we get her up."

Jacob clapped his hands and immediately grabbed his mother's skirts as soon as they hoisted her off the floor.

"Oh my gosh, thank you. I probably would still be sprawled if I'd been by myself. Watch, Jacob," she laughed, as the little fellow squealed with delight that his mother was no longer on the floor.

"This time I'm making sure you don't slip away from me." Litch looked startled at the double meaning of his words.

Caroline looked at her rescuers. "I think I'll retire. Maybe a bite to eat later, Mrs. Rumley. Mr. Bagley can bring it up."

"Certainly, Madame."

"I'll help you up the stairs," Litch offered. "I would feel better. You don't want to fall on those steps. Soon you'll need to stay downstairs. When that time comes, I can take care of Jakie."

"Of course, you can. Thank you."

She smiled at him.

Litch's closeness as they made their way up the stairs made her giddy. More than once his chest and arm touched her in support. It felt good to feel his strength surround her in a good way. She knew she was softening toward this man. He had been trying so hard these long months.

At the top of the staircase, he leaned around her and opened the door. He peered in at their bed. It had been over six months since he had set foot in their room.

"Come in, Litch. You need to."

"No."

He shook his head, almost as if he were afraid.

"Litch, we need to rid ourselves of these demons. We've had many joyful moments in this room and only one bad one. Come in."

He slowly followed her, looking around to fend off the haunts that surely would spring on him. She turned and held her hand out to him. He stalled.

"Give me your hand. I want you to help me into my nightgown. You have never seen or touched your child. It's time. It's past time."

He meekly followed her to her chifforobe, unbelief on his face. As she turned and waited, he fumbled with every button and every tie. Her clothing dropped to the floor, piece by piece. He felt embarrassed with her nakedness, as if he had no right to see her.

Chapter 15

"Touch me, Litch. Wherever you want to or need to."

His fingers inched slowly toward the most beautiful face he had ever known. Her eyes closed as he lightly caressed her face. His fingers trailed downward between her breasts until they reached the growing child. Slowly, his fingers spread to feel the life movement within. He swallowed hard and smiled. He was touching their child.

"Come lie with me tonight, Litch. I need you to," she whispered.

Never saying a word, he slipped her gown over her head and left her to have dinner with their other child.

Chapter 16

LITTLE COFFIE

Hearing his wife scream was probably the most disturbing sound Litch Bagley would ever remember in his life. Her water broke one morning, announcing the arrival of their second child, but this baby withstood all coaxing from the midwife. This time, they had decided to deliver at home. For two weeks, Caroline had lain on the starched sheets in their downstairs guest room.

The midwife pulled Litch away from the bed.

"The baby ain't turning, Mister Litch" she whispered. "You see Miss Cah'line's in a frenzy. I think we best send for Doc Frawley."

"God, what do you mean?" he whispered back.

"I mean that young'un needs to get out of there, and it ain't willing," she answered.

"You mean it's breech?"

The midwife nodded.

One moan from Caroline sent Litch out the door. Sarah looked up from her knitting in the parlor. The Cromwells had come to Raleigh to care for Jacob for the duration.

"Miss Sarah, where's the Captain?"

"He's outside with Jacob. What's wrong, Litch? You look worried."

"The baby's breech."

"Breech? You didn't tell us."

"I didn't know. The midwife suspected, but she didn't want us to worry. God, I thought the baby would turn and deliver with no complications, just like Jacob. Will you get Elijah? We need

Chapter 16

Doctor Frawley?"

"Of course. Go on back with Caroline. The Captain will get the man here like the wind."

She was already through the back hall door.

Doctor Frawley and his partner arrived in record time, both standing above their semiconscious patient, both murmuring with caution.

"If she doesn't deliver soon, I've got to take it right here," Frawley whispered. "It's too late to move her to the hospital."

"There's some chloroform and antiseptics in my bag," his partner whispered back. "Give me the word and I'll set everything up."

Frawley turned to the midwife. "Massage her one more time. If it doesn't happen, I'll operate. I'm uneasy."

The midwife nodded and stepped to the bed to begin her work again.

A frantic husband sat in the parlor. Twice he went to the door ready to burst through it; twice he backed off, knowing he would only hinder the ones who could help his wife and their child. These circumstances were positively maddening. Jacob had come so easily, but Jacob was not his child. This one was. How could he ever make love to her without fearing that he could put her through this torture again? Was it justice or punishment for their sins against each other? He felt terrible.

This birth was supposed to bring them joy, a reflection of their renewal, not a mirror of her deceit and his violence. Blaming would not get them through this hurdle, but prayer might. Litchfield Bagley clasped his hands.

"Lord, we need a miracle," he spoke aloud with fervency.

No more screams pierced the air, as Litch sat on the edge of the sofa and rocked. Elijah Cromwell paced. Sarah tended to Jacob. Mrs. Rumley wrung her hands, as she frequently peeped through the kitchen door to check. An hour passed.

The doorknob squeaked. Litch jumped to his feet. A squall

resounded from behind the door, as Doctor Frawley appeared and walked toward the bedraggled father. He himself was a mess, perspiration soaked the front of his starched shirt with a few significant blood spots intermingled, but the faint grin on his face was all Litch needed. She'd made it.

"Your wife has delivered another healthy, baby boy. You heard that squall? Good lungs, like Jacob's," he laughed.

"Caroline? Is she alright?" Litch inquired breathlessly.

"Let the nurse clean her up. Then you can see for yourself. I cannot understand it, son, but that baby turned just enough for the midwife. Once that happened, your boy came out with only a few pushes. It's a miracle."

For once, Litch had not said a word. Quickly he glanced over his shoulder at Mrs. Rumley and the Cromwells. All three smiled.

"Litch," Caroline's weak voice barely penetrated his light slumber as he sat faithfully by her bedside. She had slept for hours.

"Why, Mrs. Bagley, you did decide to wake up after all," he softly spoke as he leaned over to kiss her forehead. "You are the most beautiful I've ever seen you, my dear, but some little tyke wants his momma," he gently said.

"My milk has not come yet, but please I want that little fellow in my arms right now."

Litch jumped for the door only to meet the nurse carrying a little bundle. Smiling at the new mother, she laid the little fellow in the crook of Caroline's arm.

Litch dropped down in the chair and admired their handiwork. His heart swelled, but sudden thoughts of Jacob pressed in on him. Not once had he thought of bringing the child to her room. The Cromwells had cared for him full-time for the last two weeks. Maybe in the afternoon, he would surprise Caroline by bringing their other son to her room to meet his new brother.

"I think you should name the baby."

Chapter 16

"Would you mind if we named him after Coffie?"

"Perfect by me. You know without his help I might not have convinced you to marry me as quickly as you did."

She wrinkled her nose at him.

"The man's got unreal influence on you. In fact, he's probably stubborn enough to hang around until you bring him a great-grandson bearing his name."

This time she laughed.

"I want to go to Shiloh as soon as we can."

Weeks later, Caroline and Litch brought little Coffie and Jacob to see Coeffield King. Every visit, they wondered if it would be their last one with the old gentleman.

"Coffie? Coffie? I've brought someone to see you."

Caroline edged slowly forward with her baby in her arms. She allowed the old barrister a moment to open up his hazed eyes and focus on her and the child.

"We've come all the way from Raleigh to show you your new great-grandson."

Mini strokes had continued to sap his energy and strength until the old man rarely moved from his chair by the window at Cromwell Hall. Sarah would let her father drift into his own world, a world that could only be interrupted by his granddaughter and her offspring.

"See, Coffie, I've brought you Jacob and my new baby."

She continued, seeing a faint glimmer of light in his eye and a grotesque smile tracing his cracked lips. Coeffield King's mouth worked feebly, words pent up in him as he had sat day after day between her visits. It was as if she and the children were his only hope in life. His knurled hand began to fidget toward her as if she were not close enough for him to drink in her presence and the children's.

She held out the baby up to him.

"Coffie, he's your namesake."

The old man garbled such that saliva drooled down the

stubble on his chin. Taking her handkerchief, she lovingly cleaned him and placed the child in his lap.

"Touch him, Coffie. He's your flesh and blood. He won't break," she encouraged. "Look, he's smiling at you."

Little Coffie gurgled and cooed up into the old worn face that had once captivated jury upon jury.

Jacob hung back behind his mother's skirts.

Spotting him, the old man used every ounce of strength to extend his arm to the young boy. Withdrawing his thumb from his mouth, the child flew into his great-grandfather's arms.

"Easy, Jacob. Don't hurt him."

Coeffield King grunted. He would deal with the pain later. Right now, he relished the touch of his future.

Chapter 17
DECEPTION AND DISCOVERY

*H*ap gazed at his wife across the breakfast table, totally dumbfounded.

"Please tell me you're wrong," he muttered. "The chart? How could this have happened?"

"I-I must have miscalculated, darling," she said, shrugging her shoulders. "But listen, I've figured it all out."

Her excitement was almost contagious.

"I'll resign at the end of my school year. You'll be in your last year of school when the baby comes, so Grandfather's fund will carry us through until you get established. Now, are you not glad he was such a generous man?"

"I just can't believe it."

He kept shaking his head.

"Please, darling, be happy. You know doctors are so busy when they establish themselves. Now, I'll have the baby to keep me busy. Isn't it a wonderful plan after all?"

He despised the feeling of being out of control of his life, their life. Something about this pregnancy nagged him, but what? The year had moved along quite smoothly, or so he thought. He had even relaxed somewhat, as she constantly showed him her chart, plotting her time of ovulation. What eluded him was Pamela's second chart.

Daily, Pamela poured over both charts, figuring when she would be fertile to conceive, but what eluded her was conception. She assumed anxiety was delaying the process, but she knew it would happen. Her cycles were as regular as the mailman. If she were to conceive, she assumed that the news would thrill Hap enough to forgive her *miscalculation*.

Pamela Tyson was a headstrong young woman, whose selfishness had won her way most of her life. All those years ago, she had spotted her man on the dance floor and never relented until he was hers, free and clear of his haunting past. Their marriage finally happened on her terms. Now, she wanted the next phase of their life on her terms as well.

So, when the news broke, the Martins dined with them that weekend to celebrate ecstatically over their first grandchild; Banks danced foolishly about the house in his celebration. Hap sat stunned, observing their jubilation.

"We'll have to paint the guest room. Freshen it up. I know Miss Mandy can sew new curtains and the cradle covers. Good gracious. The cradle!" Mrs. Martin's hand flew up to her mouth. "It's been packed away since your daddy was a baby. I'm sure it will need polishing," she said. "Pammie, will you just look at your grandfather," she whispered, hiding a giggle behind her hand.

Banks was practicing playing "horsy" with his imaginary great-grandchild on his knee.

"Yessiree, Pammie. I can't wait," he laughed, his gray locks flopping with each bumping of the "horsy."

Hap's stomach churned. He felt powerless. Glancing at her grandfather, he thought, *Things will be different, old man, when I'm established. It won't be here, I can tell you.* He shuddered, thinking of Pamela's reaction to the idea of starting off somewhere fresh and anew, like Greenville or Tarboro.

Weeks passed. One night, Hap's studies absorbed him. His first medical exam loomed.

"Hap, come feel the baby kick? Ohhh...Hurry, darling."

"Please, I have work to finish," he called out. "I can't feel the baby every time he kicks."

"Or, she. You know, it may be a she," she retorted.

He never argued with her, not wanting to upset her in any way to jeopardize the baby's health. They had had only one tiff since

Chapter 17

discovering her pregnancy, and he vowed never to argue with her again. He remembered...

"Pamela, where are my chemistry papers?"

"What papers, darling?" she'd called from downstairs in the kitchen. McCloud was out for the evening for a cribbage game. She'd dismissed Lucas and his wife, for Mrs. Tyson intended to prepare a special meal for her husband.

He called out again.

"The ones that I was studying for Doc Sims' lab that I'm teaching for him tomorrow. You know the ones you hid from me last night when I wasn't paying you enough attention. I need them, Pammie, now. No joking. Where are they?"

He had come to the top of the stairs, directing his irritated voice at her.

"Look around, Hap. I'm busy trying to get our supper. You know I'm fixing you a very special meal. Really, Hap, if it doesn't just hop right out and bite you on the nose, then it doesn't exist, right? Just keep looking. Don't make me come all the way upstairs to find them for you, and they are right—"

Then, reality hit. *Oh, my God,* she inwardly cried, but he was already standing at the top of the stairs with his chemistry papers in one hand and their old chart in another. His face grew quizzical.

"I thought you threw our old chart away. This one doesn't even resemble the old one. Would you like to explain this?"

Of course, she could explain that chart. It was the authentic, factual, genuine article, the one that informed her of her chances to conceive, not to prevent conception. Her face reddened, as she started a flimsy explanation.

Hap exploded. He could not help himself. No restraint could stop it. Now, he understood her statement: "Isn't it a wonderful plan after all?"

She had planned having a child all along. She had manipulated their lives behind his back. Once more, the selfish, spoiled little girl had gotten her way. When was she going to grow up? Their life was just that, theirs, not hers, not his, but theirs. Hap Tyson could not have been angrier.

Racing to the kitchen sink, she retched violently.

"Oh, my God, Pamela," he hollered, as he ran down the steps.

Her fierce heaves frenzied them both. They clung to each other and vowed for peace for the baby's sake and health. They had another life to consider, other than theirs. He had kept his bargain, succumbing to her every wish, while Pamela, somehow, repressed her vow.

Things will be different, once I'm established. They just have to be, he thought.

Pamela Tyson carried her child to full term and delivered right there in the McCloud household with all the privacy of her own home, with her own doctor and her own nurse.

"Oh, Hap. Look at your beautiful son."

No one, not even Hap could remain disgruntled, seeing before him the joy of motherhood and the creation of life. He dropped to his knees by their bed and pushed a wet lock of hair off her face.

"You're just as beautiful, my dear, but I've got to say he does take my breath."

"Rollie. I like that name for him. Oh yes, you are a little Rollie."

She wrinkled her nose at the babe in her arms.

"What do you think, Daddy? Rollie Tyson, named for his father."

Hap started to speak, but she cut him off.

"I know, I know, that's your professional name, but it just suits this little fellow," she said as she nuzzled the child's head.

He slightly shrugged.

"Now, for his middle name. How about McCloud for my grandfather."

Hap's eyes widened.

Chapter 17

"He has let us live in his house, and he's helped us in so many ways."

Hap got up and turned away from her. His face reddened. He clinched his jaw, but he also knew she was right. Everybody would call their son Rollie. Most would never know his middle name, except family. He turned and managed a smile.

"I think it's a good idea."

"Oh, darling, I cannot tell you how much that means to me...and to him."

My God, she has already talked to him about it, he thought, sickened at the image of Banks McCloud clutching Pamela's hand, making the request.

Things will be different.

Hap's graduation finally arrived with all the accolades he had ever wanted; even being second in his class suited him. Pamela's grandfather and both families proudly celebrated and gave much unsolicited advice. The young, new doctor assured them that he and Pamela would make their own decisions. Actually, he really meant that he would make any decision since he was the doctor and head of his household. They would go where he deemed perfect for a fresh start.

Banks had different ideas.

"Listen, boy, I've figured it all out. The University needs some good teachers in the medical school. Now, with my pull, I'm sure the president will come around and hire a smart young whippersnapper like you. Doc Sims will help, too. You and Pammie, and the baby can stay right here with me until I die. Then, the house is yours. Sound like a good plan, huh?"

"Thank you, sir. Pamela and I will discuss it, but don't get your hopes up. I want to practice, not teach. It's a mighty fine offer, though," he said, choking on each word so as not to upset the old man. Frankly, he wanted to scream at him for trying to run his life. *No wonder Pammie is such a conniver, a beautiful one, but still.*

"Grandfather told me about his generous offer this afternoon. Can you believe how much he loves us? He's just one of the dearest, kindest people who breathe on this earth. Really, now, could you have ever had a more unselfish offer in all your life?"

They sat at lunch, alone for the first time in a while. Banks had rushed out to meet some cronies at the Eagle Hotel.

"Excuse me? I think it's the most selfish offer I've ever heard in my entire life."

"What?"

"I'm sorry, darling. It's disgusting what he's trying to do. He's not saying, 'Godspeed and have a good life, Hap. Remember I am always available if you ever need me.' No, my dear wife, he's really saying to stay close to him so he can always make the decisions of our lives to suit him and not us. Really, it's disgusting. He loves us but for his own selfish reasons."

He put his water glass down just a little too hard, drops sloshing onto the tablecloth.

"But—"

"No buts. I don't want to talk about it right now. I really have some serious decisions to make and I need your support."

His wife closed her mouth. She knew her husband was telling the truth. He needed time to think and any talk from her right now would only jeopardize McCloud's plan, as well as her own.

"Tarboro? You want to drag us off to Tarboro! I've never been to Tarboro in my life. I don't even know anybody in Tarboro. No, I won't go! I won't," Pamela screeched at her husband, pacing up and down the parlor floor.

"Pamela, I—"

"Forget it. You want me to go off and leave all my family and the generosity of my grandfather. Have you lost your senses? Have you forgotten that he would even give us his house? We'd never have to live in some little hovel somewhere in Tarboro, for crying out loud. I just can't believe you!"

She gained momentum in her argument.

Chapter 17

"Pammie, please, just calm down and listen. There are plenty of doctors in the Piedmont, but down east the shortage is desperate. Doctor Knight is ancient and retired. Doctor Mallory and Doctor Quiggless are the only other doctors in the entire county. I must choose a place where I'm needed to grow a practice."

"Hap, Banks has two friends that are going to retire right here in the village. He could buy one of their practices for us. He would. He will."

"Of course, the two of you have discussed this venture without consulting me. Right? Answer me, Pammie."

"Well, he did mention it after you told him you didn't want to teach... I would think you would be grateful for his looking into the matter, but, no, you have already closed your mind to anything my grandfather would do," she sarcastically retorted.

"I told you this decision would be mine. I have a vow to serve and practice. I want to birth my own, not take over somebody else's patients. I know he means well, but I want to return down east, and I want my wife and child at my side."

His face showed determination.

Frustrated, the young mother turned on her heel and left the room. He could hear her flouncing all the way up the stairs, a true mime of their small son. Gripping his head in his hands, he began to realize he was married to a very spoiled woman.

Hap shuddered, disturbed by his wife's reaction to his decision to go back down east to set up practice. He had written Mallory and even Doctor Quiggless, the only black doctor in the county. They reveled in his choice. Both men were overworked and worn down. New blood would bring life back into their own oath to serve their people. Young doctors attracted more young doctors, as they looked at Hap as the potential for medical care in Edgecombe County.

At this point, Hap had no inkling what his wife intended to do. His heart would be broken if she chose not to come. He could only pray. What more could be said? He was packed and ready for the long train ride to Wilson. He would have to take a coach to Tarboro, while his medical supplies and equipment would be shipped by water. It was funny how his whole future would float to him on the Tar.

Pamela Tyson's pronouncement floated down from the head of the stairs. "If I don't like it, Hap Tyson, I'll leave. I mean it, Hap. I won't be miserable."

She had packed furiously while he moped downstairs. Pamela actually thought he would bend and yield to her whims, but after seeing his bags at the door, she realized his intentions were solid. She had cried for hours, hoping her wailing would force a contrite heart, but not her husband, she discovered. If she wanted her marriage, she was going to have to respond to his wishes, and now.

Smiling feebly, she brought one bag down, outstretched to him. He took it, pulling her to him, and whispered, "You'll never regret it, darling." He lightly spanked her.

"Hap," she scolded with delight in her eye. Her attitude turned businesslike as she bustled around as if this decision was as much hers as it was his.

McCloud sat outside, his toe barely moving the swing where he and his wife had sat many hours, enjoying her flower garden. Pamela and the boy would be his for the rest of his days. They would give him continued life and vitality, he thought, a smile of contentment etched his face. Hearing the front door open, he swiveled, only to see his beloved granddaughter with little Rollie, her husband, and her bags. His mouth fell open as he stood.

"Now, Grandfather, you know I'm a married lady and I need to be with my husband. Why you can take that old train and short buggy ride and be in Tarboro by most half a day. I'll miss you terribly," she said as she hugged the old gentleman good-bye. He smiled at her and extended his hand to Hap.

"I like your spunk, boy. You'll do all right. You take good care of my Pammie and little Rollie. He's a mighty fine little tyke. I'll

Chapter 17

miss him, too. Now, who's gonna ride my horsy?" he asked as he slapped his knee and bent down to hug his great-grandson.

"Bye-bye, Ganpa. Come see me. Bing horsy," the child said as he grasped his teddy bear.

Chapter 18
THE RETURN

The small house Hap found for himself and his family sat only one block from the Town Common and not far from Tarboro's little hospital where he had healed from a dislocated leg years ago, miraculously maneuvered by Rufus Knight. The doctor had saved him from being a cripple for the rest of his life. The house fell short of the McCloud house in Chapel Hill, but it was a good "starter" as Hap determined for the size of his wallet. And, no, he would not touch Pamela's grandfather's fund, no matter how hard his wife pouted.

His next task was to find the perfect office to begin his new practice.

Hap discovered two rooms, nestled at the end of Main Street next to the bridge. The least expensive spaces were the farthest ones from the Town Common. He'd taken it immediately. On the good side, Tarboro's little hospital would be relatively close for any needs that he could not handle in his new office, and he'd be able to walk to work each morning from their home. Another piece of the puzzle had fallen neatly into place.

"Are you actually humming, Mrs. Tyson?"

Hap asked his wife on the fifth day of their move.

"Well, yes I am, Doctor Tyson," Pamela countered, opening a carton of linens.

He put his paper down on the table.

"You appear content, wife. Are you glad you came?"

"We'll see," she said, folding the last piece of linen and placing it in a chest. "There." She turned toward him. "Everything going

Chapter 18

well with Doctor Mallory?"

"Oh, yes."

"I'm glad you decided to help him until your supplies get here. I have to tell you that everybody has been so nice."

"I'm glad, darling."

He walked over to her and traced her shoulders with his hands. She smiled sweetly at him.

"Hap? We've gotten an invitation to go to Calvary Episcopal Church on Sunday."

"Calvary?"

"Do let's go our first Sunday. Julia Mallory dropped by and asked us. She also invited us for lunch at Mrs. Deberry's."

"But we're Presbyterians, not Episcopalians. Don't you think we should make our acquaintance with our future pastor and church? Maybe another time," he said.

"Hap, we'd be rude, and, after all, Dr. Mallory is giving you such an opportunity. How can we refuse? Just this first time, please? Mrs. Deberry's sounds absolutely wonderful, and Mrs. Mallory has already made arrangements for little Rollie."

"What? You say Mrs. Mallory has made arrangements for Rollie."

Silence.

"You've already accepted without consulting me, haven't you?" His frown made her squirm. "You're doing it again, Pamela, planning things behind my back, obligating us so we can't say no without hurt feelings. You can't do this anymore." He was irritated, but controlled his anger. She was going to be a lonely lady, especially when he had to work late hours. Launching a new practice would be no easy task and difficult on his wife and son. Biting his tongue, he waggled his finger at her and said, "Just this once. Then, on to First Presbyterian."

She rushed into his arms, but her look over his shoulder was one of control and power. Life seemed normal again, but on Sunday, Hap Tyson would not feel that way.

"How do I look, Hap?" Pamela twirled for her husband,

95

showing off her new dress for this special occasion. "Shh. Don't object. I used a little money from Banks' fund. Don't worry, it didn't cost that much. Really," she prattled, as she whirled again, admiring herself in the mirror. Hap frowned, but smiled at the same time. His wife...the enigma.

The Mallorys arrived in their carriage right on time, the driver tapping lightly on the door.

"Mrs. Mallory's planned our every breath, I suppose," Hap whispered to his wife.

"Of course, she hasn't, but I'm sure she'll introduce us to other young couples in town and maybe some new patients. Shh, Hap. Behave," she said as she bustled Hap and Rollie down the steps to the awaiting carriage.

The ride was short to Calvary Episcopal.

Alighting from the carriage, the young couple followed the Mallorys up the walkway of Calvary and through the arboretum, a tree menagerie planted in the church's early days. The varieties amazed all visitors, even Pamela.

"Dr. and Mrs. Tyson, please meet some of our dearest friends from Shiloh Plantation, Elijah and Sarah Cromwell."

Three out of the six people facing each other looked startled. Two pairs of steely eyes shot knowing looks at the young doctor. Pamela seemed unaffected by the introduction, shaking their hands as if they, too, would be her best friends.

"So, you're a doctor now?" Captain Cromwell said with stiff formality.

Somehow Hap found his voice.

"Yes, sir, I made a vow many years ago to be in a profession of service. I—I chose medicine."

He adjusted his collar.

"Pamela's from Hillsborough. We met at the university," he barely whispered.

"Darling, you're talking so low; I can hardly hear you. Yes, I was at a nearby academy while Hap was attending the university. When we married, we lived with my grandfather in Chapel Hill

Chapter 18

until after he got out of medical school. Second in his class, I might add."

She turned and wrinkled her nose at him.

Sarah Cromwell had not spoken. Quite coolly, she welcomed the two to Tarboro.

"Come, Elijah, the service will start soon," she insisted. "Julia, we'll talk later," she said, forcing a smile.

The Captain tipped his hat to the ladies and followed his wife inside.

"Shiloh Plantation. That sounds interesting. Maybe we can all go out someday for a visit, Mrs. Mallory?"

Pamela smiled broadly. *My, my, so these are the Cromwells. How convenient,* she said to herself. She continued to smile. The Mallorys had only been in Tarboro for five years and were totally unaware of these former relationships.

The Tysons and their hosts chatted their way into the sanctuary, working their way into a pew, opposite the Cromwells and slightly behind them.

What is she saying? Hap wondered, as Sarah Cromwell leaned over and whispered to Elijah.

"Can you believe the Doctor Rolland Tyson that Julia Mallory has been raving about is none other than Hap Tyson? We should have guessed it. Lord in heaven, Litch and Caroline almost came to church with us. Thank God, they stayed with Coffie. I just can't believe it," she whispered through gritted teeth.

Elijah could only grip her hand and pat her arm. Memories of his son broke the barrier that had sealed painful thoughts. Even though the young man was cleared of the murder charge, to the Cromwells, Hap Tyson was responsible for their son's death. Elijah Cromwell began to sweat and pray he could get out of church and get home without any more confrontations with Tyson, Doctor Tyson, now.

Will, you never had a chance to be a doctor or lawyer or

anything. The Captain felt twinges of hate for the young man. *The scoundrel has become a medical savior for the county.* His thoughts sickened him.

The next day Hap walked briskly to his office. Surely his medical supplies would arrive today. The post confirmed the next barge would carry everything: supplies, equipment, his future.

Later that morning, he stepped out front into the blinding sunlight. Shielding his eyes, he surveyed his end of Main Street. He waved at Toby, the blacksmith, steadying the next horse to be shod. He glanced toward the bridge and wondered how many times he had ridden or walked over it with Willie or his friends from Station House Road?

He stared at the shell of the old Station House, the ruined dreams of a man named John Constable, who'd been hung by a mob on the Medusa Tree for being kind to a lady of ill repute. He stared for a long time, his own dream formulating: a correction of blight, a revival of timbers. Its use? A medical office to serve people on both sides of the Tar. Yes, he had a dream, just as John Constable had years and years ago.

A horn upriver interrupted his thoughts. His barge was coming, his future riding in its belly. Mopping his brow, he scaled down the embankment to the dock to wave at the captain as the barge rounded the last curve.

"I see it. I see it," a voice from the bridge cried out.

"I saw it first," another chimed in.

Hap turned to see two young boys on the bridge. Both waved. Slowly, he lifted his hand to return the salute. It was as if he was seeing his youth return. He could imagine the spicy tales those two would tell about the barge captain and the new doctor. Had he not done the same? He turned laughing and waved once more at the barge, chugging toward him.

A day passed before Sarah and Elijah discussed the arrival of Hap Tyson and his new wife to Edgecombe County. A slight nod

Chapter 18

had negated any conversation about them in front of their daughter and her husband. Coffie's health was their concern. Dredging up past hurts would help no one. They would wait until Caroline and Litch returned to Raleigh.

"Elijah, we do need to talk about this new development in town," Sarah said, as she sat at the breakfast table across from her husband.

Maggie poured them a second cup of coffee.

"We're going to see that man from time to time. We need to be prepared when this happens. How do you feel about their coming?"

Elijah stared intently at his wife.

"I hate it just as much as you do," he grumbled. "Will never had a chance to become whatever he wanted to be in his life."

Pausing briefly, he calmed somewhat.

"Oh, I don't know. It really appears the young man has done something right, and he's married. He's no threat to Caroline. Our daughter's happy." He shrugged with a slightly pained expression, then it turned to one of resignation, "Maybe we need to put the past in the pa—"

"No!"

Her fist hit the table. Her face contorted.

"It's only been a few years. Can't you still feel his presence in this house?"

"Of course, I can."

"Can't you still hear his step on the stairs, his voice through the halls? Oh, God, I still feel the coldness of his body." Her voice broke. "Not yet..."

"Sarah, what good is it doing us to harbor hate? It can only hurt us, and make us hard and bitter. You know you don't want that. I—I know deep down I can't live that way. We've got to make our peace soon. I don't know when, but soon."

Sarah sprang from the breakfast table and glared at Maggie, whose eyes spoke loud and clear. *Move on with your life. Leave all this pain behind.* Sarah looked away quickly and left the room.

A piercing scream echoed through the house. Elijah looked at Maggie.

"Oh, my God, Coffie."

Both raced toward the guest room, only to find Sarah cradling her father's head. Coffie lay ashen, facing down on the floor by his chair. He was still alive.

"I can't lose him now," she agonized.

"Sarah, here, let me have him," Elijah whispered.

He handily picked up the wizened body and placed him gently on his bed.

"I'm riding to get the doctor. Hold on, Coffie," he said, touching his father-in-law's head. He bent to whisper in his ear once more, "Hold on, Coffie." Then he was gone.

The Captain hadn't ridden horseflesh like he did that morning since the war. Hitting the bridge at Tarboro, his horse's hooves clattered, foam spewing from its mouth. Several proprietors stepped out to check the commotion, the new doctor being one. Their eyes met briefly as Elijah raced by to Mallory's office.

"I'm sorry, sir," the nurse said. "Doctor Mallory's on an emergency call across town. We don't know when he'll be back."

Patients packed his waiting room.

"Hap Tyson, maybe?" she said, warily, knowing their history.

Desperately, Elijah turned his horse toward Hap's office. He had no choice.

Banging on the door, the Captain turned the knob and charged through the opening. Hap looked up from the boxes of supplies. He had taken this entire day off to get ready for business. Wiping his hands, Hap moved toward the despairing man.

"It's Mister King. He's been stricken. Can you come? Now?" the Captain pleaded, squelching any anger or pride. "He needs you. We need you."

"Of course," were Hap's only words.

He grabbed his coat and bag. Racing to the stables for a horse,

Chapter 18

Hap hollered, "Captain, I'll meet you at Cromwell Hall."

Pushing a coin in the stable hand's palm, he said, "If you see my wife, tell her I've gone to Shiloh on an emergency."

How strange it was for Hap, as he pushed his mount toward Shiloh. He trailed the man whose son had died, supposedly by his hand. This surprise was one he thought he would never have. With each jolt of the horse's stride, his mind filled with memories of that fateful day.

Cromwell Hall came into view after a few miles of flying with the wind. A youth waited to take the reins of Hap's horse. Maggie held the door open for him, respect in her eye, as he raced past her. In the hallway, Elijah restrained Sarah. Her venomous look at the young doctor chilled him. He faltered, but the Captain nodded toward the door where Coffie struggled for his life. Hap entered and went to work.

For two solid hours, he stayed with the patient before he walked out of the room to briefly speak to the anxious Cromwells.

"I've done everything I know to do to give him more days. He's resting now, but the prognosis does not look good."

Of course, they had known that to be true, but both could only nod. Somehow, the harshness in Sarah's eyes had faded somewhat.

Hap slipped back to the patient, shaking his head as he remembered the handsome lawyer who had charmed countless juries. This man was an institution in Tarboro and all of Down East.

Suddenly, King's body jerked; his eyes fluttered. Looking at the man by his side took effort, but momentarily, a sense of recognition covered his face. His mouth began to work.

"Hap?" he garbled, not Will, as he had done years ago by mistake in delirium.

Hap's face brightened as he bent over and clasped the old man's hand in his big ones. King stared and remembered the time those hands rescued him in the courtroom.

Coeffield King took his other hand and, grappling with death itself, reached up and touched the young man's tousled head.

"You remember?"

Hap was speechless. Once more he felt the familial love one man shows another, father and son, grandfather and grandson, or simply friend and friend.

"Oh, sir, you would not believe my life since we saw each other," Hap said, kneeling beside the bed for closeness.

Quietly, he began to recall all that had happened to him since his vow that day in the hospital years ago. It mattered not if the old man could hear all his story, but the feeble smile on his face and the relaxed look let Hap know that the old gentleman was glad the young man was there. Somehow, King got the gist that he had helped this youth find direction in life. Whatever it was he had done made him joyful. Once more he had inspired compassion.

Life moves forward, Coeffield King thought, *with the good and the not so good. This boy is good.* He closed his eyes.

Hap got up and tiptoed to the door left ajar. Slipping through, he walked over to Sarah and Elijah.

"I don't know how long he will last. I've left medication on the table, which should make him comfortable. If you will allow me, I would like to check on him tomorrow, or if you want Doctor Mallory, I certainly will understand."

Elijah stood up and swallowed hard. He walked Hap to the door.

"I listened through the door, Doctor Tyson. I think I owe you a humble apology. Of course, I—we," looking back at Sarah, he continued, "never knew all that you said to her father. We're so grateful you came, and, yes, please come back tomorrow. Coffie is your patient as long as he lives."

Elijah Cromwell extended his hand to receive the large one that had lifted and cared for Tarboro's favorite son.

"Sarah will come around," he whispered. "She's in shock."

He squeezed Hap's hand again and patted his shoulder.

"This is a miracle," Hap mumbled all the way back to Tarboro.

Chapter 19
DOCTOR TYSON

Little Ozzie had the croup. Shug Edmundson had wrung her hands long enough. She refused to wait one more minute to take her boy to see Doctor Quiggless. His cough would not stop, got deeper, and hurt his chest. Her home remedies had not worked.

"Mister George, I can't stand it any longer," she said, looking forlorn at the back door of Cromwell Hall. "You know Fate's been in the fields since dawn. I won't see him til midday. Can you carry us to the doctor?"

"Let me tell Maggie and get my hat. Don't you worry none. Old George will take care of everything. Just lemme get my hat."

To their dismay, Doctor Quiggless' office overflowed.

The nurse looked pensive. "You do what you want, but why not try Doctor Tyson? Maybe he can see Ozzie now," she shrugged. "It'll be a long wait here."

Shug looked down at her sick child.

"Whatya think, Mister George?" she asked. "Should I do it for Ozzie? Fate would have a conniption fit if he knew I had taken our son to Hap Tyson."

Both knew Fate's struggle with Hap's role in Will Cromwell's death; however, after a barrage of coughs, they put the little fellow in the cart.

The faint knock at the backdoor of Hap's office barely reached the nurse's ears, but when she opened the door, her mouth dropped.

"Doctor Tyson?" she called over her shoulder. "You better

come see this."

Hap appeared. "Shug? What's wrong?"

"Little Ozzie's got the croup, and Doctor Quiggless' office must have twenty-five folks waiting to see him. I just won-"

Hap smiled. "Go around and sit on the bench out front. It won't be long."

Minutes passed. The door opened. A man walked out.

"What you doing here, girl?" he asked. "Why aren't you seeing Doctor Quiggless?"

Before Shug could speak, Hap stuck his head out the door.

"Mister Jackson? Is there a problem?"

The startled man turned, "Shouldn't she—"

"Mister Jackson, you know Rufus Knight, right?" Hap asked.

"Of course, but—"

"Would Rufus Knight turn his back on a sick child?"

"Uh—" He hesitated, then scowled. "You know he wouldn't."

"Neither will I, Mister Jackson."

"Go on and do what you have to do," he growled. Jamming his hat on his head, he slouched away.

"I'll see you next week?" Hap called out, slightly raising his voice.

Jackson stopped. He turned. The scowl remained, but reality broke his expression. He needed this man for his own health. His face softened.

"I—I," he stuttered. "Yes, I'll see you next week."

"Good."

Mister Jackson looked sheepish. "I hope Ozzie gets better," he mumbled.

Shug nodded, as he shuffled away, kicking a pebble out of his way.

"Okay, Shug. Let's take a look at that young man."

He turned to her, pointing to the front door.

"Yes sir. Yes, sir. Thank you, doctor." Her grins would not quit. She heaved her huge frame up from the bench and followed Hap through the door, little Ozzie on her hip.

Chapter 19

"You did what?" Fate shouted when he returned from the fields and sat with his wife at their table. "Don't you tell me that man had his hands on my child? No, don't you tell me this!"

Fate shook his head in disbelief.

"But, Fate, we couldn't get in to see Doctor Quiggless. There must have been twenty-five folks in there, screaming children and all. It was terrible. The nurse told us to try Doctor Tyson."

"I can't believe you did this to me."

"Fate, I did it for our son, not against you. Please, just listen to how you sound. What's important here, your son getting well or your feelings getting hurt? Don't disappoint me anymore," she scolded him in her quiet way.

With his chest heaving, he looked at her, his mouth a thin line.

"The Captain gave us these few acres because of Will. How can I have anything to do with the man who killed his son?"

His face contorted.

"I just can't stand thinking about him being alive and Will being dead and gone forever. I'll pay him—tomorrow. I don't want to be in debt to the man who killed my best friend."

Slamming the door, he headed out to do a needless task.

Shug didn't care what Fate said; Hap knew his doctoring, and she would go to him again if she needed to.

Doctor Tyson made house calls to Shiloh twice a week to see his patient. He wondered if the family had ever told Caroline that he was Coffie's doctor, or even that he had returned to Tarboro. He guessed not. His new relationship with them was the present, not the past, and the present meant Coffie.

He wondered if Shug had even told Fate that he had taken care of little Ozzie. He knew if Shug ever needed him again that his door was open.

The young doctor also knew his medical ability was not the only reason he went to Shiloh twice a week. The Cromwells needed to feel that they were doing the best for Coeffield King, and he was it. Even through each visit, Sarah turned her back on him or made herself scarce. Her stinging words his first visit still plagued him every time he walked through the door. Thankfully, the Captain was his go-between, his buffer. He had clasped Hap's hand each time he left Shiloh, quite satisfied with the old man's treatment, more for his mind, than his body. Both would hear Hap telling the old man about cases he had seen during the week, as he would go through his examination, poking around with those big hands.

"Yesterday, the Browns came in with little Tom. He'd broken his arm, jumping down the hayloft. We all had to hold him down to set it," Hap said. "Surely, Mrs. Deberry's lunch crowd heard him holler." He paused. "Toby Phillips has the chicken pox. I reckon that'll run through that big family."

Telling these stories between pokes seemed to humor the old lawyer. He felt a part of this new and budding practice, for after all the old man had inspired this boy to vow to serve with compassion. The doctor certainly proved it by coming and sitting, talking, and doctoring the old gentleman. Hap never once felt he was neglecting the people of Edgecombe County by these visits. His practice was growing slowly, and he knew Coeffield King would not last much longer. His efforts were the least he could do for this family, whether satisfying his guilt or theirs.

One day, to his surprise, Sarah Cromwell turned and stiffly addressed Hap.

"Doctor Tyson?" She startled him. "Do you think we ought to wire our daughter to come? I know you have been saying that we should prepare for his not being here much longer. Give me your honest opinion."

She lifted her head to maintain control of her emotions. The Cromwells had never mentioned Caroline in his presence, not once.

"Mrs. Cromwell, I think it's time," he said, trying to hide his own emotion, for he himself had become quite fond of the old gentleman.

She nodded.

"Thank you," she whispered.

Chapter 19

Elijah walked him to the door.

"You know we appreciate all that you've done, Doctor Ty— Hap. We'll wire Caroline in the morning."

He closed the door. Elijah stood with his forehead against the heavy oaken door, his eyes shut, his face wet. Pulling his handkerchief from his pocket, he dabbed his face and turned to join Sarah.

His wife had walked quietly into Coffie's room to gaze at her beloved father. She wondered how the jolt of his death would affect them all. She felt Elijah's hands on her shoulders. Her head fell back on his chest, as both watched the labored breaths.

Hap rode toward Tarboro.

Caroline will be here soon. She'll be good for the family.

He slowed as he passed Station House Road. How long had it been since he'd seen Willie? Now was as good a time as any.

Willie smiled when she opened her door.

"My, my, look at my doctor son."

She got a long-awaited hug. She had been by his house and his office since they had moved, but this time was the first to be alone in her house. She was grateful not to listen to Pamela prattle on about the society of Tarboro or some newsy tidbit from Hillsborough.

"Tell me all about your practice, son."

He told her everything from the day the barge delivered his supplies to his first real patient.

"Want to know who my first patient was?"

"Of course."

"The one and only Coeffield King."

Willie clamped her hands over her mouth in disbelief and marveled as the story unraveled.

"Caroline's coming."

Her face clouded. "Ohhh..."

"Willie, everybody's agreed that Mister King needs her for the end."

They quieted. Both lost in thought.

"Who else have you seen?" she finally broke their silence.

"Little Ozzie."

"No. I was just with him."

"He got the croup. It hit him suddenly."

"But you and Fate."

"I know, but it was Shug and Mister George who brought him in."

*Oh, God, how you weave our lives together so. My two sons...*she thought with wonder.

"It's been a long day, Willie. I need to get on home to Pamela and Rollie."

She nodded, as they stood facing each other.

"I believe you've grown an inch," she said, bending back to look up at the tall young man. "Can I reach up high enough to hug you again?"

"Well, I can certainly bend down, Willie," he answered, bringing her close to him.

She could feel his strong arms around her. *My son*, she thought. Oh, she felt so safe in the haven of his arms. *My son...*

Chapter 20
PASSAGE

Hap had not seen Coeffield King for several days. He hoped the old gentleman had had a good weekend. As he rode up to Cromwell Hall, he wondered where the stable boy was to take his reins. Where was Maggie? She always greeted him at the door. Tying his horse to the post, he carried his doctor bag in one hand and reached for the knocker with the other, but before his hand could touch the wrought iron fixture, the door swung open with the sun hitting those golden curls that he had adored for half his life.

"Hap? Hap? It's me. Caroline."

Once more in her presence, he froze. He could not speak or think. He could only dumbly look at the beauty of her face.

Extending both hands to his free one, she pulled him through the door.

"I can't believe you are Coffie's doctor. Father has filled me in."

In gratitude, she squeezed his hand. "I can't thank you enough."

Once more her fragrances filled his nostrils.

"Caroline, I wasn—I mean Maggie usually—" he stuttered pointing at the door. "I—you look wonderful. Coffie? I'm glad I could help."

"Come. He's waiting for you."

She took his arm and guided him through the door. Both parents drew in their breaths, as they saw their daughter with Hap Tyson, a picture that looked as natural as any they could imagine. Sarah turned her face.

"Excuse us," Elijah whispered, glancing at his wife, who had risen to leave. Her sidelong glance spoke volumes, with slitted eyes, flashing hatred. The door closed quietly behind them.

"Coffie, Doctor Tyson is here. Darling, it's your favorite medical man," Caroline teased as they moved closer.

Coffie roused enough to focus on his granddaughter. She had perched on the chair by his bedside and laid her head down next to him. He touched her curls that reminded him of his Jacksie. With his other hand, King struggled to reach for his doctor's hand. Quickly leaning over, Hap extended it to him. The withered hand placed it on the golden head as well. Startled, Hap's eyes darted to the old lawyer. His patient smiled with mischief. Embarrassed, Hap stepped back in frustration.

Raising her head, Caroline smiled at Coffie.

"I'll see you when the good doctor finishes."

Rising, she turned to Hap and smiled, as she passed the end of the bed. His gaze followed her, thoughts of their youth boiling beneath the surface of his skin. It was all he could do to turn back to his patient, but he did with his hands on his hips and a frown on his face. Coffie gurgled a feeble laugh, closed his rheumy eyes, and waited for his friend to examine his wretched body.

Oh, Jacksie, the man still has feelings for our granddaughter. You should have seen his eyes following her out the door. The sparks were jumping all over the place, and she knows nothing of it. God, you have made strange creatures to walk your earth. I wish I could live to see what happens. Oh, Jacksie, the man has a deep-seated love for your grandchild, and I know exactly how he feels. I love you, my darling. It won't be long...

Hap slipped from the bedroom, tiptoeing to the family. He did not know how to extinguish their concern.

"It's a miracle Mister King is alive. I really don't have to tell you that."

Each nodded.

"All I know is that it will be soon."

Chapter 20

Their heads drooped.

Caroline raised hers first.

"Hap, come into the gardens where we can talk. Mother, Father, please excuse us."

"Caroline!" Sarah protested. Elijah's hand moved quickly to silence her.

"I really should be getting back to Tarboro before dark," he said, searching the Cromwells' faces as he spoke. Sarah's eyes flashed with objection.

"Oh, take a few minutes, Hap."

Elijah stepped in front of Sarah. "You haven't seen Caroline in years, and I'm sure she wants you to tell her more about Coffie."

His eyes were understanding.

Hap turned and simply followed her down the big hall that stretched through the center of the house. Opening the rear door, she stepped into the remaining sunlight. Both walked silently to a garden bench.

"Hap," Caroline spoke first, her voice music in his ears. "How are you?"

Her words are personal? Looking directly into those azure eyes, he told her without hesitation about Pamela and medical school. His words came easily, especially when he spoke of Rollie.

She smiled.

"I have two sons now. Maybe we'll have a girl in the future," she said in a hushed voice. She looked down at her handkerchief, fidgeting for a moment.

"Tell me more."

"We're happy," she offered with a quick smile. "Litch is a wonderful father and very successful in his real estate business. He even hints about politics, but I don't know. Maybe."

She shrugged her shoulders and wrinkled her nose.

"My boys are handfuls. Jacob is three and quite the organizer. Little Coffie will walk any day now. He may be a climber, just like his brother."

"They didn't come?"

"No. I wanted to spend every moment with Coffie. I'm so worried about him. He seems so weak."

She paused staring down at her handkerchief again, then, lifting it to her eyes to catch the tears that had been welling. Choking on her words, she continued, "I—I know he has to die, but it's so—so hard—to let him go."

Her tears spilled quickly.

His hand shook as he reached to pat hers.

"I know. I know," he whispered.

Looking up at him, she realized his own grief. Unabashedly, she squeezed his hand, sobbing openly. Both faces were etched with pain for what would happen in the big house just yards from them.

"Caroline! Hap! Come quickly. Oh God, it's Coffie!"

Elijah's voice penetrated the big boxwoods that surrounded the bench. Both jumped and dashed to the house. Reaching the backdoor, they could hear Sarah's wails.

"Coffie, Coffie," Caroline cried, as she raced through the bedroom door.

Braswell Dickens, Tarboro's mortician, opened his door. Never would he have believed that one Hap Tyson would inform him that his old friend, Coeffield King, was dead. Dickens had sworn retirement countless times, but he kept on burying the town's elders and did not feel his job was done. When he heard Hap's words, he felt confirmation that burying Tarboro's favorite son would be his last. Nodding his head, he closed the door and slowly shuffled back to his comfortable chair. Yes, he had buried the young and the old. Now, it was time to pass this duty on to another generation. He was through. His job was done.

Word spread through eastern North Carolina that the famed old lawyer was dead. On the day of the funeral, Calvary Episcopal overflowed with mourners. Their black attire matched their sadness. A profusion of flowers banked the altar of the old

Chapter 20

sanctuary, a testimony of appreciation for this man's service and compassion. Their scent hung heavily in the air. A new era dawned for this grieving family and all of Down East.

The services blurred for the Cromwells. Family and friends lined up to offer words of condolence. Hugs and handshakes momentarily comforted.

"Miss Sarah, we've lost an institution for sure. Nobody could come close to his stature in the courtroom. Lord, I remember the day..."

"Miss Caroline," another whispered. "You could not have had a more devoted grandfather. How many times we'd see him with his darling little granddaughter..."

"Captain, after your father died, Coeffield King could not have been a better friend. He thought of you as the son he never had..."

On and on the words flowed, until slowly the mourners disappeared, leaving the young doctor to comfort the comfortless. As Hap stood, he felt grateful to be able to show this family a different side of himself, one of service and compassion. If only Sarah Cromwell...

Hap sighed as he walked quietly to Coffie's grave, now placed at rest by his beloved Jacksie Thrash. Sarah noticed him first. She moved slowly toward him, a strange look on her face.

He stopped.

"I've been foolish, Hap."

She extended her hand to him. He took it.

"You unselfishly nursed and nurtured my father. I want to thank you."

Hap could feel the strength of her fingers, squeezing his with each word she spoke.

My God, she's forgiving me?

"I am so sorry, Miss Sarah," he said. "He's been important to me for a long time. I hope you know that."

"Thank you, Hap. My father was a pretty good judge of character. He spoke highly of you more than once." Her eyelids fluttered, as she swallowed hard. "I think he was right about you." She looked at her father's grave. "It may take me a while, but I think the past is buried today."

She smiled faintly, as she stepped back.

Elijah stood and shook his hand. Only Caroline remained facing Coffie's casket, yet to be covered with dirt.

"Darling, Hap wants to pay his respects," her mother spoke softly as she bent over her daughter.

"Oh?" Caroline turned, her eyes, red from weeping. "Doctor, can you heal a broken heart?" she asked, feebly smiling up at him.

Slowly, she stood. Her parents wandered toward their carriage.

"Hap, tell them I'm not ready to go," she spoke, shaking her head.

The young man chased them down.

"Caroline wants to stay a while longer," he said, then hesitated. "I'll be glad to bring her home," he spoke softly.

Her parents looked with great concern at their daughter, standing by the obelisk towering over the grave site. Nodding, they continued their way to their carriage and the sad ride to Shiloh.

The two mourners sat on the nearby bench, both lost in thought.

"Will you go inside Calvary with me, Hap? I just want to say one last prayer."

They walked arm and arm into the church and knelt at the railing, offering final prayers for the old man.

The ride home proved one of memories. When they passed Station House Road, Hap pulled on the reins.

"Whoa, boy," he said, turning to Caroline. "Do you remember the times you used to come down that road with your mother and the church ladies, passing out shoes to all the children? How many times did I hide behind a tree or a bush to keep you from seeing me."

Chapter 20

"Oh, I saw you, Hap, every time."

"Every time?"

"Yes, my friend, every time," she smiled and looked down the road.

She sighed with resignation, as if longing for the younger days, the less complicated days, the innocent days.

"How about those times in town, too? I'd see that crooked smile every turn I made."

Her voice trailed in nostalgia.

"Those days are long past, yet so vivid. It's frightening."

"I know. I know."

He smiled down at her and inhaled her fragrances, reliving memories he had laid to rest.

They moved back onto the road to Shiloh. Their silence soothed them as the horse's hooves softly stirred the dust.

Finally, she spoke.

"Thank you, Hap. I needed this time, and I could not have had a better person to share my grief."

"Of course. It helped me as well."

They rode in silence again until Cromwell Hall loomed ahead.

"Do you mind if we stop at Will's grave?"

"Of course, I don't mind. Anything."

He felt her hand on his arm as they approached the curve before the cemetery.

"I know it's a strange request, but I think I need to."

"Whatever you want," he added as he pulled the carriage over and helped her down. Walking straight to Will's grave, the young woman touched the high marker and traced the engraving. *Lord, the pain has got to stop soon...*

They stayed only moments, then moved on to the main house, both now grappling with good memories and sad ones. Climbing out of the carriage, Hap reached up to help her down, hesitating just a second before releasing her hand. Her eyes expressed gratitude for everything he had done. As they turned to the porch, Litch Bagley stepped through the doorway.

Chapter 21

UNUSUAL NEWS

On the day of Coeffield King's funeral, Litch had tried his best to get to Tarboro in time for the services. His passage on the steamboat had been delayed, ruining his chances. He had sat on the deck of the *Mary Beale*, daydreaming, holding Elijah's telegram about the old lawyer's passing. The thud of the steamboat bumping the dock jarred him from his thoughts. Pulling his watch from his pocket, he'd cursed his misfortune. His only choice was to drive to Shiloh and wait for the family's return from Calvary.

"Oh, Litch, Caroline will be so glad you're here," Sarah clasped his outstretched arms, as they stood in the entry of Cromwell Hall. "We are, too."

"I'm so sorry I missed the funeral. We were delayed."

"Shh. You're here now. That's what's important." She paused. "And the boys?"

"My parents have them. I decided it would be too confusing with all the doings."

"Of course," she agreed, glancing quickly at Elijah. "Come sit down. We have some unusual news in all this sadness."

"News?" Litch asked. His brow furrowed.

"Elijah," Sarah said, getting up and walking to a front window.

"Hap Tyson's returned to Tarboro," Elijah informed him.

"Tyson?" Litch's voice rose. He felt perplexed, yet chilled by this news.

"Yes, Litch," the Captain said. "He was Coffie's doctor."

"Coffie's doctor?"

Now, he spoke in disbelief.

Chapter 21

"I know. I know. It's been hard for us to accept, but he really is different from the scamp we knew in his youth."

"I'm just shocked. I knew nothing of this. Coffie's doctor?"

"We have to confess that, in an emergency, he did a great service for Coffie."

"Oh." Litch's face masked his irritation.

"Hap's bringing Caroline from Calvary," Sarah said, her head slightly turning toward them.

All three heard a carriage pull up; all three aware of the passengers. Litch raced to the front door only to see his former adversary help his wife down from the carriage. He stood speechless as he watched her hand touch Hap's shoulder ever so slightly. Both turned toward the house, as he walked out onto the porch.

When Litch saw his wife's face, he saw devastation.

"Litch," she cried. Lifting her skirts, she ran to him. Once more she broke down, but this time on the shoulder of her husband.

Comforting her as best he could, Litch eyed Hap over the top of her head. They nodded a silent farewell, as each returned to the business at hand, Litch to console his wife and Hap to explain to his.

Not once did Litch close his eyes that night, as he played the scene over and over again in his mind of Hap with his hands on Caroline. The morose husband, fully shocked at the jealousy that rose in his throat, choking him, pulled his wife closer as she slept a troubled sleep. Softly, he caressed her golden head, still feeling the wetness of her tears on the shoulder of his nightclothes. The dawn came none too soon for him. He wanted to take her away from Cromwell Hall and all the memories being stirred by Hap Tyson, in her and him. When would the man ever be out of their lives?

Chapter 22

THE PAINFUL PAST

Pamela Tyson looked down at little Rollie, playing with his blocks in the middle of the living room floor.

"Where's my daddy?"

"He'll be home soon, darling. He had to do something for a patient. You play with those blocks and build your mother a beautiful castle," Pamela feigned sweetness, but she was mad as the devil.

She paced and watched the window to see her husband come up the way. Hap had told her about Coeffield King's funeral. She had been disappointed not going to such an important occasion in the county, but Willie had been sick and couldn't stay with Rollie. She scuffed her shoe on the floor in anger. Hap had been with the Cromwells all afternoon.

Peering through the curtain opening, she spied his carriage slowly nearing their cottage. She dashed to the door, only to check herself.

"Oh no, Hap Tyson," she muttered. "I won't let you see my concern. I won't."

Coming through the door, Hap found a normal scene, his wife rocking and knitting, his son building something with his blocks. Listening to the cadence of the rocker, he smiled as he looked at them, grateful that he had no sadness or anger to deal with from either one. He was exhausted, especially after seeing the expression on Litch Bagley's face.

"Daddy, Daddy," little Rollie cried out and ran to hug his father. "We missed you."

"I missed you, too, son. What are you building?"

Chapter 22

"A ca-, a ca- What am I building, Momma?"

"A castle, Rollie. I told you a castle," she said, an edge in her voice. She looked at her husband with questions in her eyes.

Hap was puzzled by her look, but mainly confused by her sharpness toward their son. However, he came over and kissed the top of her head.

"I'll put supper on the table. I suppose you're hungry?"

He nodded. She got up, brushing past him. His eyes followed her.

They ate quietly, listening to Rollie's childish babble.

"Pamela, I'll tuck Rollie in bed while you clean up."

She nodded. As he walked hand in hand with their son, her nostrils quivered. Her heart pounded. Things were definitely not going as she had planned.

Picking up her knitting, she waited in her rocker. Hap collapsed in his chair by the fireplace and stared at the flames dancing up and down the logs. He got up, poked the embers, and put another log on top. The night was chilly for early fall.

"Tell me about the Cromwells," Pamela started out, trying to be matter-of-fact with her words as she rocked and stitched. His head rose a little too quickly for her satisfaction, as she peered curiously at him. He turned back, squinting at the fireplace.

"What do you want to know?"

"Well, there just seems to be so much about that family that I don't know," she baited him. "Please clarify an incident for me. In Carver's Mercantile just last week, I overheard the Carvers' daughter say something about Doctor Hap and Miss Caroline. I couldn't understand them, and they hushed up when they saw me. What did they mean?"

A dead silence.

"Hap? "

Another dead silence, as he continued to gaze into the fire.

"Answer me!"

Her voice raised several decibels.

The pain that slowly covered his face made her catch her

breath. The past was not dead. When he still did not answer, his wife slammed her knitting down and stomped off to bed, leaving her husband with his head in his hands. He heard the key turn in the lock.

The next morning, Pamela bustled around the kitchen with puffy eyes, busying herself with their breakfast and little Rollie's. She had never closed the door on her husband before, but she was angry. He didn't have a ready answer last night.

Silently sitting at breakfast, he drank coffee and read *The Southerner*. Conscious of her eyes, he finally looked up. Making sure Rollie was out of earshot, he said, "Pamela, I love you now, but I cannot tell you that I have never loved another. I will tell you everything you want to know, everything, tonight, when I come home. The office will be swamped since I closed yesterday for the funeral. Just give me until this evening, please," he pleaded. Folding his paper, he stood and paused before her, putting his forehead against hers, and closing his eyes.

"I love you," he said again, walking over to ruffle Rollie's head.

Little Rollie retired early that night.

"Come sit with me, Pamela."

Hap extended his hand to her as she came out of Rollie's room.

"I know you feel you've stepped in an unknown, mysterious world, and I'm sorry I've put you in that situation. Come, please."

His wife had stopped in the doorway and stared at her husband. Yes, they had serious matters to discuss. She walked to her rocker and sat.

Hap smiled as he sat in front of her. He had been so proud of her adjustment to Tarboro and their new way of life, but he had caused this disturbance and he needed to clear the air. Their conversation would not be easy. He just hoped she would understand. The creak of her chair and the pop of the burning logs covered their silence as Pamela stared into the flames,

Chapter 22

waiting for him to speak.

"I owe you the deepest apology. I criticized you for hiding things from me and it is I who have hidden so much about myself from you. To tell you the truth, I was embarrassed about my past and scared to death I'd lose you. Now I understand what a bad mistake that was."

He paused and leaned forward toward her, his arms resting on his thighs, his hands clasped. "I just don't know where to begin, but maybe it would be best to start when I was born?"

Her face was stone.

"My ma died having me. That was a lot to carry, knowing that I had caused her death. Anyway, I never knew her, which was hard for me. All the other children did, and I think some of them blamed me for her death. Willa Abigale Pridgen, Willie as we've all called her, had lived with us early on and was really the only 'mother' I ever knew, but she'd left us to come home to Tarboro.

"Well, I fussed and fumed for Willie and drove them all crazy until Pap couldn't take my hollering anymore, so he brought me to Willie and begged her to raise me. My Pa knew she'd given up her own baby and was barren. Now that I think about it, I can't believe she took me in and treated me as her own. We were an odd pair."

Pamela eyed her husband, still not saying a word. It was his turn to stare at the flames.

"Later on, I had the reputation of being the meanest scoundrel in Edgecombe County. I wasn't proud of that name, because some accusations were unjust, but others were true as the day is long."

Eventually, he spoke about Caroline. Pamela leaned closer.

"We were children first, polarized by our birthrights. We could never be public friends, only private ones.

"Her mother smothered her with traditions, never allowing her the freedom she craved. Me? I was just a poor moppet on Station House Road.

"Anyway, by fate or happenstance we met as young people in

a grassy area on Shiloh. I was actually trespassing on some hunting ground, but we struck up a friendship and that haven became our meeting place. I'd cut through the woods to reach the lower 40, not knowing if she would come, always afraid that someone would catch me on Shiloh property." He stared down at his hands.

"We fell in love, Pamela. It's as simple as that."

Pamela gripped her chair arms, biting her lower lip.

He continued. "Hidden and forbidden love. Now, where was it going? No-where, that's where. We were children." He stopped and looked briefly into the fireplace. His wife stared at him.

Glancing up at her, he looked startled at her face. "Do you want me to continue?"

"Oh, yes, by all means," she snapped.

Her voice shook him, but he talked on. "One day, I knew it was over. Unconsciously, she'd proven to me how different our worlds were. We were going to meet, but somehow her brother Will interfered. We fought. He fell, hitting his head on a log, and died. That tragedy changed our lives forever."

Hap settled back in his chair.

"The sheriff served me with papers, charging me with the murder of Will Cromwell. Coeffield King meant to see me rot in jail, but that was not to be, Pamela. Caroline saved me. She told the court that it was an accident, just a tragic accident."

"Then, you came to Chapel Hill?" Her words spoken with a steely coldness.

"Yes, Rufus Knight made that possible. The university gave me new meaning for my life. Pamela, I cannot tell you what it has meant to me to return to Tarboro and make peace, not only with the Cromwells and Coeffield King, but also, with the people of Edgecombe County."

Pamela Tyson injected two words. "And Caroline?"

"Caroline? What do you mean? She's married with children in Raleigh. What could there be?"

Chapter 22

His wife waggled her finger at him.

"You just don't know who you're dealing with."

She strode through the bedroom door. Once more, he heard the resounding click as the key turned.

Chapter 23
UNANNOUNCED

For weeks, Pamela and Hap were strangers, each miserable, each stubborn. She felt anger; he felt hurt.

"I'm leaving, Hap," she said with a deadened voice.

"Leaving? What do you mean?"

He looked up sharply at her from his chair, as she walked toward him. They had finished supper. Their son was asleep.

"Little Rollie and I are going to visit my family in Hillsborough. I haven't seen them or Banks in months."

Her head reared back as she continued.

"You'll get along just fine. Mrs. Deberry and her help will feed the good doctor for sure."

A sneer flickered across her face.

"How long do you plan to stay?"

"I-I haven't made up my mind, but I think you should hear a few truths."

She began to pace in front of him. Her nostrils flared as she whirled around toward him, her hands on her hips. Her neck poked forward. Her eyes narrowed.

"First, do you really think you were telling me news about Caroline Cromwell? Excuse me, Caroline Bagley."

"Well, I-"

"Well, no, Doctor Tyson. Do you think I would marry you without knowing all about my future husband? Did you really think that, Hap?"

"I—I don't know what-"

"Think who my grandfather is. Do you think Banks McCloud would not search you out? God, how naïve you are. Yes, I knew

Chapter 23

about her, but I wanted you to tell me early on. Do you think my grandfather didn't find out about your court case? Really, Hap, but I wanted to use these things to make you into the husband I wanted."

"Make me into what?"

Her skirt swished. The veins in her neck popped out.

"Fashion you into my-my-"

"Your what? For God's sake, Pamela, make sense."

His mouth hung open.

"You messed up the plan, Hap, in Chapel Hill. We were supposed to live there in the comfort I'm used to, not down here in next to poverty. Just, look at my hands."

She thrust them out in front of her but quickly hid them in the pockets of her dress.

"We were in too deep. We had a son," she whispered but gathered steam as she continued. "I couldn't even use him to keep you in Chapel Hill. No, you had to come Down East. I told you if I didn't like it here, I'd leave," she raised her voice, then quickly looked toward her son's closed door.

"Pamela, this is a nightmare."

"We're going, Hap. Don't try to stop me. Do you understand?"

"Maybe a few weeks will help us both."

She didn't answer. He watched her close their bedroom door, then turned toward the fireplace, his fingers pressing his pounding forehead. How had his life gotten into such a mess?

Pushing the door open to an empty house each night crazed Hap. His spirits plummeted every time he crossed that threshold. His wife and son were gone. Where was all this anxiety taking them? What was all of this madness doing to their son? He was so young, so impressionable.

At least doctoring the folks in the county kept Hap occupied. His practice continued to grow, endearing him to the people, slowly becoming his people with the kindness and compassion of his vow.

Weeks passed, until one day Hap succumbed and wired his wife in Hillsborough. He wired her in Chapel Hill. No return word.

"Damnit, Pamela," he cursed as he threw clothes into a valise. "You're my wife. I'm not giving up on us that quickly."

The train could not move fast enough to Carrboro. He had rented a rig and would drive by the McCloud house first. If she and Rollie were not there, he would head out to Hillsborough, no matter the hour. He wanted his family back.

The young doctor drove down Franklin Street, oddly smiling in his state of affairs at the village storefronts. A young student walked into the sundries shop where he had purchased Caroline's fragrance. *That could be me,* he thought. The corner jewelry store stirred fond memories of picking out Pamela's ring with old Doc Sims. Even the flower ladies sat in their usual spot and lifted a bouquet to tempt him. *Well, why not?*

Burrowing his nose in the posies, he gazed over at the campus. His heart warmed as he thought of Doctor Knight, Dean Perry, the Fearless Five, and all the people at the university who had molded his life.

As he turned his rig off Franklin, facing Rosemary Street, Hap was startled to see the many carriages drawn up in front of the McCloud house. Pulling up, he handed his reins to an attendant.

"You come to Mister Banks' birthday party, sir?"

"Huh? Birthday? Oh, yes...yes, indeed," he answered. Slowly, he approached the door, opened by Lucas, McCloud's manservant.

"Why, Doctor Tyson? Was Miss Pamela expecting you, sir?" he inquired, nervously looking over his shoulder.

"No, I wanted to surprise her."

Shoving his hat in Lucas's hand, he walked to the parlor door, only to see his wife in the middle of three very interested young men. She was the center of attention, clapping her hands at this comment or that one. Other friends watched the old gentleman

Chapter 23

open a present or two, as he eyed his granddaughter with admiration. He obviously approved of her scandalous behavior and her dress. Hap gawked at the low-cut neckline.

"Pamela!" his voice rang out over the clamor.

Startled, she quickly regained her composure, gushing to her group.

"Excuse me, kind sirs. I have something to attend to." She whirled and marched to her husband. Her eyes narrowed with a steely glint.

"How dare you come here unannounced?" she hissed, hardly appearing the darling bride he'd honeymooned with in this very house, not too terribly long ago.

"When do I need to be announced in my own wife's grandfather's house?" his voice pierced the air.

"Hush, please. Have you no respect? It's my grandfather's birthday. Why did you have to spoil it? Come out back this instant if you are going to let your emotions take over," she retorted as she swished to her grandfather's office. Closing the door, she turned toward him with an ugly scowl. "What's going on with you?"

Irritated, he threw the bouquet on the desk and turned with a growl.

"What's going on with you? Who are those gentlemen you were flirting with out there?"

Grabbing her arm, he continued "Why are they a part of a family celebration of your grandfather's birthday? Pamela, look at me. I don't like what I just saw. And where is Rollie?"

He paused, waiting for her to defend herself. Her answer shocked him.

"Rollie's just fine. He's with my parents." She spoke with a haughty flair. "Those gentlemen? Well, Banks has wanted to invite some young people to entertain me since he knew how sad I'd been over our situation. He just wanted to make me happy again, something you have not been able to do."

She pursed her lips at him.

"By the way, have you seen Mrs. Bagley lately?"

"Caroline? My God, Pamela, I've come all this way to get my family back and you want to dredge up the past."

"The past?" she screeched and then lowered her voice to a venomous whisper. "The past has become the present, I'm afraid. Now, you get out of this house. Banks will see you tomorrow on some business."

With this parting comment, she turned heel, opened the door, and sashayed toward her gentlemen callers.

Sickened by her words, Hap grabbed his hat from the rack in the entry hall and charged out the front door.

"I paid my respects quickly," he mumbled to the man with the reins.

Chapter 24
LEGAL MATTERS

The next morning, Hap stood on McCloud's front stoop. How he hated having to face the wiles and stratagems of Pamela's grandfather.

"Doctor Tyson," Lucas greeted him as he opened the door. "Mister McCloud is in the parlor, sir."

He nodded slightly as Hap brushed by him to meet the consequences of the day.

"Hap, be seated," McCloud coolly said, sweeping his arm toward the settee. The man stood by the mantle, arms crossed, with a scowl that Hap knew only too well. "It seems we have a situation, boy," he said, his voice laced with condescension.

"Where's Pamela, sir? She needs to be here," he said, craning his neck to catch a glimpse of her. Sweat beaded on his forehead.

"She's upstairs. She'll join us later."

"And Rollie? Where's Rollie?" Hap asked, while mopping his brow with his handkerchief.

"Still with the Martins in Hillsborough. I thought it best that they keep him for a few days. Anyway, he should not be in this house as we talk."

"Why not? I haven't seen him for two months," he said, trying to suppress his anger. "I need him. I need Pamela. You are cruel to keep me from my son." His voice rose.

"Don't get snappy with me. You're a visitor in this house and you can get in your buggy and go right down that road from where you came, you hear?"

He pointed his finger to the large window overlooking Rosemary Street.

"Sir, just get Pamela," Hap said, on the verge of losing his patience.

"Not right now, young man. We have something to discuss."

With that announcement, he walked over to a chest and opened the top drawer. Pulling some papers out, he squinted at them, as he sauntered toward Hap.

"Here," he said, pushing the papers into Hap's hands. The man stood back with an air of smugness, with the light from the window illuminating his wild, white hair. To Hap, he looked like a sorcerer ready to boil him in oil.

Slowly, the bewildered young man focused on the top sheet. His eyes widened at the first word. Divorce. The word tasted like poison in his mouth. His head jerked with such fury that the slight man in front of him flinched, stepping back warily.

"Pamela," Hap yelled. Grasping the papers in one hand, he marched to the foot of the steps. "Pamela," he yelled again, no longer caring about manners or formality. When she did not answer, he bounded up the steps.

"Now, see here, you scoundrel. Stop! You hear!" the old man hollered, but to no avail.

Bursting through the door of their old room, Hap saw his wife standing by the chair in front of the window, her head tossed back, her face distorted with arrogance and pomposity.

Once more, he felt he was looking at a spoiled child, instead of Rollie's mother.

"Well, has Banks served you with the papers?"

"Serv—? You mean you approve of a divorce? You really want this?" He shook his head. "Pamela, what has he done to you? You're my wife. I wanted you to come visit family and think things through, but didn't you miss me? Did you not miss our life together with our son?"

She didn't answer.

"Who were those men in this house yesterday?"

This time she answered.

"I told you, friends of Grandfather's." Her eyebrows shot

Chapter 24

upward, her nose in the air. "He finds them appropriate acquaintances for me, one's a lawyer in town, one's a medical professor at the university, and the other's the mayor's son. Very good stock. Well-qualified, eligible men. Don't buck this parting, Hap. You know I have to think of my future and my child's."

"Oh, no, not Rollie."

Then, quite sarcastically, he retorted, "Why, Pammie, a child will only cramp your activities when you try to snag the catch of the bunch. Think about it. No scamp to complicate matters or affairs."

She frowned, thinking about the consequence of dragging around a *young'un*.

"Grandfather," she hollered, pushing past Hap, to stand at the top of the steps. "He wants Rollie."

"What? Oh, no, the child should stay with his mother," the old man proclaimed, looking up at his granddaughter, his face blanching in alarm. His brows twitched, as he shook his head. Reaching for the staircase railing to steady himself, he murmured to her, "Not Rollie."

"But, Grandfather, my suitors."

Lord in heaven, she's already calling them suitors, Hap thought.

"They might not like my having a child around. Goodness, I hadn't thought of that."

McCloud continued to shake his head.

"Grandfather, don't worry. I can have you plenty of great-grandchildren if I want to. I'm good at figuring out the best time to be with child, am I not, Hap?" she added with a cruel giggle, turning to him. "Sure, take him, but on one condition."

"Anything," Hap said.

"He visits me whenever I want him. Understand?" She poked her finger in his chest. "Thanks, Hap, you may have increased my availability. My parents have him now, but we'll send them a telegram. They'll have him here by tomorrow."

"Pamela, are you sure?"

"Grandfather, I'm going back in my room to get ready for our caller this evening. Take care of any details. You're so good at that."

Not even telling her husband good-bye, she disappeared behind a firmly closed door.

Hap slowly walked down the steps and over to the table, papers in hand. Quickly, he dashed his name across the bottom. Never looking at McCloud or Lucas, he walked out of what he felt was a den of unhappiness and deceit. His only salvation was Rollie.

"Why didn't Mommy come?" Rollie asked his dad, as their train rumbled down the track carrying them back to Edgecombe County.

"Oh, she's staying a while longer with her grandfather. She needs more time with her mom and dad, too. She's missed them, just like you've missed me, right?"

"Yeah, Dad, but I missed you the most."

"Naw, I missed you the most."

"Da-ad! I...missed...you...the...most!"

Laughing, the father ruffled his son's curly hair. *I have my son. Thank God, I have my son.*

Chapter 25
THE GIFT

𝒥n Raleigh, life seemed to settle down for the Bagleys after Coeffield King's death. Weeks slipped by in routine.

"What are you doing, Mother?" Jacob asked one day, peeping around her shoulder as she bent, rummaging in the hall closet.

"I want to do something special for your father. Do you remember this?" she said, pulling out an old canvas she had worked on while waiting for little Coffie's birth.

"It's Daddy. You're going to finish it?"

"You are so right," she said, pinching his nose. "Your father's birthday is coming soon. I thought it would be a nice present, but, Jacob, it has to be a surprise. Can you keep a secret? And we must help Coffie to understand."

"Mother, I'm a big boy. I'm almost five," he said, puffing up his chest

"Jacob, I'm serious. We need to keep this present a secret. If you will do this, I'll let you and Coffie help me."

His hand flew to his mouth. *It was a good bribe,* Caroline thought.

Weeks flew. Litch almost breathed from the portrait, it was so lifelike. The secret remained just that, a secret.

"Hello!" Litch called from the front door. "Hello! Where's my family?" he called again, walking into the parlor. Hearing a rustling beyond the kitchen door, he smiled. "Well, well, well, did my wife hide my children? Behind the settee, maybe?"

He walked over to look.

"No. Not there. Aha, behind my chair?"

He leaned over to peer.

"No. I suppose I'll just sit here in the parlor and read my paper until my family comes home."

His voice floated through the kitchen door.

"We're home, Daddy, we're home," Jacob's muffled voice sounded out.

"What? Oh..."

The door flew open.

"Surprise, Daddy! It's your birthday!" Jacob hollered as he burst into the room with little Coffie squealing behind. Caroline trailed, a faint glimmer in her eye.

"Ask Momma what she has behind the door," Jacob urged. "Ask her, Daddy."

Looking up, he mouthed, "What?"

The boys crawled all over him, as she raised her hand for him to sit still as she returned to the kitchen and brought out the large canvas. Slowly, she turned it around, searching his face for approval.

"It's 'ou, DaDa," Coffie offered.

Laughing, he ran to the portrait and stuck a wet finger right in the face that peered out.

"How did you finish it in secret?" he asked. Putting the boys aside, he walked to his wife. "It's amazing," he said, studying the portrait. "What's this?"

"That, my dear husband, is Coffie's contribution," she smiled.

"And Momma let me paint on your face," Jacob bragged.

"I see. Thank you, family. I could not have had a better gift." Caroline beamed.

"Well, I wan-" Before she could finish her words, Litch kissed her. The boys squealed again and ran to hug their parents' legs as the two stood gazing at each other. His jealousy of Hap Tyson ebbed. They were all his.

Chapter 26

THE UNEXPECTED

"Mrs. Bagley! Good Lord, Mrs. Bagley! Something's wrong with Coffie."

Mrs. Rumley cried, rushing in through the backdoor, the listless child dangling in her arms.

"Coffie? Coffie?" Caroline shrieked, grabbing the child and shaking him. "What happened?"

"I don't know, ma'am," Mrs. Rumley said, her face pained, yet dumbfounded. "It was Jacob's turn at croquet, and I—"

"Oh God," Caroline whispered, clutching her child to her bosom. "I don't think he's breathing. Coffie?" she screamed, shaking him again.

"Go get Charlie, ma'am. He'll take you to the hospital. I'll stay here with Jacob."

"What's wrong with Coffie, Momma? I'm scared," Jacob cried, tears welling in his eyes.

He clung to Mrs. Rumley, peeping through arms that shielded him.

"Come, Jacob," Mrs. Rumley said, herding him toward the staircase. "Let your mother take care of Coffie."

The housekeeper dabbed her eyes quickly with a corner of her apron, looking anxiously over her shoulder as the front door slammed. Hysteria choked the distraught mother. She could hardly speak as she banged on her neighbor's door.

The emergency room doctors took the small figure from the mother's frantic arms. Deft fingers began to examine.

"Go, Charlie, get Mr. Bagley no matter where he is in town.

Like the wind, Charlie. Hurry!" Caroline begged, as she paced the floor, wringing her hands. Within an hour, Litch sat beside his wife and squeezed her hand.

"What happened?" he whispered.

"We don't know. They were playing in the yard. One minute he was fine and the next..."

Her shoulders slumped. Sobs tightened her throat.

"Come here," Litch said, drawing her close. Both shook, as his own sobs mingled with hers.

Another agonizing hour dragged by. Litch took his handkerchief and caught another tear. Finally, the examination room doors burst open. Doctor Frawley walked toward the worried parents. They got up slowly, their hands clasped, each hoping to diffuse strength to the other. Both strained to hear good news but feared the worst. Their faces, masks of distress.

"Caroline, Litch, Coffie is stabilized, but we do not know what his problem is. We have him in isolation at the moment, but if he does not respond to our treatments in the next few days... Well, our suggestion is to take him to the Children's Hospital of Philadelphia. They have the best doctors for childhood diseases. If I would venture a guess, it may be a bacterial malady."

Caroline and Litch looked at each other in disbelief. How could their lives go awry again in such a short time of their healing in their relationship?

"He's alive, Litch, for that we can be thankful."

Litch's breathing was short-paced.

"I need to sit down."

"Why don't you two go into the chapel where it is quiet and talk this predicament over, but I hope you take the little fellow to Philadelphia where he can get the best care."

Chapter 27
COFFIE FROM AFAR

The trip to Philadelphia was one of hope, and yet one of sadness. How could they be away from the child who had brought them together...again? For surely, they would be tested in their relationship, their marriage, their own character.

Before they left, Dr. Frawley counseled the very nervous mother and father, who sat holding hands before him.

"Listen, my friends, Coffie will be a private patient, under the care of the best doctors. They are progressive in knowledge of therapeutics and they will discover Coffie's issues. I have no doubt. I wish you well..." His voice trailed, thinking that he would hear a barrage of questions. He got none.

The hospital was small with only thirty-five beds. The Bagleys were thankful they were able to get one for their son. The hospital had been established by a Philadelphia physician, Doctor Francis West Lewis. After an oceanic trip to Great Ormond Street Hospital in London, Lewis enlisted two colleagues to found the first children's hospital in America. Needless to say, Coffie's parents' confidence grew the more they talked to the doctors and the professionally trained nurses. They had made the right decision.

"Elijah, are you awake?" Sarah whispered their first night alone after little Coffie's trip to Philadelphia.

"How can I sleep, thinking about that child all alone in that hospital. Oh, I know he's in the right place with all the doctors and nurses, but they are not his parents. Sarah, don't tell me that

Litch and Caroline can't stay there with him for the duration. I know Litch has to work and Caroline has to care for Jacob."

"That's not what I was going to say."

"Oh?"

"I was going to say that they could have lost him and they didn't. Those two have had enough to deal with. I just hate they have another issue to face. My gosh, Coffie isn't even three."

"I know, sweetheart. If they had lost Coffie, we'd be saying that at least we had Will for almost nineteen years."

"Can you think of anything worse than losing a child?" Sarah asked.

"No, except maybe losing you."

She smiled in the dark.

"Sarah, we need to stay close to our daughter and Litch. We don't want this trauma to come between them."

"How would it?"

"I don't know. I really have no idea. I just know they are hurting."

"I know," she murmured.

A tear trickled down her cheek. Elijah could see it in the moonlight.

"Come here, my love." He held out his hand to her. She rolled over and put her head on his chest.

"Do you think they've even closed their eyes tonight?" Sarah asked.

The following weeks the bruised parents struggled just to make it through each day, plagued by Coffie's absence in their home. Day in, day out, Mrs. Rumley would tut-tut and mutter, "Poor Jacob." She did her best to relieve the pressure on the child, but he needed his mother and father.

Sitting in the backyard in early spring, Caroline noticed the burst of life in all their shrubs and perennials. Little Coffie had been such life to them, the culmination of their love. With him still in Philadelphia, she'd watched her marriage turn abysmal.

Chapter 27

Only Jacob gave her sanity.

Business appeared to save Litch, yet one evening Caroline realized that business might be his damnation. With only one look, she knew he was drunk. Coldness chilled her body, as she remembered his vow to never touch another drop. He tried to hide it, but she could see through his every effort.

"All right, so I had a drink at my club, Caroline. My client and I were celebrating a deal we made just this afternoon. You know I have to entertain my customers at times. Don't look at me that way. I don't like it," he snarled, his head cocked to one side.

"You're drunk, Litch. Sleep it off on the sofa."

She walked from the room, cutting her eyes at him as she pushed by him to go upstairs. A scrape of a chair, a slammed door, then the downstairs became silent.

Chapter 28
A BAD CHOICE

Caroline's eyelids fluttered, as she tried to hold back the tears. Too much had happened and yet not enough to keep their marriage intact. Something had to give. Jacob was asleep when she heard Litch stumble up the front steps and through the door.

From the parlor, she watched him fumble with his coat, only to miss the hook on the coat stand. He uttered profanities, as he groped for it. Rearing up, he caught sight of her and felt foolish as he once more struggled to hang up the coat.

"Do you care for something to eat?" she spoke, her voice subdued.

"Noo," he slurred, reaching for the doorframe for balance.

"We need to talk, Litch," she said, still standing by the mantle. He swayed toward a chair, mumbling as he caught the back to steady himself. He plopped down.

"What, my dear wife, do you have to say?"

"Why are you doing this? We miraculously found a way to help Coffie and you are acting as if he's never coming back. Is that what you think? Talk to me."

He looked at her through blurry eyes.

"I don't know you anymore, Litch," she said. Her eyes closed momentarily.

"Well, do you want to know what I know?"

She looked puzzled.

"You have your son, yours and Hap's. My son could die. Am I being punished for my sins?"

Her eyes widened.

Chapter 28

"Hap? Oh my God, Litch, you're obsessed with that man. When are you going to let the past go and forget him?" She hesitated. "I have."

She walked over to stand before him. She bent forward.

"Litch, I love you, but I do not love the besotted man in front of me. The best thing you've done since Coffie left was to sleep downstairs. At least you've got enough decency to hide this disgust from our other son."

She walked back to the mantle but wheeled around toward him. "Yes, I said our son." She quieted momentarily. "Have you looked at yourself in the mirror of late?"

"What do you mean?"

He cocked his head.

"Just do it, Litch. You'll see what I mean."

She left the room.

Litch continued to frequent his city club for longer hours after work. Many nights he ate dinner there, or so he said. Caroline's words had haunted him. He knew his life was out of control and only a miracle could change this self-destructive spiral.

Caroline never questioned him anymore. Fight your own demons, her looks seemed to say, but at times her eyes showed fear. He couldn't stand the thought that she was afraid of him and maybe afraid for her son, Hap's son. *God, we'd come so far.* Litch shuddered. He was losing this battle. He had become a disgusting drunk.

One evening, Litch sat slumped in the bar of his club. He had consumed way too much brandy. He knew it, but he was determined to make his way home. With great effort, he staggered to the front door.

"May I call the club driver, sir?" the doorman asked. "He can bring the carriage around to take you home, or you know we have rooms."

"Listen," Litch spoke to the young man, poking him in the

shoulder. "I have yet to spend a night at this club, and I don't intend to start now."

His hooded eyes focused as best he could on the fellow's concerned face.

"I understand, sir. Then, why not take the club carriage? We can tie your horse to the back."

He gestured toward the carriage.

"No, and wipe that stupid frown off your face."

Swinging around, he attempted the steps with a little dignity, but missed one.

The doorman caught him.

"Let go of me," Litch growled, shoving him away.

The man shook his head as he watched Litch's drunken gait to his waiting horse. The stirrups eluded him, but after several failed attempts, he mounted and tipped his hat. The horse and rider faded into the darkness.

The air was damp and chilled for early spring. Little light paved the way, as the wind moved the claw-like branches overhead, cutting the silence with scratching sounds. The clippety-clop of Litch's horse resounded a cadence into the night. Not far, he spied a woman standing on the side of the road under one of the remaining streetlights. He reined his mount as she motioned for him to stop.

Never before would he have given a tart the time of day, but Litch Bagley was no longer a man in the light.

"Mister, it's such a chilly night. Let's go find a nice comfortable place to take the chill off. What do ya say? A big handsome man like you needs a lady to keep him warm."

Litch prodded his horse closer as he leaned down and crossed his arms over the horn of his saddle. He found himself leering at this young woman, succumbing to her suggestion. She could not have been over twenty, her youth struggling with her life style. Under the glow of the lantern, she opened her wrap to show off her figure and allow the gentleman to sense forthcoming rewards.

Suddenly, his expression froze. His drunken haze seemed lifted.

Chapter 28

My God, what am I doing?

Instantly, he jerked upward and spanked the horse's flank with his crop. The animal sprang to the command, leaving the young woman hollering scathing names and words that Litch hoped he would never hear again.

Caroline, I'm so sorry. Please, God, just let me get to her. Please...

Caroline lay on the couch in their bedroom, hoping against hope that Litch would arrive soon and they could talk quietly. Decent conversations didn't seem to exist anymore. She had been thinking about a trip to the coast where they'd first met on vacation years ago. Little Coffie's disease had strangled both of them. Maybe a spring vacation would be a momentary diversion where they could collect themselves and start building a marriage again for themselves and a family for both boys. Maybe he would agree to a spring trip to the Outer Banks. That time had been happy for both of them. Maybe they'd sail the sharpies from the mainland to the bank island. Maybe they could walk and ride horses on the dunes, and be carefree in the balmy air. Maybe, just maybe...

The loud knocking on the front door jarred her from light slumber. *What on earth!* she thought. Clutching her robe, she stumbled out of their room to the top of the stairs. The light from the oil lamp below cast a shadowy glow. Cautiously she took a step or two.

"Who is it?" she called out, stopping on the lower landing.

"Mrs. Bagley, it's Officer McCoy from the downtown station. I come concerning Mister Bagley."

Caroline blanched as she feverishly jabbed the key in the rim lock keyhole. The door swung open.

Chapter 29
DIFFICULT NEWS

Officer McCoy hated this part of his job. Protecting and defending the citizens? He loved. Informing them about tragedy? He'd rather be digging a ditch. Who wouldn't? He supposed it was just his turn, and besides, he was the investigating officer.

McCoy shifted his weight from one foot to the other. He could hear Caroline Bagley creeping down the stairs, then struggling with the rim lock key. The door creaked open; her face pasted with fear.

McCoy cleared his throat. "Mrs. Bagley, your husband is in the hospital. I'm afraid he's been in an accident."

"My God, is he alive?" she asked, her hand flew to her chest.

"Yes, ma'am," he said, nodding slightly.

"What happened?" she asked, steadying herself on the door frame.

"I can't say," he said, as he fidgeted with his hat.

He squirmed knowing her two questions would bind them forever. She would remember him as the informer of tragedy.

"Would you like for me to drive you to the hospital?"

"Please, oh please," she said. "My boy's asleep. Let me get my neighbor. Just give me a minute." Grabbing a shawl from the hall closet, she ran next door, banging on the door, then pleading her case. The desperate mother returned with a bustling Mrs. Boone in tow.

Breathless, the woman mopped her brow and advised, "Don't you worry one snippet about Jacob, Dearie. You go right ahead with the kind gentlemen. Everything will be just fine, I'm sure."

Chapter 29

Standing on the stoop, she shook her head and muttered, as her friend climbed into the carriage to race off into the night.

"Lord, child, what else can happen to you?"

Litch lay unconscious, his wife by his side, talking to him as if he were awake and alert. She rambled about plans for a vacation, a return to the Baker's Hotel at Core Banks, feeling the breezes blowing off the Atlantic and showing their son the beauty of a sand dollar.

"Wake up, Litch. We still have so much to do. We'll always have the scars, but the good memories will overshadow them. I promise. Wake up, Litch. Please wake up, my darling."

For forty-eight hours, he lay in shock from the fall. Their friends and family could not understand how the accident had happened.

"Mister Bagley's one of the best horsemen in this town. Sounds like it just must have been a freak accident. Such a waste," folks would say.

Caroline had heard it all, but she knew too much brandy had caused this accident. So did Officer McCoy.

His patrol had discovered the stallion grazing in a nearby park before midnight. The crop marks showed somebody had been anxious to get home, but obviously didn't make it. In minutes, they discovered the body a few blocks away in a ditch. McCoy smelled the booze and saw vomit spewed on the ground.

"You got your due, fellow, beating that horse one too many times," he mumbled as he stood over Litch.

The victim stirred.

"Stay still, sir. The ambulance is on its way."

The rattle in the chest and the bloodied head pretty much told the story: this man might not survive. "Stupid," McCoy muttered under his breath, putting his handkerchief over his nose.

The officer squatted and studied the battered torso as best he could. He envisioned the big stallion throwing its rider, then rearing above him. One swift stomp probably immobilized the man, crushing his chest. Another buck and a shod hoof must have clipped his head. McCoy knew no personal facts, but the wounded human and horseflesh reflected a raging war.

Litch opened his eyes on the second day after his accident.
"Oh, my darling," Caroline whispered.
"I—c," he choked.
"Shhhh, my love. There will be time for talking later," she murmured lifting his hand to her lips. Slight hand squeezes expressed love, transcending all past hurts and anger. Their lives now existed moment by moment.
"Mrs. Bagley, please, we need to check his vitals," the attending nurse said, trying her best to pry the desperate wife from her husband's side.
"Get some air, ma'am."
Caroline supposed she did need a break. Exhaustion weighed heavy on her shoulders, but seeing two surgeons and Doctor Frawley conferring at the end of the hall aroused hidden energy. She walked rapidly toward them, as they turned from their consultation, each face troubled. She felt faint.
"What is it?" she said, rushing into their path. "I have a right to know what's going on."
The head surgeon stepped back. "Frawley?"
Doctor Frawley smiled feebly. He took her aside and spoke quietly.
"He's stabilized somewhat, but the surgeons need to repair the abdominal damage. They don't know what they'll find, but Litch has the best doctors in Raleigh caring for him." He frowned momentarily. "His head injury worries them. They're thinking they need to open that wound and relieve any fluid pressure. They'll take one step at a time."
"Will he live?"
He patted her hand.
"We have no idea. Be strong, Caroline. He needs you."
The man turned and nodded to the doctors. They nodded back.

Chapter 29

"Surgery's tomorrow morning," he told her.

Caroline never left her husband's side, sitting by the bed, holding his hand, with her head lying on the crook of his arm. He never moved. Fortunately, the Cromwells could drop everything and come to the aid of their daughter. Both whispered around Jacob.

"Elijah, I can't believe all the tragedy befalling our daughter. And in just one year," fretted Sarah.

"I know, my dear. It's awful. Losing her grandfather, little Coffie's illness, and now maybe losing her husband," Elijah said. "She's showing such strength. God, I'm just so proud of her."

Not once did either see her falter in her belief in Litch's survival.

Dawn arrived with the gurney clinking down the hallway, startling Caroline from her troubled slumber. The orderlies pushed open the door and smiled at the woman staring helplessly at them. They glided across the floor, and in one swift move slid the battered man from bed to gurney. The motion roused the patient. He faintly smiled at his wife and mouthed indiscernible words, as she leaned over to kiss his parched lips.

Looking deep into his eyes, she murmured, "I love you, Litch. I'll see you in the 'morrow, my dearest," she whispered as they pushed him away from her through the doors of the operating room.

Chapter 30
GOOD-BYE AND HELLO

*D*ressed in her widow's weeds, Caroline smiled at the Bagleys. The three stood in her living room, each fidgety, each aware of her next words.

"I've got to close the house. It's just too painful."

Litch's mother spoke first, her voice soft and caring. "We understand, but it just compounds our sadness."

For months, they'd helped their daughter-in-law with their son's personal effects. What better way for them to deal with Litch's death than to care for their son's family?

"I cannot tell you how much I appreciate everything you two have done. I just could not have gotten his affairs in order if you had not—"

Her voice broke. She could speak no further, as they gathered her close. Looking from one to the other, she glimpsed facial expressions, the color of eyes, the shape of a nose. Litch was wrapped up in both of them.

Smiling, she squeezed their hands.

"Come sit. I have something else to tell you."

The settee held all three.

"I've decided to go back home, to Shiloh."

Silence.

"We figured at some point you would," Mister Bagley said, his face mirroring his pain.

"Your grandsons and I will visit often. I promise," she assured, dabbing her eyes with her black handkerchief.

She stood and walked toward the dining room.

"I want to give you a gift."

Chapter 30

She pointed to the heavy ornate frame hanging over the hunt board.

"Please, help me."

She motioned to Jacob, Sr.

"But—" Mrs. Bagley said.

"Listen. That man is painted on my heart forever," she declared.

"We don't know what to say," Mister Bagley said. "You know we love it."

"Then, it's yours."

Having said their goodbyes to Jacob, the Bagleys moved slowly down the street in a loaded carriage, waving to their son's wife. No sooner had she closed the door, the grieving widow leaned back for support and slowly slid to the floor, agony frozen on her face, silent sobs caught in her throat. Fortunately for her, Mrs. Rumley was doing a good job entertaining her son upstairs. Two distraught people in the household would have been way, way too much. Somehow, she gathered her wits, knowing her son's voice would soon ring out from above.

The letter from Philadelphia shook in her hands. Their son was being released from the Children's Hospital. Coffie's doctors were totally satisfied with his recovery, as selected therapeutics had worked. The child was a normal little boy again.

The tears flowed. *Litch, oh Litch, why could you not have been more patient? Our son is coming home.*

"Mommie, oh Mommie," Coffie squealed as he raced into her arms. "You have to meet Nurse Anderson. She's my new best friend. I ask her to marry me, but I have to grow up first she says."

Nurse Anderson stood a few steps back with her hand over her mouth, hiding the smile that told Caroline that her son had been in the best hands that she ever could have hoped for. Yes, her son was back to normal.

Leaving Raleigh proved more complicated than Caroline

imagined. Even though Jacob, Sr., paved the way, she still had to deal with lawyers and quickly discovered that Litch's business dealings were more widespread than she knew.

Telling Coffie about his father was no easy task, but Jacob was such a help. Both boys bonded even more so with the absence of their father.

Months passed. Jacob and Coffie grew. Caroline waited.

Samuel Dameron looked up from a neat pile of legal documents on his desk.

"Come sit, Mrs. Bagley."

The lawyer jumped from his chair to assist her. Pomade slicked hair and a pencil thin mustache matured his boyish face. Dameron stood no taller than Caroline's shoulder. She'd only met him once before and felt funny looking down at this man, who stood tall in the courts.

"Mrs. Bagley, as far as we can tell, you and your sons will leave Raleigh very comfortable. Your husband invested wisely. In fact, you'll have negligible expenditures. He made good choices."

Not always, Caroline thought.

"Thank you, Mr. Dameron. Your help has been incredible. Litch's, too," she whispered. "We'd never even discussed a will before."

"Some men do not want to bother their wives with such matters," he sighed. "But we lawyers find shared information is a good deed."

"I do feel fortunate."

"I know Jacob, Sr.'s, thoughts on Litch's holdings, but I must have your word and signature. I'd sell the houses now, but hold the land until the demand arises. Of course, it's your decision one hundred percent."

"Jacob, Sr.'s, wishes are mine. Move forward with them, Mr. Dameron."

"Done," he spoke crisply, spreading the bevy of legalities before her. She dipped the quill and inked the papers quickly. He

Chapter 30

paused looking down at his notes.

"Did I gather from Mister Bagley that you may have a buyer for your house?"

He peered up at her over his spectacles.

"Hopefully," she sighed, standing to extend her hand.

He stood reaching toward her and smiled. "Let me know if I can be of further service."

She smiled back.

Caroline left the lawyer's office and returned home to wait for her appointment. She sat on the settee in the living room, drumming her fingers on its cushy rolled arm.

Lord, please let this family love this house. I can let go easier if they do.

The door knocker clanked loudly. Her head jerked up. On the second round of clanks, she got up and walked swiftly toward the door. She breathed deeply as it swung open, only to see a family on the stoop smiling up at the lady of the house, and in that instant Caroline knew that she was going home.

The excitement of new life at Cromwell Hall invigorated her parents. After all, they were the only occupants of the rambling old mansion. For three weeks, Caroline and the boys basked in the attention of the Cromwells, but one morning at the breakfast table, they received a jolt.

"Coffie's house? But why?" Sarah asked, the hurt etched on her face.

"Mother, Jacob and little Coffie need to be close to other children. Jacob will be six-years-old his next birthday, if you can believe it. He needs playmates, and so will Coffie the older he gets. And, who better than me and the boys to air and clean out that old house on the Green? And Jacksie's yard? I would love to resurrect it. Remember that old adage she used to quote: *He who plants a garden walks hand and hand with God.* Well, your daughter needs to walk with God and heal. Forgive me?"

Elijah laughed. "Well, you're not going to China. You'd cook your old folks a pot of Brunswick stew now and then, wouldn't you?"

"Of course, " she spoke affectionately.

"My little girl, what you have endured in your short lifetime..."

Chapter 31
WILLIE'S MEN FOLK

Willie felt the earth move. She had a visitor. Elijah Cromwell's stallion kicked up a trail of dust as he came into view.

"Uh-oh, that man only comes when he's got something on his mind or has a heavy heart. I wonder which it is," she said to herself as she stood in her doorway.

It was early morning.

Willie walked out on her porch and held her hand up to shade her eyes.

The Captain sat on his horse at the rail, not moving a muscle, a sadness enveloping him, shoulders slumped, mouth turned down.

"Litch's dead," he called out.

"Mister Litch? Oh, no, Elijah, no. Come sit a spell," she beckoned her old friend.

"It's been a while, but I feel like it was yesterday. I'm sorry I haven't stopped by sooner, but we were in Ral—"

"Elijah, you don't have to apologize to me. That's what friends are for. You come when you can and I appreciate that."

They walked into her cottage.

"Sit right there and talk when you want."

Willie offered him the rocker opposite hers by the fireplace. They rocked for the longest time, eyes closed, no words uttered. The reliable creaks from the chairs popped continuously. Suddenly, Elijah stopped and looked directly at his friend as she continued to rock, shut-eyed.

"What are you thinking, Elijah?" she spoke, never missing a creak.

"I was wondering about us."

That statement stopped her rocking and opened her eyes. He hadn't said anything personal to her since she told him Fate Edmundson was their son. She opened her mouth to speak.

"Now, you just hold on a minute."

He leaned forward, shaking his finger at her.

"Don't say anything; just you listen. Suppose, just suppose, you had told me all those years ago about Fate. How do you think that would have changed our lives? I'm just supposing, mind you."

"Elijah, nothing would have been different. You would have gone on and married your Sarah and had your life just as you have had. You just would have known longer."

"I don't know. Fate and Will were best friends, just like you and me. I don't know how, but I think things might have been different."

"Elijah, go on. Why are you dragging this up? I don't want to hear that from you. What's the use? Now, we're just good, old friends."

"I just thought you might like to know that before we die."

"Hmph," Willie grunted, closed her eyes, and rocked. "Hush your fuss. We're already disgraceful."

A faint smile crossed her lips.

"Caroline's moved back," he said. This news stopped her rocking again. "She's decided to spruce up Coffie and Jacksie's house and live there."

"Captain, you're telling me she's moving to Mister King's house?"

"I am. She claims she's concerned about the boys needing playmates, but I think she's so distressed about losing Litch that somehow Shiloh has too many painful memories right now. I suppose she feels Coffie's house is a haven from all her troubles, but the child can't run from life."

Chapter 31

"Uh-oh. She ain't the only one," Willie mumbled.

"What'd you say, woman? You know my hearing isn't as sharp as it used to be. Speak louder," he said, disgruntled.

"Of course. I-I have to tell you something, Elijah, that I have kept a secret, because he asked me to."

"You are a woman of secrets. Well, what is it? For gosh sakes, spill it. I feel like the dentist trying to pull eye teeth."

"Calm down and just listen. Hap and Miss Pamela are no longer married."

"Hap is divorced?"

She nodded.

"And, Caroline's a widow—," his voice trailed. "Oh, my gosh..."

"Well, we can't do nothing, but just let 'em be. Captain, you hear me?" Sternness crept into her voice. "We all, you and Miss Sarah and me, have just got to let those two suffering souls be."

Willie could not believe she felt the earth move a second time in one morning. Another visitor? She spied Hap from her doorway and little Rollie nestled in his midsection, holding onto the saddle horn.

"Bless me," she murmured, watching them make their way to her.

Willie looked through her screen door at Hap.

"Of course, I will," she called out, smiling at him.

"You'll what? I-ha-," he stuttered, jumping down from his mount, pulling Rollie down with him. He awkwardly stood on her stoop.

"Now, don't you know I know why you came down Station House Road to see me?" she chortled and winked. "Rollie, come from behind your daddy, so I can see how grown up you are."

Rollie peeped from around the tall, strapping man, holding onto his daddy's pant leg with a vise grip.

"Come here, doll. I just might have something sweet in my house, if the doctor will let you have a taste."

She eyed her son.

"Oh, please, Daddy, please?"

Losing his shyness, he poked out his hand to the extended one. It was love at first sight.

After much conversation, Willie felt the even breathing of a sleeping child, as she rocked him.

"Tell me all about it, son," she whispered. His words were few, but her reaction was swift.

"That woman did what?" she hissed in disgust.

A vessel popped out on her forehead as she gritted her teeth, making her rock the little fellow in her arms harder as Hap unloaded his heart. Sitting across from her in what had become Elijah's chair, he held his head and wept softly, hoping not to wake the child.

"She's awful! What kind of mother wou—?"

Catching herself, Willie realized that she had done the same. She had given her own child away, too.

Rollie woke up.

"Willie?" Rollie's eyes were slits. "Where's my Daddy? I want to go home."

Rubbing his eyes dry with his coat sleeve, Hap scooped up his child from Willie's arms.

"Willie, if you—?"

His face asked the question.

"You think I'm gonna leave you high and dry, Hap?" Willie quizzed him, as she cocked her head up at her tall son, allowing the gleam to come into her eye. "I'll be at your house by sunrise to take care of your child. I took care of you, and I can take care of Rollie. Now, go get a good night's sleep. Everything's worked out."

One more time, Willie Pridgen rescued Hap Tyson.

Chapter 32
REVIVAL

Caroline blew a lock of hair off her forehead.

"God help us." She looked at Maggie and George. "I hope we don't die."

All three had taken a breather from reviving the charm of the King house. They'd dusted, scrubbed, and polished for two weeks.

It was the autumn after Litch's death.

"Oh my, look here in this drawer," Maggie said, pointing at the secretary in the parlor. "It's Miss Jacksie's wedding book. I ain't seen one of these forever. Miss Caroline, can we open it?"

"Of course, you may."

Maggie's eyes glimmered as she scanned the pages.

"Look here. It shows all her presents and who gave them. There're names here I haven't heard for years. George, here's Mr. Calhoun's. You know the man that helped your daddy get that little house your family lived in for years. Mer-cee."

Caroline smiled, as they stood by the towering secretary, but knew she could not share everything with Maggie and George. One night she'd sat on the floor by an old trunk in Coffie's bedroom, her hand caressing the worn leather. Raising the top, she felt she had unleashed her grandfather's spirit. She felt warm. Reaching in, she touched the old suede book of Poe, its cover now more brown than the original red. A bundle of letters lay under the book. Collapsing on the couch, she began to read and weep.

My dearest Jacksie,

The guys have teased me unmercifully as I pine to see you, my little darling. How I long to glimpse the sparkle in your eye, to feel the touch of your hand, to hear the whisper of your voice. They just do not understand the matters of the heart. All they want to know is the time of the next fraternity party. Silly boys. Hopefully, one day they will know the catch in one's throat and the exchange of words with a most enchanting woman. I know I have...

Eagerly, I place an X on the days of the calendar as I anxiously await our vacation. No matter the inches of snow, I will come. Jacksie Thrash, this last year of law school will not end fast enough. Plan on a special gift from me at Christmas time. I warn you now that this man will not take "no" for an answer. I tell you this so you will know my pain as I count the days until I see you again. I am one miserable man.

My regards to your parents and your family.

Your faithful servant,
Coffie

Chapter 33

SUNDAY SURPRISE

It was a Sunday. Hap had carried Rollie to church and promised lunch at Mrs. Deberry's on the Town Common. Rollie loved the tables and linen napkins laid at every place in the tearoom, and nobody in all of Edgecombe County made biscuits like Mrs. Deberry. They made his eyes bulge.

Father and son sat in the front room with a good view of the Town Common, quickly being disguised by the falling leaves of fiery red, brilliant orange, and blinding yellow. The only green left was in the towering water oaks, a few cedars, and a stray pine.

Hap gazed out onto the Commons, thinking of the last time he'd walked this bowling green with Willie. What a different direction his life had turned since that day. Here he was again, a returning son to Tarboro, hoping to serve the people who had chased him away. The young doctor's thoughts were interrupted as he noticed the handsome carriage in front of the old King house. Maybe a new family had bought it and would restore it to its glory days, he wondered.

After lunch, father and son bounded down the steps of Mrs. Deberry's. Naturally, Rollie insisted on a roll in the thick layer of leaves, Sunday suit and all. Both felt carefree as they cut through the Commons to the other side.

The handsome carriage was missing from the front of the King house, as they trudged up the walkway, kicking remnants of leaves and debris. As they passed the old barrister's home, Hap spied the front door slightly ajar. He stopped abruptly. *That's strange*, he thought. Slowly, he walked up the steps and touched the knocker, speaking softly at first, then louder.

"Hello. Hello! Anybody home?"

At that instant, Jacob Bagley opened the door wider.

"Who are you, mister?" he asked, smiling through a pronounced crooked grin. "My name's Jacob and I'm five," he said, proudly holding up five fingers.

Hap's mouth fell open, for the man stared at a replica of his youth. The hair was cropped, but the waves were there, and that smile. Backing down the steps, the man could only gape.

"Oh, who's that?" Jacob asked. "That looks like fun," the young tyke said as he raced down the steps to join Hap's son.

Totally unaware, Caroline busily cleared luncheon dishes from the table, her first preparation for her parents since her decision to leave Shiloh. Jacob. She caught her breath and ran to the opened front door, little Coffie in tow.

"Jacob Bagley, how man—"

She never finished her question. A bewildered and confused face turned toward her.

"Oh," she managed to say. Her hand flew to her throat. Her eyes darted to the boys, tumbling in the leaves.

"Jacob, why don't you invite your new friend inside?" she suggested, finding her tongue.

Checking the sidewalk, she asked, "Where's Pamela?"

The baffled young man could only shake his head. Caroline shrugged and turned to let him into her new home. She had known their meeting was inevitable, but today was a total surprise.

"Please," she gestured to him to sit in the parlor. As all three boys pushed past, she bent to speak to Jacob. "Jacob, why don't you take this handsome little man into the backyard and teach him how to play croquet? Let Coffie help. We'll watch you from time to time, all right, dear?"

Squealing, the three boys scampered through the house and out the backdoor into Jacksie's wonderland backyard. Catching the screen door, Caroline paused, shutting her eyes tightly for a moment, and turned to the man she'd left behind years ago.

Chapter 33

She found him staring up at the portrait of Jacksie Thrash King.

"She's beautiful and so alive in that portrait. The artist is very good," he said.

His arm rested lightly on the mantle, but soon his hand went up to cover his eyes.

"Where's Litch? Upstairs? In Raleigh?"

He turned to catch a pained expression covering her face, and, then, the pent-up emotion, the stress of her loss, the tears of bravery, gushed forth. She began to sob. Her head dropped down. Her shoulders quivered, and the sounds of deep anguish came up from the depths. She caught hold of the back of the couch.

"My God, Caroline, what's happened? What—come. Let me help you."

He rushed to her side.

"What in God's name is wrong?" His voice raised a decibel, anger growing with each word. "Where's Litch? Did he hurt you? Tell me he didn't hurt you."

She shook her head and waved her hand.

"Litch is dead," she croaked.

"Dead?"

He froze. Grabbing her arm, he led her around the couch and sat her down. Pushing his handkerchief into her hand, he sat beside her, as once more her fragrances filled his nostrils. The burning question in his heart about her son would have to wait.

"I'm so sorry," she said, taking deep gulps of air. "I haven't broken down like that. Not once. I guess I've held it all in for the boys' sakes. They are still young enough to know, but not to know the depth of losing a father."

Jacob interrupted the moment.

"Momma, Momma," Jacob hollered but stopped short as he flew through the parlor door. "Oh, you're crying again. Sir, my grandmother says tears help us when we're sad."

"Jacob, this gentleman is an old friend, Doctor Tyson."

"How do you do, Jacob? And, by the way, I agree with your grandmother about tears."

"Well, Momma, come see Rollie hit the ball with the mallet and Coffie is giving him instructions. Both of them will make you laugh."

Hap watched as Caroline jumped from the settee. Her hand quickly smoothed her hair, a nervous feminine gesture, he thought, and he glimpsed a slight flush on her face as she followed her son out the backdoor, drying her eyes with his handkerchief.

"Doctor Tyson, come see your son," she called over her shoulder.

"There, Doctor Tyson," Jacob said, pointing to the little fellow, who wasn't much taller than the mallet.

They all marveled as Rollie raked the ball, making up his own game and rules as he went, totally ignoring Coffie's help.

"Rollie says your name is Rollie, too, sir. If someone calls out, how do you know which Rollie they want?" Jacob demanded with the demeanor of one trying to solve a serious problem.

Hap laughed.

"Well, son, just call me Hap if you like. Most of my good friends do. I hope you will be that special."

"Momma, can I? I know you want me to call grownups Mister or Mrs., but, Momma, he wants me to call him Hap. Please. Please," he pleaded as he grabbed her around her waist.

"All right, darling. If Doctor Tyson wants you to call him Hap, then Hap it is."

"I do." His voice dropped. "I want Jacob's mother to call me Hap as well."

His look made her uncomfortable.

Chapter 34
CAPITULATION

Elijah looked curiously at his wife. "What are you thinking?" He watched her pull her gloves on and adjust her day hat in the mirror. They had been invited to lunch with Caroline and the boys.

"Sarah?"

"What?"

She swung around to look at her husband, her eyebrows arched.

"Never mind," he sighed, resignation on his face.

He knew they would have a lively conversation on their way to town. Just as Willie suspected, he had told Sarah about the breakup of the young doctor's family. Elijah looked at his wife, as he clicked the reins over the horse's flank.

"Okay, let's get this out in the open while we have a chance. I'll go ahead and tell you now that Willie thinks we should just let those two suffering souls be. Let them discover and work out anything that may or may not exist for their future. I think she's right. It's none of our business."

"Well, I have a right to my opinion, just as you and Willie," Sarah retorted, irritated that Willie had known this bit of information before she did. "It always seems that I am the last one to know anything in this family. Willie this and Willie that! Honestly. It just gets tiresome, Captain."

Sarah had tolerated Elijah's relationship with his old friend. She recognized the history they had, but still she sensed an unusual loyalty Willie felt for Shiloh and for her husband. Sarah just could not put her finger on what this strong tie was. One day, she knew she would know. Was she not Coffield King's daughter?

"Elijah, I've made up my mind."

The Captain said nothing. They rode in silence, but not for long.

"Are you trying to tell me you don't think our daughter should know about Hap and his former wife? And right now?" she demanded.

Elijah looked askance at the roadside, his mouth closed tightly.

"You surprise me," she said.

The Captain's mind had drifted from his daughter. His own secrets from this very woman invaded his thoughts. He hated it. He was treading on dangerous water.

"Look, Elijah, Coeffield and Jacksie King did not birth a fool. Everybody deserves the truth. We may be hurrying it along just a bit for the good doctor."

Elijah turned and stared at his wife as they moved up Main Street toward the Town Common. Suddenly, the truth barged in.

"Whoa!" He stopped the buggy. "Sarah, you want those two to be together, don't you?" he asked, taking her arm. "Well, glory be, your heart has softened, Sarah King Cromwell. It's about time."

She remained stoic.

"Look at me, wife, you want our daughter to marry the good doctor after the proper mourning time. Confound it, Sarah! Confess it. I know you."

He had already begun to grin and nudge her. He whistled for the horse to move on down the street, eventually turning at the Town Common toward the King house. Sarah finally spoke.

"Well, what if I do? Hap sacrificed a great deal when he cared for Coffie. He could have told us to jump off the Tar River bridge, but he didn't. We saw a different person," her voice dropped to a whisper, "not the scamp of his youth. He's totally unlike that character... Elijah, we cannot change history. We need to face the hard cold facts. Will's dead. Her grandfather's dead. Litch is

Chapter 34

dead." She raised her voice. "We need life in this family again, and frankly, I think Hap Ty—Doctor Tyson can do just that. Close your mouth, husband. You look ridiculous," she scolded briefly, then allowed the edges of her own mouth to slightly curl, her head held high.

"Stop it, Elijah. Your teasing is intolerable. Quit staring," she demanded through a grimace, wresting her arm from his grip.

As the carriage rolled to a stop in front of the King house, Elijah spontaneously reached over and kissed his wife in broad daylight.

"Captain, you are disgraceful!"

But Sarah Cromwell loved her husband more at that moment than she ever had.

Husband and wife climbed the steps of the King house, now their daughter's home. Sarah's arm stopped him from lifting the knocker. Both turned toward the spit of green laced with the towering trees and the Civil War marker, a reminder of lost sons of Edgecombe.

"I love that green. It's so beautiful, isn't it?"

"Oh yes, my dear," he said, a twinkle in his eye.

"I mean the green, you silly goose."

"Yes, and that, too," he said, still grinning at her.

She turned back to the Town Common. "I'm amazed at all the history that lies in that piece of earth. We're riding on our ancestors' coattails, aren't we?"

He continued to smile.

"It's what our history's all about. Right?"

"Anything you say," he said, continuing to grin.

The front door swung open before they could knock.

"You look ravishing, young lady," her father said, wrinkling his nose. "From the aromas of your house, you and Mrs. Fornes have fixed another gourmet luncheon for your folks. We're going to have to walk more at Shiloh to trim these waistlines."

Elijah Cromwell smiled as he greeted his only child.

"Come in, both of you," she coaxed, quickly hugging them.

Jacob pushed his way between his two favorite ladies, practically upending them. Little Coffie clung to his grandfather's legs.

"You little monkey, let your grandpa see how much you've grown since you've been away at camp."

"I have not. I've been to the hos-pi-tull. How do you say it, Mommie?"

"Hospital, darling boy."

"Yeah."

"And you are as good as new, too." The Captain poked him in his ribs, bringing a giggle that was music to all their ears.

Next, the Captain grabbed Jacob and swung him up on his shoulder.

"I think you've gained five pounds since I last saw you." Jacob's laughter filled the room.

Caroline walked ahead to the breakfast room, out of earshot.

"I have a new friend, Grandpa. Doctor Tyson's son. His name's Rollie, too, but Doctor Tyson told me I could call him Hap."

"He's my friend, too, Jacob," little Coffie barged into the conversation.

Elijah lowered his grandson to the floor. A knowing glance passed between the Cromwells, as they walked to the back of the house.

The view of Jacksie's backyard took their breath.

"Well, George has cleared every leaf," Elijah noted.

"And trimmed all the shrubs," Caroline added, threading her arm in his.

"The beds are perfect for their winter's nap," Sarah said.

"The boys and I love watching the busy birds trying to find the last insect."

She strained to catch a glimpse of a brown thrush. Every time Jacob pressed his nose against the windowpane to look, Caroline would swipe at his prints with her apron. With Coffie it was a

Chapter 34

hand print.

Chit chat dominated lunch. The food satisfied all.

"Let's have tea and cakes in the parlor," Caroline said, throwing down her linen napkin.

"Mom, I'm sleepy. I think I ate too much. Can I have dessert later?" Jacob asked through a yawn.

"Me, too," Coffie said, feigning a yawn as well.

"Come hug us before you two disappear," Sarah smiled as he dragged himself to their side of the table, with Coffie in tow.

Settling them down, Caroline returned to sit with her parents under the portrait of Jacksie Thrash.

"Thank you, Mrs. Fornes," she said, as the housekeeper carefully placed a silver tray with tea and cakes on the low table in front of the settee.

"Jacob told us he has a new friend, Rollie Tyson," Sarah said.

Elijah poked his wife.

Their daughter looked up startled.

"When did he tell you that?"

"Before lunch, while you'd gone ahead into the breakfast room. How is it that the Tysons were here?" her mother asked.

Flustered, Caroline nervously stirred her tea.

"One day last week, Jacob opened the door, which, of course, he's not allowed to do without me, and Doctor Tyson and his son were walking by on their way home. Rollie was rolling in the leaves on the green, and naturally, your grandson had to join him. They were covered as you can imagine by the time Coffie and I got to the door." She hesitated, taking another sip.

"And?" her mother injected.

"And, I invited them in, and Jacob taught Rollie how to play croquet, and Coffie gave his instructions, too."

Another sip and silence.

"And?"

"Mother, and what? Nothing. What do you want me to tell you?"

"What did you two talk about while the children were out

back? Not croquet, for sure," Sarah impatiently added.

"Really, Sarah, you are prying into your daughter's business. And speaking of business," Elijah stood before continuing, "I have some here in town before we head to Shiloh. Come along, Sarah. It's time to go."

"But, Elijah, we hav—"

"Sarah! We have business in town. We've taken up too much of Caroline's time this afterno—."

"Hap's divorced."

Sarah turned to her daughter and spoke just as casually as if they were sharing recipes.

"Sarah!" Elijah snapped at his wife.

"Wh-what?" Caroline's voice broke.

"It's true. His wife left him and took their child to see her grandfather and family. They just never came back."

"But, how did you know?"

"Willie told Elijah. Naturally, *she* would know," Sarah said, cutting her eyes at her husband.

Caroline turned to her father. Elijah scowled at his wife, disgusted that he had to be a part of this conversation. Running his fingers through his graying hair, he smiled feebly at his daughter. He knew she expected him to explain all that he knew from his lifelong friend, Willa Abigale Pridgen.

Chapter 35

MUTUAL THOUGHTS

Caroline closed the door behind her parents. They meant well, but she wished she had heard this news from Hap. Now she understood why he could only shake his head when she asked about Pamela. Both had been ignorant of the other's pain, but why was Rollie here and not with his mother?

She sat in the parlor alone and pondered. Where would all this news lead? She supposed the death of a marriage could be just as devastating as the death of a spouse. Losing a spouse is final, but divorce leaves haunting, unanswered questions. Both conditions need much healing for sure, she said to herself, as she sipped more tea. In her heart, she knew Hap and Rollie would be on their doorstep in the near future. She just did not know what her feelings would be when she saw him again.

The truth? We're both free. On the other hand, maybe too much history lies between us.

"When am I going to see Jacob and Coffie again? I like them, Daddy. I want to play croquet," Rollie said, without taking a breath, staring at his father with such pleading eyes.

Hap wished he had more time to process meeting his childhood sweetheart, his first love. He knew Rollie wanted an answer and now.

"I'm not sure, Rollie. Maybe we could invite them to Mrs. Deberry's for lunch after church next Sunday."

"Not until then? Oh, nooo—" The little fellow dissolved into tears.

Hap scooped his son up into his arms from the living room

floor and lifted him high above his head, hoping for peals of laughter, but none came. He cried louder.

"Rollie, if you'll stop crying, I'll tell you about two plans. I know you'll like both, but you have to dry your eyes."

"Okay, Daddy, I'll try."

Hap heard a few more sniffles. He lowered his son, kissed his head, and set him down in his chair in the living room.

"Son, I realize you need friends other than Willie and me. I'm going to ask Miss Caroline if Willie can sit with you and the boys some afternoons either at our house or theirs."

"Oh, goody. When, Daddy?"

"Be patient, son. I'll work it out. Look outside. It's still light enough. Let's ride to the bridge and throw a pole in the water. We haven't been fishing in a long time."

"Can we go get Jacob and Coffie, too?" he sniffled.

"Son, it's a little late for that, but your daddy promises that we'll do that very soon. In fact, your poor old daddy needed a break from the office this afternoon so he could be with you. It's a miracle that I got through with all my patients."

"Really? Well, okay, just you and me. But, the next time?"

"Next time... Maybe his mother will come, too."

"She's nice, Daddy. Do you like her?"

"Very much, son. Very much."

Father and son left their cottage, thinking strongly about the other family who lived on the green.

The next day the postman delivered a formal note. Caroline puzzled over the evenly defined script. Tearing the envelope, her hand shook. She read and reread the beautifully written message. Hap was inviting her to Mrs. Deberry's for lunch on Sunday with their children. What could she say? Surely, the rumor mill would grind madly in this small town if the Sunday lunch crowd saw the two families together. Most days, she still wore her widow's weeds in public. Maybe she should invite them to her house for lunch to avoid the gaping mouths.

Chapter 35

Nine months had passed since she'd buried her husband. She could not believe it. Was it not yesterday they had been the handsome couple envied by many? The politicos dithered over their possibilities, many knowing her to be Coeffield King's granddaughter. Litch would have served Raleigh well, maybe even at the state level. Will, too, if he had not died.

Quickly, she penned her own return invitation and hoped he would not be insulted that she was refusing his. The exchange through the post happened promptly. Rollie and Hap accepted for twelve-thirty after church on Sunday with one addendum: he had something to tell her.

The hostess mulled menus. When children sat at Jacksie Thrash's table, she always served fried chicken, creamed potatoes and gravy, baked apples, green beans, and pecan pie. What child would not like any of these choices? Her memory satisfied her.

Baking as much as she and Mrs. Fornes could on Saturday, Caroline attended Calvary's early service and rushed her sons home to finish her trimmings. She had set the dining table with colorful linens for the children and hoped for limited spills. These little fellows had to learn their graces just as she had at Jacksie's table and her mother's.

Twelve came with the gong of Coffie's grandfather clock in the hallway. Mopping her brow, Caroline straightened Jacob's Sunday tie and ran her fingers through Coffie's hair. She moved quickly through the downstairs to see if she had forgotten anything.

"Flowers!" she cried out. Maybe she could salvage some mums from the backyard. Surely, some lingered by the larger shrubbery, or maybe the sasanquas would not shed too badly.

"Jacob, stand by the door. Coffie, come with me. I'm going out back and cut a flower or two for the table. Oh, I hope they'll be a moment or two late," she hollered over her shoulder as she grabbed her shears and basket and scrambled out the backdoor.

In moments, the front door knocker clanked. The guests had arrived.

"Hi, Hap. Hi, Rollie. Come on in. Momma's out back cutting some flowers for the table. Coffie thinks he's helping. She hoped y'all might be a minute late so she could get some 'sanquas, I think she said," the young boy spoke in one breath, as he escorted them into the house, but not to the parlor. He led them right down the hall to the backdoor so they could see his mother.

Hap smiled at the innocence of the child as they all stood watching her scamper about the backyard snipping this sprig or that one, and throwing another down that did not suit her. Coffie just ran around, jumping to his heart's desire. Finally, collecting her flowers and Coffie, she dashed to the door, only to glimpse her guests watching her scurrying to complete her task. Flushed, she came through the door to gaze into the eyes and face of the handsome man who had once stolen her heart as a young girl.

"Maybe, we got here too soon?" He smiled down at her.

"Daddy, you were hurrying us from church. I told you we wouldn't be late," Rollie said.

The two adults burst out laughing. Neither child caught on to the joke, but that fact did not prevent them from joining in.

"Please, let me help you," Hap offered, taking the flower basket from her hands, his eyes fixed on hers.

"Thank you, kind sir. I just felt I wanted a little greenery on my table. Jacksie always said that a prettily set table must have part of God's natural contribution."

"She was correct. These 'sanquas' are beautiful."

Once more they laughed, relaxing with each word, as they had done so many years before, on the fallen log, on the grassy knoll, in the lower 40, at Shiloh.

Clipping the long stems, Caroline expertly placed the flower laden branches in an epergne vase and walked into the dining room to place them on the table. Hap followed. His eyes widened, when he saw the stunning table and spread before him.

"Jacksie Thrash and Sarah Cromwell have taught you well," he drawled as he watched her bend over the table to arrange her centerpiece.

Chapter 35

As she straightened up, she turned to pass by. She smiled up at him and stepped through the doorway, leaving a trail of fragrances. He closed his eyes and slightly shook his head.

Woman, your fragrances would drive any man on this earth to distraction, especially me.

With lunch over, Jacob pleaded, "Momma, can Rollie and I be excused? You, too, little brother. I want to show him our room. Our plates are almost clean," he said, tilting his for her to see.

"Of course, son. I'll check on you— Oh," she said, startled, as the boys jumped up from the table and climbed the stairs with a great deal of noise. "We've been deserted," she said, fidgeting with her napkin.

"I think we have," he agreed, unable to wipe the grin off his face.

"Frankly, I think they did quite well for their first dining experience together in the best room, as Jacob calls it. Please, may I take your plate?"

She rose and walked to his end of the table and removed his plate, placing it on the buffet.

"I have pecan pie, if you would like a slice," she spoke, not turning, but fiddling with the dishes on the massive piece of furniture.

Hap liked her busyness and felt pleased that she was fussing over him.

"By all means. I do not wish to miss one flavor."

He remained silent and watched her every move as if he were learning of her all over again.

"Coffee?"

"Oh, yes," he added watching her amusingly.

Turning, she caught his slight smile, that crooked one that had torn through her soul and body so many years ago. She flushed immediately, placing the dish down with a slight clatter. With the coffee cup, she showed more care, determined not to spill a drop. Whirling back to the buffet, she fixed her own, hurried to her end of the table, and raised her fork rapidly. They ate in silence.

"Well, whoever taught you to cook receives my applause. Perfection."

He wiped his lips with the freshly starched linen and held it, lingering with its smells of cleanliness. Her hand had prepared it just for him. Once more, the crooked smile returned, making her very nervous.

Oh, what will he say next? What will I say next?

"By the way, your menu was one of Rollie's favorites. Good choices."

Pushing his chair back a bit, he offered, "Can I help you with the dishes?"

"No. Mrs. Fornes will be back later this afternoon, but you can help me stack them for her."

"Do you suppose one of us should check on the boys?"

"Oh, my goodness. Uh…why don't you while I tidy up? Thanks. The first room at the top of the stairs on the right."

Smiling with great satisfaction, she stood and let her hand trail down the linen cloth to his place. Picking up his napkin, she folded it with amusement, as she thought of his big hands handling the china and silver with great ease. Somebody had shown this Edgecombe County boy his social graces. Briefly, she thought of Pamela Martin, rolled her eyes heavenward and, blowing a golden curl off her forehead, marched to the kitchen to organize the chaos.

Reaching the towering staircase, Hap stood on the lower step, peering upward with wonder at all the times Coeffield and Jacksie King had walked up these stairs together, perched on this very step, touching the ornate acorn finial on the lower banister. The handrail shone and glistened with the years of hands sliding up the magnificent wood. He supposed the artisan took forever to carve the embellished balusters.

Hap began the walk up the stairs, also thinking of Caroline's path each night. He shook those thoughts from his mind. He had a mission to find those boys of theirs. The door stood ajar. He

Chapter 35

peeped in and muffled laughter. In the middle of the floor, his son lay, covered by an Afghan. Jacob had flung it and his arm over his new friend as if he were the protector. Little Coffie lay snuggled up behind his brother. All were sound asleep. What a sight, Hap thought.

I've got to ask you soon, Caroline, soon.

He stood for the longest while, staring at, as he hoped, his *two* sons. His head jerked backwards, as he caught her fragrance. Smiling, he moved aside and directed her vision to the sight on the floor.

Her eyebrows flew up and her mouth opened with a delighted smile.

Captivated, she cocked her head sideways, crossing her arms, totally mesmerized, knowing for *sure* that both of those precious boys to their left were the sons of this man who stood at her side.

Laughing silently, they tiptoed out of Jacob and Coffie's room. Both turned and looked at Coeffield and Jacksie's bed.

"Your room?" He could not help, but inquire.

"Yes." Her voice was barely audible.

"The headboard is incredible."

Quickly glancing at the top baluster, he said, "The balusters have similar appointments. I assume the same master carpenter produced both?"

"I don't know. I suppose. Coffie had it made in New Bern for Jacksie's wedding present. Together they picked out the other antiques, but he wanted their bed to be special."

Suddenly, uncomfortable, Caroline reached for the handrail and began a slow descent, with the doctor following close behind. Gathering her wits, she invited him into the backyard for fresh air.

"The sun's shining, but I'm going to grab a wrap."

"Let me help you," he said, taking the coat from the rack and holding it out for her to slide her arms inside. She felt his hands briefly on her shoulders.

"Thank you." She smiled, moving to the backdoor.

They walked the paths slowly, both deep in thought.

"Sit with me a moment, Caroline," he spoke softly, pointing to the garden bench in the middle of the yard. "I have to tell you something, not very pleasant I'm afraid. I wanted to tell you the other day, but your pain was so great I just knew another time would be better. I think this is it."

Settling on the bench, Hap leaned forward with his arms propped on his thighs, his hands clasped. Caroline sat stiffly beside him, her own hands clasped, her knuckles white. His eyes shifted sidewise as he noticed her foot tapping.

"You know, don't you? Pamela and I are divorced."

Looking up into her face, he saw acknowledgment.

"I figured. This little town can't suppress news for long, and when you accepted our being together today, I-"

"Willie told my father. Then he told Mother and she just could not keep the news to herself. Forgive them, Hap. They mean well."

"Oh, it's okay. I just wanted to tell you myself."

"I'm so glad you have. How are you...in this quagmire?"

"I felt a hammer had crushed my heart. Nev—."

He stopped mid-word for that same hammer fell when he had let Caroline go years ago. She squirmed slightly and looked away.

"Caroline," he spoke again, delaying a moment, before he placed his hand on hers. "I have a question to ask you."

Both were startled by these words. Hap had wrestled with it, but he knew he must ask. The bench felt cold, but both were suddenly numb, fearing the question and the answer that would follow.

Hap picked up her hand and held it between his huge ones. She allowed him with no power to withdraw it, her legs limp, totally useless. How thankful she was they were not standing, for surely she would have fallen right at his feet.

"Look at me, please. This question is the hardest I've ever had to ask, but I have to ask it with all due respect for Litch's memory. Is...Is Jacob...Caroline, don't turn your head, please. Is that boy

Chapter 35

my son?" he choked it out, searching her face for a clue, but her face had turned to stone.

"The smile, Caroline. It's my crooked smile, and that hair. My God, when I first saw him, I thought I was looking at myself at his age. It frightened me. I know you would never keep that knowledge from me if it were true. Right? But, is he? Please, say something. I've taken such a chance asking you, I know, but I just had to. Ple—"

Before he could finish, she stopped him in the middle of his last plea. Practically jerking her hand from his, she jumped and paced in front of the bench and him.

His face reflected surprise, fringed with fear.

"No. Of course not! Jacob is Litch's son. Why, my great uncle had a crooked smile, Hap. You're not the only person with a crooked smile."

"But, his birthday is in Jan—"

"Hap, Doctor Frawley said I was just one of those women who would deliver early."

Her voice, tinged with anger, rose.

"I'm not comfortable talking about such sensitive issues with you. My poor husband has been dead less than a year. I'm afraid you're upsetting me."

She still continued to pace and wring her hands.

Jumping up, Hap assured her that he meant no harm.

"I would do nothing in this world to hurt you, Caroline. You must know that. I'm so sorry. Forgive me. I'll—I'll never bring it up again. I just hoped…"

His voice trailed, realizing that he had asked her too soon. He felt nauseated.

"Don't let my stupidity mess up this new friendship between our sons…or us."

By now, she was walking toward the house, trying to conceal the tears ready to spill down her face.

Following her quickly, he persisted, "Look, if I've offended you or Litch's memory, I'm sorry. I'll stay away, but please let our sons be together. I'll send him over with Willie, who keeps him while I work, or you can bring Jacob and Coffie to my home while I'm at work."

Still, she did not answer, as she rapidly walked up the stairs to retrieve Rollie, as Hap stood at the bottom with his head in his hands, propped up by the acorn finial.

Chapter 36
CURIOSITY

Sarah Cromwell looked across the dinner table at her husband. "Elijah, I know I saw Hap Tyson and his son go in Coffie's house. Listen to me. It's Caroline's house now, but I know I saw them. Do you suppose she invited them to lunch?"

Elijah shrugged, a hint of a smile on his face.

"I'm so curious to know what's happening. Caroline always sees us at the second service at Calvary, and since she wasn't there...Ohh, I want to know, don't you?" She paused. "Elijah Cromwell, you like to see me suffer, don't you?"

Her eyes narrowed.

The Captain made a silly face at her, thumping his nose and chanting, "Curiosity killed the cat, my dear."

"Hush. You're as curious as I am."

She frowned at him.

"Eat your lunch."

"Yes, ma'am," he said.

"Men!"

The couple finished and retreated to the parlor, the fireplace popping with red oak logs.

"Before you doze off, dear husband of mine," Sarah interrupted a nod. "It's time again to plan the Down East Cromwell Christmas."

She opened the family Bible where she kept a list. Cromwell ties were strong. Both knew not many would decline.

"You and Maggie will do it up right one more time," Elijah said, yawning again.

"Thank you, but my first concern is the list. I think I'll add the doctor and Rollie."

"But, they're not family, Sarah."

"Well, they could be," she smiled.

"You can't leave them alone, can you?"

"I don't suppose I can."

Smiling, he stretched out his hand for hers.

"What?" she said, as she placed her hand in his, only to have him raise it to his lips. "Go on. You'll have me blushing Christmas red."

"I hope so."

Sarah sat with her daughter in the parlor over tea under Jacksie Thrash's portrait.

"Wouldn't it be fun if Mother walked through that door to help us plan Christmas at Cromwell Hall?"

Sarah diverted her gaze from the portrait to study her daughter's face.

"Darling, what's the matter? You seem—sad."

"I'm just tired. Those boys of mine keep me hopping."

She offered a feeble smile, but truthfully, she had not slept well for nights, tossing, turning, plagued by her lie. The guilt weighed heavy. Why had she not told him outright, finally? Lying was too easy, too sneaky. It showed no strength or character by not relieving this man's agony. Could the granddaughter of Coeffield King really show no compassion toward Hap Tyson, when the old barrister had? She knew her love for him was rekindled, fiercely now, just as she had once before all those years ago. No offense to Litch, but he was gone. Hap and their son were very much alive.

"Well, darling, you just clear your mind of everything, because your mother is planning our Cromwell Christmas. Your father and I sent out the invitations yesterday."

Conveniently, she forgot to inform her daughter that she had invited the good doctor and his son.

"Wonderful, Mother. I need something to get my mind

Chapter 36

invigorated. Now, what can I do to help?"

"Well, I want you and the boys to come to Cromwell Hall next week and help me with decorating the tree and the house. We'll save the other greenery until a few days before. Elijah and Fate have already found the mistletoe, and guess where? The Medusa tree! It's loaded this year. One pop and we'll have enough for the entire house. Maybe you, Jacob, and Coffie can go with them."

"Mistletoe." Caroline sighed. "That reminds me of Christmas with Coffie. He used to chase Will and me until he caught us under the mistletoe. How long ago that seems."

"Daughter, I'll remind the Captain that he'll have to take up the tradition with his grandboys. He should be here any minute."

She anxiously looked at the big grandfather clock in the hallway. "I don't like traveling too much after dark."

Momentarily, the big oaken door swung open. Elijah's frame filled it.

"Have my two ladies buttoned down all the Christmas plans?" he asked with a big smile.

"You know we could talk forever, my dear, but we need to get on the road."

Sarah turned back to her daughter and took her by the shoulders.

"Whatever is keeping you awake, put it out of your mind. I don't like those circles under your eyes."

Chapter 37
YULETIDE

Willie looked at Rollie and smiled down at him. He had just finished his breakfast. It was an early December morning.

"Rollie, I want you to help me pick out a present for your daddy. Will you help old Willie?"

"Oh, yes, I will. I will," he squealed, jumping up from the table and dancing around the room. "Let's go, now, Willie. Please."

"Absolutely. Now."

She shoveled his dishes onto the kitchen counter and bundled them both with coats and mittens. Off they trudged the few blocks to Main Street.

"Willie, we got to window shop first. We haven't done that yet and you promised we would."

"I never break promises, Rollie. Which way should we go first?"

"Let's start across the street and end up at Carver's. That's my favorite store."

"It was your daddy's, too, when he was your age. I'll bet that candy jar in Carver's might have something to do with your liking it so much. Huh?"

"Well... Oh, Willie, look at that little tree in that window."

"Rollie, wait for me." She picked up her gait. "Hmph. Maybe I am too old for this chillum business," she mumbled.

Moving up the main artery of Tarboro's downtown, they oohed and aahed at every window with displays that would whet the appetite of any Santa list maker, but Carver's Mercantile always was the favorite place to shop.

The Carvers, elderly now, had brought their son and his wife

Chapter 37

into the business to carry on the family tradition. They were the third generation. The old couple still came in almost every day to spend a while piddling and tooling around to make themselves feel useful. Mostly, they enjoyed the customers. Every economic level, every ethnic background, shopped at Carver's Mercantile. Their variety pleased all accounts, but the smile and service of the shopkeepers kept their doors swinging open.

"G'mornin, Miss Willie," the younger Carver greeted one of his best customers. "And how is Mister Rollie doing this day? Son, you want a little piece of my daddy's candy?"

Rollie nodded his head so hard that both Willie and the proprietor laughed.

"Well, you stick that little paw in here and pick out the one of your choice," he instructed as he opened a gigantic candy jar. Rollie's eyes grew bigger and bigger until he found just the right one.

"Oh," he murmured with much satisfaction. "This one is the best!"

"What do you tell the fine gentleman, Rollie?" Willie asked.

"Thank you," he piped in his childish, sing-song voice.

"You're quite welcome. Now, what can I do to help you, Miss Willie?"

"Well, Rollie and I are looking for a Christmas present for the doctor."

"Oh, you came at just the right time. He was fingering this muffler the other day and commented that with the cold of the season coming on, he really needed one for his walks to his office."

"Rollie, did you hear that? Come over here and we'll choose the perfect one."

She led the child to the softest scarves Willie thought she had ever felt in her life. *Maybe Elijah would like one?* She had always given him a little remembrance for all his kindness throughout the year, the wood for her fireplace, the ham for her larder, the apples from his orchards. The shoppers made their choices and bought two.

"Thank you, Mister Carver," Rollie said again.

"Thank you, young man."

Willie smiled, just as the front door opened. Caroline and Jacob walked right into their path.

"Rollie! Momma, look it's Rollie and Miss Willie. Miss Willie, when can you bring Rollie to play with me and Coffie?" he said, rolling his eyes up at his mother, who approved his including his younger brother. "I miss him. Did he tell you about last Sunday, Miss Willie? We played so hard that we all three fell asleep. I put my blanket over Rollie, too," he proudly proclaimed.

"Well, Jacob, your mother will have to say when it's a good time."

Willie cocked her head at Caroline and raised her eyebrows. Caroline suddenly appeared uncomfortable.

"Willie, why don't you come tomorrow? I'll be expecting you two by ten o'clock," she smiled, somehow sensing that Willie knew everything. "Come along, Jacob, Miss Willie, and Rollie were on their way out."

"Yep, we're going to my daddy's office. Jacob, you want to see my daddy's office?"

"I'm sure he'd like to another time," she interrupted. "Jacob and I are doing some Christmas shopping."

"Awww, Momma. Pleas-"

"Jacob. No!" Caroline snapped too quick an answer; she felt embarrassed.

Willie hustled Rollie out the door, knowing that seeing his father was the only way to appease the young man in tears at her side.

I don't think, I know I'm getting too old for this chillun bidness.

Chapter 38
CHRISTMAS AT SHILOH

The Cromwell clan flooded Cromwell Hall. Elijah's two brothers, his sister, and their broods arrived, along with Miss Penelope, the only surviving great-aunt. All told, Sarah and Maggie had prepared for thirty-two people. Fourteen adults would sit at the dining room table with all its leaves carefully taken from storage, polished, and securely locked in place.

The young adults would scatter throughout the house; the children would settle around the kitchen and breakfast tables. Each room would burgeon with life, exactly what Sarah Cromwell wanted for the Christmas celebration.

"And the doctor's coming with his son. Wonderful," Sarah mused.

"Now, Miss Sarah, you know what the Captain done told you about meddling in Miss Caroline's bidness. I'm telling you, too. If it's meant to be, it will be by God's grace," Maggie returned.

"You, too! I am surrounded by folks, telling me what to do. Maggie, if I didn't need those invaluable hands in my kitchen?"

"You'd what?"

Both women burst out laughing.

Christmas day had arrived. The house was ready. The food was ready. The weather was perfect. What more could they ask? The carriages began arriving before noon. Maggie stood at her post at the door. Sarah and Caroline put finishing touches on the greenery in the entrance hall.

"Maggie? Have you seen the doctor's carriage?" she asked, walking over and craning her neck at the front window. "Caroline, go outside and see if you see Hap's buggy?"

"Hap? What do you mean? You invited Hap Tyson without even telling me?" Caroline demanded in a low voice.

"Oh my gosh, I can't believe I forgot to tell you, but why would you object to his being here? What's wrong?"

Feeling foolish, Caroline stuttered, "N-nothing. Truly, Mother. I'm sorry. I didn't know that you were including outsiders." She hurried to add. "Not that Hap's an outsider. I mean, oh, I don't know what I mean."

Sarah and Maggie stood, both taken aback. Shrugging, the two busy women scurried on with their pressing chores. Christmas lunch would be served promptly at twelve o'clock.

"Well, he must have had an emergency is all I can think. You know doctors," Sarah pronounced as she peeked down the road toward Tarboro. "It's time. We'll just have to go ahead. Elijah?"

"Cromwells, get your children and gather round the tree. We're going to have the blessing," Elijah announced. "Uh-oh. I hear a carriage. I suppose we can wait another minute."

Caroline heard her father as she hustled the boys into the hall. She stopped short. Her stomach tightened, her eyes glued on the door.

"Hap, Rollie, come on in," the Captain greeted the latecomers.

"I'm so sorry we're late, but Jesse Creech's finger needed a few stitches."

"Momma, it's Hap and Rollie!" Jacob pulled her hard, practically knocking his mother into his grandfather. "May we eat together? Oh, Momma, please, please, please." He grabbed her around the waist. "Jenna can look after us while you're at the best table. Okay? Please. Coffie's busy with his other cousins."

"Goodness, Hap, you better let your son follow Jacob or we'll all be fit to pay. We're all ready," Elijah said, his arm raised to quiet the crowd for introductions.

During each word, Hap's eyes gazed over Elijah's shoulder, trying to catch Caroline's eye.

"Come, boys," Caroline whispered, slipping away to conduct

Chapter 38

the eating arrangements. She glimpsed once, but her father was already introducing Hap to the boisterous Cromwell clan, as they stopped at the door to wait for the blessing.

"Now that the good doctor is here, family. Let's all get quieted down. We need to give thanks. Quiet," Elijah called out, raising his voice, "or I'll have to find Grandma's old bell to get this raucous crowd's attention."

With a few shushes, Elijah spoke, "Every two years, this family gathers here at Shiloh. I thank everyone for the effort." He nodded and winked at his sister. "But I especially thank God for clearing your path to Shiloh not just to celebrate our family, but to celebrate the birth of the Christ. Bow your heads, please."

Thirty-two people quieted.

"Lord, we've come to break bread together, to fellowship together, but we acknowledge your continued blessings on this family. Nourish our bodies with this food. Bless the hands that prepared it. Forgive us for our wrongdoings. In the name of the Father, the Son, and the Holy Ghost. And all God's children say...AMEN."

Everyone chimed in unison.

"Okay. The mistress of the house has an instruction or two. Listen! Sarah?"

"First, let me join Elijah as always to welcome you to Cromwell Hall. We love all of you and joy that you're here. All the children and young folks go into the kitchen and listen to Miss Maggie tell you about your food and your seating. All you adults need to head to the dining room, get in the buffet line, and find your name on a place card at the table."

"And, if you are first in line, hurry up, 'cause your host is hungry for some good cooking," Elijah added in the midst of laughter. "Remember it's been blessed. Eat when you find your seat. Doctor, don't be shy. Just push your way into this wall of folks," he finished, goading his guest along.

Hap strained to see Caroline, but to no avail. *Where is she? Not still helping the boys?*

"C'mon, Doctor, join us here," a friendly face beckoned.

Smiling, he fell in place but continued to comb the room for the golden curls.

Caroline stood just outside the dining room door, mopping her brow, trying to grasp her emotions. She looked around the door and marveled how at ease he was with this hoard of strangers. Of course, they were wonderful strangers full of life and laughter. No one could be an outsider around them for long, one thing she adored about the Cromwells. Whether they were judges, lawyers, planters, or whatever, they were all the same: compassionate and concerned, interested and interesting, loving and giving. No matter or manner, they were all the same.

Breathing deeply, she dabbed her brow quickly again and walked into the buffet line several places behind Hap to obscure herself until she felt control, but to her chagrin, he turned and spied her. With a smile, he slipped out of line and dropped back to join her.

"I've been looking for you. Are the boys, okay?"

"They—they're just fine," her voice cracked. "Oh, excuse me. I cheated and sneaked one of Maggie's biscuits a moment ago."

She continued to apologize.

"Can I get you some water?" he asked, lowering his head to see her face better and to catch her fragrances. He edged nearer to feel the essence of her. He could see she looked nervously from side to side.

"Caroline, did you know we were invited to come today?"

"Not exactly."

"Are we bothering you by being here?"

"No. No," she whispered, slightly shaking her head.

Encouraged, he could not help but put his hand on the small of her back to move her forward. He prayed he would not drop his plate.

Finding their names was no easy task. This uncle or that cousin had to speak to him. He hoped he was being civil, for at this point all he wanted to do was to grab her and race to the

Chapter 38

grassy knoll. They had much to say to each other. He hoped Sarah had been kind with the place cards, but unfortunately his name appeared to her right, the guest spot.

Caroline shrugged helplessly as family members nudged her along to sit at Elijah's right. Her slight wave caught his eye at the other end of the table, as Sarah's voice broke his trance.

"Hap, your family was kind to let the Cromwells steal you away today."

"They understood. I'll visit them after the holidays." He smiled at her and said, "You and Maggie have proven superb cooking skills. I know my taste buds will be totally satisfied."

"That's what this meal is supposed to do."

"Caroline certainly has had some good teachers."

"Oh, has the lady cooked for you, good doctor?" Sarah inquired arching her brows ever so slightly.

"Yes ma'am, one Sunday for lunch, after church. Rollie and the boys did quite well in the 'best room'."

"Oh yes, the 'best room,'" she laughed. "Well, Jacob is growing so that he'll be sitting at this table before we can all bat an eyelash."

Others chatted with Hap, but throughout lunch Sarah watched him, amused, especially each time he glanced down the table at her daughter.

"Elijah?" Sarah called for his attention by ringing a small crystal bell before her. "Take all the gentlemen into the parlor or out on the porch for cigars. Ladies, follow me into the entry hall. Check on children if you need to. Maggie, ask Jenna to help if you need her."

Gathering around the tree was a tradition for the Cromwells on Christmas Day afternoon. The Captain played St. Nicholas, donning a red velvet suit and a red cap trimmed in white fur. The children crowded around the tree, giggling and punching each other.

"Rollie, that's my grandpa. St. Nicholas can't be everywhere.

Grandpa's just helping him out," Jacob whispered in Rollie's ear.

Paper and ribbons filled the entry hall with squeals from the children as they opened their surprises.

St. Nicholas disappeared. Momentarily the Captain returned.

"It's communion time, everybody," Elijah urged. "Get your wraps and head for the carriages. The rector's waiting for us. I promised him we'd be there by four o'clock," he said, pulling his pocket watch out.

Most of the party would stay in town after the service at Calvary. Mrs. Deberry would feed them a light supper, and as always she would cook her finest breakfast spread the next morning. Afterward, they would scatter.

Hap and the men walked in from the parlor, cigar smoke swirling into the giant hallway. He heard laughter coming from the guest bedroom and found Caroline and the boys wrestling with coats and mittens.

"Can we come along to communion at Calvary?" he questioned her.

"Of course."

He looked at her with curiosity. How different she seemed from the other day when she had rebuffed him sharply. *Something's happened.* His mind whirred. *God, when will we ever be alone? When can we finally talk?*

"Why don't you and the boys ride with us in my buggy?" he asked. "It'll be tight, but I think we can squeeze in. Boys, would you like that?"

She smiled in resignation, knowing there was no way of denying them.

"I suppose so," she said with her hand on her hip.

"I'm sorry. That was sneaky," he whispered, leaning toward her.

"You're right." Turning quickly, she raised her voice. "Let's go, boys, and get our place in the caravan."

"What's a car—car—?" stuttered Rollie, trailing behind.

"It's when one carriage follows the other in a line, isn't that

Chapter 38

right, Hap?" Jacob asked, pulling on his sleeve, as they walked outside to find his buggy.

"Yes, it is. Come here, guys. Here's mine."

He lifted all three up into the back of the buggy. Then, he turned to Caroline and swung her up to the front seat, smiling and thinking that she was where she belonged.

Chapter 39
TIMELY MOMENTS

Fresh garlands hung on the altar at Calvary Episcopal and wrapped around the posts of the ornate brass lanterns lining the aisles of the church. Candles flickered warmly through the opaque panes of the lanterns. A hush fell over each family as they walked arm in arm into the imposing sanctuary. Caroline followed her family with Jacob on her arm and Coffie holding a hand. Hap sauntered behind with Rollie in tow. Who would have believed the reverence that spread and consumed this very vocal group? But, it happened and amazed them all every time they gathered for communion.

Old Mrs. Foley played Christmas hymns as the family filled the first four rows on either side of the main aisle, all eager to hear the familiar words and partake of the Lord's Last Supper. The Rector directed each row to come to the railing. Hap and Caroline waited their turn, moved by what they were experiencing together, the union of the Bride and the Bridegroom. Hap's eyes locked with hers. Slowly his hand reached to engulf hers, neither seeing their sons' grinning faces, but the moment broke as the Rector called their row.

He concluded the service for the Cromwells by reading from the prayer book.

"Because, thou didst give Jesus Christ, thine only Son, to be born as at this time for us; who, by the operation of the Holy Ghost, was made very man, of the substance of the Virgin Mary his mother; and that without spot of sin, to make us clean from all sin. Therefore, with Angels and Archangels, and with all the company of heaven, we laud and magnify thy glorious Name;

CHAPTER 39

evermore praising thee, and saying, HOLY, HOLY, HOLY, Lord God of hosts, Heaven and earth are full of thy glory: Glory be to thee, O Lord Most High. Amen."

But outside Calvary, the family voices erupted with excitement once more as they mingled.

"On to Mrs. DeBerry's," Elijah called, "for all who can. Some of you have other plans, but remember her breakfast feast in the morning, if you are staying the night."

Caroline's parents would remain in town with her, much to Hap's disappointment. Their conversation would have to wait for another time, but he would endure for as long as it took.

Placing them all back into his buggy after a light supper at Mrs. DeBerry's, Hap moved along in the caravan, only to drop out of line on the Town Common in front of the King house.

He leaned over and whispered, "I have a gift for you. When are we going to find time to be alone? I can't give it to you with the family sitting around, especially these boys. You know how they get these silly grins on their faces," he said, miming their sons. She affectionately punched him and put her finger under her chin in thought.

"Well, come on in. We'll put the boys *and* my parents to bed," she added with her own silly grin.

Wonderful, he mouthed.

"What's so funny, Momma?" Jacob asked from the back seat of the buggy.

"Oh, nothing, son. How would you and Coffie like for Rollie to spend the night?"

"The best present of all the holiday! Rollie, did you hear that?" A squeal from the backseat was his answer.

The Cromwells pulled up behind and were surprised to see Hap and his son get out and walk up the steps behind their daughter and their grandsons. Each looked at the other with a shrug. The day and night had been wonderful, and for some it obviously was not over.

"I told you so, St. Nicolas," Sarah chided.

"Well, Hap, why don't you and me sit in the parlor while these two ladies get those boys in the bed," the Captain suggested. Hap followed the man through the French opening into the parlor, both aware of Jacksie Thrash's eyes peering down at them.

"She was a gracious, beautiful woman. She would have liked you and Rollie, Hap. Coffie was crazy about his wife to the point of dotage. I know it's hard to imagine having seen him in the courtroom, but it was a great love very few experience."

Hap stood and stared at the portrait, but could only say, "I know."

Elijah looked at him strangely, and then, knowingly. Yes, he knew and approved.

"Mother, I love him."

Sarah's eyebrows went up, her mouth opened, but no words came out. This time she knew to listen.

"The other night, I prayed as hard as I ever have in my life. I can't deny or delay telling him any longer. We have both waited so long, too long. Close your mouth, Mother. I know you've wanted it, too." Raising her own eyebrows, she spoke firmly, "Mother, I know you too well."

With that, Sarah Cromwell relaxed and took her daughter's hand as they both gazed at the sleeping boys. Her smile voiced her approval, but what she said next startled her daughter.

"Well, child, are you going to tell him that Jacob is his son?"

"Wha—what? Mother! I—" She could not find her voice after that.

"Caroline, come sit with me in the window seat."

Mother leading daughter, they sat facing each other.

"Darling, it is very hard to mistake that crooked grin. Your father and I suspected it from the first year. We, of course, were shocked at the thought and could not imagine when, but we figured that it only could have happened at Litch's graduation

Chapter 39

before you two were married."

"You never said anything all these years."

"What was there to say, dear? It was over. You were married to Litch."

"How did you know when?"

"I went to check on my daughter in her room at the inn. I knew Litch was overpowering in all his excitement. You were very confused, but Litch was so aggressive and persuasive, not just with you, but with all of us. When you were not in your room, I suspected, but I never told your father one thing. He figured it out on his own."

"Mother, if you two have figured it out, maybe others have, too. It's so embarrassing for— I've disgraced us."

"Listen, daughter, life is too short. God does not want you to carry this burden any longer. Caroline, I'm sure you have asked His forgiveness one hundred times. Stop it now. He has. *He has.* You and Hap have two sons who love each other dearly, another great reward. Just receive and be grateful. Not many young women have lost a husband and had a deathly ill child at your young age. You deserve this happiness with Hap. I pray it will be long and enriching.

"I've been atrocious to the man in the past, but I know he can bring life into our family, Caroline. I firmly believe this. I've had a very hard time about Will as you know, but watching your father and hearing him say countless times that harboring hate hurts me more that it does the one receiving the hate. Your father has been right all along. I am thankful for his love and patience. And Will? He loved Will as much as I have. We had him for nineteen years, for which I have learned to be grateful for.

"Hap is a good man. It has taken me a long time to admit it, but your father and I saw him with brand new eyes when your grandfather was so ill. He could not have been more compassionate."

"Oh, Mother."

She reached out and hugged her as she never had before,

mother and daughter in a rich embrace.

"Now, let's go find our men."

Hearing the creaks on the stairs, both men jumped up as the ladies entered the room, each noticing an unusual contentment, a happiness between mother and daughter.

"Elijah, come put your wife to bed. It's been a long time since five o'clock this morning, but it's been worth every second."

Walking over to Hap, she reached up and placed her hand on his arm.

"Thank you, Hap, for adding to our celebration. We'll see you soon," she said with affection.

Stepping back, she allowed the Captain to guide her to their bedroom downstairs behind the staircase.

Hap and Caroline turned to each other, and very self-consciously she offered him a seat on the sofa, he at one end and she at the other.

"Now, how am I going to give you your present if you are one mile from me on this sofa? Will you at least meet me halfway?" he appealed, tapping the box he'd removed from his coat pocket. Sheepishly, she inched to the center of the couch.

"Here, open it first, and then I have a story."

"What story?"

"Oh, you'll like this one," he assured.

Tearing the paper, her eyes brightened. "Oh my, you know I love it." She glanced at him with gratitude as she lifted the bottle of perfume from the box.

"Well, not as much as I do. You have driven me crazy with the fragrance of gardenias since that first moment we came face to face in Carver's Mercantile. My nose has never been the same since," he declared, rolling his eyes, prompting her giggle. Opening the bottle, she put just a touch behind each ear.

"Woman, what are you trying to do to me? Didn't I tell you I'm already crazy?"

"Tell me your story. I promise to behave."

"When I was Christmas shopping in the village up at school

Chapter 39

one year, I passed a counter with fragrances in one of the sundries shops on Franklin Street. It drew me like a magnet. I couldn't help but purchase a bottle and carry it back to my room. I opened it and enjoyed...your fragrance. I felt closer to you and yet I knew we would never be. After—af—ter you left me when we were together in my room, the next morning I walked over to the creek behind the laundry and threw that bottle as far as I could. No longer could I, would I, allow that fragrance to pierce the air around me again, until now.

"Now, I want nothing more than to inhale that sweet aroma, because then I'll know you are near. That's where I want you, Caroline, near, very, very, near."

He reached and placed the bottle of perfume on the table. Turning very slowly, he put his arm around her shoulders. She never moved. Taking his left hand, he turned her face toward him and never closing his eyes he kissed her mouth, shocked by its forgotten softness.

Her eyes did close; her head swayed, shocked by the fullness of his forgotten mouth. The moment was tender, difficult to break. When they did part, they simply pressed their foreheads, each trying to succor the essence of what had happened. Neither could speak nor wanted to break the silence.

Finally, she did.

"Hap, I must tell you something, something very important. I feel terrible that I let you suffer recently with my answer to your...question. As strongly as I feel for you, I was very cruel. And, when my father asked the blessing and said, 'Forgive us for our wrongdoings.' I was convicted."

He held his breath through each of these words and craved only one statement to come from her lips, and it did, slowly and painfully.

"I've carried a burden ever since I brought Jacob into this world." She paused. He never breathed. Through a teary voice she whispered, "Hap, you are right... Jacob is your son."

He reached out and grasped her hand, squeezing his eyes

shut.

Her words flooded.

"I regret never having told you, but I was married, and then you were married. What good would it have brought those two other people in our lives? I tried to hide it. I cut his hair short. I prayed his smile would change, but, no, it wouldn't go away. That smile is yours, always has been; always will be."

Her face was covered with tears that had continued flowing from the moment she began to speak.

He had looked away as she confessed. Letting his head drop with his long arms propped on his thighs, he continued to grip her hand. When she stopped talking, he turned to her tear-stained face. Taking a handkerchief, he dried her tears. Then pulling her to him so her head rested on his shoulder, he let her cry all over again and release all the guilt, all the baggage. He wanted her to feel absolutely cleansed and free.

When she quieted, he kissed her forehead and turned her to face him before he spoke.

"Listen to me, Caroline; listen carefully. Yes, I would have loved knowing my son as an infant, grasping my finger for the first time, feeling the future in the strength of those little fingers curled around mine. Watching him pull up on a chair and take his first step would have thrilled me to no end, but you did what you thought was best for all. I cannot fault you for that. I do not even know what I would have done in your place. You used your best judgment.

"The important thing is what you've said to me now. I love you, Caroline. I have loved you since the first time Sarah Cromwell brought you in a carriage down Station House Road. I have loved you as an urchin, as a rascal, and later as a man. When have I not loved you?"

He hopelessly smiled at her, while raising her hand to kiss it briefly.

"We've just taken a detour from each other, but, now, we've been given another chance. I do not want anything to happen to

Chapter 39

that chance. I forgive you. It's as simple as that for me. I forgive you. Listen, from the bottom of my heart, I thank you for caring for my child. You've done a wonderful job, and I thank God for keeping both of you healthy and for once more placing you in my life."

With that, he swung himself off the sofa and knelt before her, and with love in his eyes, in the presence of Jacksie Thrash, he asked,

"Caroline King Cromwell...Bagley, marry me. *Marry me.*"

Through her tears and laughter, "yes" came from her lips, over and over again, as she pulled him off his knee and back onto the sofa. She raised her face to his as she had done long ago, and both kissed with a deep passion that seals forever. Gently, they held each other, no longer afraid. They would have each other.

"I don't want to leave you," he said, his voice strained. His face buried in her curls.

"I know, my darling, I know."

"Well, what happened last night?" Sarah spoke softly over coffee in the parlor, so the boys could not hear her. Peering inquisitively at her daughter, she prodded her to answer.

"I told him everything, Momma. *Everything!* I wanted nothing to remain unanswered between us, and he understood. He forgave me," she sniffled.

"Good, my darling, I knew he would. He has the compassion of Coffie," she said as she clasped her daughter's hand. "Let's tell your father everything. He's been so worried about you."

They walked toward Elijah at the breakfast table and drank coffee together sharing the details of the previous evening.

"I know you want to know when, but I can't marry Hap until at least a year has passed since Litch's death. We both want to be respectful to his memory, not just for Litch's family, but also for Jacob and especially Coffie. Even though they want a new 'daddy' tomorrow, in the future I want the two to feel the respect we had for their *other* father. Anyway, that's the way we feel.

Springtime, maybe."

"Whatever you want. Now, we best head home. We've got a holiday house to dismantle. Give Hap our best."

Both hugged their daughter and said their good-byes to their *three* grandboys.

Chapter 40
THE UNEXPECTED

Other than the busyness of raising three boys, Hap's work and Caroline's art salvaged their sanity, waiting for their wedding. During the week, daily routines brought them together for dinners. On the weekends, the Cromwells invited them to Shiloh for all occasions: birthdays, anniversaries, or whatever interests Sarah could generate to get them down the road to Cromwell Hall. It really was not hard, for they always accepted with enthusiasm, whether to eat one of Maggie's meals or play a hand of bridge or a game of cribbage. The contact and the bond pleased them all.

Hap's practice grew in the short duration. Many days, just to take a break at lunchtime, he would walk to the bridge over the Tar and gaze at the crumbling old Station House. He had dreamed these last few months of restoring the building for an office and clinic, but only after he and Caroline were settled in their own home. Soon they would talk about these dreams. Would she even want to leave the King house? He felt all right about that, but the remembrance of the McCloud house nagged him. Coffie and Jacksie were dead, but maybe they should start in a different house, just a totally, fresh beginning.

One late February afternoon as Hap, Caroline, and the boys sat by a roaring fire in her parlor, Rollie begged his father, "Please, please, please!"

"Rollie, you sound like Jacob." He smiled over at his son.

"He wants me to. He stayed at our house last."

"Now, Rollie, only if Miss Caroline says it's all right. We

certainly do not want to impose."

"Impose?" Caroline laughed. "Good heavens, Rollie, Jacob would be asking if you were not. Of course, we'd love to have you and Coffie, too."

Over their heads, Hap mouthed, "What about me?" with a wistful look. Returning his wistful look, she mouthed back, "Soon. Oh, very soon."

They had planned their ceremony, a small private one at Calvary in early spring, probably toward the end of March, or maybe April. When the weather would fair off, Sarah and Elijah would host a reception at Cromwell Hall. Once more Maggie and Sarah would perform their best. Spring was just a few weeks away. Everything seemed perfect.

"Is all of this real?" Caroline mused, as they came down the staircase, the boys tucked snugly into bed. "Just think. In seven weeks, I will be Mrs. Thomas Rolland Tyson. Caroline Tyson, if you will."

Turning to him at the bottom of the staircase, she took his strong hands and said, "We have waited so long, too long, for this moment. Go, now, you have a full day ahead of you."

Standing on tiptoe, she kissed him sweetly. With that, she pushed him toward the door.

"I'm counting the days when I'll carry you over our threshold. I love you, Caroline."

Reaching down, he touched the golden curls that he adored and walked off into the night. The door clicked shut.

The moon shone brightly as the young doctor, whistling, sauntered down the walkway skirting the Town Common. His spirits soared as he passed one of the guesthouses on the common.

Hmmm... That's strange. Why is a carriage with a horse still hitched to the post out front? Tarboro has some mighty late-night visitors.

Pushing the random thought from his head, he turned the corner a half-a-block from his small cottage. He did not mind

Chapter 40

Rollie sleeping over at Jacob and Coffie's, even if it meant that he would enter a quiet and empty house, but usually, exhaustion from his long day made him appreciative of moments like this one to collect himself and think of his patients.

Hap's foot hit the front stoop and in two strides his key clicked into the front door. As he turned the knob, he noticed through the window that live coals remained in the fireplace. Maybe he'd bank a few logs to take off the chill in the house. Closing the door, he hesitated, for what reason he wasn't sure. Scanning the room in the dim light, he checked to make sure he was alone.

He walked to the lamp, lit it, and started to stoke the fire. Momentarily, the live coals hissed and sparked more life, warming the air. His hand touched the back of his chair. Would he sit a while, or should he go to bed? Yawning and stretching, he decided the latter.

Turning, Hap froze. His bedroom door was shut. Neither he nor Willie ever left that door closed. Both knew the fireplace warmed the room. He could not move, gripped in wonder if Willie or Rollie had closed it by accident, or maybe someone lurked beyond. Quietly, he reached for the poker and slipped toward his room to listen for any disturbance. Haltingly, as he opened the door, the moonlight streamed down on a figure in the middle of his bed. Clutching the poker, he strained to see when a giggle from the past startled him from the midst of the bedcovers.

"Good heavens, Hap, put that poker down before you hurt somebody."

"Pam—Pamela? God in heaven, Pamela? Are you crazy? I could have killed you."

"Now, Hap, how many people would have been in your bed?" she purred and grinned like a Cheshire cat, sitting up, revealing that she did not have on one stitch of clothing.

"Oh, for God's sakes, Pamela. This is ridiculous!"

As his eyes quickly grew accustomed to the dark, he could make out the hastily thrown clothes on the chair.

"I am going outside, now. Put on your clothes and get out of my house. By the way, how did you get in?"

He only hesitated seconds.

"You kept a key, didn't you? Oh, don't even bother to lie. With all your conniving, I'm sure you did."

With that retort, he marched back to the living room, only to pace in front of the fireplace. The nerve of this woman! They were not even married anymore. How could she be this disgusting? And how could he ever have married her? Then he thought of Rollie and his shoulders slumped, as his mind raced with fear of what this evil creature behind him would be thinking.

Hearing the door creak, he turned to see her padding across the floor, not dressed in her clothes, but wrapped in the sheet.

"Pamela! What are you doing? This is repulsive. I come into my house and find you trespassing on my property. Have you forgotten that we are no longer married? By the way, what would all your suitors say if they saw you in this revolting position?"

"Hap, I've changed my mind. I—I still love you...and Rollie. By the way, where *is* my child?"

"What would you have done if he just happened to be here with me, right this minute?"

"Oh, I was watching from the window. I saw you were alone."

"If it was to better your cause, I think you would do just about anything."

"Hap!"

"Don't *Hap* me. Listen, Pamela, we no longer have any legal ties. You should not be in this house. Leave, now! In fact, I am to be married in just seven weeks. I'm obligated."

Pamela had been very still as he spoke these last words. Quietly, she walked up to him dragging the sheet swathed around her. Peering up at the young doctor with a faint smile on her lips, she appeared to be a woman in control, a woman in charge. The flames from the fire danced across her face as her eyes glowed with a reflection of untold knowledge, knowledge that soon she would share. In a very level voice, she defiantly refuted his declaration and relayed her secret.

Chapter 40

"Oh, no, Hap Tyson, you will *not* be married in seven weeks. Banks never filed our papers with the court. *We are still husband and wife.*"

With that, she wantonly danced around the room, as Hap stood in disbelief of her cruel words.

Struggling for his own control, he stammered, "Wha-what? We're—impossible! I signed the papers, and so did you! Pamela, don't mess around."

"We're still married, darling. Grandfather and I wanted to give me the chance to see if I really wanted this divorce, but, Hap, I do want to be your wife, again. Think of Rollie. He would have his real parents and we could give that beautiful boy a brother or a sister. I want to do that, Hap, and you know I can. We could be happy again. I'm sure of that."

She moved closer to him, holding the sheet looser and looser as she glided toward him, tilting her head, widening her eyes, and spreading her lips into a full smile. Realizing her intent, Hap grabbed the sheet just in time to wrap her up and whirl her around to push her into his bedroom.

"Oh, no you don't. You get your clothes back on this instant. You just can't come in here after all these months and do this to me. Get dressed!" He slammed the door shut.

For the first time, the woman did as she was told.

Hap stared into the flames. He could hardly keep from screaming as he had those years ago when he had left Caroline on the grassy knoll in sheer frustration at their last meeting. Their lives were ripped apart then and would this happen again to them?

Caroline. Oh, my God, what am I going to do?

Whether Pamela was telling the truth or not, he didn't know, but he had to find out and soon. Somehow, he would have to be nice just long enough to buy time to discover the facts. Why had he not followed up on the legality of their papers? The stupidity of it all baffled him. Everything had been going smoothly, too smoothly. He should have known better. The black cloud gathered once more over the head of the meanest scoundrel in all of Edgecombe County.

Pamela walked into the room, this time fully dressed.

"Look, I'm sorry I lost my temper," he said, standing in front of the fireplace, "but you shocked me."

He paced a little, hoping she wouldn't sense his nervousness.

"Remember we haven't seen each other for almost a year. I suppose I did look pretty scary brandishing the poker."

Startled by his softer words, she peered at him with anticipation.

"Well, I shouldn't have scared you. It was silly, but I've wanted to be your wife again for so long. I just succumbed to the temptation and since we're still married...I hoped..." Her voice trailed. Searching his face, she asked, "What do we do now?"

"Let me take you—Are you at the guesthouse right around the corner?"

"Yes, Banks is with me. He wouldn't let me come alone."

Hap almost choked. *Oh no, McCloud. Control. Just stay in control.*

"Let me walk you back," he said. "You've got to give me time to think about all of this, Pamela. I'm just shocked. Of course, I have to think of Rollie, too."

"Grandfather does want to visit family in the county, so why don't we leave and come back in a few days? Then, we can make our plans. Oh, Hap, I know we can be happy again. I do want to give you more children."

Walking out the door, they moved toward the guesthouse.

"Tell me, what happened to the young lawyer, the professor, and the mayor's son? Why, me? I'm just the same old struggling doctor."

"Oh, they were just hanging around me to get favors from my grandfather. They liked me, of course, but they liked what he could do for them better. Hap, I've been foolish. We were good together when nobody was around to bother us. Banks or Miss

Chapter 40

Ghost from the Past! I just wish we could go back to those good times."

She hooked her arm in his and nestled close. His arm was immovable. How could this woman have fooled him? She had twisted him and his emotions to the point of revulsion. He had to get away and fast.

Reaching the stoop of the guesthouse, he wrenched his arm from hers, but on the first step, she turned and swooped down on him as an owl attacks its prey. Her kiss rocked him, and once more, he froze, unable to disengage.

Pressing against him, she throatily whispered, "It could be now."

Smiling feebly, Hap pushed her toward the door and hurried into the night. Around the corner, he clung to the rugged bark of a towering oak and wretched until his midsection ached, totally sickened by this revolting development. The moonlight lit his contorted face, as he stumbled home.

Chapter 41
STARTLED

Caroline awoke with a start. Something was wrong. Alarmed, she threw back the covers, shivering as she scrambled to find her slippers by the bedside. Pulling on her robe, she walked to the window and stared into the night. The houses looked peaceful with small ribbons of smoke curling skyward, making unusual designs at the pleasure of the breezes. Wrapping her arms around herself, she sensed that all was not at peace in this sleepy little village on the Tar.

Coffield Kings's granddaughter tiptoed to Jacob and Coffie's room. For once, both lay still. She checked their breathing and wondered if other mothers did as well. Shaking her head, she smiled down at the child she and Hap Tyson had created. Touching his hair, she vowed she would always let it grow naturally. Never again would she try to disguise his identity. He was Hap's son...forever...always.

Leaving the room, she stopped at the head of the stairs. How strange she felt, sensing a pull to the lower floor. Slowly, she took a few steps, then listened. Nothing. Her hand glided over the polished rail. At the bottom, she hesitated, looking at the entry and the French opening into the parlor. How many guests and friends had passed that doorway and come into the sanctity of the King house? She recalled the compliments she'd heard back then and even today about the warmth and compassion of her grandparents.

Her head jerked. Someone moved outside. Anyone out this late was surely up to no good. Clutching her robe, she peeped around out one of the glass lights on the right side of the door. A

Chapter 41

figure moved on the edge of the Town Common, just a few yards from her doorway. Between the moonlight and the street lantern, she could make out a man pacing back and forth. Something about the figure looked familiar, but the shadows of the trees prevented any determination. Who is this?

The man walked toward the walkway ready to turn down the Commons. When the light hit his curly shock of hair, Caroline gasped, grappling for the key. It was Hap. Opening the door, she stood high on the door stoop with the chill of the wind rippling her robe. The streetlight beams hit her golden curls.

"Hap Tyson, what are you doing out here in this night air? You'll catch your death. Get in this house right now," she commanded, not knowing the agony she invited into her home.

Stunned, he came close, opening his mouth in objection, for he had no firm plan for this dilemma. The frustrated man was not ready to tell her about Pamela and McCloud, but how could he refuse her?

Hesitantly, he climbed the steps, reaching for her outstretched hand. When he stood inside the warmth of the house, gradually he pulled her toward him and looked deeply into her eyes. She was startled by his seriousness. He edged her into an embrace. She allowed their closeness for whatever length of time he needed. When he released her, he silently led her to the couch in the parlor under the watchful eye of Jacksie Thrash.

Her hand automatically moved up and down his arm as he sat on the couch, leaning over, his head in his hands. Over and over he would turn, look at her, shake his head, and run his fingers through his hair, allowing his head to drop once more into his hands.

She would wait all night if she had to, to hear the burden he carried.

Finally, Hap looked up at Jacksie's portrait. She peered back with that slight smile and azure eyes. Slowly, he turned toward Caroline. She withdrew her hand and folded it with her other in her lap. With a thickened voice he began to tell his sweetheart the unnerving revelation of his marriage.

"We're still...married," he whispered in conclusion.

Her face showed no color or emotion as she walked to the front window overlooking the Town Common.

Did Coffie and Jacksie have to face such unbelievable situations? she wondered.

Her breath on the panes grew, the longer she stood. Hap had not moved. His shoulders had begun to shake under the stress and emotion. Jarred back to reality by his woeful sounds, she strode back to him. Bending over, she cupped his face in her two hands.

"We will overcome this adversity. There is nothing we cannot survive. Remember that!"

With that admonition, she pushed him back on the sofa and crawled into his lap as a wife might do to comfort or to receive comfort. Startled, as she placed her head on his shoulder and her hand on his chest, he slowly enfolded this woman to him and cherished her as much as any husband would do. Both lightly slumbered.

At five o'clock, Hap roused and slowly lifted her small frame and carried her up the steps to Coffie and Jacksie's carved bed. How he wished he could have stayed, but he knew he had remained too long as it was. Pulling the duvet up under her chin, he looked down at the mistress of the King house. Turning to leave, he heard a rustle from the bedcovers.

"Hap? Thanks." Her sleepy voice softly emanated from her bed. He knew with one ounce of encouragement he would never leave that house. He could hear her turn over and nestle down in the covers. Breathing a sigh of relief, he quickly left her room.

Down in the parlor, he scribbled a note on Jacksie's writing desk and left it on the staircase. Locking the door, he slipped the key under one of the planters on the front stoop. With a quick glance to see that all was well with the house, he hurried into the darkness to his cottage.

Chapter 42
TRAPPED

*H*ap knew no lawyers intimately except Linc Connors from over in Greenville, his lawyer in the Will Cromwell murder trial. He needed a local to handle this affair in Edgecombe County. Carlton Phillips seemed a possibility, since he had come under the employ of Coeffield King. The next day Phillips discovered a distraught man pacing in front of his office door.

Hmmm was Carlton's only response after Hap recounted the sordid details of Pamela's display at his cottage. *Hmmm*, Carlton said over and over. It was a maddening habit. Maybe he had made a mistake, but Hap was desperate since McCloud and Pamela would return to Tarboro in forty-eight hours.

"Carlton? Is that all you can say?" he snapped.

"Huh? Sorry. My wife gets on me all the time. She says if I can't speak English, clear and simple, then I should not utter my *hmmm's* at all. Habits are hard to break," he mused. After a moment, he said, "I suggest that we approach the party in private and appeal that court exposure of private matters would be distasteful and hurtful. Many times, a party will agree to settle things quietly out of court. However, from your description of Banks McCloud, we may find ourselves before a judge. I don't think this man likes to lose."

"Correct. I just don't want Caroline or her family to suffer any more because of me. We've healed our relationship from my ordeal with Will. I can't have everything destroyed," he asserted. "We have to make Pamela and her grandfather understand that no one wants to go through anything ugly in public. They've got to see that there's no way they can force a marriage to work. I will never welcome her back into my home as my wife. Never! She gave Rollie to me. She can't just say she wants us back and a judge will let it happen."

"Hap, judges have been known to do strange things. Now, we have work to do. Tell me everything from the first moment you saw Pamela to the last. Also, I need to know everything about your relationship with Caroline, *then* and *now*."

He took his handkerchief from his pocket and mopped his brow, then looked sternly at his client. "Even if you were ever intimate. I cannot have any surprises, Hap, *none*. We just don't have that much time. Now, let's begin. I'll take some notes and interrupt as little as possible so you won't lose track. All right... Let me hear it."

He sat poised with pen in hand ready to dip and scratch his notes quickly across his paper.

Hap began, revealing his early infatuation with the daughter of Captain Cromwell. He spun the tale of their meeting on the grassy knoll, of how their relationship grew, of how it ended. He recounted the trial, his leaving for the university, his meeting Pamela there. He recalled for Carlton his anxiety in forgetting the impossible until one night when he opened his door to find Caroline in his doorway.

Yes, they were intimate, but he relayed the finality, the turning away, the moving on for both, as they strove for newness of life. Both found a second chance in Litch Bagley and Pamela Martin. Both began their own journeys, invigorated by their new paths. Children came, he said, a dimension that catapulted his soul beyond himself. And then the two journeys ran awry, Litch with alcohol and Pamela with lies. Neither relationship survived the onslaught of either.

"When did you see Caroline last?"

Hap looked up startled, but remembered the words of his lawyer, *I cannot have any surprises*. Then, no surprises.

He explained his pacing in front of her house last night and her inviting him in. He recounted his telling her about the awful

Chapter 42

situation with Pamela. They'd only held each other as a means of comfort, nothing more, nothing less.

His lawyer frowned.

"Carlton, our sons were asleep upstairs."

Carlton continued to frown. "Did anyone see you leave her house?"

"Not that I know of, but I wasn't looking for anyone. Why are you frowning so?"

"Well, if anyone saw you, they could make a case that you were up to no good, you know, and that could make you a bad father, especially with the boys right there in the house. Now, tell me about the vixen."

Caroline found the note. Slipping the key from under the planter, she turned her head slightly and started as a man standing by the Civil War marker on the Town Common stared at her. She felt conspicuous, but quickly busied herself with the plantings, in hopes of fending off the curiosity seeker's knowledge of her real task. Her eyes strayed to the commotion at the guesthouse down the street. McCloud and Pamela Tyson were departing to visit their people in the county. Suddenly, Banks waved toward the Town Common and the curiosity seeker tipped his hat in recognition.

In haste, Caroline disappeared into her home. Rushing to the window, she jerked the cord that cut the scenery and light from the parlor. The man was watching her. Her hands shook as she realized that she was captive in her own home. Somehow, she had to warn Hap what was happening, but she had the boys. She was confined.

Where was her housekeeper? She could watch over the boys long enough for her to shop and get a note down to Hap's office, telling him of her suspicions about the man on the Commons, but her lady was late. Frustrated, she paced the house and cared for the boys.

"Where can that woman be?" she agonized between gritted

teeth. The noon hour came and passed.

Surely, the lady would come early afternoon. Cleaning lunch dishes, Caroline heard the knocker. *Finally*, she thought. Pulling her sash, she threw the apron over one of the breakfast room chairs and rushed to the door.

The apologies were profuse from Mrs. Fornes, but Caroline cut her short as she hastily left instructions about the boys, informing the lady she had a most important errand. The befuddled woman scratched her head for the lady of the house had slipped out the back way, through the garden door, using a key that she had never seen before.

The key proved stubborn in the rusty lock rarely opened. Caroline struggled, but with a few extra jiggles, she pushed the creaking door ajar. Peeping around the high wall, she saw no one on the stretch of green. Quickly, she hurried across the way and up St. Andrew Street while looking in the distance with nostalgia at the Edgecombe County Courthouse and Coffie's old office building. Scooting around the corner, she hastened toward Main Street and Carver's Mercantile. At the corner of Main, she turned left, walking toward the store. Frankly, she could have walked on down to Hap's office, but with all the patients? She wanted as little suspicion as possible.

"Why of course Frank can run that errand for you. Frankie? Son? Miss Caroline has something she wants delivered to Doctor Rollie in his office."

Caroline held out the sealed envelope. A few coins brought a smile to the Carvers' son's face and prodded his steps to the door.

"Now, I can get all my other errands done. The boys have a friend at home so I need to hurry along."

Grabbing several items, she paid the storekeeper and moved to the front door. *Now where?* she thought. *Maybe the market? Of course.* They always needed foodstuff for the kitchen. Leaving Carver's, Caroline turned right and walked sideways across the street to the market on the corner near the Commons. In the market doorway, she glimpsed the stranger marching up the

Chapter 42

street toward her. Darting through the opening, she prayed that the few stray shoppers had disguised her entry into the building. Hopefully, he had not seen her at all.

"Why, Miss Caroline, a pleasure to see you today. Can I help you with anything?"

She whirled around. "Oh, I'm just going to pick up a few things, thank you."

Moving to the rear of the store, she hid behind shelving, allowing her full advantage of seeing the walkway, but any passerby would think the market was empty if he looked in. The stranger stood right in front as if he were trying to decide whether to enter or walk around the corner. He pivoted at the corner, glancing in all directions, putting his hand to his chin, as if trying to figure what to do next.

Go away, she screamed inside.

The man slowly walked down Main toward the river and Hap's office. Did he think that she was there? How did he know that she was not at home? Jacob? Coffie? Paying for her purchases, Caroline walked cautiously to the front door. Her shopping bag bulged with her packages. Somehow, she had to get out of that door without the little bell ringing. The tinkling sound could attract the attention of the stranger as he ambled up the street peering through the storefronts.

The shop owner stepped back to the stockroom. *My chance!* Caroline held the bell, as she slipped through the door and around the corner of the building. Quickly, she retraced her steps and wound up at the garden gate with the key in hand. How clumsy she felt as she fumbled with that old key.

"Madam, may I help you with your key?" Caroline whirled around to stare up into the stranger's face.

"I beg your pardon?"

"You seem to be having trouble with your key to your *back* gate door. Hmmm. This key is so rusty you must not use this way very often, do you?"

Caroline was so stunned that she never objected as the

stranger took the key from her raised hand.

"Who are you?" She paused. "Sir?" She seemed to regain a little confidence.

"Oh, I'm just someone in town for a short stay. Right nice little town on the Tar. There."

With a smirk, he pushed the heavy garden gate, listening to it squeak from lack of use.

"Your gate is opened, and might I suggest that you get another key made, so *if* you use this way again, you'll not have this much trouble."

She took the key defiantly from his hand and glared back at the smirk, a look that said, *I caught you at your little game. I am watching.*

"Hap, what in the world? What's the matter? Jenny said it's an emergency."

Hap collapsed in the chair in front of Carlton Phillips' desk, holding the note toward his lawyer. "Read this. Then, you'll know what we're up against."

Taking the note from Hap's shaking fingers, he read the finely penned message.

Dear Hap,

This morning when I retrieved the key from the planter, I spied a strange person leaning against a monument on the Town Common. He stared directly at me. There was commotion at the end of the Commons. Mister McCloud and Pamela were leaving on the trip to the country, but before they moved away, McCloud gave a slight wave to the stranger, who tipped his hat.

It seems that I am being watched under orders from Pamela's grandfather. I am scared for the boys and myself. Tell me what to do.

Affectionately,
Caroline

Chapter 42

"I tell you, Carlton, the man will stop at nothing to get what he wants."

Hap jumped up to pace with his hands behind his back. Shaking his finger at his lawyer, he continued, "We are sunk if the stranger on the Common saw me coming out of Caroline's house at five in the morning."

Once more, he plopped into the chair, grabbing his head in torment. "I just cannot bear this pressure. I am afraid I will make a mistake with my patients or with my family. What can we do, Carlton?"

"Listen, Hap, don't jump to any conclusions, but you must stay away from Caroline. Understand?"

This time it was Carlton's turn to shake his finger. Hap nodded in despair.

"Tomorrow I will wire the Orange County Courthouse to find out if the old codger is telling the truth. He probably is, so don't get your hopes up. He wouldn't go to all this trouble if a simple wire would prove them wrong. Go home; you have a son to care for. Keep Willie there. I may need to see you in the night."

Slapping him once more on the shoulder, he pulled a distraught Hap to his feet.

"Don't let that evil man take my son, Carlton? Please," Hap pleaded.

"We'll win, Hap. Don't worry. She's the one who deserted. She's the one who gave away her son. And, I may have another idea."

He tried to sound positive, because a lawyer never knew what a judge might decide when a mother was begging for her husband and her child, especially with a powerful grandfather in her corner who knows every trick in the book.

If I only had more time! he fussed.

Chapter 43
CONFRONTATION

A smile flickered on Hap's face. "Willie, thanks for staying tonight." He hesitated. "We may have a night visitor. You know Carlton Phillips?"

"The lawyer? Yes. I know the man," Willie acknowledged. "Do you want me to stay in Rollie's room while you talk?"

"If you don't mind. It may be that the less you know, the better."

Sure enough, a light knock on the door came within an hour. Carlton Phillips had come to talk strategy. He wanted more information on McCloud, Pamela, and the Martins. Whatever Hap could remember, he needed to hear, random thoughts, stories, reputation, anything, for Phillips was desperate for clues and he needed them fast. Hap smiled every time his lawyer said *Hmmm,* but this time he posed no objection. This mannerism just might help Carlton to ferret a solution for his entanglement.

"That's it. I can't think of another thing to say about the lot. What do you think? Have we got a chance?"

An exhausted Hap flopped back in his chair, extending his long legs, flexing them to release the tension in his body.

"We'll see. Now, Hap, I do have something that I want you to consider." Carlton paused putting away his notes into his briefcase. "What would you say that we put fraud on the table?"

"Charge Rollie's mother with fraud? No! I could never do that. I'm sorry, Carlton. Rollie would eventually hate me if he knew that. I just cannot. We have to move on with desertion."

"Okay, my friend, but that would cinch the case for us."

"Sorry..."

Chapter 43

"I will keep it on the back burner just in case we need to use it as a pawn. By the way, I took a note to Caroline."

Hap's head jerked upward.

"How is she? What'd you say to her?"

"Well, I didn't stay, because I didn't want the snoop to think we'd had long conversations, the reason for the note, but I assured her that you were fine and that I would see you tonight."

He glanced at his friend. Clearing his throat, he said, "She sends her...love."

"Thanks, Carlton. I think I can sleep tonight."

He stared at his hands, hands that were supposed to heal and comfort, but hands that felt helpless and out of control.

"I have to go, friend. I, too, must get some rest," he added, arching his back in a stretch. "Tomorrow will be a busy day. If I were you, I'd send word to the Cromwells. Caroline probably needs their support right now. She's scared. In fact, I may call in a favor with the deputy to move all vagrants from the Town Common."

As he spoke, his eyes twinkled as he pulled on his topcoat.

Even Hap could risk a smile.

"How did you come? Do you think that guy saw you?"

"Well, if he did, he had to totally change his position. I came up back through the old cemetery. I'll go back that way, too. When did Pamela say they would return to the guest house?"

"In the afternoon. She'll come here with great expectations, I'm sure. I dread it. God in heaven, I dread it."

The two men shook hands and stood in silence before Phillips slipped away in the darkness.

The next afternoon, Hap paced. He had not been *this* nervous on his wedding day. It seemed his shoes knew every board in the small living room floor, every rise, every notch.

"Relax, Hap," Carlton Phillips spoke as reassuringly as he could. Frankly, he was a mite nervous himself, not having had the sleep and time to find out all the facts of this case.

"Look, Hap, I think I can make a healthy statement that might keep this affair out of the throes of a legal battle. Listen, they may become reasonable. We don't know one way or the other, but let's just wait and not worry about anything until we have something to worry about."

Hap smiled feebly as he caught sight of the carriage pulling around the corner from the guesthouse.

"Well, it won't be long now," he sighed.

Pamela sat across from her grandfather in the carriage. Her face shown with happiness in the assurance that once more she would be Hap's wife and Rollie's mother. Her grandfather reached over and squeezed her hand, for he knew he would offer the young doctor any bribe to keep that expression on his granddaughter's face. Surely, no man could refuse what he could offer, and he would if there was resistance in the cottage around the corner.

Little did he know that there was a lawyer waiting to present a brief to him if the young couple could not come to an agreement. Carlton Phillips hoped this strategy of surprise would just overwhelm them so they could agree to terms and retreat to Chapel Hill.

The jostle of the carriage lulled the young woman to dream of being in Hap's bed again. Oh, she would make him *very happy*, and she knew how. Biting her lip, her eyebrows flew upward as the driver walked around to help her from the carriage. Grunting loudly, Banks McCloud crawled down after her, using his cane to balance. She turned to take his arm, to fortify their front as they approached a possible battlefield.

Hap opened the door before they could knock.

"Come in, please. Pamela. Mister McCloud. I hope you had a good trip to the country."

"Oh, Hap, it was wonderful seeing that part of our family again."

She had dropped her grandfather's arm and rushed to take his as if she was assuming her rightful place at his side. Smiling up

Chapter 43

at him, she quickly brushed her lips against his cheek before he could pull away.

"Hap, I am your wife. Wives kiss husbands—Oh, excuse me, who—"

"Uh, Pamela, come sit down. Please, sir, you, too, of course. I felt it necessary for my friend, Mister Phillips, to be—"

"He's a lawyer!" screeched McCloud. "You scalawag, we come here in peace and harmony to renew your vows with Pammie! And you present yourself with a lawyer!"

The old man had gotten outrageous in his demeanor and his squawking. Hap looked helpless toward Carlton Phillips.

"Miss Mar—"

"I'm Mrs. Tyson, sir! We are *still* officially married. I have my license right here in my purse and the documents that were *never, ever,* filed with the courts." She patted her pocketbook for emphasis. "We are still very much married!"

She, too, reached a higher, venomous pitch. Her eyes blazed; her face contorted. Feelings of rebuff and rejection triggered her wrath.

"How could you?" she screamed over and over until finally he seated her by the fire with McCloud to listen to Carlton Phillips.

Pamela sat humiliated and mortified, defied by the man she loved, or thought she loved, or wanted to love...again. Eventually she calmed somewhat, only comforted by her grandfather who glowered in silence, a silence that made both Hap and Carlton uneasy.

"Well, give us your proposal," McCloud acridly cracked.

"Certainly, sir." Carlton jumped up to make his presentation.

What a strange scene, he thought, as he drew out some papers from his case and placed them neatly on the table nearby. Clearing his throat, he stood before them and knew this plea would probably be one of the hardest he would ever make in his career. He began and spoke for almost an hour, presenting all the facts as he had heard them and showing how degrading and embarrassing it would be for all to go through the court only to reveal that desertion carried a heavy weight against the deserting party, and on, and on. Carlton Phillips was eloquent.

When he finished, Hap's face glowed with approval and satisfaction. Surely, they could not refuse, he thought.

McCloud stood feebly and said only five words jabbing his forefinger with each word.

"We'll see you in court!"

Motioning for Pamela to leave behind him, she stood ramrod and stared smugly at her husband.

"I'll make sure that you never see Rollie again when this ordeal is over. You really don't know who you're dealing with. Yes, we'll see you in court!"

Her venomous voice made Hap wonder how her love could flee so quickly.

"Excuse me, madam, sir. I have one more issue to discuss."

"What more, you ingrate?" Banks McCloud growled.

"Well, I tried to get my client to issue a complaint about fraud."

"Huh! Fraud! What fraud?" McCloud barked.

"The fraud of your not filing the papers of divorce that the judge instructed you to do."

McCloud froze, his hand on his daughter's arm.

"Sir, I want you to know that my client did not want to use that complaint, but I know that it would be iron clad in our favor. Now, I suggest that we handle this matter in front of a Superior Court Judge, in his chambers, but not in the courtroom. Will you agree to that?"

For the first time in his career, Banks McCloud faltered. "Uh, yes, we will do that."

"Grandfather!"

"On second thought, Pamela, Tyson is going for the lesser charge. Yes, we'll take it. Let's go, my dear." He turned to go.

"Excuse me, madam, I have these papers for you. I am sure your grandfather needs to see them." Pamela's eyes once more widened as she recognized legal papers. She was being served.

Chapter 44
THE OPPOSITION

Carlton filed the divorce and custody papers for Hap at the Edgecombe County Courthouse before Banks McCloud and his granddaughter could set foot again in Orange County. The timing and place meant everything to Carlton for he knew little about their system.

Only one or two colleagues practicing in the area came to his mind, one with whom he knew he wanted no entanglement. His name? Mervin Vanderclock Strawn, Carlton's nemesis at Trinity's law school. Never once had Carlton been able to debate in a moot court activity and win over Mervin. Not once in the debate societies had he and his team succeeded over Mervin and his team. Carlton wanted no part of this past thorn.

"Mister Phillips?"

"Yes, Jenny?

"Well, I know you didn't want to be disturbed, but this message just came from the wire office. Fred thought you might want to read it immediately. It's from Chapel Hill."

Carlton froze over his papers on his desk. He had been frantically trying to clear his work load so he could concentrate on the Tyson case, but he sensed the Chapel Hill folks wanted no time to burn until they could get into the courts.

Only one week had passed, and Carlton was receiving a wire from God knows whom about the case. His hands shook slightly as he tore open the communiqué. The typed print jumped out at him. His hand shook worse.

"Jenny, excuse me, please. I need to study this alone for now."

He waited briefly until the door closed quietly behind her.

The wire was sent from none other than Mervin Strawn, stating that one Pamela Tyson had retained him in divorce and custody proceedings and that he looked forward to sparring once more with his old classmate.

Perspiration beaded on the lawyer's forehead.

Surely, it's a mistake. Not Strawn! The irony is too great.

The court calendar cleared for their case in the Edgecombe County Courthouse the middle of April. Hap and Caroline would have been married by then, probably allowing Sarah to dote on them with her plans for a reception honoring their nuptials. How their life had changed in such a short time. Courts. Lawyers. These two wanted no part of such, but here they were being tossed into the arena to hear the resounding voices of the legals as they posed their points in the judge's chambers.

Carlton had ordered them *not* to make contact, except through notes delivered *only* through him. The notes of endearment wove their lives even closer through the penned word...

From her:

...each time I hear a stirring outside my door, I know it must be you. But you are not there, and, yet, I see you as clear as anything that I could name. Your infectious smile comes back at me. I look to the Green and think of my sixteenth birthday. I see you spinning me around to the music. I see you at the grassy knoll, so tall and handsome, blushing, ready to give me my precious lavaliere. I have it around my neck this moment, my dearest, holding it between my fingers, knowing that you have touched it. Was it not yesterday that you struggled with the clasp? Time flies so...but, not now, not now. I am desperate to see you...it has been an eternity...

From him:

...work keeps me sane, otherwise, I think I could run out of the office and down to the bridge and shout to the top of my lungs. Only my thoughts of you could stop me from jumping off

Chapter 44

and floating down the Tar to get away from all these unpleasant circumstances. Sweetheart, my one regret is the pain that I have caused you and our sons...soon, my love, soon...

The Superior Court Judge for their case was coming from Halifax, a little town north of Tarboro, steeped in tradition and government. Halifax, like Tarboro and other eastern North Carolina towns, hosted the General Assembly before the establishment of the permanent seat in Raleigh. Carlton was elated; Judge Latham Price would preside.

"Well, well, my friend, we've got the right man on the bench. He's as fair a judicator as we could hope for."

Hap feebly smiled still entrenched with doubts. He feared losing Rollie more than he cared to admit, not totally trusting his lawyer's words when he knew the opposition so well.

April 16th fell on a Monday. The judge would have a full week, if needed, to listen and absorb the woes of the case. Maybe it was better to hear every point without a break; Carlton certainly hoped so. If at all possible, they needed everything to go their way.

That Monday dawned with the burst of spring in the air. Tarboro was breaking forth in profusion of greenery and buds. Jacksie Thrash's garden promised the hope of renewal as Caroline walked amongst the burgeoning shrubs and bulbs. Her chest rose and fell with the deepness of the clean, fresh air. Surely, only goodness could come on a day like today.

Hap looked out his front window, able to see the guesthouse on the corner of the Green. He was sure that Pamela and McCloud chose that place as an irritant for him. This ordeal would not be easy. Hap peeked into Rollie's room and watched as Willie rocked him and read his favorite stories.

"Daddy! Daddy!" he squealed, jumping down from Willie's lap and racing to his father's outstretched arms. "Are you leaving now? Huh, Daddy?"

"Yes, son. I will see your mother today. We'll be talking about our future and some other things."

"Mommie? I—I can't hardly 'member her face, Daddy. Mommie," he sniveled slightly and then bear-hugged his father. Hap's eyes closed as he clasped his son even tighter.

Carlton Phillips gathered all his papers and put them in his case. *Well, here we are,* he thought, *the day of reckoning.* He reached for the water glass, but when he poured, he realized that the pitcher was empty. As long as she had worked for him, Jenny had never forgotten. His shoulders slumped. Everything needed to go their way, even water in the pitcher.

The sunshine hit him right between the eyes as he opened his outer door and looked over toward the courthouse. Never once in his career had he dreaded going up those steps until today. He shivered as he thought of Mervin Strawn. He would have to render the performance of his life even in just greeting this man, but he would do it. He would do whatever it took to win this case and break the agony of Hap Tyson.

Closing his door, Carlton slowly walked across the street, noticing the number of carriages at the posts outside. Sweat began to bead on his forehead. Why were so many people here? The judge would only hear the pleas, but the county certainly had a vested interest in one of the few doctors in their area. They wanted this case resolved in Hap's favor almost as much as he. Hap was one of them, now and forever. Many mumbled as they watched Pamela Tyson and McCloud ascend the courthouse steps with Mervin Strawn at their elbows. Strawn exuded such spark and confidence that even some turned their backs so they could shake their heads unseen. The situation looked bleak. For Carlton, walking Blackbeard's plank could not be worse than the thought of battling Strawn. His innards churned as he returned the man's sickening salutation from the courthouse steps.

Chapter 45
BATTLE

Only Judge Price would hear the complaints and arguments and issue his decision. The bailiff greeted the parties in the entry hall of the courthouse. "The judge awaits in his chamber."

Superior Court Judge Latham Price's appearance extremely contrasted with Hamilton Barnes, the only judge Hap was familiar with from his trial for the murder of Will Cromwell. Barnes, stately and dramatic, could have dwarfed Latham Price. Price might have been small in stature, but in the eyes of the legal community, he walked in big shoes. His stride from behind his desk to shake the lawyers' hands exuded confidence and control. The man laid the ground rules in fast order, giving parameters of tolerance, but under no uncertain terms, *he* was the final word in his chambers, as well as in his court.

"Let's be seated, lady and gentlemen. The complainant to my right, please." Everyone slipped into their respective seats at the table. "Now, Mister Philips, as representative of the complainant, you will go first and cite your client's case. Let's get started."

"Thank you, Your Honor. Judge Price, I come representing a man who wants to get on with his life and had done so before a very startling experience with one Pamela Martin Tyson, whom he thought was his former wife. We will show Your Honor facts and evidences that should prove to Your Honor that this union is no longer one of love and should dissolve. We intend to show that young Rollie Tyson, my client's namesake, desires to remain in the home, established and maintained for him by his father, Thomas Rolland Tyson..."

When he finished and seated himself, Hap placed his hand on

CAROLINE...THE CAPTAIN'S DAUGHTER

his friend's arm with approval.

"Thank you, Mister Phillips. Now, Mister Strawn, your opening statement."

Mervin Strawn rose after listening to Phillips, his old college adversary. "If the court pleases, I would like to establish my presence in this case. "

"Quickly, Mr. Strawn, please," the judge waved him along.

"One Pamela Tyson, present at this table, retained my services for the purposes of representing her in response to the allegations presented to this court in terms of divorce and child custody. My client stands alone with her grandfather, Mister Craven McCloud, presently of Orange County, to come against these so-called wishes of Mrs. Tyson's husband..."

Constantly, Carlton had his hand on Hap's arm as the master wove his opening tale for the judge. The pressure from his lawyer's hand made Hap realize the urgency for silence. Then, quite suddenly, he relaxed. The case *was* in Carlton's hands.

Strawn finished and sat.

Carlton furtively glanced at Mervin across the table and locked eyes with his opponent, whose smile was irritatingly smug. He forced his attention back to his client, feeding on his support to avoid crumbling himself.

Judge Price swiveled his chair back towards Phillips and Hap. "Sir, please present your complaint."

Carlton Phillips felt the pressure, but he also felt strength in the truth that surely would convince the judge the rightness of the issues. He began.

Carlton had Hap capturing his early life and reiterating his vow to have compassion and to serve. He masterfully led Hap through his adult life as a model citizen and a primary caregiver of the people of Edgecombe County. The approval of the Cromwells to nurse Coeffield King back to health capped Hap's professional picture. His halo shone. Even the judge smiled. Carlton was satisfied, but he knew the hard questions were coming up and now.

Chapter 45

"Doctor Tyson, would you tell of a trip you took to Chapel Hill in the attempt to get your family back? Just factual details if you will."

"Yes, Pamela had taken Rollie to visit her family since she'd not seen them in months. After several weeks, I wired her, begging her to come home. *She* never answered *me*.

"I was heartbroken, but, Your Honor, I was determined to win my family back. I even closed my practice and went to Chapel Hill. Not sending a wire to announce myself this time was a twist of fate. I walked right into Banks McCloud's birthday party.

"I confronted my wife about our situation, and she told me to get out, but to return the next day. Her grandfather had some business to discuss with me. Before I left, I asked her who all the young gentlemen were in attendance to Banks' birthday party. She told me that he had invited them to entertain her since she was so sad. She claimed they were of good stock and would make good suitors...for her."

"Doctor Tyson, did you return the next day as suggested?"

"Oh yes, but when Mister McCloud showed me the divorce papers, I got upset and called out for my wife. When she didn't answer, I raced upstairs to our former quarters. She was there, Judge Price, but she turned from me and wouldn't talk. I was devastated and confused. The woman who gave me Rollie was asking for a divorce and my son. I begged for Rollie, telling her the suitors would not want to be hampered with someone else's child."

"How did she react to this idea?" Carlton asked.

"She was shocked at first. Then, over the objections of her grandfather, she agreed and told him she could have other great-grandchildren for him any time she wanted."

"She told her grandfather that she could have other great-grandchildren for him? Am I quoting you correctly, Doctor Tyson?" Carlton asked.

"Yes, you are. My wife juggled out charts around so she could have a child. She reneged on our agreement to avoid this issue until I was out of school and established in a practice."

"Objection, Your Honor. Charts? What charts?"

"These charts, Your Honor," Carlton whipped the two pieces of paper off the table and waved them before the judge.

"Hmm," he said, as he quickly scanned them. "Mister Strawn, here, show these to your client and ask her if these documents are the ones in question."

Pamela bit her lip and nodded, barely looking at the charts.

"Continue, Doctor Tyson," the judge advised.

"I thought we were—uh-being careful until I could get out of medical school, as agreed. She lied, Your Honor," Hap said turning to the judge. "She wanted a child then and the trust fund her grandfather would set up when a child came."

"Your Honor?" Strawn stood shrugging.

"Just facts, Doctor." The judge smiled behind his hand.

Once more Carlton was satisfied. He sat down, nodding at the judge.

"Mister Strawn, do you have questions for Doctor Tyson?"

"I do, Your Honor." He smiled, stood, and looked directly at Hap. "Sir, when you decided to go Down East after graduation to set up a practice, what agreement did you have with your wife about such a move?"

"Well, I'm not sure what you are referring to..."

"May I refresh your memory? Did your wife not tell you that if you moved your family to Tarboro, in other words, plucked her from the bosom of her family and plunked her down among total strangers, and that if she did not like it, that she would leave?"

"Well, yes, she did, but-"

"Thank you, Doctor Tyson. Now, did she not come to you and tell you that she was going to go home and visit with her family that she had not seen in months and that she was taking Rollie for this family visit as well?"

"Yes."

"Thank you, again. Now, when you first met Miss Pamela's family, were you not overcome by the size and attentiveness they

Chapter 45

all had for each other?"

"Conjecture, Your Honor," Phillips injected.

"I apologize, sir. No more questions at this time."

Judge Price pulled out his pocket watch and noted that they were approaching the noon hour.

"Let's take a break and get back in session by 1:15."

Price rose; the others followed. Both sides had much to discuss.

"Hap, my wife sent us lunch to my office. We'll eat and go over a few things before the afternoon session."

The lawyer smiled as he saw the filled pitcher and two glasses in place on the appropriate corner of his desk. *Thank you, Jenny.* Serving Hap and himself, he raised his glass and toasted their success of the day. It was only the opening statements and the opening questions for Hap, but going first had given Carlton an edge to put in all the points he wanted to and with as much emotion as he felt he could.

"This is the best I've felt yet, Carlton. In fact, I sensed peace, sitting at that table listening to you. There is nothing like the truth and it was echoing in that chamber," Hap laughed, probably for the first time in weeks.

The young lawyer looked at his naïve friend and vowed silently that he would not break this mood as they discussed afternoon notes. Lifted spirits are infectious, and he needed to stay high-spirited himself.

Chapter 46

MRS. TYSON

Judge Price turned to Mervin Strawn and said, "Well, Mister Strawn? It's your turn, please."

Strawn jumped up and turned toward Pamela, who demurely looked askance at him.

"Mrs. Tyson, please tell His Honor where you are living at the moment and the status of your marriage as you see it."

Pamela turned and, with her most innocent, cow-eyed look, spoke to Judge Price.

"Sir, presently, I reside at the residence of my grandfather, Mister Craven Peacock McCloud in the village of Chapel Hill. The reason I returned to Chapel Hill was my grandfather's welfare."

Hap almost choked. Carlton quickly suppressed his client. Their eyes met briefly and then both turned to stare at this amazing young woman, who appeared to perjure herself.

"Mister McCloud's welfare? If you will, explain this to the judge."

"Well, no one really knew that my grandfather had been ill. We kept it a secret."

Oh yeah, so secretive that even his guests at his birthday party never knew he was ill. I cannot believe this!

Hap squinted pleadingly at Carlton, but his lawyer continued staring ahead and patted his client's arm simultaneously.

"Go on, please," Strawn encouraged.

"Well, my husband was busy establishing his practice that I thought it would be a good time for me to visit my family. I really had not seen them since we moved to Tarboro, and since he was not well, I could take care of my grandfather and see my parents

Chapter 46

and siblings."

"Now, if you will, tell His Honor, about your family life."

"Yes, sir. We were happy in our new home. Our precious son was beginning to be his own person. Hap was working long hours, but we made the best of the few hours in the day that we had together. We were certainly striving for private time to keep our family close. Those were such happy days, until..."

"Excuse me, Mrs. Tyson," Strawn interrupted, "Please establish for the judge how you and Dr. Tyson met. Your engagement. And your marriage."

Pamela allowed her eyes to drift off into the distance as if she were trying to conjure up visions of those first moments of contact, of their engagement at Banks' house, of their wedding in Hillsborough. Her eyes shimmered as she swiveled in her seat to stare directly into Hap's eyes, as she wove their love story.

Hap squirmed. He could not look at her any longer, staring down at the highly polished table, but never once did she divert her gaze from him. Phillips matched her stare. He knew the tactic well from law school. Strawn had not forgotten one trick.

"And your marriage?" Strawn encouraged again.

Hap got uncomfortable. *Good heavens, is she going to tell the judge what we did in our bedroom?*

His neck reddened as little rivulets trickled down his spine. He was grateful that they were in the judge's chambers and not in the courtroom. How the tongues would have wagged, passing juicy tidbits to anxious ears.

"Mr. Strawn, your client has given us ample details of the early background of this relationship between husband and wife. I'm going to ask that you bring your client up-to-date with your questions."

Hap could not raise his head. He was devastated. *My God, so many details!*

Carlton whispered, "just tactics, Hap." This time? His own neck burned.

"Now, Mrs. Tyson, would you recall the words of the letter

you received from your grandfather which prompted your return trip to Chapel Hill?"

Carlton looked quizzical, as Hap slightly shrugged.

As he spoke, Strawn fingered a document, which, of course, made everyone believe that he possessed Banks McCloud's letter.

The paper crackled; Strawn opened the letter, handing it to the judge. *It's real?* Both Hap's and Carlton's mouths dropped open.

"Of course," said the wide-eyed innocent damsel. She quoted the letter word for word. Her grandfather requested that she and Rollie come soon because he had not been well lately and felt they would lift his spirits and help him return to better health. Children are such good tonics for the elderly, he wrote.

"So, you went?"

"Oh yes, Mister Strawn. I told my husband I was going to Chapel Hill to see my family whom I had not seen since we moved to Tarboro. My son and I left the next day to attend to my grandfather."

"What happened next?"

"Well, weeks went by and we never heard from my husband. I suppose he had his mind on other things...or people."

"Do you recall when you saw Doctor Tyson next?"

"Oh yes, he barged into my grandfather's house uninvited and made demands, but-" Her voice broke as she buried her head momentarily, then raised it with mustered courage. "Banks and I had discussed my situation. If my husband had not even tried to contact me, then he—he must not want me for his wife. We devised a test. We would present him with a decree of divorce, and if he signed it, we'd know he wanted out. He signed it, Judge Price," Pamela sobbed. Strawn handed her his handkerchief.

"We'll take a ten minute break, folks." The judge practically dashed from the chamber. The man seemed to fly.

Carlton and Hap never left their seats. They were stunned that Strawn had produced a letter. Both questioned if it was even real or manufactured to ease the charge of desertion.

Chapter 46

Strawn escorted Pamela with caution and attention. He was going to win this case at all costs, repulsive theatrics and all. He knew Carlton would be bloodthirsty in his questioning of Pamela when the time came. For her blood, as well as his. But, he was not finished yet. He couldn't wait.

Chapter 47
DESERTION

"*M*ister Strawn," Judge Price said, after the break, "Please continue or conclude your questions."

"Thank you, Your Honor. May I once more thank the court for allowing a well-deserved recess. My client appreci—."

"Strawn? Proceed," interrupted the judge with a slight scowl.

Carlton Phillips smiled.

"Uh? Oh, of course, Your Honor," he said, slightly clearing his throat, while Pamela demurely looked over at Hap and then directed her attention to the judge.

"Now, Mrs. Tyson, the last point I would like for you to make for this court is to recount for us how young Rollie Tyson came to live with his father in Tarboro."

What? Is Strawn crazy? Hap thought. *Desertion, you idiot, but what will she say?*

Looking quite innocent, Pamela startled the judge by saying that she gave her son over to her husband.

"Mrs. Tyson, did you say you gave him to your husband with no fight to hold on to your son?"

"Oh, Judge Price, let me explain... First, may I have a drink of water, please?"

Her head swiveled from the judge to her lawyer with big questioning eyes. Strawn jumped to please. After a few swallows, she continued as the judge and Hap leaned closer. Only Carlton seemed to slump back.

"Hap came to the house as planned the next day. I think he stayed at the Patterson on the other side of the campus on Columbia Street. Anyway, my grandfather greeted him at the

Chapter 47

door. I just could not be present at the moment. My emotions were too great.

"My grandfather presented him with the papers as planned, but Hap ran up the stairs and barged into my room shouting. He demanded the child.

"In the heat of the emotion, I agreed, just wanting this madman out of my grandfather's house. Judge Price, that was a very big mistake on my part, but when he signed those papers and took my son away, my whole life walked out that door. I was also afraid for my grandfather's health. I felt that if we lived apart for a while, then maybe, just maybe, I could see him at a later date and all would be forgiven...until..." Her head dropped down; her eyes closed.

"Uh-Mrs. Tyson? Now, will you tell the judge *until what?*" Strawn asked.

"Mrs. Tyson?" the judge leaned over. "Until what? Mrs. Tyson, you are required to answer. Madam?"

At this time, he reared back in his chair, placing his hand under his chin, rubbing it slightly, anticipating her next words.

"We—ell," she dragged out the word for the fullest effect. "Until I realized that there was another woman in my husband's life."

Hap sat stunned. She was introducing scandal to her testimony. How damaging would her next words be?

"Would you repeat that, please?" the judge demanded as he swung around once more to lean over toward her.

"I—I said until I realized that there was another woman in my husband's life."

"I see...Go on, Mrs. Tyson," the judge urged with a furrow in his brow and a scowl covering his face.

Mervin Strawn stood back with a gleam in his eye and a slight grin on his face.

Perfect. Perfect. Oh God, this is good.

"Your Honor, I knew there was a—what shall I say? A ghost from the past? My husband alluded to that before, you see, even in our courtship, but I never knew a name to match with this—person, until we moved to Tarboro. Now, my husband is a fine-looking man. I would not expect that he did not have many ladies swooning over him before, but certainly, I expected him to respect our wedding vows. You know, 'to honor and to cherish.'"

"Go on, Mrs. Tyson." Strawn had chimed in, just to remind the judge and his client that he was in this game, too. Almost startled by the new voice in her ear, she looked back at the judge.

"Surely, all who have spoken those hallowed words in a hallowed place know the weight they carry in a marriage."

"Judge Price," Carlton said, ready to object.

The judge quickly held up his hand. "Excuse me, Mrs. Tyson. I must advise you to stick to the facts of your case and not carry on with philosophizing."

"Of course, Your Honor," she purred and knew full well that the effect was made.

"Let me see," she pondered, "I believe the first evidence of his diversified interest came during the illness of one Coeffield King. I did not suspect trysts, Your Honor. No. My husband and I were quite the married couple."

Pamela mustered up a blush for the judge. Fanning herself with her handkerchief, she took a sip of water and continued.

"At least not right away…"

"Objection, Your Honor, Mrs. Tyson knows no first-hand evidence…Please advise her of relaying fa—" Carlton said.

"True, Mrs. Tyson, I have been lenient, but you must stick to knowledge and not prognostications."

"Oh…" Allowing her voice to trail again, she looked down at her hands and wrung them profusely.

"I saw that my husband was intrigued by this woman once more when he returned from the funeral of Mr. King. For two days we had conversations about the past and the situation that seemed to be developing. He assured me that she was married and lived in Raleigh, and that was that. Judge Price, don't you know when someone is not telling you the whole truth?"

Chapter 47

"Mrs. Tyson!"

"I'm sorry, but I knew enough that I shut my bedroom door on my own husband."

The judge rolled his eyes, realizing this woman was going to get her message across no matter how many times he or Carlton objected.

"Mrs. Tyson."

Her head jerked Strawn's way. Her eyes feigned hurt.

"Did these conversations and situations prompt your taking your son out of this uncomfortable situation?"

"Yes."

"Did these situations just happen to coincide with your grandfather's plea to come to Chapel Hill and nurse him back to health?"

"Yes."

"Mrs. Tyson, did your grandfather's health improve when you returned with his great-grandson to Chapel Hill?"

"Oh, yes, immediately." Her eyes brimmed with excitement. "He changed practically overnight."

"Mrs. Tyson, was your son glad to see his great-grandfather and his grandparents?"

"Yes! He had not seen them in months. We had a wonderful reunion."

"Your Honor, I have no further questions at this time."

Mervin Strawn actually bowed toward the judge to the disgust of the man who would take over the questioning.

"Excuse me, Mr. Phillips. I will adjourn Mrs. Tyson's cross-examination until ten o'clock Tuesday morning."

Price lightly tapped his gavel and disappeared into his private inner chambers. Carlton Phillips was not a happy man. Too much had transpired against his client. No, he was not happy.

Chapter 48

MORE TESTIMONY

As her parents left for Shiloh with Jacob and Coffie in tow, Caroline sat and waited at the foot of Jacksie Thrash's portrait, looking up into those wise eyes that had blessed her life for not enough years. Closing her own, she began to think of the good between her and Hap. She smiled even as she lightly dozed, but not so deeply that she did not hear the slight knock. Jumping off the couch, she straightened her dress and patted her hair as she reached for the front door.

A weak smile greeted her.

"I've been expecting you."

They had not seen each other in two days.

"Let's sit in the parlor."

His eyes never left her head. He felt awkward.

"I had to see you."

"Well? What's happened with the judge? It's so hard not being there with you."

"You have to know what she said."

"What?"

"She told the judge that I was interested in another woman since we'd been married."

"Oh no," Caroline murmured.

"She talked about a ghost from the past but then spoke of the present and the change she began to sense in me. She said she knew I intended for you to be my future." His head dropped into his hands. "We are supposed to be married. None of this nightmare should be happening."

"My darling," she whispered and ran her fingers through his

Chapter 48

shock of hair. She leaned over and lifted his chin.

"I love you, Hap Tyson," she said and kissed his forehead.

He sat back and slid his long arm around her. Their lips met hesitantly, then with yearning.

Tuesday morning arrived with all parties facing Judge Price in his chambers.

"Mister Phillips, we will resume with your cross-examination of Mrs. Tyson."

"Thank you, Your Honor. Mrs. Tyson, was it your intent to ever return to your husband and son in Tarboro?"

"What?" Pamela's eye's widened as she turned to her lawyer.

"Mrs. Tyson, answer the question as it has been presented to you," Judge Price instructed.

"Judge, may I confer with my client?" Strawn said with a little anxiety.

"No, sir, I wish to hear her answer. Mrs. Tyson?"

"I-I didn't like it there; no, I didn't want to go back, but Rollie. I didn't want to lose him."

"So, your answer is no. Thank you, Mrs. Tyson. Now, have you ever lied to your husband?"

"Judge?" Strawn interrupted the process.

"Quiet! Mister Strawn, you may re-examine if you see fit later. Continue, please. Mrs. Tyson?"

"Are you talking about the charts?"

"Well, that for one."

"I hid the real charts and made my own ones to be in favor of conceiving a child."

"Hiding the truth from your husband is deception, an untrue falsehood, or is the act of lying to trick someone. Did you trick your husband by switching the charts?"

"Yes."

"Thank you, Mrs. Tyson. Now, speaking of hiding, did you not hide your grandfather's illness from your husband?"

"Well, we did want to keep it a secret."

"Why?"

"I am not sure..." Her voice faded.

"Okay, for now. Let's go back to your grandfather's birthday party. What was your statement about the presence of the three young men in attendance to the party?"

"He invited some younger people to entertain me since I had been so sad."

"Why did he not invite some young ladies who lived in the area, maybe some who had been in school with you?"

"I don't know."

"Mrs. Tyson, were you laughing and talking freely with the young gentlemen at this party? In other words, were you happy that day when your husband arrived?"

"Uh, yes."

"Were you happy when your husband came in?"

"Not really."

"Why not? He *is* your husband as you have pointed out numerous times. Did you bring your marriage license with you today? In your purse? To show the judge?"

"I-uh-don't have it today."

"Thank you, Mrs. Tyson. No other questions at this time."

"Mister Strawn?"

"Oh, yes, I have questions. Thank you, sir."

The young lawyer relished what would happen for the entire world to know, but, most importantly, Judge Latham Price. He had the clincher. He began.

"Now, Miss Pamela, do you know one Neal Crawford?"

Hap and Carlton exchanged blank stares.

"Why, yes I do. He's the private investigator that my grandfather hired to watch out for my interests here in Tarboro."

Hap and Carlton read each other's thoughts, the stranger on the Green. Both men wiggled in their chairs.

"Mr. Crawford came highly recommended—"

"Inadmissible. We don't know this person or anything about his credentials."

CHAPTER 48

Latham Price intervened, "True. Continue, Mister Strawn."

"Now, Mrs. Tyson, how often were you and your grandfather in touch with Mr. Crawford during the period of his employment?"

"Mr. Crawford would wire us every few days with reports. We have each wire with each report, brief, but informative."

"Now, Mrs. Tyson, do you recall the wire you two received on February 23 of this year from Mr. Crawford?"

"Yes. This wire had crucial information about my husband's behavior. I say *my husband* because at this time he was privy to our marital status."

"What did the wire say, Mrs. Tyson?"

"Oh, Mr. Strawn, I know this wire by heart. *Mrs. Tyson...husband at King house...arrived 12:30 am...left 5:00 am...Crawford.*"

With that, Pamela Tyson's head dropped.

Hap felt disgust.

Carlton's and Hap's heads practically collided.

"Mister Strawn, do you have any further questions for your client?" Judge Price queried.

"Only one or two, Your Honor."

"Please continue, sir."

"Mrs. Tyson, I think from your earlier actions that we know the answer to this question, but I must ask you for the record. What was your reaction to this news that your husband had been seen leaving the King house at five o'clock in the morning?"

"I was upset. Anybody caught in that situation is bound to be up to no goo—."

"Mrs. Tyson, stick to the facts, please," Judge Price reprimanded. "I can make my own judgments, thank you."

Pamela's mouth fell open slightly.

"Sorry, Your Honor. Anyway, my grandfather and I felt that it was our duty to come save my child from a scan—Oh! A situation."

"Thank you, Mrs. Tyson. Judge Price, I have no further

questions at this time."

"Mister Phillips? Any questions of Mrs. Tyson?"

"Not at this time," Carlton said.

"Mister Phillips?"

"Thank you, Your Honor."

Carlton stood and leaned over Hap's shoulder and whispered to *Trust me.* Hap appeared startled, but a wink from his lawyer relaxed him, even though he knew he was going to hear questions they'd not discussed. The first one was just that.

"Doctor Tyson, do you know one Caroline Cromwell Bagley?"

Even Strawn's mouth dropped open.

"Why yes, we've been friends for years."

"Go on, sir, tell the judge about your friendship."

"Well, I used to see Mrs. Bagley as a child when she would come down Station House Road with her mother, Sarah Cromwell. The church ladies of Tarboro would give all the unfortunates shoes and such, but the first time we ever talked was on the lower 40 at Shiloh. I'd been fishing. I wandered down this stream and happened on her and her pony, Nellie. I didn't have much to say, but she did. I soon found out that many people misunderstood the both of us. I suppose that was our first bond."

"Doctor Tyson, who did not understand you?"

"Well, the town had given me this name of being the meanest scoundrel in Edgecombe County, because of a few boyish pranks. I suppose I was somewhat of a skunk." He grimaced. "My reputation swelled with blame coming from all directions, some justified, some not. Trying to defend myself was impossible. I was just a scamp from Station House Road."

"Your Honor, where is this biography taking us?" Strawn interrupted.

"Excuse me, Mister Strawn. I believe you had your client make the same response. Continue, Mister Phillips."

"Thank you, Your Honor. The bottom line is the fact that you and Mrs. Bagley have been friends for many, many years."

"Yes."

Chapter 48

"Now, Doctor Tyson, are you friends today?"

Carlton had said to trust me. Hap knew he should tell all.

"Mrs. Bagley and I were planning to be married. In fact, our wedding date was April 15."

"Doctor Tyson, did you not tell us earlier that you had signed papers of divorce and so did Mrs. Tyson?"

"Yes."

"Where are these papers?"

"I have no idea. To my understanding, Banks McCloud was going to take care of all the legal matters. I assumed, regretfully, that he kept his word. Evidently not.

"On February 22, I returned to my home after being with Mrs. Bagley, her parents, and our boys, only to find Pamela in my bed totally disrobed."

Judge Price straightened up, then leaned forward. His eyebrows were arched high on his forehead.

"I was flabbergasted and angry. We were not married as far as I knew. I found her actions disgusting."

Strawn jumped up, but the judge's hand shot up. He allowed the opinion, especially after all Pamela's innuendoes.

"Facts, Doctor, facts," the judge sighed.

Collecting himself, Hap furthered his cause. "I made her get her clothes back on and told her that I was obligated and would be married in seven weeks. That's when she informed me that McCloud had never filed the papers and that we were still man and wife." Hap stopped briefly, gulping for air. "I-I was stunned, numbed beyond comprehension, but I did not want to anger her. I truly felt something could be worked out when she understood that I was no longer in love with her. When I walked her back to her rooming house, she...forced a kiss on me and talked about having more babies with me. I knew then that she wanted only to recapture family with...Rollie."

"What did you do next?"

"I returned—."

"No, Doctor Tyson, what happened next...by the tree?"

Hap appeared puzzled, then embarrassed.

"Yes, Doctor Tyson?" injected Judge Price.

"Your Honor, I left the stoop of the boarding house and..."

"And what?" asked the impatient judge.

"I must have regurgitated everything I'd eaten for two days. I beg the pardon of the judge." Hap shifted nervously in his seat, but Carlton let no time elapse with his next question.

"Doctor Tyson, did you have a virus?"

"No. I ju—."

"Doctor Tyson, if you did not have a virus, why did you get so violently ill?"

"The news. The news that I was still legally married, that I had asked for another's hand in marriage, and that I didn't know where all this entanglement was going. My body simply reacted to my mental state, both in chaos."

"Did you return to your cottage after being nauseated?"

"Oh yes. I cleaned up and tried to sleep, but couldn't. Finally, I got up, dressed and walked out for fresh air. Before I knew it, I was pacing up and down the Green."

"Did you see anybody out on the Green with you?"

"No, but that doesn't mean there wasn't somebody. I was in a terrible state."

"What happened next?"

"I'd reached the part of the Green in front of the King house. Much to my surprise, Mrs. Bagley opened the door and ordered me in out of the cold. I'd forgotten my coat. I must have looked foolish."

"All right, Doctor Tyson. Continue," the judge ordered.

"I sat in the parlor with Mrs. Bagley. I kept trying to speak, but I couldn't. She waited. I knew I had to tell my friend the terrible news. She deserved to know, but she also deserved to know that I was not going to lose hope for a solution."

"Doctor Tyson, do you remember how Pamela Tyson addressed your child when she offered him over to you?"

"She called him a 'little brat.'" Hap looked over at Pamela,

Chapter 48

who chewed on a nail.

"Please tell us these circumstances. Your Honor, some of his comments we've heard, but they will substantiate certain issues," Phillips said.

Price nodded.

"Let's see. I'd gone to Chapel Hill to bring my family home, but found her in the company of some 'suitors' as she called them. The following morning, I received the divorce papers."

"Continue."

"I was desperate. She wanted a divorce *and* my son. My mind was spinning, but I still could make *some* sense. In a futile attempt, I told her that no suitor would be interested if she allowed a child to cramp her style. She heeded my words and gave me Rollie outright even over the objections of McCloud. She told him she could give him plenty of great-grandsons."

Strawn's mouth was a straight line, his brow furrowed.

"I walked away, Your Honor, assuming I was a free man, free from an eroded part of my life. I walked away, eager for a new life with my son and someone dear to me, anxious to watch my practice grow, determined to re-establish myself with the people of Tarboro. It's all happened." Hap sat quietly.

"Thank you, Doctor Tyson. No more questions, Your Honor."

"Mister Strawn? Any questions?"

"Just one, Your Honor. Doctor Tyson, were you intimate with Mrs. Bagley, while you were married to Pamela Tyson?"

"Sir?" Hap's chair fell backwards as he stood up quickly. He looked straight at Pamela and spoke clearly. "No, never, Pamela, while we have been married."

"Let's recess for lunch. Gentlemen, let's wrap this case up this afternoon. We will have final closing statements as soon as we return."

Chapter 49
THE CLOSING

"Thank you, madam and gentlemen. We will proceed with your being first as the defendant's lawyer, Mister Strawn." The judge looked over at Strawn, pushing his spectacles up on his nose. "Mister Strawn, are there any questions you would like to ask before you make your closing comments?"

"No, Your Honor. At this time, I'll make my final statement."

"Granted," the judge said, as he reared back in his seat, waiting for persuasion.

Strawn stood behind Pamela. He looked squarely into his eyes and never flinched as he began his closing arguments.

"Judge, what we have here is a pure case of desertion. First, the desertion occurred right in the home of Rolland and Pamela Tyson. How? The doctor began deserting his wife and child in his mind." Mervin Strawn punctuated his words with his forefinger, pointing to his right temple.

"His senses faded in his responsibility, in his feelings, in his heart. My client, a mother and wife, felt this estrangement after her husband confessed that he had been interested in someone in the *past,* but, Your Honor, he never disputed his affections for this person in the *present.* That desertion reached a point that Mrs. Tyson had to close her bedroom door to her own husband."

Hap reddened and slipped down in his chair. Carlton seethed in his own way. *Disgusting! Pure disgusting!*

"Remember, please, the trip to Chapel Hill? The letter? The appeal of the ill grandfather? The birthday celebration? The uplifted grandfather by the presence of his granddaughter and great-grandson? What better way to repay gratitude than to have

Chapter 49

some young people to enliven a sad period in his granddaughter's life? The young men were friends of the family, coming to celebrate the life of a man who had extended help to many of them. Just simply a display of gratitude. The second desertion came when this man went into the arms of another woman."

Carlton's arm fell on Hap's, for surely he would have done something foolish. Hap was sick and disgusted that he'd fallen for the dirtiest trick in the book.

"Judge Price, since February 23, Doctor Tyson knew he was still a married man, yet, he visited the King house numerous times. We would like to appeal to Your Honor that no child should have to stay in this situation when the father has shown immoral conduct and shirked his responsibility as a husband to my client. I rest this case in your most able hands, Your Honor."

"Mister Phillips, as the complainant's lawyer, it is your turn."

"Thank you, Judge Price."

Carlton leaned down to his client. "No more outbursts, even out of joy for what I'm about to say."

He patted him on the arm and gave him a quick smile before his lawyer face took over. He cleared his throat.

"Judge Price, I come before you representing a young man who has experienced wonderful changes in his life. Yet, as you have heard, he's not been spared tragedy. However, let's dwell on the positive aspects of his life. In fact, let's call these positive aspects, second chances. Yes, Rolland—Hap—Tyson is a man of second chances, if you will.

"First, he received a second chance to have a surrogate mother after his own biological mother died. Second, he received the chance for schooling through his dear friend Doctor Rufus Knight. Third, he got the chance to win the hearts of Edgecombe County as a doctor himself. Lastly, he created his own chance for happiness with his lifelong, dear friend, Mrs. Bagley, with the blessings, I might add, of her parents.

"This man is no tyrant as my esteemed colleague has alluded. Ask any citizen about his reputation in this county today. These citizens praise him and count him as one of their caregivers...as well as one of their own 'sons.'

"Judge Price, not once has my client ever sought separation from his wife. Every initiative came from Mrs. Tyson. She closed the bedroom door; she deserted the household; she presented the divorce papers. She refused to give the *second chance* to my client, which he asked for countless times, even to the point of closing his practice to travel to Chapel Hill to get his family back. He made every attempt possible a man could do.

"Let's consider the child, little Rollie. He's lived with his father for almost a year now with no complaints. The doctor has cared for him in every respect with his own surrogate mother providing little Rollie with extra tender care for her son's child. Even Mrs. Bagley's own sons feel a brotherly love for this child who would be their half-brother if the papers had been filed properly.

"This very issue brings up another aspect of this case. Deception. Mrs. Tyson deceived her husband about these papers, signed, but not filed, and allowed my client to firmly believe that he was free and clear to pick up the shreds of his life and try to find another second chance for himself and his son.

"Deception? The very birth of Rollie Tyson is shrouded in deception. Switching charts, she improved her possibilities to have a child. They'd agreed to wait on family until he'd finished his schooling and established a practice. Doctor Tyson did not want to depend on anyone for his and his family's keep.

"Deception? Mrs. Tyson deceived her husband once more by working out with her grandfather a trust for herself and any children she would have. Not once, mind you, did she consult, include, or even mention such an issue with her husband.

"Your Honor, I ask you to grant my client, Doctor Thomas Rolland Tyson, his freedom through a decree of divorce and custody of the child, one Rollie Tyson, Jr. Thank you, Judge Price, for your indulgence."

Chapter 50
THE VERDICT

The next hour Hap felt was the longest of his life. He and Carlton had walked across the street to the lawyer's office to await the decision. Carlton sat; Hap paced. Finally, Carlton pulled his pocket watch out of his pocket and announced that it was time.

Judge Price entered from his private chambers with the same authority, as he'd entered the previous morning. His face showed no emotion. He sat quietly for several minutes shuffling papers, rattling every nerve in every body, as they all waited in anticipation. Finally, he spoke.

"My words will be brief. After I read my verdict, I would ask the respective lawyers to proceed with all the legalities and encourage each respective party to contain emotions as best they can. My verdict reads as follows:

"I grant the plaintiff, one Thomas Rolland Tyson, a decree of divorce on this day of April 19, 1894.

"I grant the defense, one Pamela Martin Tyson, custody of Thomas Rolland Tyson, Jr., natural child of the parties, on this day of April 19, 1894.

"The division of family is extremely difficult, but my experience of placing a child with his or her mother is more beneficial for the child. The majority of cases favor this decision; therefore, I concur. I would hope these two parties reconsider this divorce for the sake of their child. Lawyers, they have twenty-four hours to reconsider, otherwise, proceed with the details of my findings. This court is adjourned."

Tapping the gavel down one last time, Judge Latham Price

vacated the premises.

Carlton swiveled in his chair to hug Hap. He had heard the sharp intake of air as the judge pronounced the second verdict.

Hap could not believe the words, words that would change his life and his son's forever.

The jubilation at Strawn's table could mean only one thing. Somebody still had a trump card. Both men at the Phillips table began to understand the reality and the brutality of life. Strawn walked over and put out his hand to his old adversary. Carlton hesitated, but he knew ethically that he had no choice but to accept and give congratulations. Accordingly, both men had won, but only one seemed to rejoice.

"Now, Carlton, before we proceed, I think we two and our clients need to meet and talk things over right here in the judge's private chambers. Shall we?"

Carlton turned helplessly to Hap and suggested that they give audience. To their surprise, McCloud came through the door to join the huddle.

The five figures gathered around the judge's conference table, each one submerged momentarily in his or her own thoughts. Banks McCloud gloated in the win of his great-grandson. He felt more wins were in the air for his granddaughter, and whatever made her happy was all right by him, no matter what. He was a tolerant man, wasn't he?

Mervin Strawn knew Carlton outdid him in his closing comments, but after all, how many times could he slam this man in defeat? The numbers had to catch up some time, but oh, did they have another trump card?

Pamela just smiled like the innocent she wasn't and waited for the cannon fire. She knew it would work.

Hap's thoughts focused entirely on his son. How could he live a day without Rollie? How could he live just knowing McCloud had his clutches on him?

Carlton couldn't think. He could only fume. He knew what was coming.

Chapter 50

"Now, gentlemen," Strawn began. "We are all civilized people and surely the most important person does not even sit here amongst us, little Rollie. Each one of us wants the best situation for the young man, being the dependent that he is. We all heard the advice of Judge Price in his last statement. I know my client would be willing to offer her home once more to her husband and their child in order to provide the proper upbringing for their son. Mr. Phillips, would you and your client like to discuss this matter?"

"Of course, please excuse us. We'll step out in the back hall for a few moments."

Carlton guided Hap through the doorway.

"Hap, I'm so sorry. I should have known this man would try this option if the divorce did go through. The decree is not final until the judge signs it and the papers are filed with the court. You have very little time to decide."

"Carlton, I can't let my son go to Chapel Hill all alone. I'm sunk. Doomed. We won, and we didn't. They've got us in a vise. They're squeezing my heart until I think it might break."

"I know, my friend, I know. You have to call this shot, Hap. I can't decide what to do for you. I know you're thinking of Caroline, too. God, you two have waited so long to be together. It's just not fair."

With that, he slammed his fist into the wall with no apologies. He hated Mervin Strawn.

"I know what I have to do," he said, his voice dulled. He walked back into the judge's chambers.

Pamela looked up with a slight smile. McCloud still gloated. Strawn preened.

"You've won, Pamela. I don't know what you think you've won, certainly not me. Oh, you'll have a husband all right, but I'm afraid not the kind you want. I'll close my practice as soon as my new partner can get here. I suppose I can be thankful that one is coming at just the right time. Rollie will be ready to go with you tomorrow. It may take me several weeks or a month, but I'll be there...for Rollie. Carlton, tell the judge that I am withdrawing my complaint."

With no further words, he walked past all of them and made his way to tell Caroline of his decision.

Caroline had not spoken for a long time. Sarah put down her crochet needle and glanced at her daughter, started to say something, changed her mind, once more poising her needle to pick up the unattended stitch. The door knocker startled both. Scrambling to her feet, Caroline opened the door, only to stare into Hap's stoic face; hers, blanched.

"Come in," she whispered.

Relieved to find an empty parlor, Caroline offered him a seat on the sofa. She settled down beside him. Still they showed no emotion... Realization chilled her heart, as they sat as zombies for long moments, each numbed to the words that would surely come. Their numbness provided armor for the piercing words that Hap finally said.

"I won the divorce decree, but Pamela won custody of Rollie."

Caroline could only say, "Oh..."

"I cannot allow Pamela to have Rollie all alone. I cannot even think of his being with Banks McCloud all alone." He paused briefly before continuing. "I *have* to go with my son, Caroline, *for* my son. You know my heart is with you and some day, I vow, we *will* be together." He punctuated each word. "We will find each other again. I promise. God knows I do not want to do this thing, but I know of no other way to save my son."

Both internalized his declaration. He was saving his son.

She began to speak, but with a voice startling and unknown to herself. "Believe it or not, I understand, Hap. If it were Jacob or Coffie, I would do the same as you. I promise you that I am not just saying that. I would do it, too, *for Jacob. For Coffie.* Is it not amazing what we do for our children?"

She stood. Their visit was over. Awkwardly, they hugged. Hap Tyson once more left the woman he'd loved his entire life.

Chapter 50

Two weeks later, Willie looked at her son and softly spoke, "Son, I hate to bother you, but I saw Maggie and George in town today. They told me some news from Shiloh."

He put down his paper and stopped rocking by the fireplace. He felt no pain when she told him that Caroline and the Cromwells were cruising to Europe for the summer. Jacob and Coffie would start boarding school in the fall. Surely the change would help both survive this catastrophe. If only he could be sailing with them, away from the nightmare he still had to face.

Caroline's words about what one does for one's children lent some comfort, yet haunted Hap's dreams. The words he really longed to hear kept ringing in his head: *I, Thomas Rolland Tyson, take thee, Caroline King Cromwell...*Somehow his other vows interfered: *I, Thomas Rolland Tyson, take thee, Pam...*God, help me.

PART TWO

Chapter 51

1894

THE VOYAGE

"Caroline? I don't believe this." Caroline Bagley lowered her parasol from her stroll on the deck of the *Campania*, a cruise ship steaming toward Liverpool. She looked baffled.

"It's Michael Collins. Your former tutor? At Shiloh?"

"Mister Collins? Michael?"

Michael Collins was older, but much better looking than this startled woman could remember. Eight years had passed since their disastrous episode in Paris. Distinguished streaks of gray peppered his hair, as his custom-made suit complemented him. He was handsome.

"Where in this world did you go after—you left Tarboro?"

"Princeton. Thanks to my uncle, who pulled a few strings. If they keep me long enough, I might snare a departmental chair."

The tutor and his student stood in the morning sun in awe of this chance meeting.

"I just can't get over this. After all these years, the irony pushes beyond belief."

Quickly, he grasped her hand and released it just as quickly.

"Come walk with me. I must hear everything."

Chapter 51

He stood to one side, the wide promenade before them.

"You go first. I insist," she said.

"Well, I did marry a few years ago, but Lillith died last year with tuberculosis." His head dropped briefly. Hesitating, he squinted out over the blue waters. "Regretfully, we had no children, but my work fills my time." Pausing, he took a deep breath and rubbed his forehead, then carried on, "The students challenge and invigorate as you can imagine, but enough about me. Fill my ear about you and your family, and what are you doing on this ship?"

"Mom, Mom, come play shuffleboard," shouted a panting Jacob as he dashed toward the strolling twosome. Stopping abruptly, he blurted, "Oh, who's this man?"

"Jacob, come meet a former teacher of mine."

"Teacher? You don't look *that* old."

"Son, watch your manners," his mother half-heartedly scolded, muffling a laugh, but meeting a humorous look from her old tutor. "Mister Collins, this burst of energy is my son, Jacob Bagley."

Before she could remind him to shake hands, he'd done so with great enthusiasm.

"Oh my. I think you have the makings of a politician with that handshake."

"Huh? What's a po—politician?"

"Oh, you'll learn soon enough," his mother added. "Where are your grandparents?"

"The Cromwells are here, too?" Michael exclaimed in further wonderment. "I can't believe this."

He moved ahead as he recognized her parents sitting in deck chairs by the shuffleboard.

"Ah, there you are, my dear. We're glad you came to play shuffleboard," Elijah called out to his daughter.

"Captain Cromwell?"

"Sir?"

"Madam?"

Sarah looked puzzled at first, as had Caroline. Then, recognition came to her face. "Michael Collins? Oh, for heaven sakes."

She greeted him with an outstretched hand.

"How ironic to meet you on this ship after all these years. Whatever happened to you?"

"I'll be glad to tell you after I grease somebody's palm to get me placed at your table in the dining room. Caroline, will your husband join us tonight? Litch? Litch Bagley, if I remember correctly?"

Immediately, Caroline's azure eyes dulled.

"Michael, I, too, am widowed. We lost Litch a few years ago, but this is our other son, Coffie." Coffie clung to his grandmother, his thumb firmly planted in his mouth.

"I'm...so sorry," he stammered, "Of course, I didn't know," he murmured, slightly shrugging in his embarrassment.

"My dad was thrown by his horse, sir. It's all right. We've cried a bunch of tears. Mom says that helps with the healing. Our hearts sure were broken."

"I'm sure they were, young man. Mine was, too," he added, tousling the already tousled head.

"If you'll excuse me, everybody, my literary society from Princeton is sailing, too. I'm obligated throughout the day, but I shall see all of you tonight."

He tipped his hat and strode forward. Recognizing several gentlemen ahead, he flagged them down as he hurried toward the ship's stern.

Caroline watched her old tutor disappear amongst the many cruisers. How different, more polished, he is than the bumbling young tutor she'd lambasted on the deck of another ship a long time ago, making this same trek from New York to Liverpool.

The Captain and her mother had no inkling of the incident in Paris between Caroline and Michael Collins. Michael had set up a rendezvous on the grounds at Versailles, without Caroline's great aunt, her chaperone, to declare his love for her and inform

Chapter 51

her he would ask for her hand in marriage upon their return. When he made advances, she bit his lip and chastised him for taking advantage of her. No one would ever hear of that incident, especially her family. Oh, she could laugh at the bloody lip now, but not eight years ago, in all her naivety. She was so young.

That evening, Caroline found herself fussing over her appearance for dinner. She froze. *Oh, Hap, where are you? I should be fussing over you, not an old acquaintance.* She'd forced herself not to speak of Hap or think of him for weeks on end. It was just too painful. Their being together was over, done, finished.

She had to think of herself and the boys, who'd probably suffered the worse, especially having to say goodbye to Rollie. Well, tonight they were going to have fun, reacquainting with Michael Collins. The past was just that, the past. It was wonderful seeing the excitement in his face. She smiled as she thought of Jacob's comment about his age. *How old is he?* she wondered. *Six or seven years older than I? Shah! I sound so foolish.* Foolish or not, she dabbed more perfume behind her ear lobes and rushed Jacob to meet the family and her former tutor.

Michael waited anxiously, drumming his fingers on the Cromwell's table as the family moved slowly across the eloquent dining room. Changing the seating arrangements had not been easy, but his determination and a few dollars won his case. He jumped to his feet when he spied them.

The designers of the *Campania* wasted no funding on the décor of the liner, especially the dining hall. Plastered molded grids covered its ceiling. Mahogany iconic columns, slender, graceful, and decorative, rose from circular bases and extended to capitals adorned with scrolls. The Greek influence was heavy throughout the ship.

"My effort paid off," Michael called out, bowing to the ladies and extending his hand to Elijah and even Jacob. Coffie still stuck close to his grandmother.

"I do hope you find me interesting and not intrusive. I promise I'll evaporate with only a prod," Michael frowned and smiled at the same time.

"Don't be silly, Michael," Sarah chimed in. "We're delighted, aren't we, Elijah?"

"Of course, Collins. Delighted," he added as he turned to Caroline for her approval.

"By all means. We really are glad."

"Me, too, sir. Maybe you can teach me something," Jacob added.

"Me? I've got the feeling I might learn a thing or two from you, young man. Would you like to meet me in the reading room tomorrow morning after breakfast?"

"Would I? Mom, can I, please, please, please?"

"Michael? Do you know what you're asking for?" she said, leaning toward him.

"Oh, yes, I know exactly," he finished with a hint of amusement, as he looked at a face, reminiscent of an earlier one he'd tutored years ago.

Chapter 52
THE NEW STUDENT

Jacob stood in the middle of the reading room with Michael Collins.

"Wow! Mister Collins, this room is unbelievable! What are all these, these-" In his frustration, the boy ran over to a wall and just pointed.

"You're looking at real works of art. Some artisans probably sat somewhere in India and carved these panels and arches just for us and all the passengers who'll ever sail on this ship. The wood is exquisite, isn't it?"

"I don't know half of what you said, but I can't believe what I'm seeing."

Michael laughed.

"Come sit on the conversational seats, so we can talk."

"Hey, these chairs are stuck together. They look like an S."

"I believe you're right. See I told you I would learn something from you."

"Aw, gee, you know everything."

"No, I don't, but I'm interested in things...and people. How is your mother this morning?"

"Fine, sir. She's coming to write some letters while we talk. I think she'll be here any minute."

"Oh? Good, but let's talk about you. What do you like to do?"

"I like to catch bugs. Mom doesn't, but I do. They're funny. I like chasing them."

"Well, guess what? I know all about your mother's feelings about bugs."

"How?"

"When I first came to Shiloh, I wanted to begin her studies in the summer. Your mother collected bugs for a project. She wasn't too happy with the 'creepy-crawlies,' but when she caught a luna moth, she said it was worth it."

"There's Mom," Jacob shouted and scrambled to his feet and dashed her way.

Once more Michael Collins' throat closed as it had all those years ago on Shiloh. Caroline Bagley was even more beautiful than he remembered, but the memory of their last meeting clouded his mind. Squelching that unpleasantness, he dealt with the pleasantries in front of him.

"Good morning. When you didn't show up for breakfast, I wondered if you'd taken ill."

"No, Michael, I wasn't seasick."

Both laughed, remembering her green feelings from years ago.

"Mom, Mister Collins, says—"

"Jacob, Jacob, slow down and remember this room is a reading room. People want quiet," she shushed him. "Come sit on the sofa and tell me all."

"Mister Collins said you had a bug project at Shiloh a long time ago. He knew you didn't like bugs, uh creepy-crawlies. Do you remember, Mom?"

"Of course, I remember. It hasn't been that long ago."

Her eyes widened as she looked over at Michael Collins, who'd settled into the conversational chair across from them. He'd crossed his legs and propped his elbows on the plush green velvet upholstered chair arms. With his hands clasped under his chin, he watched in amusement as mother and son exchanged words.

"Now, I'll be about my letter writing while you two continue."

"Wha—oh, yes, uh, Jacob? What shall we do?"

"Shuffleboard! Oh, please, please, please!" he pleaded to Caroline's amusement and to Michael's chagrin. The man only wanted time alone with her, but not at this moment. *Duty calls,* he sighed, as Jacob Bagley pulled him by the hand toward the

Chapter 52

doorway.

Caroline moved to one of the writing tables and stared at the stationery, quill, and ink. Before writing a word, she smiled and remembered what her father had said before they sailed: *Let's see what God brings to us on this trip.* She glanced over, as Michael closed the reading room door.

"Do you know the Cunard Line's history?" Michael asked as he and Caroline strolled one of the four decks of their ship, after Jacob's shuffleboard game.

"No, but I'm sure you can tell me."

"I can if you'll allow."

He offered her his arm, pulling her closer to him.

"Of course," she smiled at him.

"The Cunard history is amazing to the maritime student. The company began as a transatlantic mail courier in the early 1800's. The founder, a gentleman named Samuel Cunard, put together a fleet of packets and cornered the mail trade from Liverpool, to Halifax, and on to Boston."

"Oh, I see," she said.

He smiled as he noticed the wind rustling with her curls trapped under her bonnet.

"With his success, he established regular steamship service between the continents. *Voilà.* Here we are, enjoying the benefits of the sweat of his brow. In fact, you and I, my dear lady, are a part of history."

"History? What do you mean?"

"Here it is 1894. She's one year old and is the largest and fastest ship afloat."

"Michael, I didn't know that."

"Oh, yes, and we may be on the fastest voyage yet. I heard rumors that we may make Liverpool in less than six days, her own record. She's a lot faster than the earlier voyage we took years back."

Suddenly, he was embarrassed that he'd stirred their memory

of a not-so-pleasant time.

Caroline turned and pointed out to the sea.

"Dolphins! Oh, they're beautiful," she exclaimed as she rushed to the railing to watch the pod race and jump, as if they laughed with each other. "What a wonderful day this is. Michael, you've added so much to our confined time on this boat. Jacob has truly been entertained."

"My pleasure. I can't believe we'll say goodbye again within twenty-four hours, but I promise to come to Tarboro for a visit. I'll figure it out. Shall we walk again?"

They moved down the promenade, once more with the tutor filling the ear of his student.

Chapter 53
LONDON

Jacob's lip poked out. "I miss Mister Collins," he whined. "Why couldn't he come with us?"

"Jacob, you know he couldn't. He's obligated to his Literary Society. We were fortunate to have him for the short time that we did. He said he'd come to visit. He'll keep his word. Come along. We have to go see Big Ben."

"Big Ben! Who's he?"

Laughing, Caroline sputtered, "It's a bell, not a man."

"A bell! Why do I want to go see an old bell?" he pouted.

"Well, it's part of a clock and one of the most famous of all landmarks in London. I promise you. You'll be glad you did."

"But Ben's a man's name."

"True. From what I've read, Sir Benjamin Hall made this magnificent bell for the Westminster Clock in London's Parliament Tower. The clock lights up at night, but also when Parliament is in session. It'll be a treat, Jacob, and when the bell tolls, you'll have something to tell all your friends at school."

"Oh, all right, if you say so, but can we go see Par—Par—," he stuttered.

"Parliament? Yes, we'll see Parliament," his mother assured. "We need to go now, Jacob. Your grandparents have been waiting and we all have to take turns with Coffie."

"Awww, Mom."

With much conniving, the Cromwells coaxed Jacob to explore London and the surrounding countryside, as well as taking a turn at helping Coffie. His favorite sights, other than Big Ben, were the castles they visited on day trips into the country. Time slipped quickly.

"Mom, will Mister Collins be on board for our return trip home?" Jacob inquired as they pushed their way up the gangplank of the *Campania*.

"No, darling, he went back a week ago."

"Well, who's that leaning on the rail? It sure looks like him to me."

Looking up into the sun, she squinted and tilted her head to one side. Michael Collins laughed and tipped his hat, only to see Caroline Bagley flush and wave vigorously.

"We thought you'd gone back earlier," Caroline said, as they all stood by the rail to watch Liverpool fade away.

"Mister Collins, I saw Big Ben. He's not a man," Jacob said.

"I know, Jacob. I was introduced to that bell a while back. Did you hear it strike?"

"Oh, you know everything. Mom, he even knows it's a bell and not a man, or a clock. Geeee."

"Come along, Jacob. We've got to get settled in our cabins. We'll see Mister Collins at dinner, I'm sure. Right?"

"Oh, yes, and I'll explain why I'm here."

"Oxford! You visited Oxford," Caroline exclaimed as the family sat over dinner on the first night of their return trip.

"Yes, I'd always wanted to go before, but just never seemed to have the time. Lillith and I were going on our last trip but just didn't. Jacob, we did go to some castles just as you did. We stayed in one of the available quarters for tourists. Don't think I slept in the king's bed, but I truly felt like a king, and Lillith was my queen." His voice lowered to a whisper.

"Gee, a king. It must have been real nice, huh?" Jacob chimed in to break the mood from Lillith's name.

"Yes, Jacob, very nice."

"What's Oxford, sir? I don't even know what that is," the boy

Chapter 53

inquired.

"Well, Jacob, the University of Oxford is the oldest English-speaking university. In fact, people don't even know when it was established, but historians guess around 1096. Can you subtract and tell me how many years ago that was?"

"Nah, Mister Collins, I'm only six-years-old. I can't do that."

"You've got Cromwell blood in you and it won't take you too long if you're kin to your mother." Michael turned. Her smile made him catch his breath.

"Mom, can Mister Collins come live with us and tutor me like he did you? Please?"

"Jacob, of course not," she gasped. "But I told you he would come visit us. He's a very important professor at a university in the States."

"Jacob, I'm flattered and if I were not under contract..." he returned with an amused glance at the object of his rekindled interest. Once more, Caroline blushed and hurriedly curbed the conversation.

"Son, ask Mister Collins the questions you have because it is definitely bedtime."

"Aw, Mom, do I have to?" he whined.

"Yes, Jacob Bagley, you have to go. How will you be able to play shuffleboard with your grandfather tomorrow without your rest?"

"Will you play, too, Mister Collins?"

"It's a date, son."

"Did you go to Oxford when you were young, Mister Collins?"

"Me? No, but many have and famous people, too."

"Who? Who?"

"Remember the old Cromwell family Bible your grandparents have on the chest in the library at Shiloh?"

"Yes..."

"The man who translated the Bible into the English language attended Oxford."

"Who was he?"

"A Mister Tyndale. William Tyndale. We wouldn't be able to understand those wonderful words without his help."

"Really? Honest? Who else, Mister Collins? Who else went to Oxford?"

"Make this your last question. You're tiring him," Caroline interrupted.

"Okay, Jacob, your last question. It is getting late. Many years ago, on the coast of North Carolina, the state where you live, a man named Sir Walter Raleigh brought a boat full of settlers to Roanoke Island all the way from England. The colonies were all known as Virginia back then. This gentleman was a statesman and an explorer. He convinced the queen to give him ships and support for his expedition. Sir Walter Raleigh went to Oxford. He learned how to be successful. I hope you'll do the same, Jacob."

"Can I go to Oxford when I'm big?"

"You probably could, but I think your mother wants you to go to the University of North Carolina. Am I correct?"

All the Cromwells nodded in unison.

"Caroline, we'll take Jacob and Coffie to the cabin. Why don't you two adults have more coffee and enjoy some grown-up conversation?" Sarah Cromwell volunteered, as she caught a faint nod from her husband's amused face.

"Thank you. Caroline, is that agreeable?" Michael inquired.

"Of course—I-but, of course."

What else could she say?

The Cromwells left with two sleepy-headed grandsons, coaxing them out the door with promises of games the next day.

"Why don't we go up to the second-deck lounge? We'll be so much more comfortable. Maybe we'll even spring for an after-dinner sip?"

"Not me or I'll fall over asleep right in front of you."

"That's fine. I'm sure they'll serve us coffee."

Elijah Cromwell felt extremely pleased with himself. This trip

Chapter 53

had been more successful than he'd ever dreamed. His "little" girl seemed distracted from her woes. Maybe, just maybe, she could see a glimmer of recovery for herself. Hap Tyson was no longer in her life. As Sarah wanted, he could have brought back life to Shiloh, but, not now, not after discovering the vise that his supposed ex-wife had on his life.

Using little Rollie as a pawn had sickened him as much as anything. How could a parent do such a despicable thing, to manipulate and use a child to force a spouse to live in a state of disharmony and distrust? What good could ever come from that situation? None, in his mind, but Caroline's words still pulsed in his head.

"Father," she'd said, "I would do the same thing if it were Jacob or Coffie. There is no way I would not have gone to protect my sons from those two. Can you imagine McCloud having Jacob in his clutches? Or Coffie? No. No! I cannot fault Hap. I would have done the same. Hard as that is to believe, I would have done exactly what he has done. I love him and I suppose I always will, but little Rollie is completely defenseless. He needs his father more than ever. We're sacrificing for the children. Maybe there will be redemption one day, but it is not to be now. Rollie must come first."

God, have mercy on all of us. Then, he wondered if Michael Collins could be part of His mercy.

Chapter 54
CHAPEL HILL...AGAIN

Hap Tyson could not even remember the train ride to Chapel Hill. His mind was a blank; his sight, a blur. Nothing registered until the conductor shook his arm and repeated for the third time that the next stop was his. Only one wire had come from Pamela and her grandfather, stating briefly that a lecturing job in the medical school awaited him at the University. Banks McCloud had arranged it all.

Of course! The old cuss! I've lost everything, my practice, my dearest friend, my whole future! I don't even have control of my own life.

A horse and buggy awaited him at the Carrboro train station, commissioned, of course, by McCloud to bring him to the house on Rosemary Street. Hap felt like a puppet with the old man pulling all the strings that governed his life.

As the buggy rolled down Franklin Street through the heart of town, Hap felt nothing had changed the years he'd been away. It seemed an age, but it wasn't. He felt it was only yesterday that he'd held Caroline in his arms in his room and cherished her as his "bride." His eyes closed as he conjured up visions of their past.

He could still hear the faint knock, see the porch light of his boarding house hit the golden curls, and feel her desperate body in his arms. And the words...

"Love me, Hap. Love me as your wife."

If only it could have been he and Caroline exchanging their vows back in Tarboro and not hers to Litch Bagley all those years

Chapter 54

ago. They had had that memorable moment and recently almost, *almost* a lifetime within their grasp. With Caroline widowed and he supposedly divorced, they had at last found each other and their time to be together. How glorious life was those few months before their comfort crumbled.

Legalities! Once again, he blasted himself for not checking on the divorce filings. Pamela and McCloud had unmercifully tricked him. Why had he depended on their honesty? What unbelievable events had crushed all their lives! Tears stung his eyes. Now, he was on a mission to save his son from God knows what. Caroline's words rang in his brain, *Is it not amazing what we do for our children?*

The stone wall along the campus edge was filled with students, many socializing, some reading, others catching a snooze during the warm spring day. The summer session would start soon, as well as Hap's duties. The passenger sighed as the buggy turned. The McCloud house stood only a block away. How stately it still appeared reveling in its own majesty as one of the beautiful old homes on the Hill. He wondered what lay behind the freshly painted door, as it seemed to announce a newness of life inside.

He stood alone in front of the residence as the driver unloaded his two trunks. He'd brought very little from his old life to his new one.

The break with Tarboro had been swift and decisive.

Shaking his head, he wondered if he should knock? He felt awkward. This house was not his home, and he certainly did not want it to be his son's. As he hesitated, the door swung open.

"Well, it's about time. Hap Tyson get in this house." Pamela was angry.

"What's wrong?"

"I want to know what you have done to my child! Start talking and now."

Hap could hardly breathe, for if she was this mad, her anger had to be about their son. *Oh, God, what has happened to Rollie?*

Keep me calm. I do not want to do anything foolish.

"Calm down, Pamela. Please, just sit and tell me what in this world you're talking about." Hap could feel his heart racing.

"The boy will not talk. Have you turned him against me? We are worried sick. Now, he was just fine when we got here. We went over to Hillsborough to visit my parents. They had planned a wonderful day with neighborhood boys Rollie's age. He was happy as a lark, but within a few days he has just curled up in a ball and will not talk."

"What?" he demanded. "You're scaring me."

"We all are, scared that is, but Banks has sworn that we'll call in the best doctors. They'll find out what's the matter."

"Matter? Rollie? Good Lord, Rollie?"

He bounded up, again demanding to be told everything.

"Quiet, Hap. Let me tell you again before you see him."

Hap was frozen in the middle of the parlor floor, not allowing himself to scream like he wanted to and shake this woman who'd ruined his life.

"All right. I'm quiet. Tell me what is wrong with my son."

"Well, he's fine, physically, but...as I've said he just won't talk."

"What? What do you mean he won't talk?" he hissed at her.

"It just happened a few days after we got home, just like I told you. He seemed fine at first. Naturally, he missed you, but Banks and I had planned all these fun things for him with the neighbor's boys and my parents. He enjoyed himself and acted normal until about a week ago. One morning I went in to get him up for breakfast and he just stared off into space—and I-I couldn't get him to say—another word. I didn't do anything, Hap. It's not my fault."

"You mean my son is upstairs in this house in some sort of catatonic state and cannot speak?"

His voice had dropped to a monotone devoid of emotion. He knew at that moment how a man could strangle his wife. Turning methodically, he went up the stairs, feeling so weighted as he

Chapter 54

dragged one foot upward after the other, dreading to see his boy, his precious Rollie in this state. Walking softly to his son's room, Hap spoke his name without the resounding response that he'd hoped for.

Father rocked son. *How could this be? My son? Not even recognizing me or speaking my name or even seeing me?* What trauma had locked this child away from all those who love him?

Chapter 55
DOCTOR GRADY

*H*ap had moved into the third bedroom in the upstairs suite on the other side of Rollie's room. Both parents had agreed that they would share the night care of their son. Neither wanted him to wake in the dark without one of them close by. At least, Hap got her to agree to that.

The agreement amongst the *three* adults in the household was an immediate conference with a child psychologist on campus. Hap hated any suggestion from McCloud, but he'd do anything to help his son.

Doctor Grady's office appeared sterile to Hap. How could someone with such stark taste have the compassion needed to deal with Rollie's trauma? Two very small paintings interrupted the monochromatic walls and seemed to salvage some warmth, one, a solitary figure, the other, a family gathering. Hap squinted to get a clearer view of the configurations. Distracted momentarily, he regained his focus on the problem at hand, Rollie's muteness.

To his chagrin, Pamela, had pleaded a headache the day of the appointment, so here he was trying to be hopeful that someone, even Doctor Grady, might have an answer for his child. To his surprise, and not his chagrin, Hap found the professor different from his surroundings.

"Mrs. Tyson is not with you?"

"Headache, I'm afraid."

"Hmm, I see. Well, please, come sit by the window," the kind voice greeted the nervous young parent. "I hear you have a

Chapter 55

silence in your house that you want erased."

"Yes, we can't understand why suddenly our son will not speak. One day he was fine and in the next few...just silence. Have you ever heard of such a thing?"

"Yes, it sounds like a separation disorder maybe," he said, slowly stretching out the word, "but I need some background on your family life."

Hap looked uncomfortable, even guilty, not to the surprise of the wise, elderly gentleman who sat before him.

"Hmmm," he said. "Trouble in the bosom of the family?"

"Well, you see..." Hap tried to begin, but seemed absolutely tongue-tied under the steady gaze of the doctor.

Laughing gently, the elderly man confessed, "Well, I suppose if I were being quizzed by another doctor, I would be stammering a might, too. Look, son, you must tell all if I'm to help you retrieve that precious boy of yours, so let's hear the story, no matter how painful it may be."

The young doctor heaved a sigh and then bombarded the man until he roared with laughter.

"Stop. Stop. Goodness, I've never had such fast cooperation in my entire life." he said with a twinkle. "Usually, ladies go first, but since the lady of the house is not present, we'll hear from the man of the house."

Hap flinched at this "title," as Doctor Grady sensed he'd hit a nerve. *Oh my, a sticky wicket, methinks.*

The old gentleman leaned back in his swivel chair and chewed on an old ivory pipe, which hadn't been lit in years. He watched Hap intently, as he wove his version of their family turmoil.

Doctor Grady thought, as he looked at the distraught man, *His wife has squashed his new life. Dear me.*

"Well, Doctor Tyson, my next sessions needs to be with your wife. Do you think she will come?"

"Doctor Grady, I have no idea."

"Then, I'd like to see the boy."

Hap jumped from his seat, eager for the session to end. With quick handshakes, he left the old professor with mixed thoughts about the stories he'd just heard. Doctor Grady sat, chewing on his unlit pipe for a long time, and peered at the campus lawn as he formulated questions for his clients. Slowly, he swiveled his chair to gaze at the little paintings. *Alone or together...these two have choices to make.*

"Mrs. Tyson, tell me about the first few days after Rollie came to Chapel Hill."

"Well, my grandfather and I—"

"Excuse me, my dear, did you tell me earlier that you live in your grandfather's house? As a married lady?"

"Oh, yes, my grandfather was very generous. He even provided us with some financial aid until my husband could get himself established. He's loved little Rollie from the very beginning as much as any great-grandpapa could."

"Go on and tell me about Rollie's return," the counselor said, micro-filing the tidbits Pamela Tyson had just revealed. *Just who is the head of that household, my dear?*

"Well, Grandfather and I planned some fun outings with some of the neighborhood boys and my family. My parents live in Hillsborough and had invited some youngsters to a picnic and games. Rollie loves my parents very much."

She smiled as she recounted the day. She recalled, too, how tired Rollie had been and knew that sleep would come quickly.

"Did you and your grandfather ever discuss your situation with your husband in front of Rollie?"

"Of course not," she said, sitting up straighter, feeling a bit indignant, even a little haughty.

"Okay. Go on."

"Surely, we had conversations, but never when Rollie was awake. Anyway, we kept telling him his father would be coming soon and we'd all be a happy family again."

Pamela clasped her hands together as she talked.

"How did you handle Rollie's having to give up Mrs. Bagley

Chapter 55

and her children?"

The woman flushed slightly. Reaching for the water offered to her earlier, she situated and re-situated herself. This woman was plainly exuding discomfort.

"I don't think I did a very good job of that, sir." She paused, not looking up at her questioner. "I'm afraid I really haven't dealt with the issue at all. He asks questions, but I've put him off. I suppose I wanted Hap to help me with what to say."

"I see. When was the last time you and your grandfather talked about your marriage?"

"Let's see." She thought for a moment. "I don't think I can remember specifically."

She remained quiet with her thoughts.

"Doctor Grady, may I be frank?"

"Without a doubt. Being frank is good."

"Well, Hap has never liked my grandfather and I'm afraid that he may have influenced Rollie's feelings. And, I am wondering if he didn't prejudice our son against me and this has caused the trauma that seems to have trapped our son." Her chin tilted up as she finished.

"I'll take that into consideration, Mrs.Tyson. Now, can we get back to my question, please? When was the last time you and your grandfather talked about your marital difficulties?"

Her brow slightly furrowed.

"Is there a time before Rollie's silence that you discussed this situation? Could he have overheard you by any chance? In fact, Mrs. Tyson, could you and your grandfather have discussed these events the night before Rollie quit speaking?"

"I-I can't re—" Realization crept onto her face. Her eyes darted left and right. "Oh my God, we did. We did!"

Her face blanched right before the professor's eyes. He could tell that she remembered and all too well. Her mouth dropped open. Her head began to shake.

Rollie had been exceptionally sleepy after the picnic that

277

Sunday afternoon. He'd slept most of the way home from Hillsborough, as the carriage jostled him, curled up in the seat by his mother. The little fellow had played hard, loving every minute, but continuously thinking how much more fun it would have been with his father there. When was he coming? He pressed his mother and his great-grandfather. Constantly, they reassured him, but no discourse could calm his elfin world.

Vaguely remembering his trip to bed, Rollie sat groggily as Pamela pulled off his clothes. Her faint prattle barely kept him upright as she prepared him for bed. He was so tired, but thirst awakened him soon after she'd tucked him in for the night. He'd called repeatedly for his mother.

Normally, she would have heard him, but Pamela was deeply engrossed in conversation with her grandfather.

Rollie froze at the top of the stairs when he heard his father's name. He strained to hear their words.

"Pamela, I think private school would be perfect for the boy next year. You just cannot start his discipline and training too early."

"Grandfather, he's still so young. He'll help me win Hap over. I-I just can't give up this opportunity," she said with firmness.

She'd turned in her seat on the sofa in the parlor to face the window where her grandfather stood gazing out on the front yard at the vibrant irises and blooming Weigela bushes.

Any other position of the two and they would have spotted the boy at the top of the staircase, but unfortunately, they did not.

"Look, I agreed to allow the man back into my house, but we both heard what he said in the judge's chambers. He plainly told you that he would not be the husband that you want him to—"

"Banks!" she injected with irritation. "I don't want to hear it. Please, sir, do not say that again. It just—has to work. I don't want to lose again. I mean I don't want to lose *him* again, especially to Miss Ghost of the Past." Her skin crawled, as she heard Hap's words again about his marrying Caroline Bagley. Well, she had fixed that. Now, she had to work her wiles on him

Chapter 55

and secure her place in her world with the doctor at her side. Her plan had to work.

"Well, if you're so fired up for this family to be, you better use Rollie as the ultimate pawn." McCloud rocked on his heels as he finished his declaration. "One thing's for sure, you can't let the boy see Mrs. Bagley and her boys again. That's a fact, Pamela. They could spoil your plans. And if it were up to me, I'd have put the pen in your hand and that man's to sign those papers to break this union. The boy's better off with us by himself. Yessir, that's what I'd a done."

Rocking again on his heels, he turned slightly.

"It'll work, Grandfather. It will," she said, with conviction.

Their words, the crucial ones, burned into Rollie's mind. The little tyke stood entranced with thoughts whirring in his head. He felt dizzy as if he could fall down the steps at any moment. *Bed, where is my bed?* Miraculously, he made it back to his room, only to crawl under his quilt, into a small ball, totally immersing himself in a cocoon far, far away from reality.

Rollie Tyson no longer wanted to think of the unhappiness in this house, with the center of this dialogue being he. The little fellow felt terribly alone without his father, who obviously did not want to be a part of this family. What had happened about Jacob, Coffie, and Mrs. Bagley? Why couldn't he ever see them again? And in the fall they wanted to send him away? He was confused. Rollie Tyson just could not handle this pain... He just could not.

"Possibly he overheard?" prodded Doctor Grady gently. "Did you check on him again?"

"Only from the door. You think it's my fault, don't you? No! It can't be. Listen, Doctor Grady, you cannot tell Hap. Please! I implore you. I am trying to make this marriage work. If you tell him, he will blame me and, and..." She could not finish her statement. Pamela Tyson could not believe there were tears on her face. The realization had finally hit her what she had done to her own child.

The elderly professor sat back,. Neither spoke.

Finally, she looked up.

Wiping her face quickly, she said, "I have to leave, sir, this appointment is over." With that, she stood up, turned swiftly, and marched out the door, never thanking the professor, never declaring her concern for the boy. She appeared to have been caught in misconduct.

Doctor Grady shook his head in disbelief and thought of the picture of the lone figure and not the picture of the family. The furrow deepened in his brow.

Chapter 56
THE SELFLESS vs THE SELFISH

*P*amela walked down the steps slowly and gazed at her husband sitting on the sofa in the parlor, the same sofa where they'd toasted their nuptials with champagne. No toasts this night, she thought, as her heels clicked on the remaining risers. Hap peered up at her.

Her face was stoic with her chin quite high. "It seems we have much to discuss. Would you not agree?"

"Yes, we do. Doctor Grady spoke with me about our situation. Pamela, I've noticed your door open quite frequently of late after my turn with Rollie. I must remind you that it will not work. You know where my heart is and I will not be-"

"I know that," she snapped. "It is not working, but actually, I have some thoughts about us; however, I am not ready at the moment to present them."

"Oh? Another plan?"

"Don't be catty, Hap. I will let you know."

Right, said the Cat to the mouse.

The fall semester had begun with the students bustling across campus. Returning from classes one day, Hap raced up the steps to see Rollie, but he was not there. Skipping back down, he met Pamela coming through the door. She looked invigorated, even excited.

"Rollie? Where is he? You're smiling. Has he had a break through?"

"Oh no, he's the same. I took him to visit my parents for a few days. We really do need to talk, and I did not want him to hinder our conversations."

"What conversations?"

"Well, since Banks has been visiting his brother in Burlington, I have been wiring back and forth with him about our situation."

Uh-oh, the drama increases...

"You will not believe his good news! He is going to a small country in Europe to finish out a term for an Ambassador, who has been taken ill. And, *he* has invited *me* to escort him there for the duration."

"What? You are going to leave? What about Rollie?"

"My dear man, he does not know who is caring for him in this state. Lucas and Corina can share the duties while you teach your classes."

"Pamela, this *plan* of yours is the most selfish one I have ever heard. It's disgusting!"

"Oh, but you have not heard the best part. My grandfather has contacted two lawyers and a judge, who owe him favors, and when he gets to Chapel Hill within the week, we shall do the deal and get the divorce that you and I have been wanting. You have said it. I have said it. This marriage is not working," she spoke with such pomposity and condescension that Hap gripped the arm of the sofa with exasperation.

"Rollie?"

"I will not contest, Hap. You will have custody, but I must have visiting rights at liberty."

And then her plan became clearer. He could see her, dressed in her finery, entertaining all the attachés, hovering around Banks McCloud, the new Ambassador.

"And when we return, Banks plans to run for mayor of Chapel Hill. He will need me to co-ordinate his events."

"Thank you, Pamela, for showing me your true colors." He got up from the sofa and headed to his room upstairs, but turned looking down at her. "Don't leave your door open tonight, lady, for it is my turn to lock my door again from you."

A divorce and custody... God in heaven, you are a good God.

Chapter 57
FREEDOM

*M*cCloud returned to Rosemary Street, preening himself as he walked through the door, just waiting for Hap's congratulations on his appointment.

What could he do, but grit his teeth and dive into the game?

"Congratulations, sir. I am sure you will serve our country well. When do you sail?" he asked with a plastered grin on his face.

"Thank you, kindly. We sail next week, but sit with me to be sure we understand each other about Pamela's situation."

Pamela's? Don't Rollie and I count? You are one strange old bird.

"Pammie says this marriage is not working. I have seen her sadness and I now think the dissolution is inevitable. She tried to make it work, but it seems your attentions are elsewhere and have been for a long time. This journey with me will offer healing of her broken heart."

Good grief, man! Hap remained silent through this discourse, amazed at his haughty conceit.

"Of course, you and Rollie may stay here in my house until you work out a plan with the University. I have instructed Lucas and Corina to care for the boy while you teach. They are capable people as I am sure you have seen."

"Thank you, sir. Now, if you will excuse me, I wish to visit with Rollie."

It was done! No slip ups! No hidden legalities! Not even any unpleasantries. Hap was free. And he had Rollie!

How can this be? My cup runneth over...

Trunks were packed. Few words exchanged. The day arrived for departure. The three adults stood in the parlor of the McCloud house, fidgety, unable to voice their good-byes. Finally, Banks did.

"I will miss my great-grandson, but you heard the judge, we do have visiting rights." He looked over at Rollie sitting on the sofa staring into space.

"Yes sir, and I will honor that for Rollie's sake." They both nodded to each other, and then Hap turned to Pamela. "I do wish you well, Pamela. I truly hope you find who you are looking for."

She smiled, with one of her knowing smiles. Never saying a word to him, she patted Rollie's head and swept out the front door, with Banks strutting behind her with his cane tapping down the walkway.

What a pair.

The University prepared his release papers, not for leaving at the end of the semester, but for leaving in the middle of the term. Fortunately, Doc Sims knew of a young doctor eager to teach in the medical program on campus. Hap could stand the months of duration just knowing that he was free and had his son. Lucas and Corina proved perfect caretakers for Rollie. Following all the prescribed activities of Doctor Grady, they embraced their part for *the little master,* as they fondly called him.

On his last visit with Doctor Grady, Hap told him that he now understood the two pictures hanging in his office. Both chuckled as they talked.

"I truly feel Rollie will wake and find a family waiting for him."

"Me, too," Hap said with a winsome smile.

Chapter 58
NEW DIRECTIONS, OLD CONTACTS

Caroline loved her art studio. She'd found the perfect two-room suite in the market building next to the Town Common. One quick walk down the Green brought her to her new workplace. Rising each day with a mission had helped heal the loss of Hap. Work and being productive were good for her mind and body.

"Classes? You mean go back to school? At my age?"

The Cromwells had mentioned the possibility one Sunday over lunch.

"Why not? Jacob will be at boarding school, Coffie can stay with us, and we can handle any issues with either, which won't happen, since our grandsons are perfect," her father assured.

"It is Jacob's first year. I don't know," she murmured.

"Look, he will be perfectly happy. Wilson is only a few miles away. Your father and I will visit him regularly. Just give it some consideration," her mother coaxed.

"Trinity might be nice. Maybe I'll audit a class and attend a couple of seminars? Then, if I would have to leave for any reason?"

"Fine, darling, just do it. You'll love it, I'm sure."

Later that day, Caroline stared at a letter from Michael. He had visited once since the European excursion and of course had enchanted Jacob. He'd made her feel uncomfortable. He was just too familiar, as were the barrage of letters that followed. Yes, Trinity would be the solution to break this unwanted tie with her former tutor, as well as to heal more from the loss of Hap.

Caroline packed her trunk, following her well-prepared list. She collapsed in her bedroom chair and recounted the last time she'd packed to go off to school. How long ago it seemed when she and her mother were making decisions for the Warrenton Academy, finding just the right fabrics for clothing and bedding. A smile crossed her face as she blew a stray curl from her forehead and recalled that fateful day in Carver's Mercantile. She'd come inches from the handsome face of the lanky, tousled headed kid who would change her life.

Where are you now, Hap? I have to know, even if you and Pamela are together, really together. A letter. What's the harm in a letter?

She knew at that moment that she intended to contact him, not as a love, but as a long-time friend. They'd lived too much of life together to allow their friendship to totally die, even if they would never be man and wife. The thought made her flinch. *Friends, just friends. I have to have that much of him at least.*

"Doctor Tyson, here's a letter from Durham, sir. There's no return address, so I can't tell you who it's from."

"Well, Mrs. Tew, it's probably from a professor over there. We do correspond from time to time, you know. Thank you. Mrs. Tew, you can give it to me now. All right?"

"Uh? Oh, of course. I was just wondering—"

"Mrs. Tew, thank you."

He smiled, as his elderly, curious secretary disappeared through his door. He tapped the letter on his fingers and glanced quickly at the handwriting. His expression changed. Tearing the envelope, he dropped into his desk chair with a slight quiver in his hand as he held the paper engraved with Caroline's name at the top.

Dear Hap,

Are you surprised? I must explain my writing to you at your office instead of at home. If you think Pamela will understand my continued interest in your family, I will openly correspond

Chapter 58

with you at your residence. Please let me know.

Can you believe it? Your old friend is a new student over at Trinity, well, just for some art seminars and maybe to audit for a while. My parents suggested that I pick up my brushes again. In fact, I have a new studio in Tarboro. It sounds silly I know to find the perfect spot and then leave town, but I just had to get all those canvases and brushes out of my house. Every nook and cranny were hiding something that spelled art. Anyway, on weekends when I'm home with Jacob and Coffie, we have fun exploring our palates. You guessed it. Jacob's begged for his own equipment. Isn't that interesting? All Coffie wants are brushes, brushes, brushes.

My son loves his school, for which I am grateful. A parent's nightmare was thwarted by getting my first-timer settled and happy. His cousins certainly help, and familiar faces from Tarboro do, too. I'm framing his first letter. It's priceless and precious. You just wait until Rollie writes your name on an envelope. Coffie pretends, but it's chicken scratch, as they say.

How is your work with the students? I still cannot picture you at the lectern, but what do I know? I'm sure you're the favorite in the medical program. Have you ever thought of setting up practice again? Somehow, I still see your compassion for service of people in your future. But again, what do I know?

I trust this letter finds you and yours well.
Fondly,
Caroline

Dear Caroline,
What a wonderful surprise to get your letter! You, a student? No, you should be the teacher, but I am excited that you are painting again and learning more about your craft. Have you thought of a degree? I know that feat might be difficult with the boys, but give it some serious thought. I guarantee Trinity would love to graduate such an intelligent lady. After all, you are Coeffield King's granddaughter, are you not?

Women are over here at the University, but only to audit classes. The guys are complaining, thinking the females will distract them from their studies. If the truth be known, they probably are afraid the ladies will make better grades. I'm sure yours would put mine to shame.

Oh, Caroline, Rollie has had a "mystery time" of late, a time of silence. For some unknown reason, he has stopped talking. However, a Doctor Grady on campus has been quite helpful. His hope is that Rollie will be one of the fortunate ones to just come out of this trauma. Pray for my son, dear friend.

Before all this happened, I was becoming a very good pitcher for him. All he wanted to do was "Play ball, Daddy!"

Yes, I must confess that I have thought about private practice. My vow with your grandfather comes to my mind quite often, but I have made no decision. The compassion of service still lingers in my heart, but those students need compassion, too. If I am this apprehensive, I'd just better bide my time.

Keep me posted about your progress and the boys. All of you remain dear to me.
Love,
Hap

He signed it *Love, Hap*. In the next second, Caroline scolded herself for reading anything into his message. Once more she read the letter, putting it against her cheek, touching something that he had touched, something that he had penned. Only friends now, nothing more, but certainly nothing less.

Oddly enough, he never mentioned Pamela or whether she would object to her letters coming for them both to their home. She would just continue to send her notes to his office until he told her otherwise, letters from two "old friends," usually once a week, being delivered by the curious Mrs. Tew.

Not once did Hap intimate the divorce. *Face to face, maybe?* How he wished his son could see such a union if it was to be.

Chapter 59
CONTACT

Caroline was showing her art at Trinity and had invited him, Pamela, and Rollie. Would this time be the right time to tell her, or should he wait just a little longer in hopes that Rollie would be whole again. *Oh agony.*

With those parting words, he grabbed his coat and hastened out the door. If he made good time, he would get to see her showing. She'd been so excited and proud of her work that he just could not disappoint her. The invitation had included the family, but there was no family, just Hap and Rollie.

When she saw him enter the gallery, Caroline's heart almost stopped as it had that very day so many years ago in Carver's Mercantile. She knew he didn't know how much he affected her. Keeping out of his view, she relished just watching him.

Hap craned his neck this way and that, but to no avail. *Where are you, Caroline*, he thought. *Did I get the date wrong?* Then her fragrance let him know that she was standing directly behind him. Turning slowly, his ever-present crooked smile crossed his handsome face. The lighting from the gallery illuminated her golden curls.

"I can't tell you how thrilled I am that you're here."

She didn't even care that he'd held Pamela and loved her. She needed to see this man. She felt shameless. *God, forgive me, but I just love him. I can't help it.*

Taking hold of her out-stretched hands, he kissed her on her cheek, stepping away just a mite too slowly. Her heart fluttered.

"Well, first tell me about Rollie, and then let me show you what your friend has been doing with her brush."

Quickly locking her arm in his, she would have sworn if she hadn't that his next move would have been to pick her up off the floor. He spoke of Rollie, as they worked their way slowly through the exhibit, until his eyes fell upon a painting that made *his* heart flutter.

Caroline had painted the grassy knoll with the fallen log and the weeping willow with its prolific fronds. Everything his brain could assimilate about the haven was there in detail, even down to the lichens growing on the underside of the tree remains. Slowly, shaking his head, he turned to her and just looked, speechless for so many moments that Caroline had to break the silence.

"Come." She once more took his arm. It seemed much warmer than it had been before. She took her handkerchief and casually fanned her neck and face. "It's a portrait of Jacob. You remember I did one of Litch. Well, I felt the urge to paint Jacob. Coffie will come later. He squirms too much at the moment." Both laughed.

She paused to let him get the full effect.

"If you like, one day I'll do one of Rollie."

Finally, finding his voice, Hap croaked, "I'd like that. Very much."

He still had her arm in his. When she tried to remove it, he put his hand on hers and held it there.

"Show me the others," he continued, steering her away, never releasing her hand.

"Well, I painted Cromwell Hall. See. In all its splendor. What do you think?"

"It's wonderful. Magnificent. I'm so impressed."

Hesitating for a moment, he told her, "Yes, I do want you to paint Rollie. I don't know when, but sometime... Oh my gosh, you are kidding me. Caroline, that's me! How could you remember without my sitting for you? I can't believe it. Well, I don't know why not. Are you not Coeffield King's granddaughter?"

Both laughed again, for that statement had become their own

Chapter 59

private joke. He steered her back through the paintings again to find a bench for them to sit.

"Your seminars and auditing are almost up? Back to Tarboro, I suppose?"

"Oh, yes, and my new studio. Hopefully, I'll find an agent and maybe I'll sell a canvas or two."

"Well, you can sell one right now. I've got to have the lower 40. You have captured it perfectly."

His face lit up.

"My office! I have to have it for my office. 'How much, lady? How much?' the anxious buyer said to the *artiste*."

Realizing that he still had hold of her hand, he begrudgingly released it so he could pull out his checkbook.

"I want to give it to you," Caroline said, as she pushed his checkbook back toward his breast coat pocket.

"That's no way to start out a new career."

"Please," she said with such seriousness. "Let me do this for you."

"I'll treasure it for the rest of my life."

"I want that."

Pulling his watch from his pocket, he knew the afternoon was ebbing.

"I have to go."

"I know. Excuse me while I get someone to prepare your new painting for travel."

She walked a short distance, took care of matters, and returned to where he stood by the bench.

"You've done a good job, Mrs. Bagley. I salute you."

Mocking a military officer, he saluted her, then clasped her hand briefly, as she walked with the gentleman and his new painting.

As he drove away, she quickly dabbed a tear that trickled down her cheek. *Goodbye, Hap. Goodbye, my love.*

Why couldn't I tell her? Why? Oh, Rollie, was it you?

Chapter 60
LEFT BEHIND AND HOME FOR REAL

The mid-term was over. *Finally!* Hap cleared his desk and book shelves and turned to gaze up at Caroline's painting of the Lower 40. *We are coming home, Caroline. I'll see you there,* he said, nodding at the painting.

"Doctor Tyson?"

"Oh, Mrs. Tew. I want to thank you for all your help during my stay."

"'Twas my pleasure, sir. I hope your boy will be well soon," she said, sniffling into her handkerchief.

"I trust that he will, Mrs. Tew, and I wish you and Mister Tew the best." He extended his hand to squeeze hers. "You've made my stay a pleasant and productive one. Thank you, kind lady."

At the McCloud house, Lucas and Corina had packed the trunks, ready for transport to the train station in Carrboro, trunks that held almost the same as when Hap arrived...the second time. Lucas insisted that he drive them there.

"We'll miss you and the little Master, sir," Corina whispered through her emotions. "We just know the Lord will break his silence soon, very soon."

"Thank you, Corina. I could not have asked for better care for my son than you and Lucas. I will send word *when* Rollie wakes," Hap said, with a hopeful smile.

The ride to the station proved an uplifting feel of freedom. They were going home, where, Hap felt, they belonged. His letters to Willie, Carlton, and Mac reflected joy that he was coming, bringing his silent son, but bringing both back to their roots, back to home. Would he regret not writing Caroline the

Chapter 60

news? *We shall see, a joyful surprise or a distressing strain to our relationship...*

The train raced along the tracks from Carrboro to Rocky Mount, where Hap would hire a coach to take them to Tarboro.

Hap talked to Rollie as if they were father and son taking a fun ride after a visit with family and friends, but suddenly, the train began to lurch.

A porter flew through the door of their passenger car, hollering, "Hang on, there's something on the tracks ahead. We have to try to stop. Brace yourselves."

And brace they did, but not before Rollie slipped through his father's arms and sat firmly on the floor between their seat and the back of the seat in front of them, bumping his head in the fray.

"Ow!"

"Ow?"

"Dad, that hurt!" the little fellow complained as he rubbed his head.

"Rollie?"

"Yes?"

"You-you are speaking?"

"Yeah, and my head hurts."

"Come here, son, Daddy will make it feel better," he said, tears beginning to stream down his fact.

"Why are you crying, Daddy? I'm the one who bumped my head. Hey, where are we? Are we on a train?"

"Yes, son. Here, let me help you." Pulling his son up into his arms, Hap could only say *I love you,* not once, but many times.

Rushing through the passenger car, the porter calmed the alarmed by announcing that a wagon had lost a wheel trying to cross the tracks. Fortunately, the driver was able to drag the broken vehicle to safety, just as the train screeched to a halt. With the all clear signal, the engineer fired up the engine and began to ease back up to speed. Hap looked back to see the farmer fanning himself with his big floppy hat.

That's not the only thing broken we are leaving behind, but oh, sir, you do not know what you did for my son. I pray your wagon can be fixed as good as new... Rollie is! What timing!

Rollie perched in the middle of the passenger car seat, peering up at his father.

"We're moving back to Tarboro? Do you mean where Willie is? And Jacob? And Coffie? And Mrs. Bagley? For real?"

Rollie's voice shrilled, as he put his hands over his mouth, just as Hap put his hands over his ears, just before he squeezed him close for the umpteenth time in sheer elation.

"Oh yes," his father declared, "we are going home."

"But Mommie? Where is she?"

"Rollie, your great grandfather needs her to care for him, just like I will care for you. We'll talk later, but right this moment, let's think about what lies ahead in Tarboro."

Hap never asked Carlton or Willie or Mac about Caroline. Why had he not told her about the divorce? Would this stupid mistake plague him for the rest of his life? He supposed he was afraid she'd have moved on or something that would be more than he could bear. What would his plan be? Surprise her? He might be the surprised one.

Chapter 61

A DARK SURPRISE

Caroline had worked feverishly in her studio to replenish her portfolio. In two weeks, she expected an agent from Raleigh to critique her canvases and advise her on marketing strategies. Her successful exhibit at Trinity had left slim pickings for review.

Memories of vacation at Atlantic Beach flooded her mind, the beached whale, horseback riding, her shell collection. She painted with a flurry of energy and anxiety to cover her canvases. Many afternoons she grew ill with the low lighting, forced to wait another day to finish an effect.

Going home totally exhausted, but happy, made her grateful, for she knew idleness would have driven her crazy after losing Litch, her beloved grandfather, and more recently Hap...again. Surely, these trials had made her stronger, and after all, she had her parents and the boys to keep her sane.

Standing on the stoop of the King House, Michael Collins straightened his bowtie as the door swung open.

"M-Michael," Caroline stuttered.

"Don't be angry, but we have to talk. You're the only person I can confide in...you know, about Lillith."

"Michael, I'm not a professional. That's the kind of help you need. I'm just—"

"My best friend," he finished her thought.

She turned from her front door, as he pushed forward behind her, closing it with the touch of his toe.

"Please, just hear me out?"

"I don't see what good I can do for you—"

"Wait until you hear the suggestion from a doctor."

She stopped and stared up at him.

"You've seen a doctor?" He nodded. "These are confidential conversations. I don't want to hear what you and the doctor have discussed. Really, this matter is getting way out of hand."

She put her hand up.

"Michael, I'm sorry, but I think you should leave."

"Leave? What do you mean leave? Caroline, you are the only one I can talk to. Please, I'm desperate! Won't you just listen?"

Pausing, she looked sternly at him, "All right. Let's sit in the parlor."

"Are the boys here?"

"No. They're at Shiloh."

"Good."

"Good?" She looked startled. "What do you mean *good*?" she demanded.

"We just need privacy."

Leading him to the sofa, they sat down in the parlor.

"All right, Michael, what did the doctor say? I'm waiting."

"I really don't know how to put it into words, but..." Looking a little sheepish, he continued, "the doctor thinks that I ought to get involved with someone."

"Involved? You mean see a woman? Romantically?"

"Yes." He searched her face.

She looked back, then broke into a big smile.

"Michael, of course, that's your answer. I think that is great. Yes. Oh, the doctor's right. You should. There must be numbers of women in your town who would love to go out with a handsome professor."

His stare was disarming.

"No, Caroline, not just *anybody*. I've told the doctor all about...you. He agrees with me that you are the *only* one who can save me from these fears about Lillith."

"*Me*? Michael, don't be silly. There's nothing between you and me."

Chapter 61

Her throat began to tighten.

"Oh, but, there could be."

As he spoke, he slipped over on the sofa to where she sat.

He was way too close. She felt trapped.

"Michael, I think you've misinterpreted our friendship. And, that's all that it is, just a friendship. If you do anything unworthy, even that friendship will be gone."

"Caroline, do you not understand me? You're the only one that can save me from mortal depression over Lillith." He paused for the effect of his words. "I need you...your help. What do I have to do? I'm pleading my case before you, and you just keep rejecting me. Hap Tyson's married, Caroline. He's not available. What are you going to do with your life? And Jacob's? And Coffie's? Sit around and mope forever. At least, give me a chance to prove myself. How do you know that you could not come to love me?"

Everything he said was true, she thought, as she stared across the floor of the parlor. What *was* she going to do with the rest of her life? The boys needed a father for sure, but she could not imagine a life with Michael Collins. However, visions of Jacob and Michael on the cruise pushed into her mind.

Shaking her head, she spoke sharply, "Michael, Michael. This situation is impossible. You must find another solution. I'm not it."

"But, what about Jacob? We get along famously, and he does need a male influence in his life. I can provide all these things for your son, Caroline. He needs me! And Coffie will, too!"

"No, Mich—"

"Caroline, are you trying to tell me that you will sit in this house, loving an unreachable man, and wither away, because you would not give another soul a chance to win your affections. I just can't believe it."

He got up from the sofa and paraded around the room, his hands behind his back. Things were not going his way. His appeals fell on deaf ears. Maybe if he just forced his affections, she would succumb. Oh no, he'd tried that before and gotten his lip bitten and his face slapped years ago, but he was desperate. He looked pointedly at her. *Why not go for desperate measures.*

"Caroline, just listen. Why not try? You've not had a man in your life for all these long months. Have you not missed the touch of a hand, a kiss ?"

"Michael, please."

"Let me help you forget Hap. We'll take it slow and easy. Nothing fast."

He'd worked his way back over to the sofa, sitting now directly beside her and reaching for her hand. She didn't move. He caressed her hand.

"Michael, I don't kno—"

"Say nothing," he murmured, bringing her hand to his lips. "Just allow me the chance."

"I'm not sure—"

She stood. He stood, never releasing her hand.

"Caroline, I promise to be the gentlest soul who ever courted you. You know this is the best for us both."

Drawing her slowly toward him, he tilted her head, bringing her face up to his. He had her thinking about the loneliness of life, the emptiness of her home without a husband, fatherless children.

Maybe he is right, she thought. He was so close, just inches. She started to pull back, but he was not to be denied. His mouth found hers. His arms enfolded her. She'd weakened and it was too late.

Once more she bit the man's lip.

"Caroline!" he shouted, grabbing his second bloody lip from the lady.

"Michael, get out of my house! This is not right!"

Twisting free from his grasp, she stumbled backwards, only to have her heel catch on the Oriental rug in front of the fireplace. Flailing arms could not stop the fall. Down she plummeted, her head clipping the edge of the marble top table. Michael heard a

Chapter 61

thump and a grunt. She lost consciousness.

Forgetting his bloody mouth, he dropped to his knees and rolled her over ever so slowly, only to see vibrant red blood oozing from under her golden curls. He pulled back in panic. *My God, she's dying.* Running to the front of the house, he threw the massive oaken door open, only to stare wildly into the face of Hap Tyson.

Both men stood suspended, each surmising the other's presence in a matter of seconds.

"Good heavens, Collins, you're bleeding! Are you all right?"

"Oh, my God, I am, but Caroline's not. She's fallen—"

"What?"

Hap pushed past the stunned man in the doorway and rushed into the parlor, spying her sprawled on her back. Flashes of Will Cromwell's fall beleaguered him. Stooping down, he picked up her limp wrist, hoping for a pulse. He closed his eyes as he detected a faint throb. Bending even lower, he tried to peek at the wound without moving her head.

Turning to Michael, he instructed, "Go in the kitchen and find me towels… cloths…anything, and chisel some ice from the box. Move, man. We don't have all day!"

Michael jumped toward the kitchen.

"Caroline, Caroline, can you hear me?"

No response.

"Please, let me know if you can hear me."

He had placed his handkerchief under her head to stop the flow of blood. *Where is that man?*

"Collins, hurry!"

Stumbling into the parlor with towels and ice in one of Caroline's mixing bowls, Michael bent down. "How is she?"

"I can't tell. Listen, run to the hospital and get a gurney and carriage to transport Mrs. Bagley to the hospital."

Hap looked up at the gawking man.

"Go, Collins. She needs more attention."

Michael hastened out the door, remembering another race to

help another injured man long ago, Hap Tyson. *Funny how life repeats itself in such strange ways*, he thought, his legs aching as he pushed down the street toward the little hospital. He prayed quickly for Caroline. He would never have had anything like this to happen to her.

Ripping the towels, Hap wrapped slithers of ice into a compress and eased it under the golden curls. A moan made his heart jump. *Oh, God, let her live*, he murmured. *She's endured so much.* He continued to bathe her face and changed the compress again and again. *Where is the gurney?* He rocked back on his heels and looked around the room. *What happened here?* he wondered. He knew it was none of his business, but he intended to ask.

"Collins, what happened back there in the parlor? I need to know...for the records." Hap held up papers in the hospital hall.

"Records? Well, uh," slightly pausing, Michael continued, his voice taking on a calculated air. "We were caught up in a moment of passion. I'd asked Caroline's permission to court her. We'd kissed and she-uh-somehow caught her heel on the Oriental. Down she went. I just couldn't catch her before she hit the table."

Then, in a very quiet tone, he whispered, "I suppose emotions just overtook us...both."

He relished in the hurt he'd just dealt.

Hap's teeth clinched. He knew his jawbone would pop through his face at any minute, but he had no rights to her affection. It was he who'd deserted her for Rollie and Pamela. Shaking his head in acknowledgment, he excused himself to his *paperwork*.

Chapter 62

MORE SURPRISES

Willie squealed, "Well, hallelujah!" Grabbing Elijah's hands, she danced him around her small living quarters. "Fate and Shug are gonna have another baby."

Both finally collapsed into chairs and rocked. The fall days had begun to chase the humidity away with the leaves painted their yearly colors of yellow, red, and orange.

They'd not seen each other for a long spell, but this news was the kind they needed to share, since Fate was their own flesh and blood.

"Yessir, Doctor Quiggless is gonna be a busy man in a few months, yessir," she said as she handed Elijah a cup of coffee to warm his bones. Returning to her seat, she gazed over at the only man she'd ever loved. Her spirit was high with this news that bonded them.

Both stopped rocking.

"Someone's coming. The house up the road is empty. Hearing hooves on the road means someone's coming my way."

Both stood to peer out the front window, curious to know Willie's second visitor.

"My God, it's Fate," Elijah uttered.

"Fate?"

He pushed the door open and stepped onto Willie's porch.

"Fate, what's the matter?"

"Captain, Miss Caroline's had an accident. She's in the hospital. Miss Sarah's with her, but she wants you to come fast as you can, suh. She thought you might be here checking on Miss Willie." He timidly looked over at the startled woman.

"Thanks, Fate, let's get going. My God, Caroline!" The man dashed out the door, never looking back.

Fate tipped his hat at Willie and followed the Captain down Station House Road.

"Hap Tyson?" Elijah called out as he rushed through the front door of the hospital. Looking up from the front desk where he was writing, the young doctor stood.

"My goodness, son, when did you get back to town?" Elijah asked, quickly shaking his hand. "Never mind. Tell me later."

He reached for Sarah's arm.

"What's happened? Fate said there's been an accident." He'd turned back to Hap.

"Come sit. Mac and I have been attending her. I had just come out, so what I say, Miss Sarah has not heard. You will both hear our prognosis together."

He led the worried couple over to a bench, the very one they'd sat on when Coeffield King was hospitalized. Looking to the doctor for encouragement, the parents waited anxiously for news of their only remaining child. Surely, she would not be taken from them as Will had? Children were supposed to bury their parents, not the other way around.

"I can't tell everything, yet. Mac's with her now. It seems she fell and struck her head on Mrs. King's marble top table. The swelling is external, which is good, but she seems to be wandering in and out of consciousness. Such a trauma to the head can cause a semiconscious state for the first crucial days. She moans, which surely is a sign she's fighting."

"Can we see her?" Sarah whispered, never expecting the man keeping them out of their daughter's room.

All three stayed the night, hoping for her to wake during one of their watches. It didn't happen. Hap wondered about Michael Collins, peering down the darkened halls, but to no avail. The man seemed to have vanished into the night.

Chapter 62

Early at the break of day, a lone rider streaked across the bridge over the Tar, only witnessed by the homeless fellows under the pylons. Popping his head over the side of the bridge, Indian Jack saw the coattails of Michael Collins flapping in the breeze.

"Jack, Jack, who you see? Who's making all tha' racket? The sun ain't ev'n ris'n," his companion complained, rolling over in disgust.

"Some fellow dos in a big hurry. Ne'er seen s'much dust. That piece of horseflesh gonna be lathered 'fore he gets to Penny Hill."

Scratching his head, the half-breed wandered on down to the riverbank, figuring he might as well toss his pole in the waters. Some fish just might take a plug out of that old fat bloodworm squirming in the rusty tin can by his pole.

"Yessir, dat man was sure in a hurry," pondered Indian Jack. "Tarboro musta been too hot for comfort. Dat man needed a breather."

Sarah looked over at Hap and her husband as they all sat on the hospital bench.

"She looks so pale."

"Miss Sarah? Captain? I'm afraid it's not over. She could have recurring headaches. Even some incidences could trigger fears of heights or falling. I hope and pray not, but it could happen."

"I know you're right. I'm just thankful she's alive," Sarah said.

"We all are." Elijah smiled at his wife.

"Well, a neighbor's staying with Rollie. Willie should be coming later. I suppose I need to tell her what's happening before I freshen up to go to my office. Will you two be all right? Do you need anything before I go?"

"No, Hap, you don't need to get us a thing, but you can tell us something," Sarah said.

"What is that?"

"Why are you and Rollie back in Tarboro?"

"Sarah?" Elijah winced, frowning at his wife. "That's his

business. Sorry, son. You know my wife oversteps her bounds at times."

"Well, we'll know sooner or later. How about sooner?"

"Pamela's in Europe with her grandfather, Miss Sarah. This time for real we are no longer married. I have full custody of Rollie. Details? Later... If you will excuse me?"

Both Cromwells sat mute.

"Oh, Hap, I'm so sorry. I am sure this has not been easy."

"Briefly, our son had a trauma that made him mute for months."

"No!" Both listeners echoed in unison.

"Yes, I'm afraid he did, but miraculously he was fortunate just to wake up."

"We're so glad...for Rollie's sake...and yours."

"Thank you. Thank you, both. Now I'll go find my son and Willie."

Chapter 63
IN THE DARK

Sarah Cromwell wrung her hands, something she usually did not do, but she was worried about her daughter.

"I just want to get her home," she said, still wringing her hands. "Who knows? Maybe something at Shiloh will jog her memory?"

They had tried everything they could think of in the hospital, but the entire past year escaped their daughter's memory. Fortunately, she remembered all the family, yet regretfully knew the sadness of losing her husband. Yet every time Hap entered her room, she'd just frown and strain to recognize anything about him.

"Don't worry," he would say, "You'll remember soon, very soon. Just rest and get well."

He'd smile, hiding his pain as best he could.

The pieces just would not come together. She'd fall back against her pillows, hoping against hope that this day would be the day of revelation and not another day in the dark.

"Hap, can we take her home now?" Elijah asked one day.

"I think it's time. She can regain her memory at Shiloh just as easily as she can here. Frankly, I want her with you all the time, until she straightens everything out in her mind. Let's get her checked out. Sounds good, doesn't it?"

"Oh, it does." Elijah hugged his wife as they followed the doctor.

The weeks flew as Caroline familiarized herself with Shiloh, but every time she visited Will's graveside, she'd fret. She could not remember how her brother died.

"You will, one day," her father said.

"Why won't you tell me?"

"I'm sure it'll happen soon, darling. Be patient. Now, let's ride the land."

He clicked the reins of his horse and led the way out into the roads that crisscrossed Shiloh. Caroline pulled up beside him.

"Father, do you realize how long it's been since I've ridden Shiloh with you?"

"I don't even want to count the years. I'm just thankful you're doing it now."

As they rode the freshly broken ground, Elijah would stop to talk to a hand, or to instruct one, or to tip his hat to the women in the fields.

"Remember how you used to beg as a child to ride with me?"

"Oh yes, and I also remember Mother's words 'Only when she can handle Nellie without George at her side.' My fussing and fuming got me nowhere."

"No, it didn't, but many a night I would hear about my headstrong daughter. Your mother knew all along that you took after her."

Both laughed.

Suddenly, Caroline pulled rein.

"What is it?" her father asked.

"I-I don't know. This woods looks so familiar and yet—," her voice trailed.

"Oh, darling, you used to ride Nellie here to be alone sometimes. There's a creek that lies on the other side of a grassy area. You roamed those woods, scaring your mother and Maggie half to death when you were late coming home. Those women fretted the most over you."

"Did something bad happen here? I have this strange feeling, but I can't quite put my finger on it."

Not wanting to coach her, Elijah took out his pocket watch.

"It's almost twelve, daughter. Maggie will ring the dinner bell

Chapter 63

any minute. We'd better head back."

Caroline stared at her father. He'd not answered her question. *Some day, I'll ride back to those puzzling woods,* she said to herself as she nudged her horse forward. She was determined to remember everything, no matter how bad. Only once did she glimpse the lower 40 over her shoulder as she trailed her father back to the main house.

Chapter 64
CHANCE MEETING

*W*illie and Hap climbed the porch steps of her cottage. He turned, staring at the woods and his old path to the lower 40 on Shiloh land.

"Willie, you got any old boots around I might borrow for an hour? I think I want to go fishing."

Willie never said a word. She walked to the shed and back and handed him a pair. He never questioned why she had men's boots and oversized at that.

"Almost perfect." Both laughed.

"Take your time. Rollie will be fine with your neighbor's child, but he's about to have a fit to see Jacob and Coffie."

"I know, but the boys and their mother will stay at Shiloh until she gets her memory back."

Willie watched her son walk back into his youth.

The path was grown over somewhat, but Hap Tyson could have walked the faint trail blindfolded. It amazed him how fast he made his way to the creek bed to find the exact crossing that led him onto Shiloh land. He found a perfect spot and cleared a seat.

His workweek had been a long, full one, but not full enough that he didn't think of Caroline. How patient could he be without somehow telling her everything that was blocked from her memory? He wanted her, but not at the risk of disturbing her. She would have to come to him with *all* her memory.

The sound of hoof beats startled him, actually felt more than heard, as his hand touched the ground. Someone was coming to

Chapter 64

the lower 40, maybe Elijah or Fate? His eyes closed. Old memories filled his head. The whinny of a horse jarred him. Putting down his pole, he scrambled to his feet and peered around the tree. Too much undergrowth hid the grassy knoll from view. He would have to walk a ways to find out who had broken his peace.

Moving quietly, he avoided briars and scrubby saplings amongst the seasoned trees. The last large oak loomed before him, blocking his view of the knoll. Ever so slowly, he sneaked a peek. The knoll itself was clothed in its full fall colors. Even the fronds of the willow still reflected a little green.

The sunbeams connected sky to earth, but the rays hit squarely on the golden curls Hap Tyson had adored since youth.

"No way," he said aloud, but there she was, a small but imposing figure in the center of the universe, seated on the fallen log. With his eyes riveted on her back, he forgot a careful approach. A stick snapped loudly underfoot, resounding like a gunshot as it echoed through the haven. He froze.

Obviously startled, the slight figure jumped from her seat, mouth opened to beckon help, hand raised to shield her eyes, eyes scanning to detect the invader. She appeared as a trapped animal, but in seconds, she spotted him and frowned, recognizing him as the doctor at the hospital. He still didn't move.

When she realized he was not approaching, she looked back at the log, then up at him. Shaking her head, she paced wringing her hands, eventually putting them to her head in hopes that something would click in her brain.

"Why can't I remember?" she moaned.

Collapsing onto the log, she looked from one end to the other. Glancing at the lichens and the partially solid center of the crumbling log, she still could not conjure up the memories.

"Come here," she hollered. "Please," she begged.

Only then did he dare move through the last undergrowth, hair tousled in the slight wind, his coat now torn by a stubborn briar.

The closer he got, the clearer her tear-stained face became. The man could not conceal his feelings. He could only look at her with the passion he'd suppressed the last few years. He stood before her, a man wanting to hold her, comfort her, and love her until he no longer breathed.

The expression on his face disarmed her, but she was not afraid of him, not one whit. She wanted to remember, but nothing would crack the wall. Both sat.

How odd the young couple appeared, he on one end of the fallen log and she on the other. His hands propped on his knees; hers, clutched in her lap. Neither spoke. Their silence strained, yet bonded them.

"Were we in love?" she suddenly blurted out.

He nodded and whispered, "Yes."

"Good grief, you would think I would remember that. I'm sorry, sir, I—just—"

"You don't have to apologize—"

"But, why won't anybody tell me any details? You, my parents, Maggie..."

He sat mute, afraid that he *would* spill his heart and unfairly sway her.

"Who is Michael?" she asked.

More silence. A sick feeling gripped him. Her old tutor's words pounded in his head, *We were caught up in a moment of passion.* He said nothing.

Jumping up from the log, she took several steps away from him. Throwing up her hands in disgust, she shouted,

"I give up! I just give up!" She heard scuffling behind her and turned.

The oversized boots restricted Hap's movements. He lost his balance. When he reared upward and backward to offset the plunge forward, he started reeling back toward the fallen log. With arms flailing, his heels hit the log as he careened, then fell into the thick grass, but as he fell, he heard her screams, not *his* name, but Will's. Over and over she screamed her brother's

Chapter 64

name. Falling on her knees beside Hap, she cradled his head and rocked, pathetically calling Will's name in agony. She would not, could not stop wailing.

Finally, Hap rolled from under her grip and lap. Her eyes were squeezed shut in shock and fear. He pulled her to her feet, just holding her at a distance with his hands on her shoulders. He dared not let her go, for surely she would fall. Slowly, he watched her contorted features relax. Minutes passed. An eternity.

He said nothing. Eventually, she opened her eyes staring straight ahead at his chest. Ever so slowly, she lifted her hand and touched him, faintly mouthing a word. Still, he was afraid to let go. Again, she mouthed the word. He heard nothing discernible, but he could feel the presence of her fingertips on his chest. His heart raced.

"Hap?"

Had he heard it? Had he heard *his* name? Not Will's? Was she saying what he'd hoped for, prayed for...his name? The sweet sound, his name.

"Hap."

Yes, there was no mistake. She'd said it. She'd said it twice. He waited for more.

"Hap, I love you," she whispered.

It was so simple, no frills, just three words. Slowly, he pulled her to him, gently wrapping his long arms around her and finally sensing their long journey toward each other might be over, but her head jerked back with puzzlement.

"Pamela?" Her brow wrinkled.

"Shhhh, my darling. I'll tell you later. It's all right. We'll be together. That's all you need to know right now. Shhhhh."

For minutes, she nestled in his arms, feeling restored in her mind, in their relationship. She'd never felt so secure and right. Yes, he could tell her later.

Glory, as Willie would say.

They walked arm and arm toward her tethered horse. He mounted first and pulled her up in front of him. Holding her against him, they rode at a slow walk toward Cromwell Hall, not caring who saw them from the fields.

Shortly, they'd be inseparable anyway.

"Sarah! Sarah!" Elijah hollered through the back door. "It's Caroline. Oh my God, you'll never guess who's riding with her? Hap! They're riding up the road from the lower 40."

He called louder, "Sarah, hurry."

"What is going on? Why are you screaming at me, Elijah Cromwell? It's who?"

She stopped beside her husband and began to shake.

"It's Caroline and Hap. Something's happened. It's gotta be good, 'cause they're riding on the same horse and she wouldn't if she hadn't remembered how much she loves that man."

"My child," Sarah whispered, as she focused on the approaching horse and riders.

Maggie had walked from the kitchen and stood by the picket fence.

"Maggie, Mother, Father," Caroline called out and waved. "No more fretting. I remember."

Pulling rein at the edge of the yard, Hap handed his passenger down to her father's waiting arms. As he hugged his daughter, Elijah slightly frowned as he glimpsed his boots on his future son-in-law's feet. That would be another story he'd hear about later.

"Please, let's sit. You have to tell us everything," Sarah said.

The four huddled on the garden benches.

"Will's accident actually jarred my memory."

"Will? How so?" her father asked.

Hap could not let go of her hand, even when she tried to talk with both. They laughed and cried as the story unfolded.

"I felt like Will reached from beyond and rattled my brain. He always was my best friend."

She smiled as she put her head on the Captain's shoulder, but held onto Hap's hand.

Chapter 64

"Are we a couple of second chances, my darling girl?"

"I'll say we are, my good man," Caroline spoke softly across the table she'd set for this special occasion. "Now, let's get down to business. Does two weeks sound long enough to get us married at Calvary?"

"Two weeks? I think I can manage that," he said with that crooked smile across his face. "And Mac says to sweep you away to the Princess Anne Hotel at the beach in South Carolina for at least a week. We can go by train."

"Sounds perfect to me."

"Walk me to the door. My day begins early tomorrow."

Standing in the doorway, he leaned down to kiss his future bride. It was a sweet kiss, not passionate, just sweet.

"You don't know what you do to me," he whispered in her ear.

"I hope it's what you do to me," she whispered back.

Chapter 65
THE INFAMOUS LETTER

Hap fingered the letter with great curiosity. Who would be writing to him from Chapel Hill? He tore open the two page letter and glanced quickly at the sender's name. Doc Sims?

Dear Hap,

I am thrilled with your impending wedding to Caroline. I just wish these old bones would allow my traveling to enjoy the celebration, but forgive me and know my heart is with you.

A colleague from Princeton recently corresponded some news that I thought you might like to hear, concerning Dean Perry's nephew, Michael Collins. It seems that Collins had a tryst with a professor's wife, was caught in the midst, and was unmercifully beaten by the husband.

The University, of course, would not tolerate such a scandal, took immediate action, and relieved him of his duties. The rumor is that he has fled the country in disgrace.

The Perrys are devastated, never expecting such behavior of their nephew. I don't think anyone will ever see the likes of him again.

I send my deepest affection to you, Hap, and to Caroline...
Your friend,
Doc Sims

Chapter 66

CALVARY

Two long tapers and a large cluster of gardenias sat on the altar in Calvary. The impatient groom had arrived early, only to pace in the Rector's study, his best man watching in amusement.

"Do you really think she'll come?" Hap wondered aloud.

Mac stifled snickers.

"Of course, she will. She's waited for you as long as you've waited for her." He enjoyed Hap's frenzy. "Never fear, my friend, I've seen the lady look at you. And, for the eleventh time, yes, I have the ring."

"I know, I know. I'm just in shock that it's really, truly, finally happening. Have you got the ring?" Hap asked his best man again.

"You're kidding? This time I refuse to answer."

"Just a joke. I hadn't asked you in five minutes."

Hap pushed his fist into his friend's shoulder in jest.

The Rector poked his head through the door and whispered, "Hap, the bridal party is coming. Are you ready?"

Before Hap could ask the momentous question, Mac quipped, "I got it. I got it. See."

Holding up the ring as a prize, he returned it to his pocket for safekeeping.

"Rollie, I can't believe this is happening. You and me will be brothers."

"I know, Jacob. We can sleep in the same room any time we want. That is when you're not off at school."

"Can I sleep in the same room, too?" Coffie chimed in.

"Well, maybe, once in a while," his older brother spoke, trying to accommodate his younger brother.

"Whoopee," an elated Coffie hollered.

"Well, Rollie, you're getting old enough. Maybe our parents will let you come to my school. We'll ask, but after their wedding night. You know they got to kiss and all that stuff."

"Stuff? What stuff?"

"Aw, they say we're too young to understand, but one day they'll sit us down and tell us these things. My mom says it's like asking me to carry something too heavy, like a suit satchel. I just might not be able to handle it until I'm bigger. Same goes for you, too, Rollie. And of course, you, too, Coffie."

Elijah and Sarah stifled giggles as they walked behind their precious grandboys, listening to this very serious conversation. They kept turning to Willie and pointing to the boys and watched as she doubled over behind them. What joy they could finally have, knitted together as a family, loving and sharing their lives openly with no secrets anymore. The three adults walked, swinging their arms, hand in hand, anticipating the joyful union ahead.

Caroline sat in the parlor of Calvary where all the brides waited before their entry into the sanctuary. For the wedding, she'd chosen a powder blue dress with white lace covering the bodice and elbow sleeve openings. The day was surprisingly mild for October.

The Rector's wife stood over the golden curls that were swept upward and pinned with her grandmother's Mother-of-Pearl combs. They'd been kept in a special box for just such an occasion, a long-awaited wedding. The woman kept playing with the curls, making sure they were just right.

Caroline picked up her bouquet of gardenias. She inhaled the fragrance and smiled. What did Hap say about her essence, simply intoxicating? Their trunks remained at the King House, waiting for the couple to pick them up and head to Wilmington

Chapter 66

where they would spend their wedding night. Hap had chosen the old Cape Fear Hotel, situated at the harbor side, giving them a beautiful view of the river. The following day they would travel to the beach below the South Carolina border and spend several days at the Princess Anne, the stately white hotel nestled on the shore overlooking the Atlantic. Everything seemed set.

Caroline looked up at the door of the parlor. She heard scuffling outside.

"Mama? Are you ready?"

She jumped and ran to open the door. Only happy and smiling faces greeted her.

Elijah remained as the others made their way to the sanctuary. He turned, a tear hanging on his lash.

"My daughter. Finally, your life will settle down. I'm so proud to take you down the aisle to be Hap's wife. Frankly, I never thought I would ever say that, but I do, my dear, with the sincerest heart...and your mother, too. We're very happy."

"Thank you, Father. I wish Coffie could see this day, but he did approve before he died. It's such a sweet story. We'll tell you later."

"Are you ready, child?"

"I am, Father. I am."

"I have it. Don't even ask," Mac whispered as Hap once more turned his way as they stood at the altar.

The old organist pounded on the keys of the pipe organ. Piercing melodious sounds leaped heavenward and resounded around the cathedral's ceiling. The entourage craned in unison to watch the brilliance of the two faces entering the coolness of the sanctuary. No face shone any brighter than the one waiting at the altar for his bride. His hand quickly cut off the path of a fleeting tear. His eyes never left her face.

Chapter 67

SOLOMON AND THE SHULAMITE MAIDEN

"Oh my," Caroline oohed as their coach pulled up to the Cape Fear Hotel. They'd ridden the entire afternoon by train.

"I decided we'd have our dinner in our suite. Does that gain your approval, Mrs. Tyson?"

"Oh, yes sir, it does."

Her eyes sparkled as the coachman and hotel doorman retrieved their trunks, another leading them through the massive entry into the lobby. Caroline's intake of breath caused Hap to turn and look at his new wife.

"Hap, what marvelous pieces of furniture! I feel as if we've walked into Louis XV's home. Well, summer cottage, maybe. Look at the shells and gilt, definitely rococo."

"Yes, definitely," he smirked.

"Don't make fun of me. I love art."

"I know, and I plan to learn to love it myself, just for you. But, what's rococo?"

"A shell motif, used by painters and furniture makers. In fact, rococo was derived from the French word 'rocaille,' which means pebbles."

Looking up at her husband, she caught him smiling at her. She could play this game.

"And did you know that people used to decorate caves with stones and shells?"

"No, but I have this suspicion that you're going to tell me more," he said and continued to smile.

Chapter 67

"Shell Motif!" she pointed out. "Quite appropriate for this harbor town, wouldn't you say?"

"Yes, quite so. Excuse me, dear. I just need to secure some things with the hotelier and then we can go to our rooms," he said, squeezing her hand as he backed away momentarily to the front desk.

"Are you ready?"

Hap had walked up to her as she continued to soak in the beauty of the room.

"Do we have a balcony?"

"Madame, I've thought of everything, and if I haven't, just tell me your wish."

Laughing behind her hand, she accused him of being as frivolous as the most decadent of the old French society.

"Oh, we are not going to be decadent this night, only cherishing. That you can bank on."

With that declaration, he led her into the bridal suite of the Cape Fear, only to hear once more the intake of her breath.

"Hap, it is beautiful."

Placing her on the couch, Hap busied himself with the dining cart that had arrived just as they had. Tipping the youth, he finally turned to his bride and heaved a sigh of relief.

"Let's freshen up and dine at our leisure," he said escorting her to the dressing area where a pitcher of water awaited her to help take the soil of the air off her hands and face. It had been a rather long ride, but they were here at last and alone.

Hap popped the cork of a champagne bottle as Caroline returned.

"Oh, you're going to ply your wife with spirits, eh? Just a toast or two for this new life of ours."

"By all means."

"Ooh, what bubbly do we have here?" She'd leaned forward to glance at the label. "My goodness, Hap!"

"The best for the best. I wouldn't let the steward open it a while ago, wanting every bubble for us."

He took a flute and tilted it slightly allowing the shiny liquid to flow gently into the crystal. "The *tete du cuvee,* Dom Perignon of Moet & Chandon, Madame. *Pour toi, ma cherie,*" he kissed the flute and passed it.

"*Merci, mon cher. Merci, avec mon coeur.*" Laughing, she added, "Don't grade me on my French."

The dinner was light since they'd had refreshments in the train's dining car. The succulent turkey slices melted in their mouths, suitably seasoned. The bliss potatoes sat bursting through their skins, while the snow peas crunched deliciously with each bite. The yeast rolls drenched in butter capped their supper. Small chocolates on a silver tray cleared their palates, washed with sips of flavored coffee.

Finishing their meal, they savored the remaining champagne on the balcony. The lights and stars twinkled, a magical illumination for this magical union. Both sighed from time to time. Neither could believe they were really man and wife, beginning a new life together, finally. She stood by the railing and peered into the far distance, imagining what her family was doing at the moment while they were sequestered away from the world.

Shaking her head to rid herself of any thoughts other than her husband, she felt his nearness. His arms encircled her waist and his head lowered to bury his nose in the golden curls, to breathe in her essences that had maddened him for all these years. He could not believe that he would be able to hold her and inhale her fragrances every day for the rest of his life. Her arm extended, wrapping around his neck, giving him room to lower his head even farther to kiss the nape of her neck and to sense the softness of her skin as he never had before. Chills ran through his body.

She turned to her husband and smiled, never releasing his neck with her arm, but lifting the other to totally encircle him by pulling gently his head to hers. She felt him lift her ever so slightly to meet his embrace. Their lips met. The shock of passion immediately electrified both. It was time to confirm their vows

Chapter 67

spoken hours before. Each disappeared into their dressing rooms.

Hap returned quickly in silken pajama pants and a robe. He sat on the settee in the sitting area awaiting his bride. When she opened the door, the lighting from the dressing room outlined her figure. He marveled at her golden curls splayed on her shoulders. He'd never seen her hair untamed. She seemed to glide toward the couch, the smile ethereal, the hand outstretched.

He rose to meet her in the center of the room. Taking her hand, he squeezed and kissed it, unable to speak. His heart pounded. He kept staring at her hand and shaking his head in disbelief of the reality of all that had happened in this last day. He'd waited so long and now all he could do was stand speechless as he did as a young boy in Carver's Mercantile, on the grassy knoll, on Station House Road.

"We've waited so long," she quietly murmured. He nodded. It was her turn to take his hand, to kiss it, to squeeze it. Still, he stood mute. Ever so slowly, she allowed her hands to trace the outline of his arms, his shoulders, his waist. Moving her arms under his, she continued to trace the sinews and ridges down his back. He did the same.

Their eyes were closed as if they wanted visions of each imprinted in their minds that would allow them to call up the sight, the touch of each part. They'd waited an eternity to really know each other.

Their first time together was a blur, but now they had all the time in the world to simply be with each other. No disturbances. None. The knock on the door startled both.

"How can this be?" Caroline uttered in astonishment, but the interruption was one of joy, a wire from Elijah, Sarah, and the children, plus a bouquet of gorgeous roses.

"*Congratulations, dear ones. We look forward to your return. Love, your family.*"

Caroline smiled dropping the wire on the table and sticking her nose in the roses. "Now, where were we?"

"I think I'd just about reached that porcelain neck. Come here, lady."

But this time, he led her to their bed. Embracing her briefly, he lifted her and placed her in the middle. His eyes never left her, as if he were afraid she would float off and disappear, an apparition of his imagination. He removed his robe and sat on the edge of the bedstead and gazed down at his fair bride.

"You know recently I read the Song of Solomon," he said.

"Oh, you did?" She smiled.

"Ole Sol had some very astute things to say about his Shulamite maiden."

"What did he say?" she asked, amused.

He paused and continued from memory. "He said, 'Behold, thou art fair, my love; behold, thou art fair. Thou hast dove eyes within thy locks...Thy lips are like a thread of scarlet...Thy neck is like the tower of David.'"

He looked from the top of her head to the bottoms of her feet.

"'Thou art all fair, my love; there is no spot in th-thee.'" His voice cracked slightly, "Solomon's feelings are no greater than mine. I hope you'll always remember that."

"I will. Oh, I will."

"I just hope I can make you as happy as—"

Before he could finish his sentence, she sat up and placed her hand over his mouth.

"You already have," she whispered. Removing her fingers, she rose up to kiss his mouth.

For this cause shall a man leave his father and mother and shall be joined unto his wife, and they two shall be one flesh. (Ephesians 5: 31)

Man shall cleave unto his wife, and Hap did, and it was well with both.

Epilogue
FIVE YEARS LATER

"Mom, Coffie and I wanna be Tysons, too. Everybody else is. Why can't we?" Jacob had questioned his mother with extreme persistence of late. Being the eldest of five children had its good qualities, but he had felt odd not having the Tyson name. Coffie was still a little young for it to matter, but he'd say anything his big brother said or felt. Jacob had watched the baptism of the three newest members of the family and heard the Tyson name ringing in his head over and over.

"Do you think my Poppa would mind?" he questioned, of course referring to Litch Bagley.

"Oh, I think your father would not mind at all," she responded, of course referring to Hap Tyson. *One day this child must know,* she thought.

"Then, please let's ask Dad to adopt me and Coffie and give us his name. I'll still have Poppa's name, too. Oh, please, Momma. Please. Please. Please."

He fidgeted so when he wanted something badly and repeated that ever present ending with pleas of *pleases,* and he was eleven.

"Did he really say that?" Hap quizzed when they were alone.

"I promise," Caroline whispered.

"I'll see Carlton Phillips next week," he whispered back. "Two more Tysons in the household. Yes, I like that."

And that's when he wanted a picture portrait of the family, the whole *Tyson* brood.

"Now, darlings, hurry. Mr. Dunn will be here any minute. Eli,

Epilogue

come here, you scamp. Hap, are you just going to stand there and laugh, or are you going to help your poor wife?"

"Oh, I was just enjoying the sight. Jacob, you're the eldest. You're in charge of Eli. Congratulations!"

"Aw, Dad, he's unbelievable today."

One raised eyebrow from Hap and the boy nodded in agreement. He knew he did have the most influence on the youngest of the Tyson clan. Smiling at his father, he marched from the bedroom in the King House, calling his younger brother.

Caroline was positioning little Jacksie's bow just right in the middle of a cluster of curls bequeathed to her by her great-grandmother and her mother. She'd been born just like clockwork, nine months after the marriage of Thomas Rolland Tyson and Caroline King Cromwell Bagley Tyson.

Eli followed two years later.

When the good doctor had heard about Mr. Dunn coming to Tarboro, he had to make the appointment. It was time for a family portrait.

As the family came down the stairs and turned to Jacksie Thrash's Garden of Eden, Hap slowed his wife and allowed little Jacksie and Rollie to pass through the door to find the other three children. Mr. Dunn was setting up in front of the garden bench where all would stand for posterity with Eli asking no less than one hundred questions.

"Darling, someone once told me you'd have a slew of children. Looka there," he said nodding toward the backyard. "Yessir, you have quite a brood of... *Tysons,* lady-friend, quite a brood at your knee."

Turning her head up toward her husband with a slight question across her face.

"Now, just who could that have been?"

"Oh, just someone from up at school," he returned with a quick peck on her forehead. Hap Tyson smiled that crooked grin, put his arm around his wife, and went to greet posterity through the camera's eye.

Acknowledgments

In my Dedication, I recognize my maternal grandmother, Mary Caroline, whose name I use for my heroine, in Book 1 and Book 2. Mary Caroline was a teacher and an artist. I always said that if I had one ounce of artistic ability, God gave it to me through her.

My grandmother died before I was born, so my only touch with her comes through the one lone painting that hangs in my entry hall. At times, I stand and soak in its essence and envision the lady with her brushes in hand, fashioning the lilies that surely are nodding their heads at me. No wonder I have lilies banked around our patio and clusters of that flower dotted around our living room walls.

I also wanted Caroline Cromwell in the novel to have that artistic love, which she pursues and becomes quite proficient in her craft.

I thank you, Mary Caroline, and Caroline Cromwell does, too.

My thanks, as always, goes to my father Connor Eagles for cultivating my love of history and preservation through family trips to historic homes, forts, battlefields, and museums.

And, thank you, Mother, for having three cousins in Tarboro who enriched our lives with that wonderful historical village.

Of course, a thank you to the Cromwell family for providing Cromwell Hall and the Cromwell family cemetery as a base for my storyline.

My gratitude for Albert Coates, Hugh Lefler, and Albert Newsome, whose books about Chapel Hill and North Carolina provided bountiful details and pictures about North Carolina.

ACKNOWLEDGMENTS

Thank you to Steven Stolpen, who put together *Chapel Hill, A Pictorial History*, which provided commentary, as well as pictures of the early University buildings, the campus, and the village.

My thanks to the Episcopal Church for its Prayer Book, which I use frequently for scenes in Calvary Episcopal Church in Tarboro, North Carolina.

I cannot forget to include the Edgecombe County Bicentennial Committee (1976) for their book *The Edgecombe Story*.

It is amazing how newspaper articles, magazines, on-line subjects could prompt and push the storyline along, but they did. Even Siri helped out occasionally!

Once more, I thank my publishers, Frank and Rhonda Amoroso, of *simply francis publishing company* for all their help and patience.

To conclude, thanks to all who have provided input and did not even know it for my writing *The Edgecombe Trilogy*. My appreciation for every life that has touched mine to give me material, whether for the storyline or historical facts. I am so grateful.

ABOUT THE AUTHOR

Joanne Eagles Honeycutt graduated from the University of North Carolina in Chapel Hill in English Education and received a Masters in Reading at East Carolina University. She taught in the Pitt County Schools and Pitt Community College before retiring.

In 2016, Joanne received the Sallie Southall Cotton Award from the City of Greenville Historic Preservation Commission for her continued dedication to preserving eastern North Carolina history through the Eastern Carolina Village & Farm Museum. For years, she has volunteered for this open air museum, a project of her father's, Connor Eagles.

Her regard for history prompted her to write *The Edgecombe Trilogy. Caroline...The Captain's Daughter* completes the sequel of Books 1 and 2. Watch for the last link of the trilogy.

Joanne and her husband live in Greenville, North Carolina, along with their son Mark and his family.

Made in the USA
Columbia, SC
26 July 2024